THE RELUCTANT KNIGHT

A novel by

H. Nelson Freeman

The Reluctant Knight

2d Edition

This is a work of fiction. Names, characters, places, brands, media, and incidents are either the product of the author's imagination or are used fictitiously. The author acknowledges the trademarked status and trademark owners of various products referenced in this work of fiction, which have been used without permission. The publication/use of these trademarks is not authorized, associated with, or sponsored by the trademark owners.

ISBN: 979-8-9869366-0-4

Cover design by H. Nelson Freeman

Acknowledgments

A special thanks to all of the incredible men and women of the Iowa Writers Corner for their full support, encouragement, and assistance in writing.

To Birdie Hawks for her daily support and help.

To Maggie Rivers, whose expertise made this and my other novels a reality.

To Dawn Hall, thank you for your invaluable help in editing my work

To my Brothers in Christ, Rev. Mickey Carvour and Rev. Dick Johnson, two of God's servants, who guide me to the ways of our Savior.

Also, by this author:

Mission: East Solomons
Mission: Santa Cruz
Mission: 1st Naval Battle of Guadalcanal
Mission: Tassafaronga
Mission: Kula Gulf
Mission: Kolombangara
Mission: Tokyo Express
Molech's Fire
VX
A New Horizon
Two Crews in One

The Reluctant Knight

A NOVEL BY

H. Nelson Freeman

"How horrible, how fantastic, how incredible it is that we should be digging trenches and trying on gas masks here because of a quarrel in a faraway country between people of whom we know nothing."

British Prime Minister, Neville Chamberlin – 1938

"Without ships, we cannot live."

British Prime Minister, Sir Winston Churchill – 1940

A TOWN-CLASS DESTROYER

CHAPTER ONE

Pounding through the rough waters of the English Channel at thirty knots average speed, the former American Clemson Class destroyer assured almost nobody would get any sleep, especially in the congested living spaces in the after-quarter of the ship. The main culprit is the powerful, loud, thumping, vibrating twin screws beneath the compartment. The rattling doors of three lockers containing heavy coats, oil slicks, and winter wear added to the racket. One last antagonistic screeching noise came from the two rudder chains inside their protective tubes, welded to each side of the deck.

Oddly enough, the men learned to sleep with the noise while swinging in their hammocks suspended from overhead.

Not all were asleep, but those who were couldn't remain asleep long. The ship-wide communications system bearing the label 1MC, which the British call the Tannoy, blasted an alert,

"ACTION STATIONS, ACTION STATIONS, ALL HANDS MAN YOUR ACTION STATIONS."

'The war had fouled our sleep again,' thought Tobias Greene, an American citizen who joined the Royal Navy to fight the Nazis while those at home sat on their hands. Toby, as he preferred, rolled out of the hammock and joined the bump and grind of men getting dressed for battle. Surprisingly, the men

exited the compartment for their stations in a timely manner, some still pulling on a piece of clothing as they made it out of the space.

After the warmth of their hammocks and blanket, the icy blast of the English Channel ensured wide-awake stokers and ratings who dropped into the engine and fire rooms.

The old warhorse and other ships in the convoy hugged the English coast as they plodded on to deliver needed supplies to Scapa Flow, Scotland. The English warships of the Home Fleet sat anchored in the protective harbor of the Scottish islands, cold but fairly free of the high winds. But it wasn't the weather the ships were concerned with; the glow in the eastern sky brought the daylight and Jerry's air attacks.

'At least the engine room warmed the cold bones of the stokers, and I'd rather be down here than freezing my tush off on deck,' ran through Toby's mind when he hit the grates.

The turbines hissed like snakes with the throttles only a few turns before they hit the stops. But the reduction gears were the howlers, reducing the high-speed turbine output to the most efficient propeller RPMs. Newcomers would express concern over the howling until the 'old hands' assured them that the reduction gears sounded normal.

Toby's job included wiping all the machinery clear of oil from around the stuffing glands, the exterior of pumps, and bearings. He also refilled the lubricating oil drip reservoirs and other tasks as directed. Toby's title indicated his work, 'Wiper.'

The senior ratings appreciated the professional way Toby went about his duties and his understanding of the operation and importance of the oil and its system.

Being the only American on the crew, Toby stood out with his accent, some phrases, slang, and his general dialect. To his credit, Toby was catching on to the dialect deficiency and altering it little by little each day. Many Officers and crew commended the young man for joining ranks with them in their fight for survival.

****

Tobias Greene lived all his life in the same home in a sparse community outside of Newport News, Virginia. His father,

Thomas Greene, became a successful banker in Newport News, and his mother, Nancy, was a housewife.

Following graduation from high school, Toby took a job with Newport News Shipbuilding, working on refurbishing and mothballing Clemson class destroyers. His work took him into the engine and boiler rooms of the destroyers. He helped overhaul, install, and remove machinery in American warships' four main engineering spaces, two boiler rooms, and two engine rooms.

Living in the primarily rural area outside the cities, the young Toby Greene took the opportunity to hunt and fish. When older, Toby helped the family cupboard with hunted food, including deer, quail, and rabbits. Following a senior class project in heritage, the young Greene developed a hobby that involved tracing his family's ancestral tree. With occasional help from his parents and history teacher, Toby traced his family lineage to England's Greenes Norton. Unfortunately, the lack of sufficient funds prevented him from continuing his quest.

Three years after finishing school, Toby watched the re-emergence of Germany into a post-World War I power in Europe. As with most Americans, the actions of the Nazis turned the Allies against the Hitler regime. Everyone watched in horror as the German Blitzkrieg walked into Austria, marched into Poland and the low countries of the Netherlands and Belgium, then rolled over France. Finally, England and France declared war, bringing on the beginning of World War II.

With the American Congress at odds with President Franklin D. Roosevelt over joining the besieged English, Toby felt compelled to go to the aid of England in whatever capacity he could. However, Thomas and Nancy Greene strenuously opposed Toby's intents, especially his mother.

The young man argued with his parents, "I love you both dearly, and no matter what, we'll have to fight in a conflict in Europe again. Everyone knows it, and we are not prepared to engage the Germans. So, I propose to join the Royal Navy and gain experience that may be transferred to our Navy when America joins the fray.

With my work and sea experience, I can serve in a better capacity. However, I certainly don't want to join the Army or Marines; my training and expertise are shipboard."

Thomas and Nancy discussed their son's proposal and supporting arguments. Then, taking in his age, the two reluctantly agreed to Toby's plan. As to be expected, the couple insisted Toby write often and keep them appraised of his adventures as the navy permitted.

Thomas helped his son obtain his passport, which was needed to join the Royal Navy."

"I planned to ask you about that; I never needed one before." With Thomas' help, the young man had his passport the same day.

Tom and Nancy accompanied Toby to the train station in Newport News. "Toby, please be careful and write as often as you can; we miss you already," Nancy Greene said, holding back tears.

Thomas shook his son's hand, then grabbed him in a bear hug, whispering, "Take care of yourself, and keep your head down."

"Yes, Dad, I know I'm putting a lot of pressure on you and Mom, but I have to do this."

"I know, and I couldn't be more proud of a son in command of his destiny. Don't forget to look up a reputable genealogist; you will be in a perfect location to learn more about your ancestry."

"That will be the fun of it."

Then the young man boarded the train as the final whistle blew, and the conductor roared, "All aboard."

During his two months in recruit training, Toby took a battery of tests to determine where he could serve most efficiently. Toward the end of his second month in a British naval uniform, the training personnel contacted the Royal Division of Engineering and reported that Ordinary Seaman Greene had extensive training and experience in working on the machinery of the American Clemson class destroyers. Accordingly, upon graduation from recruit training, Toby received his transfer orders sending him to the *HMS AMPTHILL*, a Town class destroyer.

****

The Tannoy blasted throughout the ship, "All hands stand clear of all weapons." Immediately the ship shook from the roaring reports of the antiaircraft guns, and the *AMPTHILL* rolled in defensive maneuvers.

A few men were caught unprepared for the maneuvers in the tight confines of the after-engine room and lost their footing. The men smashed into unforgiving metal objects and machinery, giving those men bruises and one man a broken nose. Then, without warning, the ship jumped at a near-miss explosion of a German bomb. Toby tightly held onto a stanchion as his body jerked first one way, then another. Half an hour later, the attack ended, and the convoy steamed on while licking its wounds.

The hatches were allowed open, and the lead Stoker told Greene and a couple of other men to get some fresh air. The air topside hovered a little above freezing, and a brisk northeast wind made it feel like ten degrees below freezing.

Tommy Fitzhenry, a gunner, joined the young American, talking about the enemy raid. According to Tommy, a gaggle of JU-8 bombers attacked the convoy.

"You look cold, mate, 'er, have a Player's," Tommy said.

Toby declined, "Thanks, but I never picked it up."

Another gunner, Jake Dobbins, joined the two, "Did I 'er ya say ya hunted back in America?"

"Yeah, I mentioned it; I hunted deer, rabbits, quail and grouse, even an occasional pheasant; why?" Toby asked.

Dobbins asked, "How did ya hit them fast flyin quail?"

"It depends on their direction of flight from where you're standing."

"Blimey, I'm tryin to lead those bleeden Jerry planes properly, but I'm not hittin 'em," Dobbins complained.

"How far are you leading them?" Toby asked.

"I put my sights right in front of them, and the shells are supposed to hit the bloody things."

"You have tracers, don't you?"

"Yes," Dobbins said.

"Use them to tell you how much further you have to lead the target. For example, if you're hitting the tail or the shells are going behind the plane, shift your aim twice the distance in front of the plane. Then you can decrease the lead as needed to begin getting hits. All you have to do is adjust your aim to fire in the same place by pivoting with his trajectory. And if he is coming straight at you, aim a foot over the nose and adjust accordingly." Toby instructed.

“Our practice is low, maybe because of all the ships in the fleet needing the practice. Could you come up and help?” Tommy asked.

“I’m sorry, mate, my action station is in the engine room, and they won’t allow me to leave on my request.”

Dobbins shook his head, “Ya need to get out of that death trap; if we hit a mine or take a torpedo in the engine room, nobody survives. The explosion would put the lights out, and you would lose direction in seconds.”

“I know, and a bomb hitting the deck will take out just as many up here. But, we all have to do our job; we took an oath to that and to obey the Captain. Whether we live or die, it’s all in God’s hands, and I trust God above all.” Toby said.

“Well, Yank, you’re a tough and cool sailor; I’ll say that for ya.”

Toby added, “Thanks, Jake. Come on, you two, let’s find some paper and pencil, and I’ll show you how to gauge your lead.” Later, on the fantail, Toby drew an outline of a plane and gave the two men the concept of leading and maintaining the proper lead on the target and how to compensate for distance and direction of travel.

“I owe you a pint, Yank, or on your case, milk,” Tommy said, bringing a laugh from them all.

“ACTION STATIONS, ACTIONS STATIONS, ALL HANDS TO ACTION STATIONS,” the Tannoy blared.

As the men began to head for their gun and the engine room, Dobbins said, “I’ll try to remember what you’ve shown us, and if I get a Jerry, I’ll tell gunnery it’s yours.”

“Be careful, you guys,” then Toby descended the ladder into the cramped engine room. The heat from the running machinery felt good to the sailor after the exposure to the icy blast across the decks.

The bell on the annunciator rang, announcing a speed change. The bridge called for thirty knots with the deck tilting as the ship began defensive maneuvers and the antiaircraft guns started barking. Toby, like the other Stokers, went about their duties. In Toby’s case, he grabbed a couple of rags, and his reservoir filling can and began making his rounds, ensuring the oil feeders were full.

The young American's mind drifted to his hobby, his family ancestry. As a project, Toby began tracing his family's ancestry while still in high school. Mrs. Holiday, the history teacher, had the students set up a family tree, and Toby took a serious interest in his ancestral lineage.

Before running out of money, he followed the family line to the shores of America. After meeting with a professional genealogist, the man said he would begin mapping Toby's ancestry.

A loud explosion jarred the ship and caused it to lurch, followed by a sharp starboard turn. The unexpected maneuver ruined a bombardier's aim, causing his bombs to fall harmlessly astern the ship. The distance the enemy had to fly from their base allowed the bombers to make one attack, then turn for home. The attack only lasted about ten minutes.

At sixteen hundred, the crew drew their ale rations, with Toby giving his to his friend, Tommy. The young Stoker stood on the sixteen to twenty watch, and following the attack, Toby stayed in the engine room until relieved for supper at seventeen-thirty. Then he returned to the space until relieved at twenty hundred hours.

After cleaning up, Toby decided to turn in early since he had to go back on watch at zero-three-forty-five. The sea's state had deteriorated, but the ship headed directly into the heavy seas, giving it a see-saw movement. Toby was happy to get back into the engine room near the center of the vessel, relieving the effect of the worst of the ride.

Within an hour, the seas began mellowing, and the convoy had weathered another storm. The icy blast of air had fallen to ten knots and maintained a southern direction, pushing the much smaller waves in front of it.

"Now hear this, Action Stations, Action Stations." The time to prepare for the best hunting hour for U-boats had come. Accordingly, *HMS AMPTHILL* and the convoy began moving among the islands leading to Scapa Flow, the anchorage of the Home Fleet.

The escorts received directions to replenish their fuel bunkers for the trip south. Much to their delight, they were relieved and ordered to Devonport, their home station. Since the *AMPTHILL* was the only Town class among the escorts, she took the last position in the line of ships departing Scapa Flow.

Two days later, the ship made Devonport and steamed in with the crew manning the rails. The next day Greene stood in the shore leave party, awaiting inspection. Upon leaving the ship, he hopped a ride in a taxi to the genealogist's business in Plymouth.

The master of genealogy met Toby at his door. "Come in, young man, come in. I have interesting news for you."

"Good afternoon Mr. Kensington; I trust you have been well while I was away." Toby asked.

"Quite well, thank you. You said you were going on a ship. But I didn't catch the name."

"I am posted on the *HMS AMPTHILL."*

"What kind of ship is that?"

"She is a former American destroyer, now flying the Royal Navy ensign. I cannot say anything more about the ship or my work, but she is visible in the harbor."

"That is the proper position to take; we cannot take security for granted. However, what I have to tell you does not fall into that category."

"Were you able to follow the work I began?" Toby asked.

"Yes, I have found sound lines of your ancestry into prominent English families. Your ancestral line leads to the DeBoketon line, Geoffrey la Zouche, and his spouse, the Princess of Britany, Constance De la Zouche. From there, a direct line leads to Maud Beauclerc and her father, Henry I Plantagenet, King of England."

Toby looked around him, then spotting a chair; he sat, his mind reeling with the magnitude of Mr. Kensington's revelation. Then, with a stuttering voice, the young man stammered, "I'm in the bloodline of Henry the First?"

"Yes, sir, and when we followed the line further, it extended to William the Conqueror, Robert the First, the Magnificent, and beyond."

"That can't be; I'm Toby Greene, an American serving the King."

"Yes, I can see you are in the service of the King and doing a fine job at that." Kensington decided to test the sailor, "You aren't from around here; your voice indicates you are a Yank."

"That I am," Toby proudly said. "I'm from Virginia, sir."

"May I ask, what are you doing here?"

"Well, sir, like many others, I saw the war coming, and there is no doubt in my soul that America will become involved again; it's just a matter of time. I know my heritage is English, and I saw the people of this county fighting with their backs to the wall. So I must do what I can to help."

"Oh, my boy," the elderly man said, "You are indeed in the line of giants. You are doing your heritage a great honor, in my humble belief. I've no doubt the King himself would shake your hand."

"Oh, I don't think he would do that; I'm just an ordinary person, nobody special. But, tell me, have you finished your work?"

"I'm afraid not; I still have work to do, but it will be easier now because the rest is already history and known. I would hazard to guess I can finish in a fortnight, maybe two."

"If you could tell me your bill for your work, I would be happy to pay you."

"I'm afraid I do not have a tally yet, it would be better once I have finished, and I will make good for you at a rate you can afford."

"That's very kind of you, sir. I don't want to take advantage of you; I believe in paying you a fair wage for your work."

"We can put it all to rest when you return."

"I'll be back as soon as I can. Right now, it depends on our schedule."

"If needed, I think I could find you," Mr. Kensington said.

"Thank you, sir, and thank you for being so kind."

"Oh, my boy, thank you for helping to defend our country. God be with you in these dangerous days, and be careful."

"I will; thanks again."

Toby Greene left the business, his mind reeling with the heady information given him. *'Just think, me in the line of the greatest Kings of England, who would believe it?"*

Then he stopped in mid-stride, "Nobody."

The sailor decided to keep it all confidential, feeling it would bring him disbelief, criticism, and trouble.

Toby walked around town, looking at the architecture, all the while keeping an eye out for a place to eat. Finally, after a short time, the sailor found a small pub with food, and despite the rationing, the food was good.

Toby caught a taxi driver looking to end his day heading toward the housing not far from where the ship moored. The driver engaged the sailor in the normal taxi talk, then learned he was a Yank. At the front gate of the naval base, Toby tried to pay the man for the ride.

"No, Yank, you came over here to fight for our country; I'll not accept any money. Any time you need a ride, you call me." Then he handed Toby a card. "It will be my honor to take you anywhere in Plymouth. Besides, I live over that hill," he said, pointing to the north. Toby stepped out to try paying for the ride, and the taxi drove off, the driver waving and yelling out the window, "Call me anytime."

The following day after quarters, the stokers began working on the machinery. Stoker First Class Styles instructed Toby to lap in the seats of a steam valve that developed a leak.

The Tannoy blared out, "Hold on the shore leave section," the First Officer said, "All shore leave is canceled; we will rearm and top off the fuel bunkers as soon as possible. Sorry about the shore leave, men. The war will not wait. All officers and Chiefs assemble on the pier in fifteen minutes. That is all."

The lead Stoker called Toby, "Get that other valve lapped in straight away."

"Right first," The American picked up a can of lapping compound and rags, then headed toward a steam-driven pump.

GERMAN Bf-109f

CHAPTER TWO

Robert Kensington, the genealogist who worked on Toby Greene's documents, felt the pull of indecision. The older man acknowledged Toby's wish to remain anonymous regarding his heritage. Yet, Kensington believed anyone, especially a young lad from another country, who would travel here to fight for England in her time of need, was a rare breed of man. Then, to be in the line of the Kings of England should be recognized as a national hero, something needed in these perilous times.

Kensington's brother served in Buckingham Palace; the decision to send him Greene's information overpowered his silence, and he sent a copy of his report to Buckingham Palace to see if anyone considered the young American's acts worthy of recognition.

****

Stoker Toby Greene finished the work on the valve; the Lead Stoker examined the work and smiled, "Mate, you're an excellent mechanic; I'm glad to have you with us."

Toby stowed his tools after cleaning them off; then, checking the rest of his assigned area in the engine room, he wiped down the machinery and cleaned himself of grease and dirt. Finally, the

Lead Stoker Petty Officer released Toby from the engine room as a reward for his excellent work.

Greene stopped by his locker in their berthing compartment for his letter-writing gear. Sitting at the small table, where another Stoker read a magazine, Toby penned a letter to his parents. He brought them up to date on his activities, minus any mention of his work or his visit to Mr. Kensington. His letter was in the proper wording to avoid rejection by the censors. Unfortunately, his letter ran short because he wanted to post it before the ship had to get underway.

While the *AMPTHILL* rested, moored to the pier, it had a slight roll. The ship's narrow beam, only slightly short of thirty-one feet. But the vessel's length reached three-hundred-fourteen and a half feet, making it slim and prone to rolling.

Finally, the order filtered down to the Stokers to light off the engineering plant and prepare to get underway. The ballet began, and when the auxiliary steam reached three hundred pounds, the steam-powered pumps came online. As the rest of the crew prepared their part to get the destroyer underway, the boilers and turbines warmed to normal temperatures and pressures for full operation. The plant stood idling for only a short time before the bridge called the Engineering Control in the forward engine room.

"Main Control, bridge, secure the jacking gear, and prepare to answer all bells."

Stokers shut down the jacking gear motor and threw the engagement lever. "Spinning main engines," called out the throttleman as he cracked open the astern throttle valve. Steam shot from the nozzles in the astern elements, and the shaft began to move. Throttleman David Hallen closed the astern throttle and cracked the ahead throttle, immediately closing it. Cracking the astern throttle again brought the shaft to a halt. Then they waited for the first bell. If it didn't come in five minutes, the engineers had to spin the engine again to avoid warping the turbines.

On the bridge, the pilot appeared and said, "Captain, get underway when you wish."

Captain Champs ordered the last lines aft thrown off, and the Captain moved the ship away from the pier. When clear of all obstructions, the Captain turned control over to the pilot, who conned the vessel to the mouth of Plymouth harbor, then he turned the control back to the Captain and disembarked to a small boat.

As the destroyer reached the English Channel, the wind and waves buffeted the ship, causing it to roll, pitch, and yaw.

With the ship clear of the land, the Captain said, "The Tannoy, ship-wide, please. Your attention, please. One of the escorts to convoy H43 suffered an engineering casualty; we have been called upon to provide the escort. We will rendezvous with H43 at Liverpool, then turn toward Gibraltar. That is all."

No sooner than the Captain hung up, the Boatswain's Mate of the Watch cried out over the Tannoy, "ACTION STATIONS, ACTION STATION, all hands to ACTION STATIONS, repel air attack."

With most of the crew already at their action stations as required by condition two wartime steaming, the remaining men only took seconds to prepare and report ready. In seconds the pom-pom of the forties could be heard throughout the ship. Then, what seemed like an instant later, the twenty-millimeter Oerlikon cannons joined the fight.

Messerschmitt Bf-109s ran antiaircraft suppression attacks on the destroyers to prevent the cannons from shooting down the incoming JU-87 Stuka dive bombers. After three passes, two of the twenty-millimeter guns and a forty-millimeter twin cannon sat quiet, the gunners lying on the deck, blood seeping from wounds. Finally, the Assistant Gunnery Officer moved men to man the forty and one of the twenty-millimeter cannons. The second remained silenced for lack of a gunner.

Gunner Tommy Fitzhenry called to the Gunner's Chief, "Chief, I know a man who c'n shoot that cannon and hit the target."

"Who are ya talkin 'bout?"

"Stoker Toby Greene in the after-engine room."

The Chief hurried to look up the Assistant Gunnery Officer. "Sir, we c'n get a Stoker from the after-engine room; he's said to be a good marksman."

"Good work Chief; I'll speak to the Captain about putting him on the gun."

"Straight away, sir," the Chief bumped the edge of his tin cover in a salute and headed aft.

At the bridge hatch, the Lieutenant requested to see the Captain. "Sir, we may have found a sailor to man the stern twenty."

"What do you know of him?" the Captain asked.

"Sir, he is the American Stoker Tobias Greene in the after-engine room. He helped other young gunners with some excellent advice on aiming."

"The Yank? That would make sense, coming from America's farm country. Most of the farmers there have weapons and are excellent shots. Have the messenger fetch Stoker Greene and bring him to the bridge forthwith."

"Aye, sir."

Within five minutes, a mystified Toby Greene stood before the ship's Commanding Officer. "Stand at ease, Stoker Greene. I understand you have a sound understanding of handling firearms; is that true?"

"I'm pretty good with a rifle but a little less with a handgun."

"Do you think you could shoot a twenty-millimeter cannon?"

"Yes, sir, with a little familiarization and a couple of practice rounds. We touched on the weapon in training, sir."

Mr. Rutland, take Stoker Greene to the twenty-millimeter mount, and see if he can handle it."

"Aye, Captain. Stoker Greene, follow me."

"Aye, sir." Toby snapped the Captain with a salute, which the Commander returned with the slightest of smiles.

After recalling the training process from his near photographic mind a few minutes later, Toby checked the weapon properly. Then the American tightened the straps of the heavy cannon to hold him in place and wiggled around to let the straps settle in more comfortably. Finally, having ensured a full magazine sat attached to the weapon, he awaited the Officer's orders to fire.

The Tannoy sounded, "All hands stand clear of the stern during test firing the twenty-millimeter cannon."

"Stoker Greene, you are clear to shoot."

Toby fired off four bursts at wave tops, adjusted his seating slightly, and fired another two shots. Finally, he held his hands up, signaling he had completed his firing.

Mr. Rutland told the Chief and Toby, "Have a loader and talker here to put this weapon into commission, then standby for the next attack."

Both men acknowledged the Officer, and the Chief threw a few questions at Toby. Then, he turned to the Sub-Lieutenant, "Mr. Rutland, I believe Stoker Greene is ready to engage enemy aircraft."

"Very well, Chief, all we need to do is wait; Jerry will return soon. Talker inform the bridge the stern twenty-millimeter cannon is ready for combat."

"Aye, sir."

"Stoker Greene, we need a good gunner at this station, and if what I am told is true, you should do well. Good luck."

"Thank you, sir."

Toby's baptism of fire wasn't long in coming. The ship's Tannoy announced the arrival of another wave of enemy aircraft. This gaggle of death headed for Devonport. As they flew near the ship, a half dozen broke from the flight and turned toward the *AMPTHILL*.

"Enemy aircraft approaching from green zero-eight-five-zero true, at about a thousand meters."

Toby swung the big cannon to the left of the stern, and in the distance, multiple specks slowly grew in size. The young man licked his lips, only to find that his tongue and mouth were as dry as a desert bone.

"There are at least two Bf-109s in the group," reported the talker.

Toby pushed the wax earplugs snuggly into his ears, tightened the tin pot on his head, and grasped the gun handles with his right fingers posed over the trigger.

Greene looked through the gunsight, trying to place the inner circle a hair over the oncoming fighter's canopy by a couple of inches.

"Shoot," yelled the talker.

Toby fired half a dozen rounds, watching two tracers disappear over the plane's canopy. He lifted the handles ever so slightly; as he pressed the trigger, he noticed the winking lights on the enemy fighter's cowl and wings.

Toby's fingers grasped the firing trigger and the big gun jumped in recoil faster than he could imagine. The .78-inch shells lanced out toward the fighter and flew by the left side of the fuselage. The Stoker pulled to his left and held the trigger down as a line of German bullets and larger shells raced toward the ship. The American watched through the gunsight as the plane seemed to shudder under the impact of the heavy ammunition. TNT high explosive rounds exploded on contact, shattering and ripping away the canopy. Follow-on shells tore into the pilot, bringing instant death in his dismemberment. The twenty-two-year-old flyer's body fell forward, discontinuing firing the plane's weapons and pushing the stick forward. The aircraft's elevators rotated down from the stick's movement, putting the plane into a terminal dive. The sleek fighter disintegrated on impact, sending a column of water a hundred meters into the air.

The talker and loader congratulated the young gunner with back slaps, howling, and yelping. Toby felt uncomfortable with all the attention.

Captain Champs watched the Nazi machine begin its strafing run from the bridge. He saw the tracers fly over the top of the aircraft as the fearful knot began forming in his stomach at the thought of having to write another two or three condolence letters.

The plane's machine guns rattled loud enough to be heard, and the Captain witnessed the line of shells raising splashes in the sea as they screamed toward the ship, promising death and mayhem. Only the distance allowed the Captain to see the flight of tracers begin slamming into the nose of the 109, tearing the yellow spinner away, dissecting the front of the plane, and working back to the pilot. Suddenly the aircraft ceased firing and dove into the wake of the ship. The remaining planes changed course, deciding to go after less aggressive targets.

The Captain turned and looked at Mr. Rutland, who had a look of disbelief on his face. The Sub-Lieutenant turned toward the Captain and saw a small smile form on his face as he returned to conning the ship. The word of the Yank downing the enemy fighter spread quickly, along with cheers and clapping among the younger crewmen, with the 'old salts' silently cheering for the popular sailor.

Tobias Greene was never one for loud felicitations. His upbringing instilled a modest streak in his characteristics, causing him to shun such celebrations.

Tommy Fitzhenry respectfully requested that they could paint a black Balkenkreuz Cross on the splinter shield. The Gunnery Officer brought it up to Captain Champs, who approved; however, he restricted its size to no larger than fifty millimeters square and in the upper right corner. Tommy couldn't wait to get the cleaner, paint, and brush.

The ship secured from air defense, and Toby headed for the engine room. When he arrived, he found the stokers were no less celebrative than the deck sailors. After enduring a respectful time of compliments, the sailor grabbed his rags and oil filler can and headed on his rounds with a slight shake of his head at all the hullabaloo.

The air, the ship's hull, and everything seemed colder when they hit the St. George's Channel, then turned toward the Irish Sea. Toby was no fan of the cold and felt content to stay in the warm engine room, even when off watch. So, the sailor passed the time wiping down his assigned area.

The on-duty wiper stopped at his feet, "Hey, mate, why are ya hangin down 'er when you're off watch?"

"I'm not working; it helps pass the time; besides, it's warmer down here; I hate the wet and cold decks."

"I guess ya have a point there; it's a bit more comfortable but noisier."

"I'd go to the compartment, but during the day, it's secured, so I just stay down here out of everyone's way."

"I hear ya; by the way, where did you learn to shoot like that? I heard you nailed Jerry on the first burst."

Toby smiled and gave a light laugh. "First of all, it wasn't on my first or even second burst. Both missed but gave me a reference point to adjust the next burst. As far as learning to shoot, me and all the guys I know back home had to hunt to help feed the family. It's called survival, but I never thought I would shoot a huge gun like that twenty millimeter, let alone shoot down airplanes."

"I heard you were as cool as an iceberg up there."

"Where do these guys come up with that stuff? No, not at all; I almost forgot to press the trigger; I'm still shaking over it all."

Toby held out his hand, the adrenalin rush still causing a slight trembling effect.

"Yank, I would have thought you wouldn't be afraid of anything."

"Where do you get that? I'm no different than you or anybody else aboard. I get scared. Everyone does; it's natural. The key is keeping the fear under control, which isn't easy. Anyone who tells you they ain't afraid is either a liar or crazy. In either case, stay away from them; they'll get you killed."

"Blimey, I never thought about it like that. Back home in London, nobody admits to being afraid of anything."

"Yeah, that's almost always false courage and lies. Nobody wants to appear afraid, yet it's normal; I guess it's like that everywhere; admitting fear of something is equal to being a coward, and it's not true."

"Can I ask you something?"

"Sure, Don."

"What's that little book you keep in your pocket? I see you reading it now and then."

"It's the Book of Proverbs, from the Bible. It gives me a lot of information on how to live and how to behave in times of stress."

"Oh, you're one of those people."

"One of what people?"

"A churchgoer, a Bible thumper."

"Yes, I am a Christian, and my beliefs help me immensely, especially like today. And, as far as being a thumper, I'm not. But, you ask, I told you. So, if you ask another question, I'll give you an answer. But I won't try to push anything religious on you."

"You sure are different," Don said. "Well, I better get back to work."

Toby waved and went back to cleaning a pump.

"First, the bridge called for Toby's presence," the throttleman said to the First.

The Stoker First found Toby wiping down a pump on the lower level. "Toby, you're wanted on the bridge; are ya gonna leave us, lad?"

"Not if I have anything to say about it, First; I'd rather be down here."

"I'm glad to 'er that. You're a good man, Toby, and you're in line for a promotion; I would hate to see you go."

"Thanks, First, I've learned a lot from you, and I like my job."

"That's good, we'll talk more when you return, and I want you to begin learning the responsibilities of your new position when you get back."

"Thanks again, First, I'd better not keep the Captain waiting."

"I would think not."

Toby donned his heavy coat and climbed the steep ladder to the main deck. He made his way forward with an icy wind blowing into his face.

After climbing the exterior ladder, Toby asked permission to enter the bridge, and the entrance was granted. The OOD went to a bank of voice tubes and blew on one cap, causing the opposite end to whistle. The Captain answered.

"Sir, Stoker Greene has arrived."

"Very well."

A second later, the ship's Captain entered the small confines of the bridge. "Captain on the bridge," announced the Bo'sun.

Captain Champs motioned for Greene to join him at one corner of the bridge, with the XO following. "Sir, Stoker Greene reporting as ordered."

"At ease Stoker Greene. I want to congratulate you on your first downing of an enemy plane. It's a good start for the first time behind a twenty."

"Thank you, sir, that's very kind of you."

"Not at all; you've earned it. I'm assigning you to that gun as your Action Station. Right now, there isn't enough room in the gunner's quarters; I'm afraid you will have to remain with the engineers."

"Sir, may I speak?"

"Yes, go ahead."

"Sir, I appreciate your confidence in me. I am happy to serve at your command at the gun and will do my utmost to defend our ship. However, may I request to remain at my post in the engine room other than at Action Stations? I have trained in the engine's operations and maintenance. With your permission, sir, I could retain the job I was qualified for and still man the gun as needed. It is only a few steps from the engine room.

"Now, that's a bit irregular; let me think it over; I will discuss the matter with Mr. Rutland and Mr. Hemsford, the Chief Engineer. That's all for now; dismissed, Stoker."

"Aye, sir." Toby took a step back, did an about-face, put on his hat at the hatch, and left.

Turning to the XO, the Captain asked, "What do you think?"

"He is a bit different, sir. But I see no reason we can't leave the ship's roster as it is and change his action station. He proved he could shoot straight; we need more of that."

"You're a good man and an excellent Executive Officer, Samuel. Make the changes on the ship's roster and keep the Stoker in the after-engine room."

"Aye, sir."

Captain Champs looked through the small window at the bow crashing through the waves, wondering, *'This is a spooky ship to conn, with both screws turning in the same direction and an inadequate rudder. How could any marine designer fail to see the foolishness in it? We're in for a long voyage, which will require seagoing refueling, and I'll dread every second we need to spend alongside another ship.'*

The destroyer steamed northward until a lookout called the bridge. "Bridge forward lookout, smoke on the horizon, red three-five-zero."

"Bridge, aye," the talker repeated the message to the OOD. The news brought two sets of binoculars to the eyes of the Captain and OOD. As the Officers watched, the smoke drew closer, then materialized into the mass of ships.

The destroyer approached the convoy while the signalmen read the flags flying from a cruiser's yardarms. Captain Champs, an excellent ship Captain, easily read the orders. He ordered the *AMPTHILL* about as they passed halfway along the convoy, then smartly pulled up to their assigned position on the after-port quarter.

The long slow trek to Gibraltar began.

GERMAN Ju-88 BOMBER-TORPEDO BOMBER

CHAPTER THREE

A high-pressure front swept across the Atlantic and the convoy, raising the temperature under the sun, but it would take time for the air and even more time for the frigid water to warm. Moreover, the breeze came out of the north, giving the ship a fore and aft pitch with minimal roll. Still, the only comfortable places for temperature were the main engineering spaces.

The convoy steamed southwest about a hundred miles off the coast of Lorient, France, at a maddening eleven knots. In the engineer's berthing compartment, some men were preparing their white summer uniforms with shorts. Toby always felt he looked stupid in white shorts.

"ACTION STATIONS, ACTION STATIONS; REPEL AIRCRAFT FROM RED ZERO-EIGHT-FIVE," boomed the Tannoy. The off-watch crew hurried to their combat stations to bolster the condition-two men.

Stoker Toby Greene made his way to the stern twenty-millimeter gun station, where he donned his flash-protecting gear, then checked and readied the big cannon. His last adjustments were to set his earplugs tightly and adjust the mounting straps. Then, after wiggling around, the young American felt ready to fight the enemy.

Captain Champs looked over his ship from the bridge, his steady eyes setting on the stern twenty station. A small black dot on the twenty-millimeter splinter shield was the black German Luftwaffe insignia commemorating Stoker Greene's first victory over a German aircraft. A smile curled his lips at the thought of the rising morale the young American created.

A lookout reported, "Bridge, after lookout; fifteen aircraft at red zero-eight-zero, five-thousand feet, speed, about three hundred-fifty kilometers per hour."

The talker repeated the report to the OOD, and Captain Champs acknowledged overhearing it.

The antiaircraft guns pointed toward the enemy flight as the alarm went out. The OOD looked down at the gunner station on the left side of the ship below the bridge, "Gunner," he called out.

"Sir?" the man with his hand on the trigger responded.

"Please be mindful of us up here when firing that weapon."

"Aye, sir, we checked the transverse stops, and they will prevent me from bearing the cannon toward the bridge."

"Thank you, and bless you for your thoughts," the OOD said with a smile.

Tension gripped the crew as the German bombers drew closer, hands sweating slightly less than their bodies under the heavy combat gear. Those men inclined to believe in faith prayed for safety and salvation; others gritted their teeth, determined to beat the enemy. Some professed atheists even found comfort in prayer.

Approaching aircraft dropped to two thousand feet and headed for the convoy. The gunner on the stern twenty-millimeter cannon pulled the gun around on its track and zeroed his sights on the closest fighter. Then, four Messerschmitt 109s veered off toward other destroyers; the remaining two continued after the *AMPTHILL*.

"Shoot," yelled the talker, the signal Toby waited to hear. He depressed the trigger, and the big gun began blasting out .78-inch diameter cannon shells directly toward the lead fighter at over twenty-five hundred feet per second. The remaining antiaircraft guns on the ship opened fire simultaneously. The forty-millimeter gave forth their recognizable POM…POM, as they threw up a curtain of two-pound high explosive shells. The steel curtain winged its way toward the enemy aircraft, yet somehow the planes came through, but not unscathed. Pieces of the aircraft and a panel flew off one of them. The tight German specifications of fit and fastening served the planes well and made them tough to knock down. The two fighters pulled off as the guns started concentrating on them. The fighters, suffering from limited range, carried fuel sufficient for only one strafing attack and were forced to turn for home.

The Captain's voice came through the Tannoy, "Men, our two attackers must have felt the concentration of gunfire too heavy for survival. We are far enough offshore to force the escorts to head back to their base or fall from fuel starvation. Therefore, they were unable to fire upon us. However, the bombers are a different story, they have a longer range, and we must take them down; good shooting."

ACTION STATIONS, ACTION STATIONS, MANY ENEMY BOMBERS BEARING RED ONE-FIVE-FIVE DEGREES, AT DIFFERENT ALTITUDES, SPEED TWO-NINE-ZERO METERS PER HOUR.

The First Officer came on the Tannoy, "Lookouts, remember to pay attention to the bomber's tactics. They can be in three roles: horizontal bombing, glide bombing, and wave-hop to launch torpedoes. Be sure to add any tactics you see in your report. First Officer, out."

"Bridge, starboard lookout, Ju-88 on the deck, torpedo configuration Green two-zero-zero degrees, course zero-two-zero, speed three-seven-zero kilometers per hour."

Spotters, gunners, and command swung in the sighting direction and immediately spotted the bomber. The forward and starboard guns began firing as fast as the men could load. Geysers jumped a hundred meters into the air near the plane and began tracking the craft. Finally, the aircraft passed two hundred meters in front of the ship's bow and into the range of the antiaircraft batteries.

Toby aimed in front of the plane and squeezed off a half dozen shells; their lead was excessive. Then in Greene's peripheral vision, he saw the cargo ship's men running across the deck. Backing off a hair and held the trigger down, sending a hundred rounds toward the Junkers. Toby saw the lead tracers pass a few feet across the front of the aircraft; then, the mottled-painted plane seemed to shudder as the glass cockpit blew apart. The destruction by explosive twenty-millimeter shells devastated its port engine and mid-section. The shudder became worse as the aircraft faltered from the buzzsaw of doom. Incendiary shells started a blaze in the nose of the plane that quickly spread aft. As the torpedo bomber lost speed, the port wing dropped until the tip of the aircraft's wing hit a small wave, cartwheeling the machine across the water and throwing pieces in every direction. Both F5 torpedoes disengaged from the bomber, and one exploded, causing the sympathetic detonation of the second in a thunderous double clap of chaos. The resulting rain of shrapnel injured men on the cargo ship and two on the *AMPTHILL*.

The Ju-88, following the decimated leader, pulled up and away from the fatal track of his commander. Then he returned to a wave-hopping flight evading British antiaircraft fire. Finally, the pilot radioed their fighter escort for another suppression attack on the small destroyer.

After checking his fuel supply, one Messerschmitt descended from a cloud bank, lining up the destroyer for an end-to-end suppression run. Two twin forty-millimeter cannon stations opened fire on the enemy plane, but gunfire from the cruiser shredded the 109s after section and tail and drove him off. The erratic flight of the aircraft testified to the seriousness of its damage.

Toby's assistants at the stern twenty slapped the American on his back, congratulating him with glee on his second downing of an enemy plane. Captain Champs watched the celebration from the port bridge wing, a smile crossing his face, revealing his approval and fondness for the young stoker-gunner.

"OOD, I will be on the stern for a few minutes if you need me. Call the stern talker and have him meet me with the paint and brush; I want to present it to the gunner myself.

"Aye, Captain," the Officer of the Deck said, with a raised eyebrow, to conceal his desire to smile.

"Sir, a message from the Convoy Commander," as he handed the Captain a folded sheet of paper.

To: All vessels H-26C

Change of voyage track

With the discovery of our location by the Luftwaffe, we will alter our passage as follows:

At thirteen hundred hours, the convoy will come to 247.5^0 for 765 Km.

Turn to 355.6^0 for 901 Km.

Turn to 97.75^0 for 501 Km. the Strait of Gibraltar.

H-26C sends.

Captain Champs read the message twice, then initialed and took it to the Navigator. "Mr. Webley, here are new orders; plot the courses and have them listed as an alternate, identifying this message as the authority for the new steaming orders."

"Aye, Captain."

Captain had the Bo'sun open the ship-wide Tannoy. "This is the Captain; the Convoy Commander has changed our track to take us out of the active zone of Luftwaffe patrols and attacks. We will disappear into the south Atlantic during the afternoon, especially tonight. Our primary adversary will be the U-boats; adjust your watch activities to that effort. Our destination is unchanged, and as for the time of arrival, the Navigator will announce the arrival time when he determines it. Good show to everyone for defending the Convoy and this ship; well done. Captain out."

Stoker Arledge Blodwell rigged a fishing line and talked a cook into giving him a piece of old meat for bait. He let out about forty meters of line with a steel wire and hook trailing behind the ship, making the meat a tempting snack.

"Hey, Arle, you gonna catch a shark?" Markie Stone, a deckhand, asked.

"I hope not, but maybe something a bit better; I'm hoping a marlin or tuna will jump on the bait," the Stoker said.

"I doubt it, Arle; I've only known sharks to follow boats and ships to root through the garbage for food. They're pretty crafty devils, they are."

"Even so, Markie, a shark would be better than bully beef every night. Blimey, it's a big one!"

Arle's fishing pole bent to the breaking point under the strain of a heavy bite. The fish began to run to throw the steel hook, causing Arle to release the brake to prevent the stress from parting the line or destroying the pole.

"Hey, you blokes, Arle has himself a fish, and I'll wager it's a big 'en," Markie called out to anyone who would listen. It wasn't long, and a gallery of watchers wondered if the Stoker or the fish would win. Forty-five minutes later, a large silver fish flashed in the sea-subdued sunlight; it looked like a tuna. Markie had disappeared, only to reappear, now holding a homemade harpoon.

"Boat's get a line ready to slip over his tail when we get him alongside."

One of the assistant deck officers called out to the group, "Watch your step, Tars; we'll not be lowering a boat for yer hide if ya go in," he lied.

Arle reeled the big fish alongside the ship without the speed of twelve miles an hour being an impediment. Markie launched the harpoon, burying the barb deep enough to hold the fish. The Boatswain's Mate slipped a line around the tail, securing the tuna to the ship's hull. Additional men dropped a line behind the two pectoral fins and then blocked and tackled the fish aboard.

Four sailors set the large tuna on a sailcloth attached to a chain with hooks in grommets, then suspended through a single block. The opposite end supported marked weights, and the men deduced the tuna weighed over six hundred pounds or two-hundred-seventy-two Kilos. Nevertheless, the Supply Officer, Chief Commissary Petty Officer, and two cooks looked the prize over pessimistically.

"Sir," the Chief got the Officer's attention; "Are we gonna cook this beast? There is enough to feed two ships here."

"I'll be back," and he headed for the bridge.

"Sir, I need to see the Captain regarding a sizable amount of food."

"Enter the bridge, and for your information, the Captain mentioned he liked tuna steaks," the OOD said.

Mr. Beals, the Supply Officer, rolled his eyes, knowing what would come next. "Captain?"

"Is there sufficient tuna to feed the crew?" the Captain asked.

"It will dress out to at least two-hundred-seventy-two kilos, sir. It could feed two ships."

Smiling, Captain Champs said, "I prefer my tuna steak cooked through and slightly browned."

"I'll have the Commissary Chief begin preparing for an evening meal of tuna steaks."

"You may wish to consult with the fisherman. If he does not wish to share, we can't have a dead fish fouling the ship, can we?"

"No, sir," The Supply Officer took his leave to carry out the orders for a busy afternoon.

The Signal messenger arrived, "Captain, a signal from the Convoy Commander."

"Thank you, Seaman; standby for a reply." Captain Champs opened the folded paper.

"What did you catch?"

CC

After checking the sun's rising and setting a schedule, the Captain wrote his reply to the Convoy Commander;

"Sir, you are invited to tuna steak dinner beginning at seventeen thirty."

MC

"Send this as my reply, Seaman."

"Aye, Captain.

A minute later, the messenger returned. The message was short.

"Be there at seventeen hundred."

Small white caps appeared randomly as the convoy entered the Straits of Gibraltar as the light breeze of the Atlantic gathered a little speed through the straits. The convoy ships went to piers to unload while the escorts tied up to the fueling piers to top off the tanks. Following refueling, the vessels moved to buoys; provision lighters arrived to replenish them with dry provisions and food. The first items to be transferred were the mailbags.

Stoker Greene stood in line with the other sailors waiting to see Gibraltar. When he stepped up for inspection, Sub-Lieutenant Trevor Herrington said, "Stoker Greene, you are looking well today. Enjoy yourself, but exercise restraint with the pints."

"Aye, sir, thank you." Toby tagged along with three other engineers, looking at the sights on the mountain. The large colony of wild monkeys presented plenty of laughs at their behavior and antics. The men stopped at curio shops and purchased souvenirs for families back home. Time always seems to fly when they enjoy their time ashore.

Upon arrival at the ship, the men displayed their purchases to ensure the Officer of the Deck knew they weren't trying to smuggle contraband aboard. Then, with their booty stored for safety, the men stowed their caps in the boxes they came in to keep them shaped and clean.

Dinner piped across the Tannoy, and the men found the evening meal consisted of tuna steaks. The crew members ate, worked, played, and fought together, resulting in a family mentality. Sometimes not all goes well, as two men returned intoxicated, and on the quarterdeck, they became involved in a fight. The OOD brought charges against the two men, and they would face the Captain in the morning.

Immediately after breakfast, the offenders stood before the mast and answered the Captain for intoxication and fighting. After hearing the charges and evidence, Captain Champs asked each man for his side of the story. Both men admitted drunkenness and fighting and threw themselves at the mercy of the Captain.

Captain Champs thought for a few minutes, then decided to set an example. "Tars, you disrespected your ship, your shipmates, and the Crown. Hopefully, you have learned your lesson; if you fail, you will have time to think about it. A fortnight's loss of shore leave when we return to Devonport and immediate loss of one rank. You do not want to repeat this offense. Dismissed."

"Excuse me, Captain; this just came in," the First Officer handed the envelope to Captain Champs.

The Captain opened the envelope, and after reading the material, he said to the First Officer, "Call the department heads together and prepare the ship for getting underway," then turned the steaming orders over to the First Officer. Twenty minutes later, the ship's tempo changed as the crew went about their duties to prepare the *AMPTHILL* for sea. In the Engineering Department, the Chief Engineer had the ship's machinery lined up and warming to steaming temperatures.

The clock stroke twelve hundred hours, and the pilot backed the ship from its mooring and headed for the open waters of the Straits of Gibraltar, where he departed in his pickup boat. While still in the straits, the convoy formed up, and the *AMPTHILL* fell in on the after-port quarter. When the convoy entered the Atlantic, it sailed five hundred miles due west before turning toward England. Their estimated travel time, including antisubmarine tactics, would take almost six days.

HMS GLASGOW, the convoy command cruiser, called the attention of all the ships, "Surface contact Greene zero-eight-zero, possible U-boat, range."

On the *AMPTHILL*, Three of their four main battery swung to the coordinates, followed by the twenty-millimeter cannons. Bright searchlights stabbed out from the cruiser, *AMPTHILL,* and two other destroyers and swept across the black waters, looking for the sinister U-boat.

Then, light from one of the other escorts slashed back, settling on the trail of bubbles rapidly heading for an intersection with the 'Old Horse.' Captain Champs, using information gleaned from American Intelligence, Called out, "Both engines full astern."

The men in the four engineering spaces jumped to the commands, turning hand wheels and watching gauges. Then, with the twin screws acting as a brake, the bow plunged into the sea, causing the shooting solution to fail as the torpedo crossed in front of the small destroyer.

"All ahead, flank," Captain Champs said, clearing the area for the more advanced destroyers to use their electronics to find and deal with the submarine.

Another escort's light found the U-boat, and with the *AMPTHILL* having moved out of the way, the remaining three destroyers opened fire.

Captain Champs' actions saved the ship from a torpedo and removed her from the shielding effect she caused by being between the larger destroyers and the U-boat.

Water and condensed moisture shot fifty meters into the air in front of and behind the conning tower of the U-boat as the diving valves popped open.

But the rising geysers of several four-point-seven-inch diameter shells exploded below the surface around the submarine, marking her demise. A follow-up volley of high explosive and armor-piercing rounds began crashing into the boat's steel hull, and five fatal hits on the submarine opened her hull from bow to stern. Finally, the doomed submersible rolled over and quickly sank into the cold, clear water of the Atlantic Ocean, taking all hands with her.

"Message, Captain," the Signal messenger said as he handed Captain Champs the flimsy paper.

CC
AMPTHILL

Inspect the sinking site for survivors and evidence, then rejoin the convoy at your best speed.

CC sends.

"OOD, have the Navigator route us back to the sinking site for a sinking survey and alert our medical team. And have the First Officer contact the bridge, direct him to oversee the Search and Rescue evolution."

"Aye, sir."

Calm but colder conditions greeted the convoy as they entered the bottom of the Irish Sea. The *AMPTHILL* received her expected release and steamed separately toward Plymouth. The rolling ship entered port, and the harbor pilot boarded to guide her past the defensive minefield to her berth.

The post, having high priority, awaited the ship on the pier and hauled aboard straight away. Captain Champs entered his small cabin to find a handful of correspondence stacked on his miniature desk. One letter stood out; the return address identified the sender as the Admiralty.

The Captain looked at the envelope and raised an eyebrow, *'Now what would the Admiralty want with a lowly Town class destroyer?'* he wondered.

With questions creating a frown on his chiseled face, the ship's commander opened the envelope, and a set of orders fell out. He opened the official papers and saw the order's subject was Stoker Tobias Greene.

As the Captain sat on his small chair, he muttered, "What has our young Stoker gotten himself into now?"

The letter ordered the Stoker to report to the Admiralty, where he would receive special training. Captain Champs sat back, "This is highly irregular," he muttered again, the mystery becoming intriguing. Then the orders identified young Greene's instructions were for an appearance at Buckingham Palace.

Captain Champs stood and reread the orders, finding he did not misread the papers. "What the bloody hell is going on here?" It was then he noticed the orders came from the First Sea Lord himself. *'The First Sea Lord, the top ranking Officer in the RN, is ordering a lowly Stoker, and a Colonial at that? To prepare for an audience at Buckingham?'*

A step away stood the voice tube to the quarterdeck; Captain Champs removed the cap and blew into the line. A distant voice answered. "This is the Captain, have the First Officer and Stoker Greene report here straight away."

"Aye, Captain."

Two minutes later, a knock on the Captain's door brought a response from the commander. The First Officer entered, "You wanted to see me, sir?"

Saying nothing, the Captain handed the First the orders. About five different expressions crossed the First's face; then, the Officer looked at his commander.

The Captain's shrugged and showed a nondescript face as much as said, "Don't ask me."

Another knock and the CO nodded to the First, who opened the door, allowing the sailor to enter, "Sir, Stoker Third Class Greene reporting as ordered, sir." Toby Greene held a straight face, but his voice declared his trepidation.

WHITE HALL-WWII ADMIRALTY

CHAPTER FOUR

"Son, what have you gotten yourself into? And stand at ease."

"Sir, I have no idea what you are referring to."

Captain Champs handed the orders to the young sailor. After reading the communications, Stoker Greene said, "Captain, I have no idea what this is all about; am I in trouble?"

"I don't believe you are; this is an order for you to appear at the Admiralty in London to receive training for an audience at Buckingham Palace. Do you know anyone at Buckingham Palace?"

"No, sir, I have never been to London or Buckingham Palace. But I may have an answer to all of this."

"Go ahead, son, speak up."

"Sir, I have a hobby I started years ago as a high school project, tracing our family's ancestors. I became interested in continuing the family history, but the trail went cold in Boston. All I knew about the family ended there, except that they came from England in the sixteen hundreds. So both of my parent's family trees have direct ties here, in England.

Before we set sail to Gibraltar, I found a genealogist, Mr. Robert Kensignton, in Plymouth while on shore leave. After we returned, I stopped to see if he had found anything. The man acted excited, saying my bloodline led directly to William the Conqueror and subsequent Tudor kings. Of course, I laughed it off; I'm a colonialist and don't even have British citizenship. Besides, I didn't believe it all and asked what I owed him for his work. The genealogist asked what I was doing in England, and I told him I had joined the RN. I was in my uniform, and at that point, I felt I should leave. I returned to the ship, and now this. He must have sent the information to his brother an Buckingham, it's the only explanation, and someone in the palace picked up an interest in his report."

"Well," said the Captain, "That answers many questions. I'd wager he did forward his report, and you may be right; someone took an interest in the facts. So pack your bags, and we will arrange your transportation to London."

"Sir, does that mean I'm off the ship for good?"

"Your orders are under the directive of the transfer clause. And even if you are still attached to this command, there is no telling how long you may be gone. But, in the meantime, if the *AMPTHILL* sails, your clothing would go with us, leaving you without your uniforms."

"Aye, sir, I'll pack right away. May I speak freely, Captain?"

"By all means."

"I don't wish to transfer from the *AMPTHILL*; I belong here; everyone here is…family to me."

"I appreciate your candor, Stoker, and I feel the same way. I would like to retain you aboard; we need men of your caliber."

"Thank you, sir."

"Now run along, Stoker. First, check in with Mr. Higgins, and give him a copy of your orders. He will arrange the transportation and give you the authorization needed and your personnel file. You will need it wherever the Navy sends you."

Thank you, Captain, and you, First Officer Atwell, for all you have done for me." Toby stepped back, completed an about-face, and left with a troubled scowl across his face.

****

After leaving the ship, Toby caught a ride to the train station. Once aboard, he found the train had an aisle on the side of the train, and four passengers sat enclosed in cabins. Toby sat down in an unoccupied red and glassed-in cubical. No table separated the two seats. The sailor opened his orders and reread them for the third time, going over the events leading up to his train ride. The American surmised Mr. Kensington passed the ancestry file to his brother, disregarding his request to drop the matter. Thinking about it, Toby decided he didn't hold the man's actions against him; he was doing what he felt was in the country's interest. Finally, the sailor thought about the training he was about to undergo, feeling it would be different. Toby secured his orders and sat back, trying to relax.

The knob on the cabin door turned, and the silent hinges allowed the entry of a woman. Only the rustle of her clothing revealed her presence. Toby opened his eyes to see the intruder.

The sailor sat up as the Lady asked, "Pardon me, may I join you; there seems to be no other seating available."

"By all means," Toby replied as he rose in a gentlemanly way. The uniformed man's courteous manner didn't go unnoticed by the young Lady. "Tobias Greene here, but I prefer Toby."

"I am pleased to meet you, Mr. Greene. I am Lady Amanda de Lacy," she said, using her title to set the tenor of their conversation.

Lady de Lacy sat across from the sailor and asked, "Are you in the Navy?"

Noting the lack of wedding rings, Toby adjusted his vocabulary to the proper noun. "Yes, miss, I was attached to a destroyer but am en route to another assignment."

"Where might that be?" the Lady asked.

"I'm sorry, but regulations prohibit me from discussing such information with non-military personnel. But I can tell you I am a Stoker and work in the ship's engine room."

"I understand; I hadn't meant to pry."

"Oh no, it's just a military requirement. And I'm not involved in any restricted endeavors."

"Every member of the armed forces is important; otherwise, you wouldn't be there."

Their conversation continued as they tried to overcome cultural differences and life stations. Toby looked into her aqua-colored eyes, finding them more than attractive. He saw intelligence, and a quick mind, readily grasping unusual situations or complex mechanical concepts. Lady Amanda was blessed with a clear, natural complexion of peaches and cream; any cosmetic would detract from her beauty. Toby found himself engulfed in her beauty, intelligence, and gracefulness.

The young English Lady didn't fail to take in the available attributes of this navy man. She watched his mannerism, noting he was polite, almost to a fault, and not in any way a braggart, a trait Lady de Lacy disliked as immaturity and egotistical. Amanda felt herself falling into his near emerald green eyes. Due to his accent, she was having trouble connecting his name Greene with Norton's Greene. The more she listened to this handsome man, the more she noted that his pronunciation was not English.

"Can you tell me where you call home?" Amanda asked.

"Yes, I'm from a small farm town in rural Virginia."

"You're an American, then?"

"Yes, I am."

"Please call me Amanda; I dislike ma'am since I am single, and titles are a bore."

"Yes, ma…Amanda," Toby corrected himself.

Amanda smiled, showing Toby, the perfect white teeth of a well-kept person. Then he noticed the twinkle in the aqua eyes of a happy and possibly naughty young lady. His eyes didn't miss her dress's poor job hiding her Aphrodite figure.

Changing the direction of the conversation, Amanda asked, "What does that patch mean?"

"It is an identifier of my rank and rating. For example, I'm a Leading Stoker in engineering; the red propeller indicates I work and operate the ship's engines."

"And what does this patch mean; it looks like a cannon?"

"It means I am also a gunner; I shoot at the enemy."

Amanda raised her eyebrows, "You mean one of those big guns you have to crawl into?"

"Oh no, I fired a twenty-millimeter cannon on my ship."

"But you said you worked in the engine room; that does not make sense. Gunner shoots guns, and mechanics run the engines," Amanda insisted.

"I do work in the engine room, and when we are at Action Stations, I man the stern twenty-millimeter cannon. The Captain can utilize men where he needs them to ensure the ship's safety and complete her mission."

“I thought only the gunners shoot the guns.”

“Normally, they do. However, in this situation, our ship was strafed by a German fighter, and the pilot wounded the men manning that cannon. The fact that I could shoot had gotten around, and the Captain assigned me to man the gun. Therefore, I work and stand watches in the engine room, but I man the gun when we fight.”

“That’s strange; I’ve never heard of such an arrangement; gunners are gunners, and Stokers are Stokers.”

“You seem to be rather knowledgeable about naval rates and ratings.”

“Oh, I wasn’t going to let on. I’m from a military family, the Navy, to be exact,” Amanda said with a look of embarrassment.

“I take it you have family in the RN?”

“Yes, our family has sailed the seas for over two hundred years. My grandfather is in the Navy today.”

“What about your father? Is he in the Navy?”

A look of sadness spoiled the woman’s beauty, “He lost his life in the Battle of Jutland.”

“I’m terribly sorry; I didn’t mean to pry or cause you such pain.”

“Thank you, Stoker Greene; I hardly remember my father; he spent most of his time aboard ships. My mother suffered his loss; it broke her heart, and she never recovered from his loss, passing from a broken heart.”

“I have no words to express my regret for opening that wound. But, please, call me Toby; Stoker Greene sounds so formal.”

The hurt Toby saw in Amanda’s eyes came from her mother’s grief and loss more than the loss of her mostly absent father.

Amanda smiled at the sailor, thinking, *‘This sailor is so kind and sensitive to others’ emotional distress. What a change to meet a man her age with empathy. Those she had met in recent years were all about themselves. Now with the war on, it is the center of their conversations. But unfortunately, these men are so ego-driven that they miss life’s true values.*

The two young people continued their conversation, exploring their present and future goals and ‘what ifs.’

Toby had subconsciously tagged Amanda as his 'Sea Flower.' The sailor fell under her spell of beauty, intelligence, and caring.

Amanda had slipped under Toby's aurora of gentle strength and a strong ethical foundation needed for the security a woman required at the time. In Amanda's eyes, he appeared as the poster-grade sailor the Royal Navy needed. In addition, Lady de Lacy had the beginnings of serious thoughts about the Yank, as the English called Americans. Two traits that stood out impacted Amanda's intellect, Toby was pleasantly different from the young men Amanda knew, and his sincerity was real.

Their hours of conversation ate up the kilometers, and the train pulled into the big city of London. As they neared the Paddington Rail Station, Toby pulled his cap from the small overhead bin, and when he turned around, Amanda stood next to him. She grasped his cheeks and kissed him. Then pressed a folded paper into his hand.

"Take care of yourself, Toby, and drop me a line now and then." While the sailor tried to recover, the beautiful dream disappeared among the disembarking crowd.

Toby opened the note to find her name, address, and telly number. Her residence was in Nottingham; Toby wondered what she was doing in Liverpool, where she claimed to visit family.

A black taxi pulled up on the street at the station's entrance, and the driver stepped out. "Where can I take ya Mate?" Toby showed the driver the address on his orders, and the driver said, "Let me place your bag in the boot, and I'll have you there in a flash."

In the taxi, the driver said, "That's the Admiralty Mate; you're not an admiral in disguise, are ya?"

"I've been called many things," Toby chuckled, "But being an admiral is not one of them. I'm just a lowly Stoker; the top dogs probably want someone to start their tea heaters." They laughed, then Toby fell silent as the driver pointed out famous buildings Toby had only read about in magazines and books.

"You're a Yank, aren't ya?"

"Yes, I am."

"What are ya doin in the King's service?"

"I got this call one day, 'go fight the Germans,' and here I am."

"The devil, ya say?" the cabbie blurted.

"It's true, the voice said; Hitler was killing people in an unrighteous war. So I joined the Royal Navy, and now I'm in it with all of England."

"That it is, mate, he's an evil one, he is. Well, good luck to ya. The main entrance is over there, where the sandbags are stacked up. And mind yer self and do what the Marines say; they are a hard bunch and won't take any sass."

"Thanks, mate," Toby said, returning the man's kindness.

The taxi driver pulled Toby's seabag from the boot while the sailor pulled some money from his pockets.

The taxi driver held up his hand, "No, sir, you came a long way to fight for us; I'll not take a shilling from you."

"Well, thank you, sir."

"It's nothing compared to what you're putting on the line for us." The smiling taxi driver hopped back into his black taxi and drove off with a wave.

Toby hefted his seabag to his shoulder and walked across the huge open marching field to the sandbagged entrance. Two armed Marines stood stock still as statues, Lee-Enfields at the ready, their eyes never leaving the approaching figure, particularly his hands.

"Stop where you are, sailor," one barked with authority.

Toby froze, trusting these men weren't trigger-happy.

"State your business," another order blared at him.

"I'm Stoker Tobias Greene and have orders to appear at the Admiralty."

"A Stoker, you say?"

"Yes."

"Set your bag on the ground, and stand at attention." Toby complied, his brow furling in concern.

One of the sentries made a circling approach toward the sailor while the other drew a bead on him with his seven-point-seven millimeter rifle aimed at his heart. The Marine frisked Toby for weapons, then asked, "Where are your orders?"

"They are inside the bag, on the top of my clothes, in the large envelope."

"We will retrieve your orders, stand at ease but do not move around, and maintain silence."

"Aye."

Toby didn't see the signal from the Marine behind him, but the second sentry came out at a trot, his bayonet-tipped rifle still pointed at the sailor.

The first Marine located the American's orders and read the top page. He said, "You can relax now; sorry about the reception. We had no notification of your arrival, and our job is the safety of the Admiralty."

"No explanation needed; I fully understand. And I'm as much in the dark as you."

"Follow Corporal Hermes, Stoker Greene." Toby hefted his bag to his shoulder again and marched behind the first Marine, with the second taking up behind Toby in a defensive position. As the three men marched through the opening in the sandbags, Toby saw a reinforced bagging system creating a maze-like path to ensure nobody could shoot directly into the building's entrance. However, the sailor did get a glimpse of a machine gun nest about fifty meters to his right and another in the other direction.

Several steps within the entrance, a spotless desk with two flags staffed behind it stood one on each side, and on the desk was a phone, what looked like a register book, and a light.

"What's your business here?" asked the Sergeant seated at the desk. Toby gave him the same information he gave the previous two.

"Your orders?"

One of the sentries who originally stopped Toby stepped up, handed the envelope to the Sergeant, then turned about and left. The Sergeant read Toby's orders and said, "Set your bag against the far wall and follow Corporal Henshaw."

"Aye, Sergeant, thank you."

Stoker Greene followed the strait-laced Marine, who led him to an elevator. Unexpectedly, the elevator dropped beneath them rather than up. The elevator whisked floor after floor past gated hallways in front of the elevator. Finally, the elevator came to a stop ten floors from where they began; when the door opened, more Marines stood, all armed with Sten guns, guarding the entrance to a concrete maze. Inside the hallway stood an officer.

Toby came to attention and removed his cap since he was inside the building.

“Who is this?” asked Sub-Lieutenant Myron Hallsworth.

The escorting corporal handed the Officer Toby’s orders.

After reading them, he asked, “Your name?”

“Stoker Tobias Greene, reporting as ordered, sir.”

After a couple of additional questions, the Lieutenant ordered, “Follow me.” Toby fell in behind the officer and marched in step into the maze. Sub-Lieutenant Hallsworth made a sharp left turn and stopped. Toby pulled up behind the officer and saw another Marine snap to attention and render a salute, which the Sub-Lieutenant returned.

“Inform the First Sea Lord that Stoker Greene has arrived.”

“Aye, sir.” Then the Marine disappeared behind a thick solid English oak door. Seconds later, the door silently opened, and the Marine beckoned the two into a clean, sparse office.

Sub-Lieutenant Hallsworth stood at attention and said, “Sir, this is Stoker Greene, reporting as ordered.”

“Thank you, Sub-Lieutenant, “I’ll take it from here.”

“Aye, sir.” Then the young officer stepped back and retreated through the door, which closed with an almost silent thump.

First Sea Lord Brian de Lacy thumbed through the sailor’s personnel file; while Toby stood at attention, his heart racing, he stood before the most powerful man in the Navy.

Admiral De Lacy looked up, and Toby looked into Aqua-colored eyes. He had seen those eyes before on the train from Plymouth earlier in the day. His nameplate on the desk said Admiral Brian de Lacy, the same last name as Amanda de Lacy. *‘My God, this must be Amanda’s grandfather, she mentioned.’* Toby’s blood pressure spiked, not because Amanda had kissed him, but because she’s in a powerful and influential family, and her grandfather is the First Sea Lord.

Admiral de Lacy’s deep yet soft voice punched through the mesmerized sailor’s thoughts, “You shot down two enemy planes and one a fighter?”

The shaken sailor answered, “Yes, sir, I had been assigned the stern twenty-millimeter cannon, and I guess I got lucky.”

After reading a little further, the Admiral said, “No, not luck Stoker, skill. Your Commanding Officer recommended you for a decoration you have yet to receive. Congratulations on your shooting. Do you know why you are here?"

"I have my suspicions, sir."

"It appears we learned you are officially in the bloodline of Norton's Greene, the Tudor Royal family, and several of their monarchs, including William the Conqueror. That is impressive. The King has ordered you to appear before him."

WESTMINISTER PALACE

CHAPTER FIVE

Toby's eyes were popping by then, "Me? I'm just a Stoker on an old Lend-Lease destroyer, sir. That's what I do."

A questioning mask crossed the Admiral's face, "You're a Yank, aren't you?"

"Yes, sir."

"That could complicate matters; however, I have my orders, and now I am going to give you your orders. "You will undergo training in the appropriate conduct and protocol for a person in the presence of the King," the Admiral said.

"Yes, sir, I will do my best."

"Tell me, Stoker Greene, why are you here?"

Toby repeated his story for the Admiral, and from time to time, Admiral de Lacy would arch his eyebrows as he looked up, revealing his captivating aqua eyes. "Sir, may I ask a question?"

"Go ahead."

"Your name is de Lacy, isn't it?"

"Yes, it is."

"Do you have a granddaughter with the name Amanda?"

"A granddaughter, yes. Do you know her?"

"Well, I don't know her in-depth, but we were on the train from Plymouth and had a pleasant conversation during the trip."

"Amanda went to Liverpool to visit her aunt, who lives there," the Admiral explained.

"During the conversations, I learned she had connections with the RN, and her family was Navy all the way."

"Did she tell you about her parents?"

"Yes, sir, as I told her, sir, I'll tell you, you have my condolences on your loss of loved ones."

"She is my ward now. I need to be her father figure and mentor at the same time; I find it a consuming task," he confessed.

"Yes, sir, I got the feeling she is a bit headstrong, not to be impertinent, sir."

"No offense taken; you're quite right, you know. Well, Stoker Greene, I'm going to call in the man who will instruct you. You must be ready tomorrow; your audience will commence at thirteen hundred hours with some Royalty in attendance. The audience will be quick and easy; the King is quite busy these days."

"Yes, sir, I can only imagine his stress. Thank you for your guidance, Admiral, and may I say Amanda thinks the world of you."

"You are a polite young man, especially for a Colonial. Good luck to you. When your audience is completed, Stoker Greene, you will be returned here for reassignment."

"Sir, if I may, can I request being reassigned to the *AMPTHILL*?"

"I see no reason why not; your request is approved."

"Thank you, sir."

A short talk on the intercom brought the Sub-Lieutenant into the Admiral's office.

"Sub-Lieutenant, prepare this sailor for an audience before the King at thirteen hundred hours tomorrow."

"Aye, sir. Stoker, follow me."

Toby duly followed the officer to another room, where he read and signed several forms. Finally, the Sub-Lieutenant handed Toby a thick pamphlet describing the requirements and protocol for the audience. Then he stepped out of the room, only to return in less than three minutes.

Toby sat upright in his chair, waiting for the next part of the instructions. "Are you going to read the protocol instructions, Stoker?"

"I did, sir."

"You didn't have it that long; it's twenty-two pages; tell me, what did it say?"

Toby stood with his hands clasped behind him and began to recite the handout verbatim until he reached the halfway point. Sub-Lieutenant Hallsworth held his hand up to stop the Stoker.

"I believe you, but how did you do it?"

"I have a photographic memory; I remember what I see or read."

"I say that would come in handy." The Sub handed Toby two thin books, each about seventy pages. Less than ten minutes later, Toby reported he had read both books.

The training continued until seventeen hundred, when Toby proved he had prepared himself for the audience.

Admiral de Lacy came from his office and said, "I hear you are a walking memory expert."

"I just remember what I see and read, sir."

Admiral de Lacy began taking a liking to this young American. But then, he started thinking about the sailor's future. *'It would be a shame to hear Stoker Greene had lost his life on that ratty old destroyer.* "How about some supper, Stoker Greene?"

"Really, sir, that would be great; I am a bit hungry."

"Come along," the Admirable said with a touch of a father figure.

Toby grabbed his cap and trailed behind the taller, broad-shouldered Admiral. They stopped once to retrieve Toby's seabag, then continued to the elevator. During the ride to the surface, the Admiral and Toby engaged in idle chit-chat, mostly a soft grilling on Toby's pre-service life. On the surface, Toby maintained about six feet distance behind the Admiral, enjoying the responses of the Marines as the two passed. The sailor also enjoyed the anonymity of being unseen. A large black, heavy-looking sedan awaited the Navy's Top Officer. Before the driver could exit the driver's door,

Toby opened the rear door and smartly saluted the Admiral. Admiral de Lacy smiled and returned the required honor; then Toby sat in the left front.

The driver routed them through the more affluent neighborhoods before pulling through a pair of ornate gates and unto finely crushed limestone drive. The drive was circular to allow visitors to see the magnificent mansion, then led to the front steps. Toby quickly hopped out, hurried to the right rear door, and swung it open. The Admiral stepped out of the auto to another salute from Toby. Admiral de Lacy walked up the fifteen steps with a wide smile at the show Toby had been putting on.

"Follow me, Stoker Greene."

"Sir, my seabag?"

"Seaman Hart will take it to your room."

A manservant opened one at the massive front doors as the Admiral approached. "The Stoker is with me, John; have him set up in a spare bedroom and some evening attire, if you will."

"Yes, Admiral."

As they crossed the threshold, each man uncovered, and John took their caps. Toby looked around, thinking, *'Wow, this is really the up and outs.'*

John quietly said, "Please follow me; I will show you to your room." Toby complied with John's directions. John led Toby up a large flight of stairs; the Oak steps, railing, and trim reflected a satin finish, giving the wood an expensive appearance and mating well with white-painted walls. All the door latches and handles bore a late eighteen-hundreds design and were made of solid, gleaming brass.

John introduced Toby to additional help, addressing the sailor as Master Tobias. Toby went along with the unfamiliar settings and speech patterns to keep from rocking the boat.

A selection of scented soap sat in dishes next to the bath. Toby selected the least scented, manly soap from the choices available. The sailor donned fresh underclothing from his seabag and slipped into sharply pleated trousers, a soft shirt, and a tie. John knocked on the bath door and entered at Toby's response. John helped the sailor into a dinner jacket, which doubled for evening attire. It had bronze threaded highlights with contrasting lapels.

John escorted the American to the dining hall and said, "Remember, be yourself, with politeness. Follow the Admiral's lead. And should a lady enter, stand and face her without staring."

The Admiral waited while reading an evening London paper. Finally, John seated the guest, and Toby whispered, "Thank you for all your help." John responded with a slight squeeze of his shoulder.

Toby's eyes scanned the large dining room. As with the rest of the mansion, English hard Oak and brass fittings adorned French-styled windows and railings. Each wall supported magnificent oil paints from bygone years. The white paint walls seemed to give each painting an added frame.

The sailor had seen the dinner table when he first arrived. It appeared to have been finished with spar varnish, then buffed to a glossy finish. English Oak provided England's people with an almost endless supply of world-class wood for furnishings and house trim. The young man sat with his hands in his lap as the Admiral began giving introductory comments on the house and its history, explaining the house and grounds didn't belong to him; the owner turned it over to the Navy for use by a responsible person of stature.

Admiral de Lacy returned to his soft interrogation of Toby, learning the religious history of his family, which was close to de Lacy's preferences. As the two men talked, they heard the approaching rustle of clothing accompanied by the click of a woman's shoes.

The striking young lady entered the dining room, her presence gathering all the male eyes. Upon seeing Toby, Amanda de Lacy lit up like a sign, and her beautiful smile glistened like white diamonds as she locked eyes with the American. The men stood facing the new arrival. Amanda went to her grandfather and kissed him on his cheek, then sat across from the young man that stirred her from their first meeting.

Brian de Lacy could not help but notice the magical attraction between the two. Although he maintained a straight face, he smiled within. Then, a single thought flashed through his superb mind, *'Could it be this simple?'*

During the meal, the three discussed many topics; the war took the greatest time. Amanda succeeded in redirecting the conversation and asked Toby about his family.

Finally, the Admiral announced he was adjourning to the outside garden for his evening cigar. "Care to join me, Toby?"

The American stood; nobody in their right mind would fail to see the Admiral's statement held an undefined order. Toby followed his senior officer and took a seat after the Admiral had done so.

Toby accepted a cigar from the outstretched box of premium cigars. Having never smoked a cigar or other tobacco product, he carefully watched the actions of the Admiral as he prepared the La Aroma de Cuba cigar and clipped the end from it. As John had suggested, Toby mimicked the senior man, and to his surprise, the Admiral held a match beneath the cigar.

"Did you know these are one of Prime Minister Churchill's favorite cigars?"

"No, sir, I did not."

"Your first?"

The slightly embarrassed Stoker Greene nodded his innocence. "Yes, sir."

"We all must start somewhere. First, don't inhale; let the smoke roll around your mouth, then exhale it gently."

Amanda made no pretenses at stealth as she entered. The bold young woman wasn't about to let her grandfather monopolize this American.

The men stood in respect as Amanda asked to join them. "By all means," the Admiral agreed. He noticed his granddaughter was more than interested in the American. *'This could be good or troublesome,'* he thought.

As the evening progressed, the trio covered many subjects, none of which would impact the world. But, except for one reoccurring item, one of the three would occasionally crack a joke or bring up a fun-filled incident, resulting in genuine laughter. The senior Lacy saw the evening as the beginning foundation of a future for the two young adults.

By eleven-thirty, the small group opted to turn in, for the next day promised to be extraordinary for Stoker Tobias Greene. Toby brushed his teeth twice to clear off the taste and odor of the cigar.

It wasn't as bad as he thought it would be, but he thought, *'I doubt I'll make the cigar addiction to my lifestyle.'*

Zero-five-thirty found Toby wide awake. He had succumbed to the time schedule of the Royal Navy. He was back to the bathroom to ready himself for his audience with the leader of the UK. Toby's mind returned to the oversized bed, *'I think that was the most exciting dream I had. But was it a dream or for real? Surly, Amanda didn't come to me during the night, and...no, she wouldn't do that, would she?'* The sailor dressed in his blue uniform he found freshly cleaned and hanging on hangers. *'This place is amazing; they must also have a cleaning service on the property.'*

The sailor felt unusually refreshed and lightly descended the wide stairs. At the breakfast table, the Admiral asked, "You're looking spry; I take it you had a good night's rest."

"Yes, sir, I haven't slept in any bed or hammock as well as last night." Toby glanced at the strangely silent Amanda, who appeared to glow, and had an exceptionally shy demeanor. Everything about her behavior brought back his questions about his dream.

Admiral de Lacy asked, "Toby, do you have the medals which came with the ribbons you wear?"

Toby's right hand reached up to the two ribbons on his uniform, then answered, "Yes, sir, I have my entire wardrobe in my seabag."

"While we are changing our clothes, fetch the ribbons and exchange the ribbons for the formal meeting."

"Aye, sir."

Later, Admiral de Lacy came down the stairs, escorting Lady Amanda. The Admiral stood tall and magnificent in his dress uniform and was decorated with many awards. But, on the other hand, Lady Amanda would turn all eyes on her when she entered the Court of the King in her light yellow dress and hat. Again, clothes could not hide her Aphrodite figure, which seemed to highlight the glow on her face and the shyness of her being. Her radiant smile for Toby more than captivated him; it changed his world.

Buckingham Palace is unmatched in the United Kingdom and most of the world. Splendor and pageantry are their hallmarks, and

Buckingham's formality maintains the permanence of the atmosphere. Yet, after the introductory address, including the immediate audience participation, Toby still did not understand the whole purpose of all the pomp and circumstance, followed his training, and stood at attention before King George VI.

King George addressed the attendees, " The Village Norton, as you know, was purchased by Sir Henry de Grene from William the Conqueror in the 14th Century, bestowing on the acquisition the title Grenes Norton, which is today known as Greenes Norton. Our guest, Tobias Greene, was born in the colonies, and his direct ancestral line to Greenes Norton has been confirmed by licensed Genealogist Robert Kensington, Esquire.

Stoker Tobias Greene came to us as an American volunteer to join the fight against our enemies. As a stoker on a Town class destroyer, Stoker Greene's action station normally kept him in the engine room. Fortunately, his upbringing required him to help feed the family by hunting, making him an expert marksman.

His ship came under air attack, wounding a gun crew. Stoker Greene's skill was related to an officer who reported the fact to the Commanding Officer, Lieutenant Commander Michael Champs. Stoker Greene volunteered to man the gun and promptly shot down the attacking German aircraft.

During the next encounter, an enemy torpedo bomber was making a run on a cargo ship. It, too, was destroyed by Stoker Greene. Stoker Greene is credited not only with destroying two enemy aircraft but saving a cargo ship loaded with valuable supplies and, more so, saving the lives of many brave English seamen.

Commander Champs has recommended an award for Stoker Greene for a later date. However, in light of the voluntary effort of one man, all the requirements by Stoker Greene have been considered and approved for another award."

"Tobias Greene, kneel."

Following traditional dialog in French, the King said, "Arise, Sir Knight." Having problems believing what had happened, Toby stood at attention, his knees shaking. He gave a glance toward the Admiral, his mentor and strength. The fatherly figure had an ear-to-ear smile, and Amanda held a lace hanky in her hand to dab her eyes while her smile rivaled her grandfather's.

"Ladies and gentlemen," King George said, "I realize this ceremony is short. However, we took the precaution to protect all who were here.

"Ladies and gentlemen, meet Sir Tobias de Greene."

The applause shook the rafters for the somewhat shaken sailor. However, it quickly quieted down as the King remained standing.

King George slightly moved his hand, and a man brought forth a shield with the colors of Greenes Norton. The man stood before Toby and helped him don the heavy metal shield.

He said, "I am Sir Reginald de Greene of Greenes Norton. Congratulations on joining our fold. If you have sufficient time, we welcome you to attend a reception at the Village Norton Inn."

"Thank you, Sir Reginald; it will be an honor. May I ask if Admiral de Lacy and the Lady de Lacy will attend?"

"Most certainly, Sir Tobias. Sir Brian is an old friend; we haven't seen the Lady de Lacy in some time."

"Thank you again, Sir Reginald." He looked at the shield, not knowing what to do with the heavy object.

"Let me take this shield. All the current Knights of Greenes Norton have their shields mounted in the castle."

"I would appreciate having this shield standing alongside its brothers," Toby said.

"It will be an honor to have it displayed. You have become a hero to the village, you know."

"I had no idea, Sir Reginald; this is an unbelievable set of events for me right now."

"I understand," the Greenes Norton Knight answered as he took charge of the artifact.

"Sir Tobias, please, walk with me," the King said.

"Your Majesty, I admit to being unprepared for this honor; it was a complete surprise; I wish to thank you from the bottom of my heart. Sir, you have changed my life for the better, and I shall always be indebted to you."

"Thank you, Sir Tobias; you are a fine gentleman and would make an excellent ambassador for the United States. It was a last-minute decision, and I think it turned out exceptionally well. And, I would suggest you pay serious attention to Lady de Lacy; Amanda, I dare say, has become seriously taken with you, and you could not find a better loving woman in which to have a wonderful life together. But it is only a suggestion."

"Thank you again, Your Majesty; I will follow your suggestion. One last thing, Sir. You would like my father; you are both cut from great stock. By your leave, Sir."

"Sir Tobias, your request to return to the *AMPTHILL* is granted, providing you take as much precaution as possible for a safe return. I know you must do your job; at least you will be able to fire back at the enemy." Then the King of England turned away and walked down a passage as a staff member took charge of the new Knight.

The staff ushered Toby into another room where the Admiral and Amanda waited. Both stood as he entered. Finally, Admiral de Lacy said, "We must depart for Village Norton and your reception immediately. I can only recommend you remember who you are and exercise politeness, dignity, and patience. I understand you are to return to your ship in three days; it will provide you with the time you need to acquaint yourself with your new status, and we can help you adjust to your responsibilities."

"Yes, sir, there is an issue I would like to speak to you about when we have time," the sailor said.

"I'm sure there will be more than one; now, we must leave."

In the drive, the Admiral's driver expressed shock when the Admiral said, "I'll ride up front with you, and please close the privacy window to the rear seating."

Toby held the door for Amanda, then followed her into the back seat. As they looked around the luxurious rear accommodations, they noticed the driver raise the privacy window.

Amanda removed her wide-brimmed hat, giving Toby full access to kiss her with no interference. The new couple spent the next miles discussing their future and taking the time to be together.

Toby added, "I will do my best to remain safe, but I have a sworn duty to uphold; even the King recognized that. When we return to port, I'll head for the mansion."

Amanda held her finger to his lips to silence him. "We have a grand home on the outskirts of Plymouth, and I will move there. We will have the use of the property as long as we need. And that will give us plenty of time to plan our future. First, however, there is one undisputable fact you must understand."

Red flags popped up in Toby's heart, but he said nothing until he heard Amanda's exception.

"I have no doubt we will marry in a short time, and it is not only my duty but my desire to go anywhere you wish to live without discussion or fanfare. We will be one, and you, Sir Knight, are the man of the family."

The reception, attended by most of the villagers, turned out to be a gala affair, with many of Amanda's friends and sailors turning up from the *AMPTHILL,* including Captain Champs. Tea-time came at sixteen-thirty, ending the reception, and the Admiral, Amanda, and Toby headed for the mansion.

That night, the grandfather clock in the vestibule struck eleven-thirty. The door to Toby's bedroom opened enough to let a shapely shadow slip in for the night to seal their future.

GERMAN HEINKEL HE-111 TORPEDO-BOMBER

CHAPTER SIX

After the trip to Village Norton, Amanda took up sleeping in Toby's room. If anyone noticed, nobody uttered a word.

HMS AMPTHILL's stern gunner finished breakfast, then completed his packing. He was at a loss for what to do with his sword and sash, left over from his Knighting ceremony. The sailor's shield already hung in the castle's great hall. A second shield stood in its crate.

Amanda and he looked at the colorful shield, seeing history before their eyes. The Greenes Norton shield had a simple yet distinctive design. Three stags in a bronze hue on a field of blue. His sword was a full-size steel weapon with chrome plating and the Knight's name engraved on the ornate blade.

"Toby, my dear, we can keep these treasures here for the time being. Then, when it's time to return home, they can be properly crated and shipped, and you won't need to worry about them."

"That's a relief, Amanda; thanks for coming up with it. I think I have everything packed." Toby still felt unsure if all the events he had gone through in the past few days were true or a good dream.

Amanda sensed her betroth's brief confusion and questions. She stepped up to him and lovingly raised her smooth hand to his cheek. "Darling, this is no dream; I know you have been through a great deal these past days, but we are here, betroth, and you are

Sir Tobias of Greenes Norton. Our times alone were certainly real; of this, I can attest. Our promises are more than words; they are a bond to which I am forever committed. At breakfast, grandpa approved of our engagement; even I was surprised. He has grown fond of you, and as much as I would rather remain with you, I know you have a job. Now, we must catch a train.

The two lovebirds and the Admiral sat in his official car, with the Admiral taking the front passenger seat and letting his granddaughter and Toby have the private rear seat. The two lovebirds sat, holding hands and talking softly. Amanda wore a comfortable dress and a warm wool coat she laid across her lap. The smiling woman guided Toby's hand beneath the coat, holding it between her thighs, and then lay her head on his shoulder.

The driver dropped the Admiral off at the Admiralty and then headed back on the road. Unfortunately, Toby wasn't paying attention to where they were going; Amanda's actions ensured that.

The sailor finally looked at the countryside flowing by the vehicle's windows. He sat up; they weren't on the right road to the train station. Then he relaxed; he knew someone, probably the Admiral, had pulled strings for Toby to fly to Plymouth.

Sure enough, the almost silent vehicle pulled into the entrance to an RAF airfield. After the driver informed the guard, who had been forewarned of the passenger's arrival, who he was and displayed his ID card. The guard waved the auto through the gate, and the driver drove to the second hangar in a row of fourteen identical hangars. Inside sat a Lockheed Electra passenger plane. Toby looked the aircraft over, taking in the camouflage paint that smoothly transitioned from one color to another.

Amanda and Toby stepped aboard while the driver and an air crewman loaded their luggage and seabag. A modification on the Electra provided private seating in the aircraft's rear. Toby didn't miss Amanda's interest in that feature.

After boarding the aircraft, Sub-Lieutenant James ensured Amanda and Toby's seat belts had been properly secured. "Sir," he said, "We have your baggage stored in our cargo section. Our flight will take less than an hour, your ship will get underway today, and transportation will be waiting at the airfield."

"Thank you, Sub-Lieutenant; my concern is she will get underway without me."

"Admiral Lacy informed us the ship is awaiting your arrival."

"What's wrong, my dear?" Amanda asked.

"The Captain isn't going to be happy waiting for a Stoker rating to arrive before he can get underway. Anyone else would miss the ship's movement and face a court martial."

"You aren't anyone else, Toby; you are now a Knight of the Realm, and the Captain received his orders from the First Sea Lord; he won't say a word."

"I'll remember you said that, sweetheart."

The twin engines roared; the acceleration pushed the two further in their soft seats. Then, after leveling off and turning southwest, the roar subsided to more of a growl as the Electra reached her cruising speed.

Amanda couldn't get her hat off fast enough; "I have no fondness for hats, and that's why I shun activities in London, where hats are a must." Looking around, the two moved to a wider seat, where they enjoyed holding hands and trading kisses, which progressed to caresses and Amanda's quivering whispers of promises to come, her voice revealing the arousal that coursed through the two of them.

A small Tannoy crackled, then a voice said, "We are approaching the RAF Roborough Airfield in Plymouth; we should be down in fifteen minutes."

Toby, seeking to use his authority for the first time, grabbed the mic and said, "This is Sir Tobias of Greenes Norton. Would you circle the city a couple of times before we land?"

"Yes, Sir Tobias, please let us know when you wish to land."

Toby turned to see Amanda had unbuttoned her blouse and had a hungry panther's look in her eyes. Holding out her hand, she said, "Come, we have very little time left, and I feel it will be some time before I see you again." The door to the private seating section swung open.

To Toby's surprise, a bed sat behind two chairs. After their initial session, Toby said, "Amanda, we must get married as soon as I return; I don't want to mar our wedding; it would embarrass and hurt your grandpa too."

"I agree, and when you return, nothing will keep us apart. But right now, we have to finish what we started."

It only took a few minutes for Amanda and Toby to make themselves presentable, and Toby asked the pilot to land.

RAF Roborough housed Spitfires and Hurricane fighters for the southern end of England and the Channel entrance from the Atlantic. After landing, the camouflaged Electra taxied to a shiny black limousine, where a man stood by the front bumper. Two men unloaded the cargo area and helped load the luggage first, then the seabag. Now dressed as a Stoker, Toby saluted the confused pilot and thanked him for their ride. Surprisingly, Amanda stood just to the right rear of Toby, adding to the officer's confusion.

A Navy Rating ushered the two into the rear seat and rushed to the driver's door. He didn't pay attention to the speed limits; his orders were stated with all haste.

Within a few minutes the gate guard of the Plymouth Naval Base waved the black car with rolled pennants on the front bumpers through to the piers. The driver spotted the *AMPTHILL* and pulled up to the gangway.

Amanda and Toby exited the vehicle, and while the driver retrieved his seabag, the Stoker received a lasting kiss of promises to come from his woman. She took particular joy in ensuring the sailors on the ship watched what Toby had, and they didn't.

The sailor broke the kiss, grabbed his bag, and swiftly negotiated the gangway to the quarterdeck. Toby saluted the Ensign and the OOD, asking permission to board the ship.

Acting Sub-Lieutenant Marc Leighton returned the salute and took Toby's papers. Then, a heavy cable, a pelican hook, and a lifting cable were attached to the gangway and swung away. Toby spotted the car a hundred feet from the pier, with Amanda standing by the open rear door, watching the ship get underway. Amanda shifted her glance toward the bridge, and seeing the Captain watching the scene, she waved to him, and surprisingly, he returned the wave.

Toby took his gear and papers to the Administration Office to check-in. When the process was finished, the rating David Addington said, "You are to report to the bridge as soon as we leave the harbor."

"Thanks; I imagine the Captain will have me keel-hauled."

The admin rating looked at Toby with a raised eyebrow, "The Navy doesn't allow keel-hauling anymore."

"That's good; I can swim back to shore when he orders me thrown overboard. You don't know what I've been through, the past three or four days have been as bizarre as they get, and the Captain was there."

"What are ya talking about, Yank? You ain't making any sense?"

"Don't mind me, mate; it's been rough. I'll take my gear to the compartment, then see the Captain."

"The Captain told the Chief Engineer to save your hammock spot," David called out to Toby as he left.

AMPTHILL and another destroyer gave up their harbor pilots and headed southwest toward the Atlantic.

"Stoker Greene is reporting to the Captain as ordered," the sailor told the Bo'sun, who met him at the hatch. The duty Bo'sun turned to the Captain, who nodded.

Toby stood before his commander and handed him a letter from the First Sea Lord. Captain Champs read the letter twice, which confirms the King knighted Toby.

"That ceremony, although short, stands above all others. I'm glad I didn't miss it, it was splendid. And, like you, Sir Tobias, I had no idea that would happen. Tell me, did that vehicle you arrived in have official plates?"

"Yes, sir, I'm afraid Admiral de Lacy ordered that to get me here before the ship sailed. I don't know if it's because he didn't want me to miss the ship or he wanted to ensure he could keep me away from Amanda."

"Amanda, as in the First Sea Lord's granddaughter, Amanda de Lacy?"

"Yes, sir. I'm afraid so."

The Captain smiled, "Sir…."

"Captain, may I request something?"

"Certainly."

"Forget the King Knighted me. If that gets around the ship, it will cause chaos. Amanda's intended behavior was to ensure the men knew this lowly Stoker has a lady in his life, and she was successful; Lady de Lacy is a scamp; I understand that. I can deal with a lovely woman in a fancy vehicle, but the ship is not a good place for a Knight's shield. It will disrupt order, and if the Huns find out, it will put a big bull's eye on this ship, and I would be responsible for every injury and death."

"You make a valid point, so what am I to call you?" the Captain asked.

"Sir, this is a big request because it will place a large responsibility on your shoulders. Call me what you called me before I left the ship. I'm Stoker Greene, and Lady de Lacy and I are betrothed if the question comes up in the wardroom. But if the latter is forgotten, just as well."

"I see no problem with your analysis and solutions. I agree, and you are Stoker Greene. You might want to become a barrister; you have a gift of delivering a solid case."

"Thank you, Captain; I need to check the watch bill in the after-engine room by your leave, sir."

Carry on, Stoker Greene, and welcome back."

"Thank you, sir, and just between us, there was only one thing keeping me from pushing to stay with Amanda."

"And?"

"My promise to fight for England against all odds, and my promise to come back the *AMPTHILL."*

"Thank you, Stoker, you earned your spurs." The two saluted, and Toby headed for the berthing compartment to change and go to work.

The men on the bridge maintained a quiet demeanor; this time, the ears strained to hear the words.

Captain Champs had earned his spurs earlier in life. "OOD, have the hatches closed for a few moments."

"Aye, sir." Two thuds marked the closing of the hatches. "Men," the Captain got everyone's attention. "If anyone here overheard any words between Stoker Greene and myself, you are ordered to forget them and never repeat them. Lives are dependent on your silence. There will be no mention of our meeting or my statement; that is all. OOD, take command; I will check the ship while we sail to the rendezvous."

Toby dropped into the after-engine room, expecting the barrage of questions about the beautiful lady who almost devoured him on the pier.

Toby took their ribbing with a mixture of goodwill and friendship. After many questions, Toby admitted Amanda, and he became betrothed. That renewed the questions.

Finally, Styles cut in and sent the men to their stations to take care of the ship's business. Toby gathered his rags and filled the oil can, then began his rounds of the machinery.

Part of the Captain's rounds took him through the engineering spaces. When he entered the after-engine room, the watch was at their stations, and the other crewmen were working on assigned chores. Styles jumped to attention and began to announce the Captain when he waved him to silence.

"How are things going down here, Petty Officer Styles?"

"Smooth, Captain, this machinery may be an old design, but I believe we got the best ship in the package."

"I tend to agree with you. Keep up the proactive work, and I think we will come out on top. How's our gunner doing?"

"Stoker Greene," Styles began, "Returned from his days off, and after a few questions regarding a kiss from a lady, everyone returned to getting underway."

"He didn't mention anything about his activities, did he?" the Captain asked.

"He finally admitted he became betrothed to the kissing lady, which seemed to be the main subject of the questions."

"I'm afraid the lady set him up for some teasing. He called her a scamp."

"I would agree; I would say she wanted her man to brag about having a first-class woman on his hands, not meant to be mean, but maybe ornery."

"Good selection of words Petty Officer. Take care of him for me, will you?"

"Aye, sir, the honor is mine."

Toby went about his job of wiping down the machinery and refilling the oilers. Finally, it gave him time to think. *'Why am I feeling so good? Maybe the time off did me some good. But there have been some serious changes in my life, and I should have thought them through a little more. Toby, you have made life-long changes; it's serious; now get your head screwed on tight. I have to take my time, think through everything I have opened myself to and plan to carry out each responsibility. I'm making this promise to myself; I intend to follow through on all my oaths, promises, and responsibilities. Not because I should, but because I want to keep my word, which is my bond.'*

EOT bells rang, and the annunciator specified the speed ordered. Once again, the little destroyer headed into harm's way.

Town-class ships rolled due to the nature of the hull configuration and lack of larger stabilizing fins. But, the men rolled with the ship, these blue water sailors 'sea-legs' keeping them upright and their stomachs in check.

Toby's watch ended, and he headed up to the main deck, where he ran into the Chief Engineer. "Good evening, sir."

"Good evening, Stoker Greene; how was your shore leave?"

"Rather hectic, but everything turned out well. I found London a unique city and well kept."

"London is all of that, and hopefully, you will find there is a great deal more to the big city."

"I most likely will, sir; I'm looking forward to returning to that interesting city."

"I'm glad you like London. By the way, you are still the primary gunner on the stern twenty."

"Thank you, sir; I figured as much; I had intended to check with the Gunnery Division Petty Officers or leading seaman to make sure."

"Take care out there; we don't want to see you hurt; you're a hero to the men."

"Yes, sir."

After supper, Toby went to the stern, finding the gun wrapped in oilcloth to keep it ready. The Stoker spotted something red on the splinter shield. He hurried to the spot, thinking it was blood and someone might have been hurt. Instead, Toby saw two crosses for the planes he shot down, and an enterprising sailor painted a set of red kissing lip-prints next to the crosses.

Toby chuckled, then headed for the compartment and a shower.

The shipwide speaker, the Tannoy, crackled and came alive. "This is the Captain. We are going to be away from home for a while. Our destination is the Java Sea; once there, we will be taking assignments from the famed Force Z. It is going to get warmer, and when we get to Gibraltar, we will switch to summer whites with standard trousers. When we join the convoy, the ship will go to condition two, wartime steaming, with all guns and action stations half manned. After that, we will switch to twelve hours on and twelve hours off watchstanding. Sleeping on deck is authorized, depending on the sea condition. Engineers will continue wearing their blue work uniforms.

We will conduct drills on every casualty we may face; the exercises will continue until the ship can withstand attacks of any nature. And we will drill on the abandonment of this ship because a greater force than we can handle possibly pressures us to leave her.

There will be antiaircraft live fire practice as we can arrange it. In addition, we will be involved in antisubmarine warfare, and our greatest asset is our lookouts. Unfortunately, we have little information on the Japanese submarine force; therefore, it behooves every man topside, lookout or not, to keep an eye on the air and sea for signs of attack. We must accept that the Japanese submarine is as vicious and deadly as the U-boat.

While we're attached to Force Z, we will sometimes work with our brother-in-arms, the Australian Royal Navy, the Dutch, the Americans, and even the Free French Navy; they have a few ships down there. I expect we will see some good liberty ports, Brisbane, Melbourne, Singapore, and others.

I won't lie to you; it is going to be hot, humid, and dangerous, and remember, all aircraft are the enemy unless proven otherwise. Captain out."

Still, the convoy had been shadowed by two high-speed boats a hundred miles west of the French coast. Everyone aboard expected an attack from German aircraft. They weren't disappointed.

The Convoy Commander came across the TBS, "Silence on the TBS frequency," he bellowed. Three seconds later, all was quiet. "This is the Convoy Commander," he began, "A flight of unknown aircraft is coming from France and expect to be overhead in about twelve minutes; all vessels prepare for air attack, maintain distance between ships at one kilometer to take advantage of antiaircraft fire from the escorts. All escorts prepare for maneuvers as per Escort Commander Davidson. All convoy ships stand clear of TBS frequency unless it is an emergency, as described in the pre-departure briefing. That is all."

"OOD, turn TBS to AA frequency, channel five. All orders will come in over that frequency. Sound Action Station air attack from red zero-nine-zero."

"Aye, Captain.

The Captain turned to the talker, "Tell Main Control to put all boilers on the line and prepare for heavy maneuvers."

"Yes, sir," the surprisingly calm voice of the young talker caused the Captain to look at the sailor.

The Tannoy blared the alert, sending men to fill the few open positions at action stations. Toby Greene reached the stern twenty to relieve the secondary gunner, and wiggled into position behind the big weapon, then swung it to port.

Toby noted two transport ships carried troops heading for North Africa and ensured he knew where they were in the convoy. As the aircraft closed the convoy, they identified them as Heinkel 111s. They broke into two plane sub-elements on the air commander's cue and headed for their selected targets. Then, two twin-engine bombers began dropping to sea level in a torpedo attack on the troop transport a kilometer from the *AMPTHILL*. The Gunnery Officer directed the ship's weapons toward the attackers.

Toby led a bomber and held down the firing switch, sending half a dozen ranging shells toward the plane. Unfortunately, its velocity appeared slower than it was, and the tracers flew over the top of the midsection. Toby quickly opened fire and began swinging the gun to increase his lead. A line of an inch to an inch and a half holes appeared halfway down the side of the plane and continued to the tail, where the bulk of the rounds chewed up the Nazi's rudder. The pilot felt the controls jerk from the impacts of the shells, and he pulled up and away from his attack. He headed east out of the combat zone, dropping his torpedo into open water.

Seeing his leader's plane shot up in front of him, the wingman followed the wounded aircraft to the east. Toby watched the retreat, thinking, *'Me thinks me needs some practice.'*

HMS HOWE IN SUEZ CANAL

CHAPTER SEVEN

Tommy, Toby's relief, arrived later than usual, "Sorry bout not getting down 'er, they've been keeping me busy. But, hey, is it true, ya have a mate?"

Toby smiled, nodding, "I do."

"Good for ya. You deserve a fine lady."

"Thanks, Tommy; let's hit the chow line."

"I heard ya got a Heinkel in the raid."

"Naw, I chewed up his rudder, though. I need a little practice."

"Either that or your mate had her hooks into ya tight," the Jack said.

"I don't think that's bothering me, just out of practice," Toby assured him.

The men continued their talks over supper, then went their way for duty. Tommy pulled a lookout station, with Toby heading for the engine room. Again, the convoy steamed closer to Gibraltar, this time not stopping as their track bent slightly south to line up the canal.

The hours seemed to drag by, and the Mediterranean warmed as they closed Suez, raising the temperatures in the engineering spaces. Once they arrived, the convoy began the fourteen-hour trek to the Pacific end of the waterway. The crew of the small destroyer appreciated the canal; their alternative would be to challenge the stormy Cape of Good Hope and Cape Agulhas at the southern tip of Africa.

The Convoy track took the ships from the Suez Canal at Suez, Egypt, into the Gulf of Suez, south to the Red Sea, then through the Bab al-Mandab Strait. South of the Strait is the Gulf of Aden, leading into the Arabian Sea, where they turned southeast to the Indian Ocean. After transiting that large body of water, the convoy turned southeast into the Malacca Strait to Singapore, the home headquarters of Force Z.

"This is the Captain speaking; these past few days have been like a cruise, maybe even boring. Axis submarines continue to be our primary adversary. As we close the Java Sea, Japanese aircraft, submarines, and surface contacts will become more prevalent. With this in mind, we will begin conducting action stations and combat casualty drills. We are going into the enemy's backyard, and they will not take kindly to it. That is all."

Petty Officer Styles called the engine room crew to the throttle board. "You've all 'erd the Capt'n, The Petty Officer in charge of each watch, get your men together and begin going over the books on dealing with the possible casualties; that way, when we run drills, it will be smoother and successful."

"First," the throttleman raised his hand, "C'n ya tell us what's happening out 'er?"

"From what I've 'erd, the trip to Java 'as created a lot of rust, and we need to get time for the deck boys ta clean and preserve the hull and exposed equipment. But then, I picked up a report that came in. Z, the battle force, is expected to blunt the Japanese move southward; they have two battleships and four destroyers. So I think we are goin' to see a lot of steaming and fightin'.

Second Class Petty Officers and Leading Stokers, Make a close check on all pumps, their bearings, and stuffing boxes. Next, make a list of required maintenance, then review the history of those needing attention. Following that, write up a recommendation on each piece of machinery, and I'll turn it over to the Chief." The engine room crew answered and began the lengthy chore before them.

"This is the Captain; I have additional information regarding the Southeast Asia area. The Japanese became a part of what is now called the Axis Powers, currently consisting of Germany,

Italy, and Japan. This pact is a mutual defense treaty where if one signatory becomes involved in a war, the other two will go to a third party's aid. England and France already declared war on Germany on 3 September 1939. With the Tripartite Pact, Japan is at war with England and France. Any ship or aircraft flying Axis identification is hostile, and you may fire upon them. It is also important that each gunner makes a positive identification before shooting to ensure they are not US or UK aircraft.

The Americans suspended supplying oil to Japan for their attacks on China. Instead, the Japanese will push for Dutch oil, rubber, and bases in the Dutch Indies, New Guinea, Java, and possibly the Solomon Islands. My interpretation of the current situation is not an intelligence analysis. That is all."

The intrepid little destroyer steamed in its assigned position in the convoy as they neared the peninsula of Malaysia and the likelihood of getting into a shooting war in the Orient.

Their track took them north of Sumatra and into the Malacca Strait, turning southeast to Singapore on the southern tip of Malaya.

Three hours out of Singapore, the *AMPTHILL*'s solid reliability shattered when a gasket in a main steam line failed. The men in the forward fire room scampered to the main deck, where they closed the emergency valves. The lower level watch pulled the emergency shut-down devices on the pumps and burners, then abandoned the space. Luck was with the Tars, Only one man lost his life, and five men suffered first, second, and one man, third-degree burns.

Captain Champs requested assistance from a repair ship or shipyard, and the convoy commander forwarded the request to the British Material Officer in Singapore. The answer returned in record time and approved replacing all main steam line gaskets and other machinery repairs. However, each space could only open one section at a time in the event of an emergency sortie. Upon arrival, the destroyer moored to a repair pier, where men waited to board her for their survey.

The Stokers and seamen prepared the ship for upcoming operations, which may not allow them time to do the same work at sea or under combat conditions. Meanwhile, the shipyard personnel replaced the main steam line gaskets at their best speed.

As in any engine room of ships worldwide, valves required seats lapped in for steam and water-proof surfaces. Stuffing boxes must-have new packing to replace old or worn packing. Lube oil sumps on steam-powered pumps were cleaned, and new oil was installed. Then there was the need for constant cleanup to reduce the fire hazard of oil and fuel.

Not one crewman believed the yard period would last the sixty days granted. Everyone worried the Japanese would attack before they could get out of the yard. So intelligence sections and the commanders of every ship monitored all known frequencies to get any tidbit of information on enemy movements. Tensions were rising by the minute, and the engineers on the *AMPTHILL* moved to a twelve-hour shift, working around the clock. Nobody expressed an interest in shore leave, partially because they didn't want to be left behind by an emergency sortie.

The Herculean effort by the crew and yard workers succeeded in replacing all the main steam gaskets and completing other planned and unplanned maintenance.

At twenty-four hundred hours, the quarterdeck watch began a new deck log. The OOD wrote the date as Saturday, 8 December 1941.

AMPTHILL's crew completed maintenance and dozens of small repairs and felt as exhausted as the shipyard workers who replaced the main steam line gaskets and additional renovations. After the shipyard personnel departed, the crew received the remainder of the day off; the Captain halted all shore leave. The ship's company crashed; some men could eat regular meals, but the majority were already asleep.

****

A shrill whistle caused many Jacks to jump from their hammocks in confusion at the call to attention. Then, a familiar voice came across the Tannoy; "Now hear this. This is the Captain; at zero-one-fifty-five local time, Japanese forces attacked the naval station at Pearl Harbor with carrier-based aircraft. There is no information on ship damage or personnel casualties at this time. I expect a sortie by zero-eight-hundred, but it may come earlier. All hands prepare the ship for an imminent combat sortie.

That is all." The call turned out all hands, some not yet fully awake.

"ACTION STATIONS, ACTION STATIONS, ALL HANDS TO ACTION STATIONS FOR AIR DEFENSE." Those men in the deep-sleep fog were now fully awake and heading to combat stations. In the four main engineering spaces, the crews slowly brought the boiler and steam lines up to temperature while watching the gasket joints for signs of leakage. None occurred.

The call-to-action stations sent Toby hurrying to the stern twenty-millimeter gun. The sailor donned his flash gear and helmet, then wiggled into the harness and strapped himself tightly to the weapon. The Colonial prepared himself to do his part in defending the ship, despite his hardly knowing the opponent's and their weapon's capabilities. While scanning the still dark skies, several Tars stopped by with condolences and encouragement on the Pearl Harbor attack.

Daylight broke over the eastern horizon, with the sun promising another warmer-than-usual day. "Set the inport security watch," blared over the Tannoy. "The ship will maintain an antiaircraft defense cover, secure from Action Stations. The ship is on standby for an immediate sortie."

In the Engineering Control room, the talker responded to a message, then turned to the Engineering Officer of the Watch, "Sir, the bridge ordered engineering to remain in a split plant configuration and with a full underway watch. With one boiler online and the other on standby and warmed up in each boiler room, the Jacking gears engaged. We will be getting underway at ten hundred hours."

"Very well, pass the orders to the other three spaces."

At zero-nine-thirty, the Tannoy blared, "Set the Special Sea detail." The destroyer slipped her lines at ten hundred, blew her horn, and got underway. At the mouth of the harbor, the pilot departed, returning control to the Captain. The convoy Commander issued the orders for the *AMPYHILL* to fall into the trail position behind the last destroyer of a task force consisting of Dutch and New Zealand cruisers and three British destroyers.

Petty Officer Styles had the messenger of the watch add checking the new main steam line gaskets every hour when they took hourly readings. The old horse steamed proudly in her assigned position, easily maintaining twenty knots as the calm sea helped quell the ship's tendency to roll.

Three days later, the signal flags on the cruiser's yardarms popped open the return to base signal. The column turned in a mile circle to retrace its path to Singapore and maintain the positions of the escorts. The return trip to the Malaysian city passed without enemy contact. Upon mooring at designated berths, fuel and provisions lighters nuzzled up to the warriors, topping off their fuel tanks and restocking provisions.

Orders went down to the engineers to maintain the steaming watch, with one boiler in each boiler room on standby.

Petty Officer Styles hauled himself up the ladder to the main deck, then stepped back into the engine room, followed by the Chief Engineer. "Call Stoker Greene to the throttle board," the officer said.

Toby worked his way to the gauge board and stood at attention before the Engineering Officer. "Stoker Greene, I hate to do this," he handed over a packet of papers. "You are to pack your gear; you are transferred to active duty in the American Navy, but I suspect you expected this would happen with Pearl Harbor."

Toby stood aghast and slammed his open mouth shut, recovering from the unexpected orders.

"You will have two weeks' leave, and you are to appear at the Admiralty on arrival in London. Your ultimate destination is the San Diego Naval Training Center in California."

Toby stammered, "I…I'm sorry, sir, I don't know what to say; I don't want to leave the *AMPTHILL*; these men are my friends."

"Speaking for the Captain and First Officer, we appreciate your loyalty and will miss you. You have been an inspiration to the entire crew, and your expertise in the engineering division and at the stern twenty will be sorely missed, Stoker Greene. And anytime we are in the same port, please, stop by for a visit, Sir Tobias."

"Sir, what is my travel uniform?"

"Travel in summer whites as far as Gibraltar; you switch to dress blues there. Your first stop will be the RN Administration building on the base; they will provide you with an itinerary."

"Thank you, sir; my time here will not be forgotten."

The Engineering Officer shimmied up the ladder and disappeared. Styles shook Toby's hand, "I'm gonna miss you, Yank. But, by the looks of these guys, they will too. So, turn your tools in before you leave, Sir Tobias."

Toby looked around; the engine room crew crowded around the sailor, wished him a safe trip, and told him to remember to stop by whenever they were in port together.

The word of Toby's departure spread around the ship, bringing many to the compartment to say their goodbyes. The Chief stepped up to shake the American's hand.

"You can turn your gear in here; all you need is a couple of changes in clothes, your kit, dress blues, and hats. I have an extra travel bag I'd like to give ya; it'll make travel easier."

"Thank you, Chief. I forgot to ask Styles to send my packs to my Plymouth address. Could you take care of it for me? There is only a couple in the storage void."

"I'll see to it. You get yourself back home to England in one piece, and could you drop this off in the post?" He handed the sailor two letters.

"Consider it done."

"Be off with you and be careful; you have a fine lady waiting for you back home."

"Aye, Chief, and a wedding."

"Congratulations, Sir Tobias, and my best to your Lady."

Shaking hands again, Toby acknowledged the Chief and made a mental note to drop the letters off in person.

After clearing the Quartermaster, the American, toting his duffel bag and regulation gas mask, headed for the quarterdeck, thinking, *'I wonder if Captain Champs or the First is still aboard, I'd like to thank them for all they've done for me.'*

When he stepped through the hatch to the quarterdeck, the first people he saw with the Captain and the First. Toby dropped the bag and saluted the officers.

"At ease, Sir Tobias; we couldn't let our Knight leave the ship without seeing you off."

Toby answered, "You are too kind, sir, and it is an honor to be a member of this crew and to have you and the First as the top commanders. And if I may, I want you to know I will miss the guidance and help you have both offered me."

"The honor has been ours; you have provided the crew with outstanding help and guidance from gunnery to engineering. You have upheld the honor and expectations of a Knight of Greenes Norton and the rare admiration of the King of England as well."

"Thank you, sir; I wasn't aware of that."

"Here are some additional papers for your records. May we inform the crew?"

"Of course, Captain, and thank you for keeping this between us."

"Not at all; you have brought great pride to this ship with your accomplishments; safe sailing, Sir Tobias."

The First Officer offered his hand, and Toby took the strong grip of friendship. "Sir, you and the Captain are an inspiration to me; thank you."

"We shall miss you, Sir Tobias. The auto at the gangway is for you; the driver knows where you need to go; safe sailing."

"I don't think I'll ever get used to all this," Toby chuckled.

Toby turned toward the gangway, then noticed the rails lined with the friends he'd made while aboard. *'At least all this pomp and circumstance will give them something different to tell their kids.'*

Toby saluted the OOD, "Permission to leave the ship, sir?"

"Granted, Sir Tobias, safe sailing, sir."

As the American Tar saluted the British Ensign, the Bo'sun blew his whistle and announced, "Sir Tobias de Greene, of Greenes Norton, departing." Toby walked down the gangway, his face a crimson flush, and heard cheering. At the pier, Toby turned to see the ship's crew had turned out to wish him a safe journey. The young man was overwhelmed with the emotion of friendships that matured aboard the *AMPTHILL*.

Toby dropped his bag, turned, and snapped a salute a King's Marine would honor to the ship's men. They, in turn, answered the salute like the professionals they were.

The American grabbed his bag and quickly hopped into the waiting vehicle before his emotions got the best of him. The driver negotiated the streets of Singapore like a professional race driver. It didn't take long to get to the large ocean liner. The driver jumped out and opened the door for Toby. Slightly unnerved, he smiled and thanked the driver, then turned, almost running into a man dressed similarly to a sailor. "Pardon me," Toby said.

"No, sir, I should have been back a step or two. Are you Sir Tobias Greene?"

"Yes, I am."

"Welcome aboard, sir. The purser will be right along. Is this the extent of your luggage?"

"Yes, I planned on purchasing some clothes aboard ship."

The purser led the way up the gangway and through the first-class section to a suite. Again, Toby felt the results of the First Sea Lord at work. The purser indoctrinated Toby on the ship's arrangements for food and drink and the store locations. The sailor quizzed the man about the dress expected in the first class sections, to which the purser took the time to educate the American. With a proper tip and thanks, the purser promised to make himself available anytime the Knight needed him.

Toby wasted no time looking for the clothing venues, where he purchased three changes of outer clothes and six sets of underclothing and socks. Then there was the need for an evening dinner ensemble, which a tailor could only fit.

After cleaning up from his trip, the Stoker dressed in a conservative pair of slacks and an open-collar shirt, then headed for the open deck to watch the ship get underway. The process, very much like any ship, had gone unseen by Toby; as he worked in the engine room.

When the last line cast off, the ship's horn let out a deep blast notification that she was moving under power. On the pier from where the passenger liner pulled away, a crowd of well-wishers and dock workers milled around, watching and talking. Now at the deck's railing, Toby took in the sight with the same excitement as the crowd. Looking over the superstructure, the sailor spotted two men on the flying wing of the bridge. One looked like a Captain, and the other was probably the harbor pilot.

With the help of four tugboats, the huge passenger ship turned toward the harbor's mouth. Toby found himself looking at the Old Horse, the *AMPTHILL*, for the last time. He saluted the two-toned camouflaged ship, noticing his vision blurred with emotion. Then the image of Amanda flooded his mind, making him feel warm and happy, knowing the ship would take him to his second home.

The ship's track took the liner far away from established shipping routes to lessen the likelihood of encountering Japanese surface units or submarines. Nevertheless, the fourteen-hour trek through the Suez Canal seemed to drag as mile after mile of desert sand slipped by silently.

The liner entered the Mediterranean at the northern exit of the canal and there joined a well-armed convoy headed for the ports of England. Toby received an invitation to dine with the Captain in the first class dining room; the dress would be black tie, at eighteen hundred. Toby felt vindicated for the money he put out for the evening dress.

As the American arrived, the Captain stood, "Ladies and gentlemen, may I introduce Sir Tobias de Greene of Greenes Norton."

Toby sat at the behest of Captain Myron Bevington. Three of the younger women began the question-and-answer session after a few minutes of salutations and raised goblets of light wine. The table crowd didn't take long to learn he served in the RN. Toby took the approach of military restrictions to avoid questions about his role aboard the ship. Most men were more interested in the vessels and weapons the RN faced in defense of Java, Borneo, and Australian areas.

The conversation picked up interest when an older couple revealed they attended Toby's knighting. For the first time, Toby got a glimpse of the ceremony from the gathering's view.

The Lady Martha de Thornton announced, "Tell us, Sir Knight, what was it like to shoot down the two German airplanes?"

Most of the ladies present whispered about this Knight's bravery, and the three younger ladies almost drooled over Toby's looks. But, again, the information sparked the men's interest.

"I must be honest; I do not recall any particular feelings during the combat. Like any man in a similar circumstance, my concentration centered on stopping the fighter and bombers from killing our people and me. But for a while afterward, my hands shook from shooting the cannon and adrenalin rush."

"You mentioned cannon. Can you tell us what kind of weapon that is?" asked the Captain to help the ladies and non-military experienced men understand.

"A Nazi fighter made a strafing run on our destroyer, the *AMPTHILL*, wounding the after stern twenty-millimeter gun crew. The Captain picked up information I had some shooting experience and asked if I would try the weapon. He accepted my abilities and assigned me to the cannon. It fires different shells, armor piercing, incendiary, and high explosive. The gun can deliver the rounds at about three-hundred-twenty per minute, which leaves the barrel at eight-hundred-twenty meters per second and can reach out to four thousand meters. Their impact is devastating."

"Impressive, Sir Tobias."

"Yes, sir, it is an impressive and fearful weapon."

"I refer to your recall of the gun's specifications."

"Thank you, sir."

Thankfully, the rest of the evening fielded many other subjects, allowing Toby to withdraw. But not quick enough for one of the three interested young ladies to attempt to latch onto him.

After a not-so-discrete offer for the night, Toby politely refused, "Thank you for your gracious attention, but I must decline, being betrothed to Lady Amanda de Lacy."

"Oh, I'm terribly sorry, but do envy the Lady de Lacy," she returned to the gathering after glancing back at the sailor. Her one saving grace in her error would be telling the other two huntresses the Knight was off the market.

The great ship turned up an easy twenty knots, and under the guns of the RN escorts, it and the convoy cargo vessels docked at wharves in Liverpool.

Toby donned his blue Royal Navy uniform and white cap with *'HMS AMPTHILL'* for the last time. In their brief encounter, the forward lady looked surprised to see Toby was not an officer but a Stoker. However, it didn't reduce her desire, which still burned within her. Toby smiled at her as he walked down the gangway, toting an oversized piece of luggage containing his clothing and gear.

The sailor spotted a sign held by an RN driver, 'Greene.' Toby walked up to the driver, "I'm Tobias Greene."

"Sir Tobias Greene?"

"Yes, that's me."

"Sorry, sir, I was expecting an officer."

"That's alright; it happens all the time."

The driver looked at Toby, "I'm Seaman Jan Horn."

"Glad to meet you, Seaman Horn, or should I call you Jan?"

"Jan is fine when no brass is about; then it's best to be more formal."

"I understand. Where are we headed?"

"Let me load the luggage; I'll take you to the cottage."

"Thank you. Mind if I sit up front?"

"Oh no, sir, I'm not a back seat man unless I have my girlfriend."

"I agree there," the sailor said."

Jan started the official vehicle and pulled into traffic.

Toby asked, "How has the war effort been going? I just now returned from Java."

"The so-called Battle of Britain has ended, and Jerry removed his invasion barges from the coast. From what I've heard, crazy Adolf is attacking Russia. Hitler is doing pretty good, but he may have bitten off more than he can handle."

"Some people never learn. How about the Atlantic war?"

"Jerry is now sending out 'Wolf Packs,' where several U-boats attack a convoy at the same time. We have the destroyers the Americans sent, but they are only holding their own. We are still losing too many men and ships. Say, are you a Yank; you don't talk like us?"

"Yes, I am a Yank, but I came here to fight the Nazis."

"Thank you for that, Sir Tobias. Now that America and Germany declared war, we have a chance to beat Adolf. It will help put more destroyers in the Atlantic."

"That's for sure, and not a minute too soon, I would say."

The black vehicle pulled up to the de Lacy country home outside Devon. The driver opened the door, and Toby thought, *'I'll never get used to this service.'*

After Jan removed the luggage from the boot, as the English call the trunk, Toby said, "I'll take it from here, and I appreciate your efforts and friendship."

"Thank you, Sir Tobias," said Jan; "You can reach me at this telly number. It's in Devon, and I am on full call for you."

"Thanks again, Jan."

Toby didn't see anyone in or near the structure, so he retrieved the key from its hiding place and stepped into the comfortable house. Fond memories flooded the sailor's mind with images of Amanda and their times together.

Toby pulled his luggage behind him to the bedroom Amanda, and he, used and fully opened the door to get the bulky luggage through the frame. He heard the rustle of soft clothing and turned in time to receive the full weight of fresh smelling woman smothering him in kisses.

The smiling Amanda stopped long enough to kick the door closed, gave Toby a hungry look, and resumed showering him with wet kisses. Finally, the excited woman pulled Toby toward the bed, and before they reached the soft platform, the sailor had her in his arms and turned, falling atop her in one smooth move. They urged one another on, each undoing and removing the clothes of the other. Later, while lying in a tangle of arms and legs, Toby asked, "Amanda, will you marry me?"

"I thought you would never ask, and if you didn't, I would ask you," she growled, ending her words with a deep kiss. "I have been your woman since we first met. But I'm not fond of big weddings; they're so overdone. And I'm afraid I'm not going to have my way on this."

"I can understand; your grandfather loves you very dearly and only wants to make you happy. One of the ways he wants to show it is with a proper wedding, with all the trappings of your station. And come to think about it, it's not that often the First Sea Lord gets to walk his granddaughter down the aisle," Toby said.

"Yes, I agree, and my Mum and Dad would turn over in their graves if he failed to give me away. Now tell me, when do you have to leave?" Amanda asked.

"I have two weeks' leave to use; then, I'll have to board the liner for the two or three-week voyage to New York. I don't live far from New York and wanted to stop by and see my parents. I haven't seen them since I arrived in England almost two years ago.

"Do you think your parents would mind if I stayed with them while you're away?"

"I have no doubt they would be delighted to have you. I know they would want to be at the wedding, but they understand the war prevents that. But, come to think of it, I better tell Mom and Dad of our wedding and confirm you're staying with them, so they can get our room ready," Toby thought out loud.

"I feel bad about taking the road of an up-tight, proper lady when I'm the opposite. I'd rather be a home wife, taking care of our children and keeping our home clean and tidy. So, I have no time for sitting around all the time, primping, looking down noses at others, and babbling gossip like the woman around the gatherings in London do these days."

Toby smiled, "You surprised me; I wasn't quite sure what to make of you during our first meeting. And I've never been a top-hat kind of man. But now, I find we are kindred souls. I wanted to be a farmer and own a farm with a wonderful wife and family. And, after the war, there will be a great need for food, more than now. And I would like to raise cattle and chickens for food to go along with what we grow and sell. So, I researched the subject and found some of the best soil for farming is in Iowa. But my biggest concern lately is what you think of farming as a way of life?"

"I have never been farming but love animals and have always enjoyed growing flowers. Farming intrigues me because there is so much about it, I don't understand."

"That sounds great; I've met some farmers from Iowa and found them well-grounded in manners and thoughtfulness. They come from a solid stock of people who farm for a living. The family is paramount; everyone works the farm, even the young. The men and their wives work as a team. It's truly a family-oriented way of life."

"That sound more than interesting and something I would like, but only with you as my teammate," Amanda confirmed.

"The first thing to order is an engagement ring; every betrothed woman needs one."

"Toby dear, I don't want anything big and flashy; it's not me; besides, I'm quiet and shy," she said with an impish smile. And you know grandpa is not going to let his only granddaughter waste away as a maid. You also know Grandfather is very keen on you; he sees you as the son he always wanted."

Toby chuckled, "He sounded like a father more than once than your grandfather or First Sea Lord. He treated me like family from the first day he discovered we had met. I'm only worried about him discovering we have been sleeping together when I'm here."

"Oh, don't worry; grandfather knows, but he trusts you, respects us as a couple, and we are destined to be married. So, when he learned about your orders to transfer to the American Navy, he began planning our wedding," the smiling woman said. "Enough of this chatter, Toby, we have been apart too long, and I don't want to miss a second of precious time with you."

QUEEN ELIZABETH PASSENGER LINER

CHAPTER EIGHT

Two days after arriving in England, Toby de Greene looked over the church full of people he didn't know. Everything up to then had gone smoothly, but now a bit of insecurity set in with the intimidation of a large crowd. Possibly because so many people looked at him as a specimen under a microscope.

'Get a grip on yourself, Toby. You have been in combat and faced-down death more than once, and these people are not the enemy,' forced him to settle down. After all, it was his wedding day, a time for happiness and the future.

Toby shook the cobwebs from his mind along with the insecurity. Then he noticed his shirt collar was stiff and chaffing; he decided he hated the thing. To make things worse, he felt almost like an overdressed chauffeur.

Standing next to the First Sea Lord, full medals shining on his dress uniform, Toby thought of the three lonely medals pinned on his chest. Admiral de Lacy introduced Toby to dozens of couples, many of whom had positions in the Royal Court.

Soft angelic music began to float through the air about the Methodist Church, causing nearby residents and pedestrians to stop and listen. Many clustered about the intersection, watching the accumulation of high people and startled at the arrival of the King himself.

A voice rang clear and loud over the crowd:

"His Majesty, King George the VI, King of the United Kingdom of Great Britain and Northern Ireland, and Emperor of India."

Immediately everyone fell silent and faced the King. Then, the men bowed in the front, and the women curtsied. King George shook hands with the men and addressed each lady by her title and proper name.

Dressed elegantly in his bemedaled uniform, the King walked up to the First Sea Lord, who offered honors to his commander.

"Sir Brian, this is a most special ceremony for you, I'm sure."

"Yes, your Majesty, I only wish Sir Nigel and Lady Martha could be present."

"Yes, I miss them both, and I know Amanda would give everything for their presence," King George said.

Recalling his protocol, Toby bowed before the King, "Your Majesty, thank you for the honor of your presence; no finer gift could be given to Amanda and myself."

"Thank you, Sir Tobias; you honor me. Unfortunately, I understand we are to lose you to the American Navy."

"Yes, your Majesty, in a word, I was drafted."

"It's the agreement the UK has with America; any US nationals in the service of the King must be returned for induction into their service should they become involved in a war."

"Yes, sir, I hated to leave my ship and, most of all, the crew; they are more than friends. But, on the other hand, I had a good run and learned so much. Best of all, I have a second family whom I have come to love. It has been an honor to have served you, your Majesty."

"Sir Tobias, the honor is ours; we need men like you, and thank you again for serving in the Royal Navy. I have something for you; it would be an honor if you accept these documents in the spirit England offers them."

King George handed a thick official envelope bearing the seal of the King. King George nodded for Toby to open the gift. The contents of the heavy document included a certificate of authenticity for the Conspicuous Gallantry Medal and a case with the medal. The sailor also found a personal letter from the King and official documents making Toby an official citizen of England.

"Now, Sir Tobias, I believe there are others who wish to meet the dashing colonial that swept the beautiful Amanda de Lacy off her feet."

"Thank you, your Majesty; you're too kind." Toby bowed respectfully, and the King moved on to fulfill his duties.

Admiral Sir Brian de Lacy said, "It's time, my boy, your opportunity to run has expired. Here, you must have the King's medal pinned in front of the other two awards you have. Happily, the Admiral pinned the new gleaming medal in its proper position.

Toby smiled at his new grandfather-in-law, "Never, sir, only a fool would run from Amanda. I have been called many things but never a fool."

"Amanda tells me you two are going to farm in a place called Iowa when the war is over. Where is Iowa, anyway?"

"Iowa is in the heart of America; Des Moines is about three-hundred-fifteen miles west of Chicago and hundred-seventy-seven miles on course 196 degrees to Kansas City. Iowa means 'Beautiful Land' in the native Sioux language. The state is bordered east by the Mississippi River and west by the Missouri River."

"Very good, Toby; you know your geography. I am surprised that Amanda has an interest in farming; it's hard labor and long hours, but an honorable endeavor. My granddaughter could live here in luxury, and you too if you stayed. But, alas, I know she is not that kind of woman; spurs and a cowboy hat would suit her fine."

Toby replied, "We call a woman with those traits a 'Tomboy,' and she fits that description better than 'Lady.'"

"I agree with your description; it's quite accurate, and you both shall get along just fine," the Admiral chuckled.

"Sir Brian…"

"Toby, when we are at home and family is present, call me Grandpa or Grandfather. When there is company present, we better stick with the normal formal titles.

"I understand, Grandpa. As I was saying, Amanda and I want you to move in with us when the war is over, it will keep the family together, and it can mean a new world for you as well; it will also provide a quiet place to consider your memoirs or suggest more efficient operational procedures for the RN."

"I might look into that. With Amanda moving to America, no family will be left for me in England, and the travel can give me plenty of fresh air. It sounds inviting. But, it will have to wait until this war business is over."

"Yes, sir, we'll both be busy."

****

The music signaled the beginning of the ceremony in the chapel, and the crowd drifted to bench seats of the church. King George was seated in the front row of the balcony at the rear of the great hall, his personal guards and attendants scattered throughout the assembly in traditional garb. The seating was open to all without family members of the bride or groom, as conservatively dressed couples filled the seats. Then The Admiral left, leaving Toby in the hands of a trusted friend.

Toby's driver Jan stood nervously at the front as the best man. Across from Jan stood three gorgeous bride's maids in identical pale blue attire. One, Mary Beth Bayford, stared into Jan's blue eyes, making contact with his soul. Deep in the young lady's being, she knew he was the one for her.

Sub-Lieutenant Hallsworth had developed a respect for the young American and volunteered to help with Toby's wedding. The Sub-Lieutenant looked like a walking Navy poster display in his immaculate uniform as he ushered Toby to the front of the church. Then stepped behind Jan, Toby's best man.

Quiet draped itself over the church as the congregation waited. Then, almost unexpectedly, the pipe organ thunderously rocked the church with Wagner's Bridal Chorus. The bride appeared through the archway adorned with a low-centered diamond tiara holding her veil securely upon her head. Behind the tiara lay a silk Union Jack, saluting the King. Amanda floated alongside her escort in a pure white silk gown trimmed in cherry red. Across her bosom was a white silk scarf with gold fringes and a simple gold-fouled anchor of a Seaman in the center. She held a clutch of red, white, and blue Carnations in her hands, a tribute to her husband-to-be. Amanda's petite shoes had the thinnest of heels, supporting a white silk design and inlaid pearls shaped into hearts. Amanda slow-stepped, firmly supported by her loving grandfather, the impeccably dressed First Sea Lord, Sir Brian de Lacy. As the bride and Sir Brian reached the front of the church, Sir Brian released his granddaughter and stepped back to sit in the first row of seats. Amanda advanced a step and faced her betrothed. The world about them ceased to exist; somewhere in the distance, the minister began their binding words.

Amanda and Toby exchanged solemn words of devotion during the ceremony and lit the unity candle. When the minister finished with the final words of the wedding ceremony, he pronounced them husband and wife and said, "You may kiss the bride."

As the new couple turned to the audience, they glanced up to the balcony, and a smiling King George looked down upon them, memorizing the scene of the granddaughter of his best friend, Brian Lacy, and Toby Greene, a colonial, who stood in the King's heart as a son.

"Your Majesty, I present Sir Tobias de Greene and the Lady Amanda de Greene." The King arose, "I am honored."

The organ exploded into Mendelssohn's Wedding March as the couple walked down the aisle and stopped briefly to talk to friends along the way. Toby and Amanda glanced up toward the balcony, where King George stood smiling; he nodded his approval. Toby gave a bow, and Amanda curtsied, then the newlyweds made for the exit.

The wedding party was reunited for tea and cakes with family and close friends at the castle in Nottingham. The King sent his apologies; duties required his presence elsewhere. With the war-making extended pleasantries non-existent, the close-knit family and friends gave their blessings. Then, they departed to pressing responsibilities, leaving the Admiral, Amanda, and Toby together for a private discussion.

Sir Brian asked, "When will you have to leave, Toby?"

"My ship leaves Liverpool at twelve hundred hours in five days, sir."

"Much too soon, but the fortunes of war wait for no man or woman. Are you going to accompany your husband to America, my dear?"

"Yes, Grandpa, we made contact with Toby's parents, and they were more than happy for us and asked me to stay with them while Toby was away."

"Good, a couple, especially newlyweds, should be together as long as possible. The time you will have on the cruise to New York will give you a solid beginning in your marriage. And by staying with Toby's parents, Amanda, you can cement your future life together and develop the best of family foundations. It seems your road through the clouds of war is leaving a silver lining for others to follow. So, during your next few days, gather as many photographs as possible, and take or have them sent to Toby's address as you can. It will be a gift for the Greenes' to see the wedding."

"That is a grand idea, Grandfather; I believe we can do that, can't we, Toby?"

"I agree, it's an excellent idea; I know my Mum will appreciate it."

Amanda giggled, "You're sounding more English than American."

"Yeah, I've been hanging around you guys for some time now. But don't worry, we'll all sound like Yanks in time."

The Admiral turned serious, "I want to wish the two of you the most wonderful life together. Merriam and I had that, and there is no substitute. So now I am going to give you your wedding present. You have talked about taking up residency as a farmer in Iowa; is that correct?"

"Yes, sir," Toby answered.

"You know," the Admiral continued, "I am privy to a great deal of information, and you must prepare for an extended war between the Allies and the Axis powers. So with that in mind, and Toby in the American Navy, with you staying with his parents, I have done some advanced planning for you." He handed Toby a thick envelope, "Here are documents giving you access to funds for your new home in Iowa when you can settle down. As I said, this will be a long war, and we need to keep that information here; these funds will earn good interest on the initial investment and will more than cover what you will need to begin operations on your farm.'

“Oh, Grandpa, what are you going to live on, all you will have is your service pension, and that won’t be enough?”

“Not to worry, my dear. I will have plenty to get by, and I also have plans. Your grandmother and I set this up the day you were born, and it has been working ever since. We had it all planned out and were delighted to have you when you came to live with us. Merriam loved you so much; she looked upon you as a daughter, more than a granddaughter. You were always so energetic, and as Toby described, you were a Tomboy.

My dear, you could not have picked a better man than who you have in Toby. He is a fine gentleman and will make you a grand husband.

Toby, I don’t say much of this, not because I haven’t had the opportunity. But, I want you to know I am exceedingly pleased you and Amanda have married. Toby, you and Amanda were made for one another; neither of you could be happy with anyone else. I have no fear of harm coming to my granddaughter with you at her side.”

Sir Brian stood, shook Toby’s hand, and then grabbed him in a fatherly bear hug. Amanda stood, tears of joy streaming down her face. All her fantasies had come true.

“Welcome to our family,” the Admiral said, with a tinge of quiver in his voice and wet eyes.

“Thank you, Grandpa; I would have never guessed all this would happen the first time we met.”

“Neither did I, at first, but by the time you knelt before the King, I knew it was all in the offering. Now, the time has fled us, and we shall have a sherry to bind us; this old man is past his bedtime.”

The Admiral poured three glasses half full with Sherry, saluted the newlyweds, and then took his leave.

Following a half-hour of rehashing the events of the evening, Toby led Amanda on a fox chase to the upper bedroom, where he carried his wife across the threshold.

****

The next days slipped by almost without notice with their preparations for the move to America. Toby wired his parents with the ship's docking schedule but cautioned them to check with the steamship's office for last-minute changes before driving to New York. The next day, the Admiral had to attend to fleet issues and could not participate in the newlyweds' departure.

At the full dockside, the driver, Jan, pulled up to a flagged parking spot near the ship. "I cannot proceed further, Sir Tobias, but as you can see, the gangway is a short distance away. I'll have the ship's crewmen deliver your luggage to your room."

Amanda and Toby thanked Jan for taking them safely wherever they needed. "How long will you be the Admiral's driver, Jan?"

"I don't know, but I hope to stay on as long as possible."

"I seem to recall you had quite a silent communication with Mary Beth Bayford at the wedding."

"Yes, my Lady, we have since been betrothed."

"Well, congratulations, Jan," Toby said as he shook Jan's hand.

Amanda asked, "Have you set a date?"

"Yes, my Lady, we will marry in three weeks."

"That's wonderful, Jan; I wish we could be there, but we had no idea, and Toby is under orders."

"I understand; at least I have an idea of what I'm in store for; I watched your wedding from the back of the church, and it was a grand wedding; ours will be smaller; we don't have that many attendees."

"Have someone take photographs for us, if you will."

"I will, and if you forward your new address to me at the Admiralty, I'll have copies made and sent to you."

"I'll do that, Jan," Amanda promised.

"Sir Tobias…."

"Jan, we are both Tars, its Toby, as you say when we're alone."

"Of course, Toby, I want to tell you how much pleasure I've had driving for you. It has been an honor to meet a real gentleman from America. Most American military men I have met are far short of your standards. Thank you for your service to the King and England."

"Thank you, Jan. That's the nicest comment I have heard, and we're looking forward to seeing you some time in the future. We have some plans for the future to come back for a visit, and when we do, we want you and your family to join us for dinner."

"Oh, I don't know if I could do that."

"Sure you can, we are friends, and it's an invitation, and you will have a fun time with our plans," Toby said. "Besides, you wouldn't want Mary Beth to know you, and she had an invitation to a dinner engagement, would you?"

"Toby, wouldn't that be blackmail?"

A sly grin slid across Toby's face, "That's exactly what it is."

A short time later, Amanda and Toby stood at the edge of the deck overlooking the pier. They spotted the car and Jan and began waving at him. He returned the waves, then stepped into the vehicle as the ship's whistle blew its departure signal.

The mighty screws of the liner stirred up the bottom mud of the harbor as the ship backed away from the pier. Amanda and Toby watched the official black sedan disappear into the crowd of well-wishers, then enjoyed the start of their voyage.

The forecast was for cold weather on the North Atlantic crossing. Toby and Amanda took advantage of the cold to snuggle beneath heavy blankets to protect only their skin. However, the two generated their own heat to stay comfortable.

The newlyweds walked the decks, making acquaintances and a couple of new friends. The shops provided various souvenirs and gifts the couple purchased and mailed to friends and the Admiral. Amanda and Toby kept those gifts for Toby's parents in their room for the voyage.

As the ship plowed into the North Atlantic, the ship's Captain ordered the required abandon ship drill for all passengers and crew. Toby took notice of all the lifeboats lining both sides of the vessel. New laws of the sea have changed shipbuilders' and ship owners' requirements since the 1912 disaster of the Titanic.

The meals aboard the liner showed the professionalism of the chefs and crew talents. Nightly entertainment was the norm for all but two restaurants aboard the ship. They catered to a quiet setting for guests who enjoyed such an evening environment. The two did enjoy the nightclub dancing and dinners as well. They walked the decks in the brisk cold air, then warmed in the soft feather bed of their cabin.

The track of the ship was considered top secret for two reasons; first, the ship's classification is RMS, or a Royal Mail Service vessel. Second, too many liners sunk by U-boats had an excessive loss of lives. As a result, the ship traveled far from normal shipping lines and maintained radio silence and unplanned zigzags and courses. These factors made the eight to ten-day crossing a full two-week voyage.

The great liner docked in New York amid the hustle and bustle of the city that never sleeps. Thomas Greene spotted his son as he emerged from the ship's double-wide side hatch; Nancy Ella, Toby's mother, clutched her coat about her neck with one hand and waved with the other.

The Purser summoned a porter to load the luggage into the Buick's oversized trunk, allowing the four to sit comfortably in the cabin.

Toby's parents, especially his mother, immediately took a liking to the beautiful daughter-in-law Toby brought home. Moreover, they were highly impressed with her title, Lady Amanda de Greene of Greenes Norton.

Amanda explained how she came by the title, marrying a Knight of Greenes Norton in the Tudor Royal bloodline.

Nancy's eyebrows raised in question, "Royal bloodline? What do you mean, is Toby in the Royal bloodline?

"Oh, Mum, Toby's ancestry is traced clearly back to William the Conqueror and beyond. The same for one or both of your family's lines," Amanda explained.

Tom and Nancy looked at one another, their faces clouded with questions that bubbled to the surface. "We have never thought about our heritage."

Toby joined the conversation and explained how he hired a certified genealogist to continue his work on the family heritage and further presented the genealogist's findings.

Amanda continued, "Then, the Royal Family wished to meet Toby for several reasons."

"The Royal Family? As in England's Royal Family?" Nancy asked.

"Yes, King George the VI, King of the United Kingdom of Great Britain and Northern Ireland, and Emperor of India."

"Oh, my, such a long title and a huge responsibility," Nancy exclaimed.

Amanda continued, "Yes, our Toby was summoned before the King due to his volunteering to fight for England, shooting down two enemy aircraft, saving a valuable cargo ship and the lives of the seamen aboard the vessel, and damaging a third aircraft, and of course, his heritage. Then, King George knighted Toby as Sir Tobias de Greene of Greenes Norton.

"Knighted?" Tom and Nancy chorused. "You're a Knight of England?"

"I was going to surprise you with it all when I got home. There is one other thing; King George made me an official citizen of Great Britain."

Tom stepped up to Toby, "Son, you have brought great pride to our family. But, most of all, you have married a beautiful, intelligent lady who has already become the apple of your mother's eye."

Nancy said, "Now all this explains the package which arrived. I almost sent it back."

"What package? Where is it?" Toby inquired.

"We have no idea, son; we didn't open it," Tom answered Toby's question.

"It sounds like there are a lot of surprises for everyone by our coming home."

Amanda sat smiling, knowing more than she let on. Then she added, "My grandfather is the First Sea Lord."

Nancy and Tom looked at her with more questions on their faces.

"The First Sea Lord is the head of the Royal Navy and answers to the King and the Prime Minister," Amanda explained.

"You are both up there with the elite of England, and the socialites, aren't you?" Tom asked.

"I suppose that's true. However, Toby and I prefer to keep a low profile," she said.

"This is all so exciting, our daughter-in-law, a Lady, our son, a Knight, and you know the King, and your grandfather is the head of the Royal Navy; it's all rather heady," Tom said. "And we are in the Royal Bloodline too."

"Well, at least you are; I don't know about Mum." She said.

"Mum?" Nancy asked.

"Yes, our use of Mum is the same as a mother," Amanda said.

Nancy smiled, "I like it and am flattered you addressed me as such. Tell me about your parents."

Amanda's head dropped, "I lost both my parents when I was very young. I was a ward to my grandfather, and he and grandma were as real parents to me. Then I lost my grandmother a couple of years ago to illness."

"Oh, please forgive my intrusion."

"Oh no, you should know; I was too young to remember them."

"Well, my dear, you have our love as well, and Toby adores you."

"You're both so sweet; thank you for taking me in."

"Tell me, son, what is your future looking like now? Will you have to serve again?" Tom asked.

"I'm afraid so, Dad. I received a discharge from the RN to uphold a British law and agreement with the US that all Americans serving the King must return to the US in time of war. So, I'll leave for the Naval Training Center in San Diego in three days. All I can do is let you know what's going on as I find out myself."

"Amanda dear, what will you do? Could you stay with us while Toby is away?" Asked Nancy.

"Oh, thank you, I would love to stay with you. I thought I would seek employment in one of the factories near here."

"That won't be a problem; the factories are screaming for help now with the war on. There is no doubt you can have any job you want," answered Nancy.

"That's wonderful; I intend to pull my share of the responsibilities. I couldn't bear to sit around like the gossips in London, the ladies who pass judgment on other people's looks or look down their noses at those of the lower classes. So, I refused to be seen with them."

"You're a lady after our hearts," Tom offered. "We'll put you up in Toby's room; there is plenty of room for the both of you," Tom suggested.

A few minutes later, Tom pulled into the drive of a modified colonial-style brick home with white wooden trim. The property sat in a rural setting outside Williamsburg, Virginia. Everyone pitched in to unload the sedan and settle the new couple into their room. Tom and Nancy were intrigued by Amanda, and Tom felt great pride in his son's maturity since leaving for Canada.

Three days later, the family drove Toby to the train station. He only took an overnight bag, as directed by the Navy Recruiters. Toby kissed the two women and hugged his father, "I'll write as much as I can." Then, he boarded the train at the call of the conductor. Sitting in a window seat, Toby felt forlorn with the two women he loved standing on the siding, tears in their eyes. He watched them as long as he could, then they disappeared from view as the train rolled into a curve.

Naval Training Center, San Diego

CHAPTER NINE

Every military-bound man or woman requires a training period to adjust to and learn the requirements of life in the military to ensure the mission's success and the individual's survival.

Toby settled in for the three-day train ride toward the southwest coast of California. He looked at the other passengers, almost all male, and judging by their conversations, some had joined, others drafted, and yet others were in transit to new assignments. Several poker games sprouted up, but Toby steered clear of them. While serving in the RN, he learned he would never be a winner.

Toby and another sailor-to-be struck up a friendship when the youngster learned Toby served in the RN and expressed interest in the differences between the RN and USN.

Finally, the Santa Fe train pulled into the Santa Fe station in San Diego, California. Several blue buses stood waiting to transport new recruits to the Naval Training Center.

A khaki-dressed Chief Petty Officer called for the men to line up in ten-man rows, five rows deep, tallest to the left. He bellowed to be heard, "Welcome to the San Diego Naval Training Center. You will be our guest for the next ten weeks. I am Chief Petty Officer David L. Palmer, your Commanding Officer, and you will address me as 'Sir, or Chief Palmer. From now on, you will preface every utterance from your mouth with "SIR," and you will end that utterance with "SIR," understood?"

Various answers came from the men, including a few "Yes, Sir."

In a louder voice, the Chief said, "I didn't hear your answer."

More answers came from the lines of men, with more now saying, "SIR, YES, SIR."

"I still can't hear you; are you deft? I said, begin your utterance with, SIR, and end your utterance with, SIR."

This time there was a change, "SIR, YES, SIR," growled the men.

"Welcome to the Navy," Chief Palmer answered.

The men received their famous recruit haircuts after the orientation and sea bag issue. The first phase of tearing down the unorganized lifestyles of the recruits finished. After that, the conversion to organized sailors, whom all responded to their superiors' orders, began.

While marching, Toby noticed his gait brought him almost into contact with the man in front of him. Then he had to adjust the swing of his arms. In the British Royal Navy, he learned to make a full swing, level in front to level in the rear. The US military arm swing was more in the natural movement of the arm.

Chief Palmer came alongside Toby, "Greene, what are you doing? You're marching like a Limy."

"Sorry, Chief, it's a habit from the RN."

"WHAT?"

"Two years ago, I wanted to fight the Nazis; with America on the sidelines, I joined the Royal Navy."

"You're jerking my chain."

"No, Chief, I worked in the after-engine room of a Clemson class can, and my action station was the stern twenty-millimeter cannon."

"Now I know you're jerking me around."

"No, Chief, check my records, and I'll make it a point to correct my marching."

"You do that." And he was off to correct another recruit.

The man next to Toby asked, "Were you really in the Royal Navy?"

"Yes, I was."

"I'll bet they kept you in some dark hole and watched you all the time."

"Where the heck did you get that? I did work in the engine room, and we were called Stokers, and I did shoot the stern twenty."

Then another recruit said, "Imagine that, now you're here, getting ready to do it all over again."

"Like everyone else, I'm doing what I can."

Later that evening, while the men prepared their gear for the next day's training, Chief Palmer walked up to Toby, "follow me," he quietly said.

Chief Palmer led the way to another structure serving as the administration building for the recruit companies. "Wait here, Greene, I'll be right back," then he went through a door with the sign, 'Division Commander' on it. Minutes later, the door opened, and Chief Palmer motioned for Toby to enter.

Toby stood at attention in front of a wooden government-issued desk with a nameplate at the forward edge, 'Lieutenant Commander Mark Enders, USN' on its face.

"At ease, sailor." The Commander returned his attention to the sheaf of papers before him. A minute later, the officer looked up. "I'm, impressed with your military history. We received a copy of your duty with the Royal Navy, and I noted you received credit for shooting down two Nazi aircraft and damaging a third. In addition, you also received credit for saving a cargo ship and its crew. In our Navy, that action would get you a bronze, if not a Silver Star. Congratulations, any commander would love to have you in their command."

"Thank you, sir; it almost seems like a dream."

"What's this? Holy cow, this says you are a Knight?"

"Yes, sir."

"What is your official title?"

"Sir Tobias de Greene of Greene's Norton."

"I've never met a Knight before; this is a first for me."

"Me too, sir," the Chief cut in, "How are we going to address this at the morning formation?"

"Sir, may I speak?" Tobias asked.

"Granted, please do."

"Sir," Toby began, "I request that all information we have discussed remain confidential. It can only create problems in the company, and maybe further. Can't we bury it in the papers and let me be Recruit Toby Greene? No special treatment, no more, no less than any other recruit, and no notoriety. I'd rather not cause problems.

"I understand where you're coming from, and I agree, it would probably create an issue; even worse, if it got out and the media picked up on your status, we'll have newspaper reporters from all over the United States wanting an interview," Commander Enders postulated. "We'll all be in the soup."

"One other thing, some of the guys heard me explain the marching issue with the Chief, and they know I was in the RN, but not combat; I said I shot the cannon, not shot down aircraft. So, I would hope that if we left it in oblivion, nobody would be the wiser."

"We can do that, I can seal it, and only a JAG judge or I can unseal it. But I want you to know the Base Commander looks through the new recruit's personnel records, and he will find it. Then the questions will fly. So, I recommend you let me bring him into the fold. And I'm sure he will keep your confidence and not release anything until graduation."

"Yes, sir, thank you, sir."

"Good luck Greene; I'm expecting leadership from you."

"Aye. Sir, oh, Sir, yes, sir."

"You're dismissed. Chief, keep this between us and cut off any scuttlebutt you hear regarding this issue." Toby stepped into the darkened hallway and sat on a bench.

"Yes, sir, it's a bit of a shock. I'll bet that young man carries a lot on his shoulders."

"I agree with you on both counts."

The Chief escorted Toby to the barracks. On the way, Chief Palmer asked, "What was that destroyer like in the Brit Navy?"

"Most of the fifty destroyers sent to England should have been scrapped. As it is, they stripped some parts and scrapped rusted hulls. A few hadn't been in mothballs for twenty years, and they took up a large challenge and are coming through by doing the job. Their main duty is escorting convoys, thereby releasing larger and newer destroyers for other assignments. On the Lend-Lease destroyers, The Admiralty converted the bridge to an open design and tore out the enlisted bunks for hammocks.

Another area the British altered the destroyers was to install forty, and twenty-millimeter antiaircraft weapons; the four-inch-fifty main guns are good for surfaced subs and shore missions but can't elevate to reach aircraft.

"Personally, you have my respect, and I want to congratulate you on downing those Nazi planes. I'll be looking for your help in pushing these youngsters through their basic training. None of these guys have prior service, and you're way ahead of them."

"I'll do what I can, Chief, and thanks for everything."

"All right, here's your barracks, get some rest; I'll be back at zero-five-hundred."

"Good night, Chief; see ya in the morning."

The training continued, with nothing said of Toby's unique circumstances. From time to time, the Chief used Toby in his duties, which included identifying potential leaders and men with experience. The rest of the company accepted Toby's leadership, knowing he had served at sea on a destroyer and fired an anti-aircraft weapon. Most believed he had seen combat from his wounds which left visible red scars while showering, but he wouldn't talk about them.

The San Diego Channel enters and exits a short distance west of the training center. The recruits saw destroyers tied to buoys off the channel, and when cruisers came or went, they stood well above the destroyers. Aircraft carriers looked like the Empire State Building floating by on its side. Finally, Navy aircraft landed and took off from the north Island Naval Air Station on Coronado Island, west of the harbor.

One day after the mail call, Toby showed the Chief photos of The King, Amanda, his shield, sword, and himself. Chief Palmer said, "I'm at a loss for words; maybe you should write a book about it all."

Toby chuckled, "Nobody would believe it; I would have to pawn it off as fiction. And let's keep these photos in the dark too."

Weeks seemed to disappear off the calendar without notice, and it was the day before graduation. Chief Palmer stepped into the barracks and saw Toby finishing up the packing of his sea bag.

"Toby, you have a visitor at the admin office."

"Thanks, Chief; any idea who they are?"

"Fraid not," he turned and left so Toby couldn't see his smile.

Toby got to the admin building and stepped through the door. His jaw dropped as Amanda rushed into his arms. His beloved wife almost squeezed the breath from the former Stoker, then showered him with kisses and soft words that changed Toby's face into a scarlet light. Tom and Nancy Ella stood aside, smiling and remembering their separations and happy reunions. The two lovebirds joined his parents, and everyone tried to talk at once. Finally, Toby managed to get the reunion out of the building and saw the Chief coming toward them.

"Chief, I want to introduce my parents, Tom and Nancy Greene. Then he turned, with Amanda holding tightly to her husband's arm. Chief, this is Lady Amanda de Green, my wife, and dear, meet Chief Petty Officer David Palmer, my chief instructor.

Chief Palmer couldn't keep his eyes off the red brunette, whose presence caused heads from every direction to stare at her beauty. Finally, the Chief gathered his wits and secured his mind into a professional mode; "Lady Amanda, it's a pleasure to meet you, I've heard amazing statements from Toby, and all were short of the truth."

After a few minutes, Tom Greene said, "I thought since Toby has many things on his platter, we would look around San Diego, then stop back later."

"Where are you staying?" the Chief asked.

"We planned on a hotel in town."

"Forget it; tomorrow is graduation day, and the hotels have already filled. Let me make a phone call before you do anything."

Palmer reached the nearest base phone and called his wife.

"Patty, how's the house look?"

"What kind of a question is that? You know I bust my butt keeping it Navy clean."

"I know, and I do appreciate it too. Remember the recruit I talked about who served in the Royal Navy?"

"Sure, he will be graduating tomorrow."

"That's the one. Greene's parents and wife are here, and the hotels have already sold out their rooms. Normally I wouldn't suggest this, but we have an opportunity to spend an evening in the company of first-level people who know and talk with the King of England, and one is a genuine Royal Knight and his wife."

"Oh, my, by all means, I'll find something to eat."

"No, you check the spare bedrooms, then put on your going-out clothes; we'll go out for that once-in-a-year fancy dinner."

Then Chief Palmer called his boss, Lieutenant Commander Enders. "Sir, I have a plan and request regarding Recruit Greene."

"Let's hear about it," the officer said.

"Greene's wife and parents are here. With all the events and graduation tomorrow, the hotels are full. So, I've arranged to have them stay with us; we have two spare bedrooms. We planned to take them out for dinner but haven't set that up yet," the Chief explained.

"What do you want me to do?"

"This is the perfect time to bring the Captain into the mix, and the hook is Greene's Knighthood. I figured with the Greenes, you and your wife, the Captain and his wife, we'll have eight people."

"You're quite a schemer; I'm glad you're on our side. Let me get back to you."

"Don't take too long; good places to eat will be gone."

"Roger that." The phone went dead.

The Chief rejoined the Greenes and announced the arrangements.

Tom immediately spoke up, "Chief, you shouldn't put your family out for our stay."

"My boys are off to college, and it's only my wife, Patty, and I. With the citywide events and graduation, unless you made arrangements in advance, there isn't any room."

A messenger ran up to the Chief, "Sorry to interfere, but the Commander is on the line in your office."

"Excuse me; I'll return in a few moments."

Toby called out, "Chief, I'll take my family over to the Gedunk stand for some tea."

"I'll meet you there."

Toby guided his parents and wife to the refreshment stand as the Chief disappeared into the admin building.

"Chief Palmer speaking."

"Chief, this is Enders; you aren't going to believe what's happened."

"At this point, nothing would surprise me."

"The Captain found out a short while ago about Greene; I was able to keep my head on by some quick talking. But here is where it gets good. The Captain's overjoyed at meeting a Knight and is springing dinner at the Marine Room for all of us. We'll meet there at nineteen hundred; we're part of the Kelsing party; you have a black bow tie and suit?"

"Yes, sir."

"What about Greene?"

"Only his Uniform."

"Get him over to the Exchange clothing department and have them do what they need to put Greene into a black bow git up. I'll call ahead and put the charges on my tab, and we can figure out what to do with the cost later."

"Aye, sir."

'Man, what have I gotten into? This is beyond my pay grade,' thought the Chief.

Chief Palmer found the Greenes sitting in the shade at the Gedunk stand, sipping iced tea. "Here is a plan my Commander and I worked out. First, where is your luggage?"

"It's in a secure area at the train station; I have a key." Do you have a black bow tie suit or tux available?"

"I have one at home, but not here."

"We have a fund, and my Commander has authorized me to outfit you and Toby in black tie dinner suits."

Toby's Mum said, "You boys, go do what you have to; we will be here or close by."

The Chief called a Petty Officer from the office. When he arrived, he handed him the keys to his vehicle. "Here is a key and an authorizing letter from Mr. Thomas Greene; go to the train depot where they are holding the luggage of the Greenes; here is the ticket for the luggage. Then take it to my house; you remember where it is?"

"Yes, Chief."

"The Mrs. is home and expecting the luggage. I would appreciate it if you would take it into the house. Here is something for you to enjoy later." He handed a folded twenty-dollar to the youngster. That brought a smile and life back into his bones.

By the time the clothiers finished the suits, it was nearly closing time, and the Petty Officer returned with the Chief's keys, then left for the admin building to check out.

The Chief signed the suit receipt and placed it in his wallet. Chief Palmer laid the suits in the trunk to keep them pressed and allow the passengers to sit in the back seats. Everyone piled into the vehicle, and the Chief headed for home.

After showers, shaves, and makeup, the four looked one another over in the living room and again loaded into the vehicle; the Chief headed around the entrance to San Diego Harbor and south to the Mariner Room.

A valet took charge of the Palmer vehicle at the plush restaurant, and the party entered the hi-society establishment. The Chief, now asked to be called David, spoke with the Maître d, who took the four guests to a table easily capable of eight or ten adults next to the large glass windows overlooking the unsettled seawater.

The ladies, Amanda on one side of the table and Nancy on the opposite side, had a first-person view of the seawater coming straight in from the ocean through the wide mouth of the harbor.

Looking every bit, a Knight, Toby sat next to his wife; then Tom sat next to Nancy across for the newlyweds. Finally, Patty was seated between Tom and David. The arrangement left room for another couple, who hadn't yet appeared. The rounded shape of the thick glass table gave the guests the impression of looking directly at the sea.

The four sat drinking water and chatting when the Maître d escorted a slender yet regal-looking lady to the table. Toby's training at the Admiralty took charge, and he rose to meet the lady's presence, followed immediately by David and Tom. The Maître d seated the lady, and when the six foot two hundred pound man sat, so did the other men.

David rose, Tom, Nancy, Amanda, and Toby, may I introduce Captain Andrew Merrifield, Commanding Officer of the Naval Training Center, and his distinguished wife, Doctor Wendy Merrifield. David continued, Captain, Mrs. Merrifield, may I introduce Mr. Thomas Greene and his delightful wife, Nancy? Across the table are Sir Tobias de Greene and Lady Amanda de

Greene of Greene's Norton, England, now established in Virginia."

The evening began with rank left at the door. Amanda was staring at the Captain, but discreetly so.

Later, during dinner, Wendy said, "Amanda, please forgive my ignorance; I sometimes become confused by all the titles in English history, but how would one become a Lady?"

"To be honest, the only way I could set it all out is with a program of some sort. I received the title when my father became a Knight. When we lost him in the Battle of Jutland, my mother soon followed with a broken heart, but I retained the title. My title has changed to Greene because I am Toby's wife."

Captain Merrifield said, "In my travels in England, I met several middle and ranking officers, one of whom now commands the Royal Navy. Unfortunately, our acquaintance lacked time to develop due to a dinner engagement, but I'll never forget the fine gentleman."

Amanda whispered to Toby, and he said, "Captain, may I fill you in on the Admiral?"

"By all means, Sir Tobias."

"Please, sir, can I be Toby? Titles don't grow on me very well."

"Certainly, my boy, you've earned it, Toby, so tell me, what do you know of the Admiral?"

"I first met the Admiral when he found out our family's ancestry reaches to William the Conqueror and beyond." The Captain and his wife both looked at Toby and his parents.

"Earlier, Amanda and I met on a train to London, and we parted ways on arrival; end of the story, I thought. At the Admiralty, I took training to make an appearance before the King, for what I had no idea. If anything, I thought it had something to do with shooting down a couple of German planes.

The Admiral had me tag along to his home that night, not having any quarters or even a meal. There is a great deal more to England than anything the schools here teach. Then, at dinner, in walked Amanda; needless to say, I was stunned. Sir, my grandfather-in-law, Amanda's Grandfather, is Admiral Brian de Lacy, the First Sea Lord under King George VI."

The Captain and Wendy sat mesmerized at the unfolding story.

Captain Merrifield blinked at the potential of power a couple of feet before him. “Then the King knighted you?”

The knighting came about for many reasons.”

“May I speak, Captain?” Amanda asked.

“By all means,”

“Toby hasn’t fully come to understand the depth of gratitude England has for him. He is a Colonial, and some, still view the United States as a breakaway collection of Britain’s. However, Toby and others have joined the RN to fight a common enemy that speaks highly of character. A friend of Toby’s learned he was an excellent marksman. When a strafing fighter injured the regular gunner and his team, the Commanding Officer ordered Toby to man the cannon. In doing so, he destroyed the planes and later damaged a third, which other ships destroyed. That saved a cargo ship and its crew from a torpedo attack. Lastly, Toby and his parents have direct bloodlines through William the Conqueror. And I suspect Grandfather, a good friend of the King, talked together.

And for you, Toby’s parents, your son is a hero of the Village of Norton; he has found a second family in England, a wide-ranging family. My Grandfather has grown quite overjoyed with Toby; he thinks of him as his second son to help him over the loss of my father. He also touched the heart of King George, who had no sons. So the King knighted Toby and had him walk and talk with him privately, and His Majesty honored us by his presence at our wedding.”

The Merryfield’s sat in stunned silence at the almost fairy-tale story. “And now you plan to serve our Navy as well?”

“Yes, sir, it’s my duty.”

GLEAVES CLASS DESTROYER

CHAPTER TEN

The following day, men in each barracks put the finishing touches on their dress uniforms. Fireman Toby Greene was the lone recruit wearing three white stripes of piping on the blue cuffs of his white jumper, with a red seam band at the root of the left arm. Toby's prior RN service and experience had him start ahead of the recruits. In addition, the sailor wore three foreign awards over his right breast, the only serviceman aboard the NTC authorized to wear such medals. Earlier, Chief Palmer gave Toby a short letter from the base Captain dated for the graduation:

To whom it may concern:

Fireman 1/c Tobias Greene is authorized to wear medals or ribbons for the following foreign awards:

Conspicuous Gallantry Medal	England
Distinguished Service Medal,	England
Pacific Star Medal,	England

/s/
Andrew Merrifield, Captain, USN
C.O. NTC San Diego, CA.

"You will carry this authorization letter whenever you wear those English awards. All law enforcement personnel have the authority to stop and question you regarding foreign awards, and the Shore Patrol leads the pack."

"Thanks, Chief; if anyone is to be stopped and checked, it will be me."

Toby returned to packing his sea bag, ensuring every article of clothing was accounted for and tightly folded and packed. When finished, he still had sufficient room for his shave kit, a small towel, and his personnel file.

Chief Palmer walked in, "Fall in at the front of the barracks."

The company hustled to fall into the man he knew and expected to be to his right and left. The Chief looked at the outgoing company, then said, "Greene, front and center." Toby hustled to the front. "You will march abreast of me to my left. We both will salute the CO on the podium when we pass in review. "COMPANY, RIGHT FACE." Then the Chief ordered the march to begin, "Left; Left; Left; Romero, take over."

Recruit Raymond Romero turned out to have a strong voice that rivaled a megaphone and practiced classic marching orders. He became the caller during all the marches. After reaching the drill and graduation field, the company fell into numerical order with other graduating companies.

Following the ceremonies, Toby met with the families and walked to the admin building, where the men could find their duty assignments. Toby followed a line from his name to *USS JASON L. MANNING (DD-525)*, Bath, Maine.

"That's a new construction destroyer on the east coast; maybe she will be homeported in Norfolk, not far from home," Toby hopefully said.

Amanda cooed lustfully, "I'd rather like that," hungrily, looking at her hubby. The red crept up Toby's cheeks while his parents turned away with smiles.

Chief Palmer offered to take the family to the Santa Fe terminal, and the Greene's gladly accepted. Tom secured passage with their return tickets and Toby's one-way transportation at the train depot. Their train's schedule to depart showed two hours, and Tom asked the Chief to join them in a luncheon since he didn't have a company of recruits to worry over. He gladly accepted the offer.

Santa Fe's black, red, and orange painted steam engine sat, hissing like a snake; the big steel drive wheel with an off-center rod and solid steel counter-weight on the opposite side seemed to quiver with stored energy, waiting for the engineer to open its throttle.

A conductor checked their tickets and helped the family into the Pullman Sleeping car. He noted that the sailor's ticket was a government issue, not for the Pullman. Then he saw the wedding rings on the young couple and waved Toby aboard, "Complements of Santa Fe," he said.

Toby was about to offer to pay the difference in cost, and the conductor said, "I lost my son at Guadalcanal; he paid for your ticket."

Toby's face fell, then he looked the conductor in the eyes, "I promise to do my best to finish what your son began."

The conductor's eyes glistened, and he mouthed the words, "Thank you, son."

****

Amanda sat on Toby's lap as they passed through the western countryside in the gondola atop the Pullman. It was all new to both the newlyweds, but it didn't stop intimate times between them when they were alone. During the restful periods, they commented on unusual sites and sightings, and at night, the cloudless skies provided unusually clear views into the depths of the Milky Way.

At times they slept in one another's arms under the stars until one or the other suggested moving to the bed on the bottom tier of the car, where the soft noise of the train was the loudest and covered their enjoyment. With stops in each state, the train traveled, the trip stretched into five days; then, the family began seeing familiar locations.

The family reached home in the afternoon on their trek's fifth day. The work to convert Toby's room of earlier days had produced a work of art and craftsmanship, now ready to provide a home for a new couple to begin life together.

Time respects no human emotions or schedule. Two days before Toby shipped out for Maine, Amanda woke before Toby after a serious night of love. She felt exceptionally secure and the happiest she has ever been. The Lady de Greene bathed alone that morning, enjoying the silence and privacy. Then she dressed in her 'Tomboy' attire, having come to the feeling of completeness in the rural environment.

Amanda lightly skipped down the stairs and headed for the kitchen, where she began a pot of coffee; The woman had acquired a taste of another American drink. She drank it black, thanks to the coffee-drinking habits of Tom, Nancy, and now Toby. The English Lady leaned against the large table, sipping the steaming coffee and gazing across the meadows through the French-style windows.

Nancy silently descended the stairs, wearing homemade, heavily padded slippers. She heard humming from the kitchen and stealthily looked around the archway corner, watching her daughter-in-law sipping coffee and smiling between small drinks.

Nancy noted her bright eyes and glowing complexion; the young woman's naturally red lips curled at the ends in a smile, revealing inner contentment only a woman can enjoy.

The older lady backed away and made an audible sound announcing her imminent arrival, then acted sleepy as she came through the archway.

"You look chipper," Nancy said.

"I'm feeling very well, thank you, Mum."

Nancy slid over to her daughter-in-law and wrapped her arms around Amanda, looking regal, even dressed like a Tomboy.

"Are you all right, Mum?"

"Yes, my dear, you have brought much happiness into this home, and we love you as a daughter."

Amanda set the coffee on the table and embraced her mother-in-law, "I hardly remember my real parents; Grandma and Grandpa tried their best and were wonderful. But, for an unknown reason, I feel this is where I should be, with you and Dad."

"As it should be, dear," Nancy said. "Now, let's begin breakfast for our men."

The departing day had arrived, finding the family on the railroad platform. The center of attention, Toby Greene, stood holding his wife, Amanda, and his parents. His father's smile didn't hide his grim feeling, while the two women in his life wept with his return to the war, fearing he may never return. The four reminisced about their days at ball games, fishing, and walking together.

Earlier in the car, Toby and Amanda sat in the rear seat, holding one another, whispering back and forth about the wonderful nights and days they spent together. Then one or the other would make a promise of what to expect on his homecoming, getting a rise out of their partner.

The conductor called loud and clear, "ALL ABOARD," signaling the breakup of the group. Toby's sea bag was already in the luggage car, and he carried a book to read when he got bored watching the miles increase between him and home.

The American sailor transferred to his third and last passenger train destined for Bath, Maine. This train carried mostly naval personnel. Toby sat with a few Fireman third-class sailors out of boot camp the same way he did. They were in other companies and were strangers until then. Toby found out the two would be heading for the *MANNING* as he.

Toby expected the questions that came at him about the three foreign awards, and he told the sailors enough to satisfy their curiosity. The sun had set about two hours before the train pulled into the small station in Bath. As the sailors disembarked from the train, they waited by the luggage car for one of two men retrieving sea bags to call the name on it. Then, Toby's name came up; he grabbed his bag and began looking at the blue Navy buses, each bearing a ship's name. Finally, he spotted the *MANNING* and climbed aboard. The driver, a seaman, counted each person who boarded, ensuring he wasn't overloaded, then closed the door and started the former school bus.

The trip wasn't that far, but the road made up for the ride with the bus's stiff suspension. Finally, the blue beast stopped near the gangway, letting the sailors disembark. A Second Class Boatswain's Mate took charge and had the men form into five-man lines, with the senior men to the left and in the first row. When formatted as the Boat's wanted, the first row grabbed their bag and headed up the gangway. The next row stepped out when the last man stepped aboard, with Toby at the rear.

Toby saluted the Officer of the Deck and requested permission to board, as per protocol. The Officer spotted the odd row of ribbons and motioned him aside.

"What with these ribbons, sailor; we've never seen them before; are they something new?"

Toby explained the ribbons and asked, "Sir, may I pull a letter from my sea bag, which should explain the authorization for wearing them."

"Certainly," the Ensign said. Toby handed him Captain Merrifield's letter of authorization, and the Ensign read it with questions clouding his face. "The letter merely authorizes the wearing; my question was for what deed."

"Yes, sir," Toby explained the circumstances without mentioning his knighthood or relationship to the First Sea Lord.

"I congratulate your success against the German planes; I see you're now going into engineering; what rate are you striking for?"

"Machinist Mate, sir."

"That's good; we'll have time to talk again; I'm the M-Division Officer, Ensign Hanover."

"Pleasure to meet you, sir."

"I see you wear a wedding ring; I take it you have a family back home?"

"A wife, Amanda, sir, we haven't been married that long."

"That's good; as nice as it would be to have a full family, I don't think now is the time; there will be plenty of time after the war; that's what I'm doing. Okay, Greene, the X-division duty Petty Officer is here, he will get you a bunk for the night, and tomorrow we'll have you bunked in the engineer's compartment."

"Thank you, sir." Toby saluted the officer, grabbed his bag, and followed the Petty Officer. When they arrived at the X-division berthing, there were no empty bunks.

"Did the OOD say you would be in Engineering?"

"Yes, I'm a Machinist's Mate."

"Let's get you a bunk with them, and I'll tell you where to muster for quarters in the morning to get you signed in."

"That will be great, thanks."

The following morning, after quarters, Petty Officer Mark Hall took charge of the three new men. Each man had a bunk and associated locker assigned to him. Their heavy Pea coats, bearing their name on the inside back in white paint, hung on a hanger in a converted void. After making their bunks, they placed a piece of masking tape on the aluminum frame, where they printed their name and rate. Petty Officer Hall took the men back to the Engineering Office and finished signing them in. Chief Machinist's Mate Devon Foley checked the billet sheet, sending one Fireman Third Class to the forward Engine room. Fireman Third Class Lawrence Webb and Toby went to the after-engine room.

Petty Officer John Carter, the Petty Officer in Charge of the engine room, assigned a lower-level work section to Webb. Toby acquired the cleaning station on the upper-level, starboard side.

Carter asked Toby, "I see you're a Fireman First. Did you serve on another ship?"

"Yes, I was on a Clemson class destroyer and worked in the after-engine room."

"Those old ships were the real Flush decks," Carter noted.

"Not to mention they rolled and pitched like a floating whale," Toby added.

"Where was your ship ported?"

"She flew her home port flag in Plymouth, England. The *HMS AMPTHILL* is a Town class destroyer escort, part of the Lend Least fleet which went to the RN."

"You were in the English Royal Navy?" blurted Carter.

Taking the response in stride, Toby explained, "After high school, I went to work at Newport News building and repairing components for the engine rooms of Clemson and a few Gleaves ships for almost three years. Like everyone else, I saw the war coming, and when England found herself alone in the European Theater, I decided I wanted to fight the Nazis. So, I joined the RN in Canada. Not a happy move by me for my parents."

"How did you like England?"

"Great country and wonderful people; many were scared but determined never to give in. Most regular folks saw the war as a continuation of World War I. Then December 7th happened, many Americans helping out received notices to return home for duty, and I received orders to San Diego, and after Boot Camp, here I am. Another Clemson Lend Lease ported in Plymouth had half its crew consisting of voluntary American sailors; they all returned for new assignments."

"I heard something about that but figured it had to be scuttlebutt."

"Naw, it's real, and I understand she had a rep for being a mean fighter."

"I saw you earlier, and you had a ring on; did you take it off?"

"I don't wear it in the engine room; too easy to lose your finger that way."

"Smart move, you're right; I heard about a snipe losing his finger that way on another ship just the other day. So, I take it you're married?"

"Yes, her name is Amanda, and she's staying with my folks in Virginia." Toby showed Carter Amanda's picture.

"You did well, Toby Greene. Better get to work; we're getting underway in two days."

Toby's cleaning area was already shining and ready for work; he looked the plant over, noting the Gleaves class destroyer presented a clear generational leap from the Clemson four pipers.

Toby soon learned the plant's steam pressure had a gauge pressure of six hundred pounds per square inch and used superheated steam with a temperature of eight-hundred-fifty degrees. The ship's design created the first staggered engineering, cross-connected capability design. Two boilers in the forward boiler room provided steam to the forward engine room. As a result, that plant's isolated in what is called a split-plant operation.

The second boiler room duplicates boiler room number one work for the after-engine room. The engineers can open the proper valves if either boiler room receives sufficient damage to put it out of commission. The ship can continue with both screws in operation with one boiler room but at a lesser speed.

Each engine room contained a cruising turbine, high and low-pressure turbines, double-locked reduction gears, and a turbo generator. Toby read the top speed rating and settled at thirty-eight knots, or about forty-three miles an hour.

"Greene, here is the information pamphlet on the ship's layout. I found it in the admin office, left over from the commissioning ceremonies."

"Thanks, John."

Fireman Third, Larry Webb, asked, "Toby, is that the ship's info you asked Carter to dig up for you?

"Yes, it is."

"Read it out loud, Toby; I'm not the best reader aboard."

"Sure," the Virginian began giving Webb a verbal outline of the ship's capabilities. "We know her main battery consists of the four five-inch dual-purpose guns on the main deck and the 01 deck for use against a surface, air, and shore targets."

"I'll bet the whole ship shakes when they fire those guns."

"I doubt nobody will sleep through it," chuckled Toby.

"What about air defense? From what I've heard, there's never enough antiaircraft guns."

"According to this handout, they only have six of the fifty caliber machine guns. We had better than that on the *AMPTHILL;* I'll bet we pick up some twenty-millimeter and a couple of forty-millimeter cannons before we tangle with the enemy. Half a dozen fifties aren't enough."

"Are ya gonna tell 'em that?" the youngster asked.

Laughing, Toby asked, "What makes you think anyone is going to listen to a lowly Fireman?"

"Oh, I thought you were an ace," Webb blurted.

With a full laugh, Toby asked, "Where on earth did you get that?"

"I dunno, maybe because you wear those funny-looking ribbons on your jumper. I saw them the other day when we came aboard."

"Forget you ever saw them; they thought I was a good boy on their ship."

Toby thought, *'I thought someone spilled the beans on my actions on the AMPTHILL.*

At zero-three-thirty, the Main Control messenger made his rounds in the engineer's compartment. "Time to get up and begin lighting off the plant and getting underway at zero-eight-hundred." The Snipes dressed, stopped by the head, then headed for the engineering spaces. There, the scripted ballet for warming the machinery began once the hundred-fifty-pound steam system had about a hundred-forty pounds.

Noise in the four spaces increased as steam became available for the oil heaters, turbines, and a dozen other pumps, air ejectors, and generators started coming alive.

Toby began his qualifications for messenger, learning which logs to prepare and finding the gauges to record temperatures, steam, and flow pressure readings. Toby's earlier experience gained while working for the shipyards gave him a substantial start over his contemporaries. But, wisely, Toby avoided taking the high road by listening to the Fireman assigned to training him rather than telling his trainer he knew what the parameters were saying. Such behavior would prove counterproductive.

Once at sea, the drills began, taking untrained individuals and bringing them together as a coordinated acting team. The one thing Toby felt happy over, he remained in the engine room during the GENERAL QUARTERS and combat drills.

In a few days, toby qualified for messenger. He made a point of correctly logging all the readings, knowing they formulated a baseline for identifying a potential problem with a piece of machinery.

An occasional test question from Carter regarding a particular reading of abnormal circumstances kept Toby on his toes. In addition, some questions created follow-up questions when answered, forcing Toby to answer increasingly more difficult questions. As a result, the sailor could see suspicious looks at the more complex explanations.

MM1 John Carter came from the small town of Mentor, Ohio, east of Cleveland, Ohio. "Toby, where did you pick up all your knowledge? You're far ahead of any Fireman aboard this ship in operations and maintenance."

Toby took a drink of coffee, mentally aligning his points and putting his answers in order. Finally, Toby told Carter about his experience in the shipyard and joining the RN. He explained his work and watch-standing duties on the converted Clemson. But refrained from mentioning his gunnery duties, knighthood, and the attached social status thrust upon him.

Toby ended his story, "I wanted to learn from Gleaves class experienced men. There are large differences between the plants of the four pipers and the Gleaves. I didn't want them to think I was upstaging them."

The two talked between trips to fulfill his duties and taking readings. But when the story finished, Petty Officer Carter realized he had a qualified Second Class Petty Officer in a Fireman's billet.

Toby learned engine room operations, repairs, and maintenance faster than any of his peers, due not only to his experience in the shipyard and RN service but also to the gift of a photographic memory.

Carter scratched his head, unable to understand how anyone could remember the complex machinery and operation of the engine room in such a short time. Yet, he watched the young Virginian soak up knowledge like a sponge soaking up water as he read through machinery and plant manuals. If the young sailor continued, he could easily become a First Class or even a Chief Machinist's Mate before the war ended.

There was something else about Greene that made him different. It wasn't a bad trait; he stood above the other men in maturity and was surer of himself. He exercised command of his life, despite the efforts to make Toby a cookie-cut sailor. Then Carter remembered Greene wore a wedding ring outside the engine room; yes, that's it, his maturity drove him.

GLEAVES DD REFUELING FROM HORNET

CHAPTER ELEVEN

Three island-camouflage-painted destroyers plowed through the six-foot swells and waves of the Atlantic Ocean as the destroyers steamed for Norfolk, Virginia. The new ships carried a mixture of old salts, those transferred in from other ships, and the green-gilled recruit graduates. The latter ensured they had a good supply of crackers until they developed their sea legs; others included a bucket.

"Toby, what are you doing to keep from losing your guts the way this ship is bobbing and weaving?" Larry Webb asked.

"I got my sea legs on another destroyer in the North Atlantic and the English Channel long before I came aboard the *MANNING."*

The ship made Norfolk, and all hands turned two for the next two days, loading supplies, stores, and ammunition. Then the three ships nuzzled up to the wharf at the torpedo station and loaded ten Mark fifteen torpedoes each. A last-minute revision caused the destroyers to return to the piers and take on a huge load of forty and twenty-millimeter ammunition. The next day started a week of modifications, where two twin forty-millimeter mounts, one on each side of the after stack, and five twenty-millimeter cannons replaced the fifties. In addition, two guns appeared in front of the bridge, each on a port and starboard platform. Two additional twenties were mounted outboard the centerline on podia, and the final twenty sat mounted to the deck after the fifty-four gun.

During the modification period, Toby made a few phone calls home. He kept any mention of the ship, its modifications, and schedule out of their conversations on the possibility that a censor listened in. Amanda had become his parent's answer to wanting a daughter, and Nancy forgot her status as a daughter-in-law. On the way back to the ship, Toby eyed the additions as a great improvement in the *MANNING's* antiaircraft defenses.

The three cans entered their training phase and went on a two-week training cruise. During the days, shipwide drills covered every damage, fire, and flooding condition the fleet experienced during the war's early part.

During the evening and night hours, the three engineering shifts underwent casualty control drills, including more fire and flooding, with the men building, shoring, and fighting fires with trained men riding along for the exercises. The critical firefighting training required training to excellence, especially since you can't call a fire department at sea; the sailors are the fire department. After two weeks of intense training and gunnery practice, the crew yearned for some liberty.

The three Gleaves turned their bows toward Norfolk, and the annunciators called for thirty knots. Two hours later, the cans pulled into Navy City, tied to a buoy with another ship. The duty deck crew and Motor Machinist's Mates readied the two motor whaleboats for water-taxi service.

Toby called home and arranged to meet his family at the main gate of the Naval Station. Toby watched the big car drive up, thinking, *'What a saloon, betraying his cultural change while in the RN.'* Then, finally, the big sedan stopped at the entrance where the lonely-looking sailor awaited.

Amanda carefully exited the vehicle to avoid damaging her newly made dress. The Lady de Greene oozed excitement as she wrapped herself around her hubby. Nearby, a group of *MANNING* sailors watched, their mouths hanging open in envy. Then Toby hugged his mother, and Tom whispered, "We better get you and your wife in the car and head home, so those sailors don't have a heart attack."

Toby chuckled, knowing he'd get the twenty-question treatment when he returned to the can. But he had more important things on his mind. He and Amanda slid into the spacious rear seat. Tom started the straight eight-cylinder engine, and the comfortable ride began. Amanda drew a light coat she had brought along and draped it across her lap. Then the saucy lady from England held onto Toby's hand and guided it under the jacket, where she slid his hot hand up her thigh. Toby stopped the movement as he looked at his wife with wide-open eyes. Amanda smiled and gave him a double dose of arched eyebrows as if saying, "Well?" Amanda had only the dress covering her. Toby looked at her, jutted his jaws, and snapped his teeth together. Amanda smiled with satisfaction.

Toby looked at his parents, who seemed exceptionally concentrated on the road. Then, finally, he began a neutral conversation to allow his emotions to recover from his delightful wife's actions.

The two days off came rapidly to an end, and the family made the short trip to the Naval Station entrance, where after their farewells, Tom drove the car toward home while the women rehashed the times spent together.

At one point, Nancy whispered, "that was a wonderful surprise you gave Toby when he got in the car. I wish I had thought of something like that when Tom and I were just married."

As Toby expected, the word of his stunning wife made the rounds on the ship, and he spent a short time assuring the men, both Amanda and he, were off the market in matrimony, and they would have to look elsewhere.

****

Navy training prepared the crews of the three destroyers for everything they may encounter. Now, it's up to them how they use their training. The trio of destroyers married up with a twenty-ship convoy steaming due south toward the Panama Canal. A one-way trip through the canal took the destroyers almost ten hours. The canal track is forty miles from the Atlantic to the Pacific Ocean. While the cargo and troop ships transited the canal, the destroyers ran antisubmarine search patterns on the Pacific end.

The convoy commander laid in a course for San Diego, California, once the convoy became reconstituted. A convoy speed of fifteen knots held the speedy destroyers in check; with the relatively calm Pacific, the soundmen experienced better than fair results from the new equipment. The radar systems on all three destroyers searched the seas out to the horizon; with the taller mounted antenna on the command cruiser, the distance extended to fifty-two miles. In addition, those vessels having Fire Control radar continued to practice ranging on the convoy ships. As a result, they were a good asset for close-in objects, such as surfaced submarines, with small returns. The zigzag track of the convoy to San Diego could take ten-to-twelve days at fifteen knots, depending on contacts with submarines.

At the southern city of San Diego, the destroyers received orders to proceed to the 32nd Street Naval Station. There, they tied pierside with their sister ships moored along port side of the *MANNING.*

Toby pulled his first liberty in several weeks. The sailor hopped on a public bus and made his way to the NTC, where he was hoping to find Chief Palmer. As the sailor walked near the reviewing stands at Preble Field, he heard the unmistakable bellow of Chief Palmer. Rounding a set of bleacher seats, Toby stood, watching the Chief work.

The Chief finished working with the recruits and turned toward the bleachers, where he spotted a sailor watching him. “What are you looking at, recruit? Are you lost? What is your company number?” The Chief began stomping toward the sailor, who didn’t move. As the charging Chief came closer, he recognized the face, now wearing a squared white hat, set at a slight port list and two fingers above his eyes. It was a fleet sailor, not a recruit. Then he spotted three ribbons on his right breast; only one sailor wore those ribbons.

Smiling, Chief Palmer said, “Do I salute a knight or say, by your leave, Sir Tobias?”

Toby returned the smile and held out his hand, “It’s good to see you again, Chief.”

The Chief grabbed the sailor’s hand, giving him a solid shake. “What are ya doing here, Toby?”

"I'm on a destroyer currently berthed at 32nd Street. I see you're still pushing boots."

"You aren't too soon, Toby, a month from now, I'll be shipping out too. My detailer assigned me to a cruiser; she's tied up at 32nd Street."

"I saw her after we shut down the plant, and I got up for some fresh air. She looks like a fighter." Toby noted. "Are you happy about going back to sea?"

"Yes and no. Obviously, the no has to do with the family; Navy life puts a lot of strain on families, even those with supportive spouses. But, on the other hand, the yes is easier; I'm a sailor, and a sailor belongs at sea."

"I understand; fortunately, Amanda comes from a navy family and is both understanding and supportive," Toby said.

"Yes, I remember; your father-in-law was an English sailor and KIA at Jutland," Palmer said. "And her grandfather is a high-ranking Admiral, right?"

"Yes, he is the First Sea Lord and answers to the King and Prime Minister."

"Your wife has some high-power relatives," the Chief noted.

"Did she return to England after you went to sea?" he asked.

"No, Amanda is living with my folks in Virginia; they wouldn't let her leave; they've fallen in love with her as the daughter they always wanted. She wrote in one of her letters that she had taken a job with my father's business to pull her share of the responsibilities. Amanda couldn't fit in any better," Toby crowed.

"You have a fine family, Toby, and it couldn't happen to a more deserving person," Palmer praised. "So, what are your plans?"

I'm off to call home; everyone in Virginia should be home now. Then I'm going to hunt up some tools."

Tools?"

"Yeah, we have navy tools in the hole, but they're communal tools and aren't well taken care of. So I decided to pick up my set and a toolbox. My First Class has a toolbox, and he has them if he needs them. He said he doesn't loan them out; otherwise, they seem to walk away. So he got them because more than one man needed the same tool, and it always seemed it was the same time he needed a particular tool," Toby explained.

"It sounds like a good plan, but make sure you keep a receipt for everything you have. The Navy will confiscate any adrift tool with no proof of ownership. One other thing, stand clear of those clowns on the strip; their only tools are junk, with no guarantees. Instead, go to a reputable hardware store."

"Good idea, Chief. Good luck with your new ship. If we're in the same port down the line, we'll have to get together."

Later, Toby called home, and his Mom answered, "Greene's."

"Hi, Mum."

"Are you all, right?"

"I'm doing very well. I'm in San Diego and thought I would call. How's the family?"

He heard his mother call out, "Amanda, Tom, it's Toby."

Toby spoke to his three family members, during which they asked Toby several times if he was all right. Amanda sounded like a giddy schoolgirl in her excitement. However, everyone knew the restrictions on any potential security information and kept the conversation neutral.

Toby's time ran out, as other sailors wanted their calls too. They said their goodbyes and sent their love, then were gone. Toby felt good hearing the family so chipper. But he wasn't going to allow his duty to ruin his disposition.

The sailor spotted a blue bus stop and waited for the base bus. He took it to the main gate, where he sat on a bench waiting for a bus heading downtown. He arrived on Broadway and walked east, only to find bars, cheap jewelry, and hustlers. Finally, he found directions to the nearby USO location. Some questions later, he learned of a good hardware store.

The owner turned out to be a retired Chief and helped Toby select tools of good quality but at a reasonable price. Toby knew what he didn't need and worked around the old Chief's suggestions. Once he made his purchase, he locked the toolbox with the receipt in his jumper pocket. Then, rather than deal with the crowds and busses, Toby hailed a taxi and paid the price to 32nd Street.

The sailor was tired and looked forward to the evening meal and maybe a movie. At the quarter deck, the OOD asked for proof of ownership of the tools. Toby broke out his receipt. After the expected questions, Toby cleared the quarterdeck and headed for the engine room. He stowed the locked box behind Carter's toolbox, bearing his name on the top, in fresh paint.

The Fireman headed for the engineer's berthing compartment in the stern, where he changed into dungarees, then fell into the chowline. This ship was a far cry from the Old Horse. The Navy allotted more money per man for food than the RN; the results showed a wider selection of food and larger proportions. It wasn't that the RN starved the Tars; the food system in the UK is different in style and taste, yet nourished the Navy personnel to their needs.

As for the ships comparison, the Clemson was an earlier Wicks class with modifications. The Gleaves were longer and wider, giving her a better ride and fighting platform, with much better weapons.

Following the evening meal, Toby dropped into the after-engine room, where he looked the plant over and checked the bilges. Even though his rank didn't call for him to do it, it had become a habit.

"OOGAA," the ship's phone bellowed.

"After-engine room, Fireman Greene speaking, sir."

"Greene, good. This is Mr. Berridge, the Engineering Officer; you're just the man I was looking for; lay to the Engineering Office immediately."

"Aye, sir," Toby said into a dead phone.

'Now what?' the sailor thought. *'How can I get into trouble for being in my own space?'*

Toby opened the door to the Engineering Office, and upon seeing the EO and Chief Foley standing watching, he sensed trouble, "Fireman Greene, reporting as ordered, sir."

"Is there anything I should know about before we see the Captain?"

"No, sir. Unless it's about some tools I brought aboard, sir."

"Do you have a receipt for the tools?"

"Yes, sir." Toby pulled the sales slip and list of tools from his wallet and handed them to the officer.

"Why did you do this? Don't you have issued tools in the engine room?"

Toby repeated the story to the Chief Engineer. "Okay, be sure to hang onto that receipt; otherwise, the tools will be confiscated if ownership cannot be proven.

"Aye, sir."

"Let's head up to the Captain's cabin to see what he wants."

Toby had a sneaking suspicion his previous duty and knighthood may lay at the bottom of the Captain's inquiry.

Toby stood at attention in the Captain's Cabin, with the EO and XO standing by. Toby's suspicions weren't wrong. He spent ten minutes laying out his time in the RN and the events which occurred. Then he added his request to restrict the knighthood information on the same bases he used at the NTC.

The Captain, Lieutenant Commander Robert C. Drake, wore an academy ring. He was all Navy. Being his first command, the *MANNING* would be special to him, hence the possibility of a little over-protectiveness. Captain Drake stood six feet even and came in at a hundred-ninety pounds. His rugged, weathered face made him a standout, handsome devil, and any number of ladies stood in line to end his single status. His two characteristics marked a good leader, Confidence and capability, but not to excess.

The Engineering Officer, Lt. Henry Berridge, graduated from the Merchant Marine Academy, and the law required him to be in the USNR. However, he now wanted to switch to USN for a Navy career.

"Fireman Greene, I have been reading your military history with great interest. So, we are all on the same sheet; please correct me if my information is wrong. You joined the Royal Navy to fight the Nazis, and in doing so, an air arrack wounded the gunner and loader on your ship, the *HMS AMPTHILL,* a Lend-Lease Clemson, and you jumped in and shot down the fighter, is that correct?"

"Yes, sir," the slightly red-faced sailor admitted.

"Your Captain, Lieutenant Commander Champs, asked if you would man the gun during their action stations; you shot down a second plane and damaged a third. As a result, you were summoned to Buckingham Palace by King George. For shooting down a couple of planes?"

"No, sir. My hobby was our family genealogy, and I had a certified Genealogist finish the work I started. He found out I was in the bloodline of the Tudors, all the way up and past William the Conqueror, and passed the information on to his brother, an employee in Buckingham. So, the knighthood was a last-minute decision based on the ancestry and shooting down the aircraft as a colonial in the RN."

Then Toby requested the restrictions on the knighthood apply to the ship, and he outlined the issues.

"Fireman Greene, we are sailing into war, and you are probably one of only a handful of men aboard who have combat experience. We are a couple of hands short in Gunnery and need a gunner on the stern twenty if you want it."

"Sir, as I told Captain Champs, I serve where the ship needs me, and the Captain wants me, and I wouldn't mind manning the gun until regular gunners are available."

"Henry, any problems with the Fireman trying out the gun?"

"No, sir, we can spare him."

"Sir, may I speak?"

"Certainly," the Captain replied.

"May I remain working in the engine room and stand my regular watches if I am assigned to the GQ gunner's billet? The gun is but a few steps from the engine room hatch."

"I'll think about it, but let's see how you do in next week's live fire exercise."

"Aye, sir."

"This meeting, especially the personal record information, is confidential and not for discussion. Dismissed."

"Thank you, sir." Then Toby did an about-face and left the Captain's cabin.

Captain Drake smiled, "I like him. I didn't touch on his other accomplishments, but he is married to the former Lady de Lacy, granddaughter of Admiral Brian de Lacy, the First Sea Lord for the British fleet, and a personal friend to King George. And a little bird told me the King had private talks with the Fireman and thought highly of him. And if you ever see him in dress uniform, he wears the British Conspicuous Gallantry Medal, Distinguished

Service Medal, and Pacific Star. He has also received wounds in combat, but the UK has no equivalent to the Purple Heart."

The XO said, "He does grow on you. One thing has surfaced, he is what he says he is, and I'll bet he doesn't even know how to lie."

Then the EO added, "There aren't many like him anymore."

"No, Henry, there aren't. We better prepare things for next week; how's the plant, Henry?"

"Ready to go, sir; she is anxious and ready for thirty-plus knots on your order, Captain. All machinery in commission."

"Very well, Lieutenant. Tomorrow, have everyone go over everything twice. Then, right after gunnery practice, we'll return to 32nd Street to rearm, refuel, and replenish all supplies. Then we head west to join a fast convoy for Hawaii."

The following day, the ship was underway before zero-eight-hundred, and the three cans prepared for the live fire. All the destroyers steamed at thirty knots to the live fire exercise area, where the practice began.

The Bo'sun called "GENERAL QUARTERS, GENERAL QUARTERS; ALL HANDS MAN YOUR BATTLE STATIONS FOR THE LIVE FIRE EXERCISE."

Toby strapped himself into the twenty-millimeter gun harness, then adjusted his helmet and earplugs. He charged the cannon with a live shell when ordered, then waited.

"Toby, Gunnery Control says we're up next; get ready," the talker yelled.

A plane towing a target sleeve a thousand feet behind it flew past the ship from the bow to the stern. Each forty-mount fired when ordered; then it was the twenty-millimeter gun's turn. First, the port forward and mid-ship guns fired, then the plane returned, and the starboard guns fired.

"Toby, this next run is ours; he will be coming left to right down the starboard side," the talker called out.

The sailor knew the aircraft was at three thousand feet; he estimated the speed and began tracking the sleeve. "Clear to fire, Toby." Toby followed his set routine and began chewing the sleeve apart from the tail-end to the center. Everyone, including those on the bridge, watched where the shots went. Finally, the plane flew off to its base with a third of the original target in tow.

While his crew hopped up and down at Toby's shooting ability, the Gunnery Officer and Chief stopped at the gun mount to congratulate the sailor on his accuracy.

The normal wartime steaming watch took over, and Toby went to the engine room, where he received more salutations on his shooting; after that, he began his duty watch.

"Greene, you're wanted on the bridge; see the Captain," the talker said.

"Okay, thanks."

Toby identified himself at the bridge hatch. "What do you want?" the messenger asked.

"The Captain sent for me."

The messenger started for the Captain, who was sitting in his bridge chair, then the messenger saw the Captain wave the Fireman onto the bridge.

"Fireman Greene, you are as good as your record said; congratulations, you're now the stern gunner."

"Thank you, sir; I'll try not to let you down."

"I'm sure you won't, and good luck," the Captain said.

"Aye, sir." Toby saluted and left for the engine room.

The OOD, Lieutenant JG Harold Harper, said, "There goes a young man with some humility and respect."

The Captain answered, "He has more humility and respect than the whole ship."

IJN A6M2 ZERO

CHAPTER TWELVE

Convoy 17C consisted of two cruisers, several destroyers, military cargo ships, converted passenger liners for troop transport, dry provision cargo ships, and an oiler. The convoy formed off San Diego under the watchful eyes of the escort destroyers, Navy aircraft from North Island NAS, and two lighter-than-air ships, also known as blimps, for antisubmarine patrols. Their destination, Pearl Harbor, Hawaiian Territory, lay about twenty-three hundred nautical miles from San Diego. An indirect route, with an unplanned zig-zag track; and a speed of fifteen knots, figured into a fourteen-to-sixteen-day trip. Every ship in the convoy carried sufficient fuel to make the trip without refueling.

Most of the *MANNING's* crew had never been to the Islands, and those who had, seen the damage of the December attack on Oahu.

The Snipes had settled into their transit routine in the Gleaves' main engineering spaces. In the after-engine room. Toby pulled the twenty to twenty-four hundred and zero-eight hundred to noon watches of a three-section watch force. Training continued throughout the ship, preparing her and the crew for war.

The sea temperatures had moderated as they closed on the Hawaiian chain of islands, and the temperatures in the spaces rose accordingly. As a result, the areas under and near the vents had become favorite spots for the men to linger if not on watch.

Fireman First Class Sean Anderson, a youngster from Cleveland, Ohio, said he relished the warmer climate. "Where I come from," he said to Toby, "I've seen my share of snow; when the cold winter storms come in over Lake Erie, it collides with the warmer moisture temperatures; and the clash dumps several inches of snow at a time from the so-called lake effect. It can get very deep east of us in Buffalo. I've heard of them getting a fifty-inch annual snowfall. Then, behind the storm, we usually get the sub-freezing temperatures brought down from the arctic, and it gets nasty cold."

The convoy slipped between the islands of Molokai and Oahu and skirted Waikiki on its way to Pearl Harbor. The destroyers stood guard on antisubmarine patrol as the convoy ships headed for either a pier or anchorage, according to the port authority and pilots aboard the different vessels. Then it was time for the cans to enter the port.

"John, what's the chance Larry and I get a look at our first glimpse of Pearl Harbor?"

"Go ahead, but don't stray from the hatch in case we have a casualty; going into or leaving harbor is the worst place to have one."

"We'll be within earshot of the hatch," Toby promised.

Toby and Larry Webb stepped onto the main deck and into the warm sunlight. Although they were aware of the air strike on Pearl, the extent of destruction stunned the two men.

With the fires extinguished, the stark reality of the destruction of war shocked their senses. The *USS NEVADA* remained beached at the head of the channel, its bow deep into the mud. The battleships *CALIFORNIA*, and *WEST VIRGINIA*, still sat on the harbor floor. *ARIZONA* sat crushed into the muck, and Oklahoma capsized, her screws in the air. Tennessee received damage but remained afloat, and Pennsylvania suffered a fire in a dry dock with two trashed destroyers. Finally, the old Ogalala sunk at a pier. Buildings, hangars, and plane skeletons littered Ford Island. Everywhere the evidence of fire scorched ships and buildings black.

"I wonder how many men and women were killed and wounded?" asked Larry.

"I don't know," mumbled Toby. "But it had to be hundreds or even thousands."

Honolulu still had bars and some places to eat available, and those men lucky to get to them ate and drank, many in silence. Many sailors were glad to return to their ships for the first time. Many swore to do whatever possible to exact vengeance.

After their first long voyage, the engineers checked every pump, valve, and gauge. The plant was well-built and normal maintenance made it ready to continue. The first order of business took the destroyers to the untouched fuel depots to refuel the fighters. Then they returned to their previous berths, where food and dry store awaited loading by all-hands working parties. Two days later, messengers woke the lighting off watchstanders, and they worked until relieved for breakfast. Finally, fresh crewmen took over and readied the warships for the first bells to signal they were underway.

At zero-seven-fifteen, "Set the Special Sea and Anchor Detail" came across the 1MC, bringing the M-B-Division Officer, Ensign Eric Hanover, to the after-engine room. At seven-forty-five, Main Control received the order to disengage the jacking gears and prepare to get underway. A couple of spins later, the first bells came down, and the 1MC blared, "Shift colors." Fireman First Class Tom Watson worked the throttles as called upon from the bridge. The sleek destroyer backed away from the pier and into the clear waters of the harbor; the ahead bells propelled the destroyer toward the mouth of Pearl Harbor to the Pacific Ocean. Once past the torpedo net, the pilot disembarked, leaving the Captain to conn his ship.

Ensign Hanover and MM1 Carter sat on the large grey toolbox, sipping coffee. Then Carter called the messenger, and when he arrived, he said, "Find Greene and have him come up to the throttles."

A minute later, the Virginian appeared from the lower level, "You wanted to see me, John?"

"Yeah, how did you get yourself assigned to that twenty-millimeter on the stern?"

Toby laid out the story from the *AMPTHILL* and how it became part of his permanent record, and Captain Drake was trying to be proactive about possible events.

"That's highly unusual," Carter noted, "Do us a favor, and don't get your ass shot off."

"That's my number one priority. I've been there and done that and certainly don't want to repeat it," Toby said.

"I didn't know you had a Purple Heart."

"I don't, I got hit while on the *AMPTHILL*, but the RN has no awards for being wounded in action."

"That's a bucket of crap; spill your blood for them, and nothing to see from it."

"I wouldn't say that; I'm still alive. I only want to do my part and go home to my family."

"Do you like being a Snipe?" Carter wondered.

"Oh, yes, after graduating from high school, I worked for three years on ships in shipyards before I joined the RN."

"Did you work on this ship?"

"No, I was already at sea with the RN when the Bath Shipyard built this ship. I worked at the Newport News yard across from Norfolk."

"What did you do in the yards?" Ensign Hanover asked.

"I started on the pump installation team. I installed a lot of pumps with one other man after the transfer team moved them to their proper location. Then I went to steam turbine installation and repair. I did that for over a year on Clemson's and some Bagley's and Gleaves."

"Hell," the Division Officer said, "I'm impressed; he's had more experience than anyone here, including the Chief Engineer."

"What did you do in the RN?"

"I got assigned to the *AMPTHILL's* after-engine room and started at the bottom, like everyone else. We were called Stokers; some worked with the boilers, and others with engine room turbines and pumps. First, we had to change all the main steam line gaskets because the twenty-year layup dried the original ones, and they would blow out. After that, we repacked valves and pumps as needed, not much different from what we do."

The Ensign looked up, "Main steam line gaskets? The yards do those."

"Yes, they do, but we had to get them done because we were the only destroyer available to replace a can that had a casualty. The RN doesn't accept excuses."

“We need to get this man advanced to Second Class as soon as possible.” The Ensign said.

Further conversation halted at the call of the Bo’sun on the 1MC. “Now hear this.” A brief silence, then the baritone voice of Captain Drake blared over the sounds of the engine room.

“This is the Captain. Now that we’re underway, I can tell you where we are going. Our first destination is Bora Bora, where all the vessels in our convoy will refuel, but before that, all slimy Pollywogs must pass muster before Neptunus Rex, Ruler of the Deep. The ceremony will take place at the Ruler’s doorstep, the Equator. All Shellbacks will observe and take note of Pollywog violations to bring forth charges against said Pollywogs. And it’s sad to say, but the Navy no longer allows keelhauling the wanting.

After refueling, we will head for Espiritu Santo Island in the Vanuatu chain of islands in the northern New Hebrides. It is a staging location for operations. We may become detached from this convoy or pass on to another command for operations.

Between now and our arrival in Big Bay, Espiritu Santo, we will continue drills covering every casualty, flooding, and fire throughout the ship, except the main engineering spaces. As the Engineering Officer prescribes, they will run their training from eighteen hundred to zero-six hundred. Once we get to Big Bay, there will be no further drills. All General Quarters and directives will be real-world, and no training. More on that after we leave Vanuatu. Captain out.”

Toby turned to the Division Officer, “Sir, having been through the initiation while in the RN, will I have to do it again?”

“No, once a Shellback, always a Shellback. Now that I’ve supported you, I trust you will put in a good word for me?”

Toby looked at John Carter and knew him to be a Trusty Shellback. Carter’s scowl said all there was needed.

Toby pulled out his pocket notebook and began writing on a new page entitled Ensign Hanover.

The Ensign took an immediate interest in what Toby wrote in his book, “What are you doing?”

“Your first offense; attempting to bribe a Trusty Shellback, sir.” Then he turned and headed for the lower level.

The stunned officer looked at Carter and shrank a little at the sardonic smile on his face.

On the bridge, Captain Drake addressed the OOD, "Ensure the steaming orders include requesting two-thousand-yard separation between this ship and all others during the time of engineering drills at night, of course, any contact with submarines or unaccounted for surface ships, will cancel all drills and revert to real-world war response."

"Aye, Captain."

The day of reckoning arrived, and the Pollywogs, officers, and enlisted stood together as Neptunus Rex, Ruler of the Deep, strutted down the deck. The ceremony lasted most of the afternoon, then their duty to the war took the forefront, and the ships continued to Bora Bora. Toby's records held a fine colorful certificate confirming Fireman Greene as a Trusty Shellback of the *HMS AMPTHILL's* crew. The only crewman of the *USS MANNING* to have such a document and lay to rest any question of whether or not Toby Greene served in the Royal Navy.

The arrival of convoy 17 C in Vanuatu was without fanfare. After refueling, the three Gleaves destroyers received orders to supplement the escort of twelve empty cargo ships to Brisbane, then proceed to New Caledonia's Moselle Bay, where a Destroyer Tender had availability for any repairs and updates the ship required and allowed the crew some much-deserved liberty. New Caledonia is also in the New Hebrides chain of islands and under Free French control.

The island became valuable due to large deposits of Nickel and Chromium, important ingredients in making stainless and specially treated steels, and its location in the war effort.

On the strategic value of New Caledonia and Vanuatu, as well as the rest of the New Hebrides, if Japan were allowed to capture both islands, they could plan the invasion of Fiji and Samoa, from which they could cut the US-Australia supply line and give the enemy bases to attack Australia. And the Allies knew it.

In the web of political and military strategic planning and calls for manpower and supplies, the US Army and Navy were locked in a battle for resources. President Roosevelt went along with England in defeating Hitler in Europe, the top priority. However, the Pacific forces would have to fight a delaying conflict against the world's third largest Navy, manned by centuries of sea experience, and successfully defeating the Russians in their 1904-1905 war; it promised not an easy task.

In their march to seize the rubber and oil resources in the Dutch East Indies, the Japanese snatched Rabaul and Tulagi in the Solomon Islands. In addition, intelligence sources found the Japanese had started a new airfield on Guadalcanal.

A calendar in the engine room showed a new day at midnight, 5 August 1942. The destroyers rendezvoused with other ships from Fiji, New Caledonia, Vanuatu, and Australia to make up an invasion fleet of eighty-one vessels southwest of Cape Esperance. Heavy cruisers and destroyers turned southeast out of the Cape into the bottom of The New Georgia Sound two days later. Guadalcanal was on their starboard side; they passed Savo on the port side, and further aport lay the Florida Islands, one of which is Tulagi.

The pre-dawn bombardment began with all the warships lashing the island of Guadalcanal with eight-, six-, and five-inch-high explosive shells. The Snipes in the after-engine room of the *MANNING* heard the guns blasting out fire and death, but only one could see the bombardment, Fireman First Class Toby Greene, at the stern twenty-millimeter gun.

Toby Greene's new loader, Jerry Masters, a seaman, came aboard in Noumea. When he heard the gunner was a Snipe, he took offense and questioned the intelligence of the man who put him there.

Jack Huffman, a helper, looked at Masters and said, "Because he's the best shot on the ship and the Captain assigned him to the billet."

"Oh, I didn't know that," Masters mumbled.

"Yeah, he's cool as a cucumber and instinctively knows where to place the shells."

"We'll see when the Nips get here."

Jack turned to Toby, "You get a Japanese attacker today, and the first drink is on me."

"Jack, you know I don't drink, but I'll take a Cocoa Cola any day."

Masters chimed in, "You don't drink? Everyone drinks, at least now and then."

Toby straightened Masters out, “I just don’t like the taste of it, and after seeing guys come back from liberty all liquored up, acting weird, and getting sick, I figured I was way ahead of the game.”

“Come to think about it, I hate those hangovers and wondered why I did it,” Masters admitted.

“I’ll bet you wouldn’t miss it a bit if you stayed away from it for a while.”

“Probably, but that’s like asking a hooker not to play their games.”

“Is that what you call it, Jerry?”

“Yeah, I was trying to be polite.”

“Tell me, Jerry, how many times have you had to use the red seat (reserved for those men who contracted an STD).”

“Just twice, how about you?”

“Never and never will,” Toby said with assurance.

“Yeah,” Masters said, “you will see, one of these days.”

“Naw, I’m married and wouldn’t dishonor my wife.”

“Married? I didn’t know that; I never saw a ring.”

Jack chimed in, “I’ve seen her picture, and if I caught him messing around, I’d shoot him for being stupid.”

“My wife hired Jack.” Toby teased. “Working in the engine room can be a dangerous place. I didn’t want to catch it in a pump and lose my finger.”

Masters got the last words, “You’re sure a careful one up to now, and here you are, getting ready to face a killer enemy head-on.”

“Yeah, go figure.”

They came from the northwest, from Buin and Rabaul’s airfields. The first to become visible were the G4M Betty bombers because of their size. Then other, smaller single-engine planes materialized from the clouds, white AM6 Zero Navy fighters.

Before they could get into position to attack the American ships, F4F Wildcats from the carrier Wasp jumped the enemy. Lingering off Cape Esperance, three Bettys tried to use the island’s background to hide their approach and were escorted by a pair of Zeros.

Greene yelled at his talker, "Torpedo planes are going after the transports on the deck from the northwest." The Snipe swung the big cannon around to engage the bombers.

The 1MC bellowed, "All guns open fire, and be mindful of friendlies."

Toby ran off a half dozen rounds, watching the tracers. Then the Virginian adjusted his swing and held the firing switch down. The L70 cannon rattled out .787-inch shells at 2700 feet per second. The high explosive shells weighed 4.3 ounces, and the high explosive tracer rounds came in at 4.1 ounces, giving them a plane-stopping punch at 360 to 450 rounds per minute. The gun bucked but stayed on track.

Jack also acted as a spotter. "Continue firing; you're on target," he yelled.

The heavy rounds chewed into the starboard engine, shedding parts and then exploding into a blossom of fire and thick black smoke. The pilot may have panicked and pulled up before the bombardier could drop the Italian made torpedo. Two guns on the targeted cargo ship opened up on the bomber, making short work of destroying the aircraft. The shredded G4M went head-first into the water with his one good engine at full throttle. Disintegration began at the nose and proceeded along the axis of the frame, but the torpedo exploded in an ear-shattering detonation that sent out shrapnel in every direction. The second plane dove above the water's surface and flew at maximum speed to escape the deadly fire.

The loader turned and yelled, "I owe you an apology Greene; you're as good as Jack said.

The attack ended as fast as it began. But then, the chatter of machine guns drifted from the sky, northwest of the fleet. Toby and his crew looked toward the sound in time to see a speck flutter earthward like a shot bird. Then, in seconds, the guns of the air battle fell silent.

Crewman cast a look across the wide southern bottom of the Sound and saw four columns of smoke from damaged and burning ships.

Half an hour later, the word filtered through the fleet to step down to condition two but keep guns manned. Then, finally, the smoking lamp was lit, allowing men who smoked to light up.

Toby called Masters, "Can you get some salt tablets from the medics and a gallon jug of water to wash them down with?"

"I'll be back in a jiffy," and disappeared up the port side.

Masters took about ten minutes and returned to let each man dump a couple of pink salt pills into their hands, then down them with several gulps of water. "The medic who gave these to me said not to exceed the recommended dose, and water is unlimited."

"General Quarters, General Quarters; Set condition one, air defense to port," blasted from the 1MC. The hustle began anew with men hurrying to their battle stations and strapping into guns and gear.

As expected, the fighters appeared as green-painted Zekes, another name for A6M-2 Zero, to spray the decks with their 7.7-millimeter bullets and, when closer, opened up with their 20-millimeter cannons.

A Zeke bored in on the *MANNING*, this one taking his time to line up on the bow to allow him a wide spray of gunfire by alternately tapping his rudder pedals. The destroyer's two forward five-inch guns began firing at the Japanese fighter first, then the two twenty mounts forward of the bridge opened up.

The Japanese 7.7-millimeter bullets are in the same .30 caliber size as the 30-06 rounds of the US forces, a little less powerful, but not enough to matter. The Japanese had a license to manufacture the 7.7 (The British .303 round) from WWI but ignored the license's expiration and put it to use throughout their armed forces.

The machine gun bullets began to ricochet off decks and bulkheads, many finding their marks, bringing cries of pain from young men. The heavier twenty-millimeter shells punched through the thin metalwork until they reached the engineering area. There the denser STS steel plates succeeded in defeating the deadly projectiles. Yet some penetrated the decks as the plane passed overhead and were in point-blank range.

The Zeke was in front of, over, and past the ship in a blink of an eye. The stern twenty-millimeter mount took several hits, downing all three men.

IJN MITSUBISHI G3M 'NELL' TORPEDO BOMBER

CHAPTER THIRTEEN

The Zero pulled up aft of the destroyer, leaving the *MANNING* with several wounded men, two seriously. As the plane began to gain altitude, the fifty-four-mount fired. In a million-to-one shot, the shell smashed through the tailwheel assembly and exited behind the pilot without detonating. Kinetic energy shredded the frame's coverings and tore through the upper main stringer, equivalent to severing the aircraft's keel. The few remaining stringers separated under stress and split the ship in two. Both pieces fluttered to the Sound's surface to be met by the murderous fire of two twenty-millimeter cannons and two fifty-caliber machine guns.

"Cease fire," blasted from the 1MC. In the quiet that followed, those on deck only saw pieces of plane and body, no larger than a hand, some floating, others beginning to sink into the deep.

Corpsman Sean Halverson moved between the three wounded gun crewmen. Fortunately, their wounds weren't life-threatening, and all would survive. Greene took a graze to his thigh, removing a small chunk of muscle. Masters, also hit in the leg, suffered a bullet gash across the inner thigh, leaving him faint with the thought of where he almost hit. Jack Huffman suffered multiple splinter wounds, painful but easily healed. Halverson quickly applied sulpha and tight bandages, leaving the men to remain at their cannon. The Corpsman disappeared to attend to other wounded sailors.

The loader from the port twenty leaned over the splinter shield and, in a poor mocking English voice, said, "You blokes gonna be, okay?"

"Yeah, it was close, I swear, that guy was aiming right for us, then he must have kicked his rudder and turned toward you at the last second; you guys, okay?" Toby asked.

"Pretty much so; our spotter took one in the guts. The Doc said he'll be out of the war for a few weeks, but he'll make it."

Toby added; that bloody bastard was trying to take out all the gunners so the bombers could get through. I'd wager a quid that's their standard play, so watch for fighters to make AA suppression strafing runs first."

"I think the Snipe is on to something there; it makes sense. I heard a couple of guys jawing about something called antiaircraft suppression runs; that must have been what they meant. Where did you hear about it, Toby?"

"I experienced it on the *AMPTHILL*; that's what the Huns do."

"Huns?"

"The Brits and Allies call the Germans a couple of pet names, Huns, Jerry, Boche, Fitz, Hans, or Krauts. I'm sure the reverse is true. One thing I did learn, except for the politicians, leaders, and their followers, the people of all lands are down to earth and good people."

"You could be right, but if a plane comes over showing a black cross or red meatball, it's all guns fire at will."

"I hear ya," Toby agreed.

"Quid and bloody bastard? That doesn't sound like you, Toby."

"Yeah, the Hun pissed me off, and my leg hurts like hell; I guess I slipped back into my RN days."

"Keep it up, Toby, and we'll make you into a Gunner's Mate yet," Masters said.

A lookout was shot in the chest and most likely laid up for several weeks, then a decision to keep or discharge him would take place. A few other men received lesser wounds and stayed on their stations. Fortunately, the crew fared well against a strafing plane; the ship's company could have suffered numerous deaths.

When John Carter heard the enemy plane hit the stern mount, he called Tom Watson to the throttle board. "Tom, Toby's mount was strafed, and he's down. Check him out occasionally and see if he needs anything. He's stubborn as a mule, and I wouldn't be surprised to see him trying to get down here to go on watch. Let me know."

"Will do; he'll talk to me; we get along pretty well."

Watson returned about twenty minutes later, "His leg has a groove in it. He told the Doc to wrap it tightly, and give him a pill and let him get on with my job."

"That's Toby," Carter said.

The sun quickly turned the decks and bulkheads into oven walls, forcing the men to use every trick in their books to keep cool. Toby took refuge from the fiery ball beneath the front of the fifty-four mount. The air moving across the ship felt perfect, and a shot from the Corpsman blunted the pain in his leg.

Watson located his friend under the fifty-four mount, "Come on, hero, let's get you something to eat."

"I'm not going to argue; my stomach's growling as it is." Tom got his buddy set in a corner seat, where his outstretched leg lay between a bulkhead and the mess hall table. "I'll be right back with some chow. Would you like some coffee?"

"You bet; I feel like I've been on a fasting binge without some joe."

Tom made his way back with the coffee, then headed for the galley for a food tray. The mess cook, a Snipe on temporary duty, put together a tray with more than the average food. "We gotta take care of the star gunner."

Tom smiled, worked his way through the crowded mess hall, and then returned for his tray. "Toby, I know the Doc said you could return to the hole, but John says no."

"Why not; I can hold my own."

"I know it, Buddy, but that leg will get stiff as a board, and any working the muscles will hurt more than you want, you know. And if you insist on staying at your gun, you won't be able to get up and down that ladder into the hole. You could cause a logjam of men in an emergency, and nobody would get out. And by staying on deck, you're only a few feet from the gun if we go to GQ."

"Yeah, I know you're right; I sometimes get stubborn."

"Ya thinks?" Tom's words disappeared in the shrill Bo'sun's whistle; then, an announcement boomed from the 1MC.

"This is the Captain. We and one of the other destroyers will patrol the northeastern edge of the New Georgia Sound from the southwest shore, northwest to the Manning Strait, and back. If we make contact with surface vessels, we report it to Cactus Control. Submarines usually run on the surface while recharging their batteries and conducting housekeeping chores. Consequently, enemy subs are free targets. Get what rest you can on stations; we have no idea how long we have before we must go to general quarters, condition one. Captain out."

Toby relaxed next to the stern twenty, enjoying the light breeze as the ships swung to three-zero-six degrees, beginning their patrol. Their speed remained at ten knots, giving the soundmen the best chance at hearing a sub.

Clusters of men gathered on the decks to cool off. Conversations occurred in near whispers on the darkened ship. The smoking lamp was out on all weather decks to avoid one person revealing their presence with the flare of a match or lighter flame. There wasn't much difference in conversation from one cluster to another. Home, family, girlfriends, or wives left behind. One group centered on Toby and consisted mostly of Snipes.

Stories and memories bounced back and forth, but Toby didn't say much about Amanda due to her family connections. When he did speak about them, the range of family influence ended with the death of her parents and a loving grandfather who raised her without mention of his life. Nothing indicating his knighthood and connection to the King of England left his lips.

After a while, the number of men in the conversations dwindled as the sailors tried to get some rest or sleep. However, the atmosphere remained warm, and the humidity increased as the fog drifted into the Sound. Then a messenger from the bridge stopped by and told everyone that rain was moving into the area. Toby forced himself to get up and move about, limbering his leg for the ladder he had to negotiate to get to the berthing compartment. Tom Watson helped his friend down the ladder like a faithful Golden Retriever. Once in his rack, one of the names for bunks, Toby wiggled around, then fell into a deep sleep. By dawn, the clouds began breaking up, and the clearing sky promised a warm day with a hot sun.

"GENERAL QUARTERS, GENERAL QUARTERS, SET CONDITION ONE, AIR DEFENSE," blared the 1MC. Toby woke with a start and began to wiggle to exit his bunk, only to find someone had strapped him in.

With a growl, the sailor worked his way free and ignored the pain in his thigh. It took two minutes for Toby to make it to the gun mount, where his crew waited.

"We hoped you would make it; we already called in manned and ready," Jack said as he helped Toby get strapped in.

The *MANNING* cranked up her speed to twenty-five knots as three G3M 'Nell' torpedo bombers dropped to wave level, heading for the X-Ray Assembly Area of Guadalcanal.

Stress caused pain in Toby's leg, but the doctor's snug bandage and a pain tablet helped him ignore it. Then, finally, the sailor swung the cannon toward the aircraft, and he got some rounds in the slim bomber to no avail. Finally, a forward five-inch gun fired in front of the closest plane, causing a towering column of water to shoot upward into the starboard engine, causing it to stall. The bomber glided into the sea, skidding to a halt. The crew exited the plane and began firing at the ship. As the number fifty-one gun began to turn toward the downed craft, the forward starboard twenty-millimeter cannon opened up, punching fist-sized holes in the cabin area, starting a fire in the fuel lines, and the flooding began to take its toll. The crew stood their ground and died, taking on a destroyer.

F4F Wildcats from the Wasp jumped into the furball and scored a few victories, but ten American aircraft were lost, with the disposition of the pilots remaining unknown. Gunners on the escorts had to identify the aircraft they aimed at to avoid firing on friendly forces. The planes from both sides seemed to disappear into the gathering clouds as suddenly as they appeared. The distant chattering of machine guns confirmed the fight moved toward the northwest.

"Check with radar on all aircraft in range," the Captain said half an hour later.

"The only aircraft in the air is over Henderson, sir," the OOD confirmed.

"Set the modified condition one, OOD, and double the lookouts on a two-hour rotation," The Captain ordered.

Jack relieved Toby for lunch when Tom showed up to escort the limping sailor. With the threat of another attack at any time, lunch consisted of soup and a sandwich washed down by the ever-present coffee.

Toby made it back to the gun mount to relieve Jack for lunch, and Tom helped by taking the talker's phone. The heat built under the bulky kapok life jackets caused most men to either untie them or remove them to take advantage of the breeze. Unfortunately, the bulky life jackets couldn't stay off long, or sunburns would result.

Toby, Jack, and their talker stood the twenty-twenty-four-hundred watch on the cannon. The word of anticipated action kept the crew at General Quarters. Toby used a pair of binoculars to scan the not-so-distant growth on the Florida Islands. He expressed amazement at the size and range of colors of the Orchids growing wild on the islands. The trees teemed with colorful parrots and parakeets, chattering and darting limb to limb. It provided an unending scene of colors that rivaled the rainbows that frequented the islands. The sailor noted the water changing from its normal deep blue through the green shades as the water became shallow.

General Quarters downgraded to condition two, allowing the gunners to take charge. Toby gratefully headed for the berthing space, then to the showers, and back to his bunk. His pain meds helped him get into a night of good REM sleep until the messenger woke him. "Time to relieve the watch."

Toby, now qualified as a Top Watch in the engine room, sat on a toolbox where he could see all the gauges on the throttle board. He slowly worked on a cup of coffee and listened to the machinery. An unexplained change in machinery sound could be a warning of a potential failure and require immediate attention. It proved to be a quiet watch, which the men always appreciated.

Four hours later, Toby stopped by the head, then went directly to his bunk. He gingerly lowered himself onto his bunk, wiggled to get comfortable, then the exhausted sailor fell into a deep sleep.

Within an hour, the 1MC blared out, "General Quarters, all hands man your battle stations."

Toby rolled onto the tile deck and struggled a little to get dressed. Finally, he grabbed his binoculars and hauled himself up the ladder to the main deck. Reaching the mount, the sailor donned his life jacket and strapped on the WWI-style tin helmet.

Jack slapped a fully loaded magazine into the breech, then Toby jacked a fresh round into the weapon, making it war-ready. They waited.

A snap and hiss came from the 1MC system, "This is the Captain. Men, an unknown composition or size enemy force, is attacking the cruiser-destroyer task force off Guadalcanal, southeast of Savo. Be prepared for surface action with enemy warships." The Captain added, "We are also seriously concerned about submarine action in the area."

Like a magic wand, the Captain's words swept across the crew, converting them from tired sailors to fighting US Navy crewmen. Everywhere the clang of weapons becoming charged for use. Initial armor-piercing shells filled the breeches of the main armament. Dozens of sets of eyes peered across the waters, eager to be the first to see and report the enemy's presence.

Distant lightning jumped between clouds and occasionally lashed Savo Island and the waters of the Sound. But the rain stayed to the south. Weather conditions could not veil the flashes of non-flashless gun powder nor silence the sharp crack of large caliber guns discharging and the crump of their shells exploding. A line of machine guns and cannon shells arched across the sky as gunners fired at aircraft dropping flares southeast of Savo Island.

In the Operations Center, the TBS frequencies rapidly became jammed with cross-traffic, making sense of the confusion an impossibility.

"Bridge, Sound, we picked up what sounded like several large underwater explosions bearing one-six-three to one-seven-three degrees, estimated at about forty miles. That would put them somewhere south and east of Savo Island."

The OOD looked at the Captain, "Sounds like torpedoes, Lieutenant; get everyone watching for submarines in earnest."

"Aye, sir. Bo'sun sound ASW alert."

"Aye, sir. GENERAL QUARTERS, GENERAL QUARTERS, SET ANTISUBMARINE ALERT."

"Bridge, Sound; we have searched every degree around this ship and have nothing to indicate a submarine within our range."

"Bridge, aye." The talker repeated Sound's report to the OOD, with the Captain hearing. Captain Drake looked out the window, trying to put together a reasonable explanation from the information.

"Bridge, aye, sir," the talker addressed the OOD, "Radar report an unknown casualty is causing the radar to malfunction; they are working to correct the problem now."

"Very well."

Captain Drake felt the hair rise on his neck and head.

"Bridge, aye, sir, Radar is now getting intermittent returns on their equipment."

"Very well." Captain looked at the OOD, barely making him out in the dim, reflected instrument lighting.

The premonition of doom swept over the staunch man like a black blanket. He closed his eyes and made peace with his creator. A soundless air silenced even the breathing of the men.

"Bridge, aye, Sir, Radar reports three large ships passing us to port, bearing, two-three-five, course three-one-zero, speed twenty knots, distance, five miles."

"It's too late." Captain Drake mumbled.

****

Nobody saw nor reported the invisible three-ton monster rushing toward the *USS MANNING* ten feet below the surface at fifty-one knots. The torpedo was one of three twenty-four-inch fish launched by Japanese cruisers exiting the northwestern corridor between Savo Island and the Florida Islands group. The Type ninety-three torpedo packed an explosive punch with over a thousand pounds of high explosives in its warhead.

At fifty-one-knot, the nose of the torpedo struck the frame separating the forward fire room and engine room at almost fifty-nine miles an hour, punching a hole through the hull and bulkhead. The half-second delay in the firing sequence allowed the warhead to enter the hull before the thousand-eighty pounds of Type 97 high explosive detonated.

In the blink of an eye, the blast killed the crew in the forward fire room and created massive amounts of shrapnel that shredded deck 01 to the top of the Fire Control director. The main deck cracked and opened above the fire room across the beam of the vessel. Nearly all the ship's personnel in the path of the blast perished, including the entire bridge watch and Captain. In addition, boilers 1A and 1B were driven through the bottom of the ship, snapping the keel.

With the bulkhead between the fire room and forward engine room ruptured, those men in that space perished as well and devastated the turbines. Blades from that machine penetrated the after bulkhead mincing both boilers in the number two fire room, and the added destruction wiped out the after-engine room.

Between the damage caused by the two forward boilers and torpedo detonation, only three steel stringers held the two halves of the Gleaves together. Then, when the ship slammed back into the water, the forward inertia of the *MANNING* forced the bow half to fold back on the starboard side, snapping the three stringers. As a result, the ship became two independent halves, riding alongside one another.

Still strapped to the twenty-millimeter cannon, Toby suffered severe conflicting twists and wrenching of his muscles. Those men not secured to the ship found themselves catapulted out to a hundred feet from the wreck, many dying from the blast and flying shrapnel while still in the air. Those that landed in the water responded as if they had landed on concrete, causing extensive, life-threatening injuries and death to several men.

Toby, heavily dazed by the shock of the blast and thrown like a rag doll, lay limp in the gun's harness, a large sliver of steel protruding from his back. As he struggled with partial consciousness, he became aware of more pain than he could remember. He didn't believe the human body could withstand such pain from every limb of his body. Finally, the ship settled down long enough for the dazed sailor to release himself from the gun, where he fell to the deck, crying out in agony.

Water washing over the low deck brought the Petty Officer around, and after moments of slow movements, he looked around.

A question formed in the fog of his mind, *'Why is the front half of the ship moving in a different direction than the stern? And why is it next to the stern?'* Then he watched in horror as the torn and destroyed forward half of the ship rolled over and plunged below the surface of the black water. Toby's mind screamed at him, *'Get off this ship; it's going to sink and fast.'*

Before the sailor could move, the stern section rolled with a sudden twist that acted like a slingshot, throwing the sailor over twenty-five feet away from the dying hull. The water was warm and soothing in Toby's mind. His life jacket held his head clear of the water, allowing him to look around. He could see something like a ship or boat heading toward him.

Toby Greene began a modified breaststroke to get away from the vessel or boat. His greatest fear welled up in him; he knew he'd suffered injuries that bled, and swimming in known shark-infested waters would be fatal. Then he felt a bump, and something grabbed his arm, then blackness overcame everything.

USS SOLACE (AH-5) USN HOSPITAL SHIP

CHAPTER FOURTEEN

"SHARK, SHARK," Toby Greene screamed as he woke up, flailing at the monster below the surface of the black water. Then his brain centered on the bright light in his eyes. Finally, his mind whispered, *'Heaven's light, you have lived the good life.'*

Strange, masked faces moved through the bright fog, and he heard, "Toby, Toby, can you hear me?" Then only darkness.

The sailor took long strokes to reach the surface, his lungs beginning to feel like they would burst. Once on the surface, the light returned, but not as bright as he remembered.

Toby heard distant voices, "He's coming around."

That angelic voice again said, "Toby, can you hear me?"

The sailor cautiously opened his eyes, the light a dim glow; he felt hot and musty, his mind still in confusion. Toby moved his eyes, looking around, trying not to move or reveal his position. He blinked, and his eyes focused a little. Toby blinked again, twice, and twice; each time, his vision cleared until everything stood in clear sharpness. "Where am I," he rasped through parched lips and dry mouth.

"Toby, can you hear me?" that angel-like voice asked.

Again, the sailor croaked, "Where am I?"

"Toby, I'm Lieutenant Carol Darcy; you're on a hospital ship. A medical team brought you here after a torpedo struck your ship. You suffered some wounds. How are you feeling?"

“Horrible, my left side and shoulder hurt.” Toby felt with his hand until a soft woman’s fingers brought it to rest at his side.

“Don’t try to remove the dressings; you needed surgery and must heal before you touch that area. I know it hurts,” her voice full of genuine concern, “but we’ll get you something to help shortly. You had a piece of steel go through your life jacket and into your back. And some smaller ones around it, down to the top of your legs. You will be sore for only a short time.”

“What did you say happened to me?” Toby asked.

“Your ship took a torpedo and sunk; apparently, you were injured and thrown overboard, where men in a boat recovered you. Unfortunately, we had to remove the steel piece and other fragments and splinters during a couple of surgeries.”

Toby looked at his left hand and arm, where Doctors secured it to a frame, which they attached to his waist with a heavy belt.

“If you play your cards right, you might get a medical discharge and stay home for the rest of the war,” the Lieutenant said.

“No, Lieutenant, I can’t do that; I have to return to my ship; I have a job to do.”

“I’m sorry, Toby, but your ship is gone, sunk; when released from medical care, you will begin thirty days of survivor’s leave, and medical authorities will determine whether or not to discharge you.” The nurse smiled at the sailor, “I want to wish you the best for what you want and congratulated you on your determination and loyalty.” Then, after cleaning and redressing his wounds, she smiled and said, “You’re already showing signs of healing.”

After two weeks under the care of Nurse Darcy, he found himself attracted to the beauty. Through the days which followed, Toby and Nurse Darcy grew closer.

One day, as Carol pushed Toby’s wheelchair to an empty sunny location on the main deck, she said, “We have to talk.”

“I know, we’re getting serious in a short time.”

“Yes, but that’s not what we must do. You probably know of the Navy’s position on relationships between Officers and enlisted personnel.

“Yes, it’s taboo.”

"Exactly. My feelings for you clearly violate the regulations, so we must be careful because I'm not about to let you go, even if we have to wait out the war."

Toby took the woman's hand, "Carol, I love you, and if I must, then we will make it until we can be together."

"Deal," she said with a radiant smile.

Despite his feelings for this woman, something gnawed at him; something was missing from his past that was vital to his future.

Toby found out he and the hospital ship sat anchored in Moselle Bay at Noumea, New Caledonia, of the New Hebrides Islands, and his stay depended on his ability to travel.

The sailor rested in the warm sun, not thinking of the war or how he became injured. Then unexpectedly, his eyes flew open, he looked at the blue sky, and it all came back in a rush of sensation, horror, and a sense of terror. After that, Toby's memories stopped swimming in a kaleidoscope of images.

Fireman Greene searched his memories as they were. *'A monster of an explosion came from the vicinity of the forward stack, rendering the heavy tube into shards of metal going in all directions. For some reason, it hurt to breathe, and for some reason, I felt as if I'd been clutched in the teeth by a huge wolf and shaken like a rat. I picked myself up, and the pain felt like it drove me back to the deck. I had a vision of the front half of our ship alongside the stern, which made no sense. Somehow, I found myself in the water, looking at the stern of the MANNING. The stern began to roll over, and I swam as fast as possible, but my left arm wouldn't work. Then, I felt a bump against my leg; it must be a shark, but I woke up here.'*

He held his head in his hands, "It's all so confusing," he muttered. Then, finally, the sailor made it to his bed and fell into a troubled sleep. Flashes of light and thunder shook the man's thoughts, causing him to flinch. Then all was quiet, and Toby slowly woke to a new day, with the form and scent of Carol Darcy bent over him, adjusting his covers. She straightened up, and a red line crept up from her neck when she realized he woke when she bent over him. Toby smiled, and Carol ran her tongue over her upper lip as she turned away, not wanting to create a scene.

That day, Doctor Jeremy Allen wrote orders on the sailor's chart for Toby to begin short walks on deck to help restore his circulation. Over the next two weeks, the soreness from the small wounds dissipated, leaving his shoulder his only source of discomfort. However, some of that ceased when the Doctor removed the heavy bandages and applied light coverings.

Toby looked at his ring finger, but he couldn't recall why he thought it looked bare, and his memory of all events before the torpedo blast remained an enigma. Finally, the sailor returned to the sun's warmth on the deck and slept comfortably in a lounge chair.

The Fireman awoke with a start; he looked around in confusion, then the images of the torpedoing returned, this time with the full recall of the sailor. *'The explosion, the pain in his back, and briefly watching the first stack lift and disintegrate. The images jumped to water, and he used a one-hand breaststroke to get away from the suction of the stern going down. Toby remembered thinking how much he wanted to live to see Amanda again. Amanda, my wife, at home with my parents.'*

The sailor shook as shock began taking hold of him, his eyes becoming vacant.

Nurse Darcy walked up the deck to check on her patient and saw that he was in distress. She hurried to him, "Toby, are you all right?" Kneeling in front of him, Darcy checked his pulse, finding it racing. She called a nearby orderly, "Call for help, patient in need of assistance, possible shock."

"Toby, can you hear me?"

The Fireman looked into the Nurse's blue eyes and heart-shaped face and then at her auburn hair.

"Toby, what happened? Are you hurting other than your shoulder?"

"N…no, I guess I got shaken up when everything came back to me; I remember everything now."

A Doctor and two nurses trotted up to Nurse Darcy and Toby. The Doctor asked for a sitrep from the Lieutenant, and she filled him in on her observations and the things she and Toby said, along with checking his pulse and checking him over for any additional injuries.

Turning to Toby, the Doctor said, "Toby, I'm Doctor Allen; how are you feeling right now?"

"I'm feeling better, sir, I've been pushing myself to remember what has happened to me, who I was, and it all came crashing in at the same time, but I'm feeling much better now. I'm sorry to have created all the commotion."

"No, don't be sorry; it's our job to be ready at any time help is needed with small or large issues. So, tell me, who are you?"

Toby gave the Doctor the full rundown on who he was, including his official status in England. Doctor Allen took a patronizing stand with Toby, thinking he still suffered from delusions.

"Sir, I'm quite lucid; I am a Knight of the Realm." Then he filled the Doctor and nurses in on surprising events which only fortified their beliefs. "Sir, are either the Captain or XO of the *MANNING* aboard?"

One of the arriving nurses confirmed, "Lieutenant Mark Carvour, the ship's XO, is aboard in Officer's Country."

"Can you check on his condition, and if he's ambulatory, ask him if he would consider coming down here. Then, explain the situation to him," ordered Doctor Allen.

The nurse quickly walked toward the bow and disappeared into the ship. A couple of minutes later, the nurse reappeared, pushing the XO, who sat in a wheelchair.

"Fireman Greene, how are you doing?" asked the XO.

"Getting better, sir. May I ask what happened to you?"

"When the torpedo hit, everyone flew in different directions, partly from the shock and ship's gyrations and partly from the impact of shrapnel. Everyone on the bridge died, yet somehow I survived; I shouldn't have, but I guess it wasn't my time. I held onto a handrail when the forward half of the ship began to roll; my other arm was useless and shredded. How about you?"

Toby filled the Officer in on his story, explaining how he had just recalled almost all of his memory.

"Are you going to remain in the Navy?" the Officer asked.

"I want to, but the board to determine that won't meet on it until I finish my recovery. And you, sir?"

"I got the long face from my Doctor; my arm suffered too much damage for saving; the final decision will come after the board convenes."

"I'm sorry to hear that, sir; I looked forward to serving with you, the Captain, and the crew again. But that's all gone now. If the Navy retains me, I'll ask for another destroyer," the Fireman said.

"I'm glad to see you came through that mess. But, of course, the King wouldn't be happy to find one of his best Knights died."

"Thank you, sir."

Doctor Allen addressed the Lieutenant, "So, Fireman Greene really is a knight? I must ask, though, if Fireman Greene is a Machinist's Mate and assigned to an engine room, what was he doing behind a gun?"

"Doctor, you're in the presence of one of the best gunners in the Navy. When he was in the Royal Navy, he shot down two Nazi planes and damaged a third, which saved a cargo ship and its crew. And if I recall correctly, he has added enough kills on the *MANNING* to qualify as an Ace."

"My apologies, Fireman. I should have listened better before I made an assumption. We will do our best to prepare you for your next assignment, but in the meantime, we need to prepare you for your thirty days of survivor's leave."

"Thank you, sir; four weeks will seem like heaven, all spent with my wife. But, unfortunately, we never had the opportunity for a honeymoon; I want to take her to Niagara Falls."

"I'm happy to hear you're both feeling well. Enjoy the rest and treatment we can provide, and we'll get you headed home very soon."

"Thank you, Doctor, and thank you, ladies, for your fast response. Thanks to your expertise and compassion, I want to take this opportunity to tell you that I am fortunate to be alive and will forever keep you in my prayers."

The care keepers talked a little, then returned to their duties; one nurse, Carol Darcy, looked back at her patient and smiled.

The XO and Toby sat and talked about their event and their losses. The two reminisced about the times they spent on the new Gleaves destroyer, committing as many memories as they could into the corners of their minds. Toby said, "I think I'll spend the next couple of hours writing about the things we have shared. In time my memories will fade, and details will be lost; this way, I can at least refresh them."

"That's a good idea, I might try that, and other things will pop up."

The men shook hands, comrades in combat and survival, then the Lieutenant began to turn his chair, and the nurse that fetched him came from behind a lifeboat to wheel him to his room.

Two days later, Toby and the Lieutenant prepared to leave the hospital ship for a passenger ship to San Diego via Pearl Harbor. Nurse Darcy assisted Toby in packing his two changes of clothes and shaving gear in a cloth bag. With all the supports and casts removed, Toby felt like his old self for the first time.

Nurse Darcy said, "Hold my arm; I'm required to assist you until you step off this ship." With that, the two slowly walked toward the exit in the ship's hull. As they neared the large open area of the access point, Darcy guided Toby into a small head. She closed and locked the door, then turned to Toby.

Before she could speak, Toby clasped her hands firmly between them. "Carol, I want to share something with you before I leave. Until I felt the rush of memories of whom and what I am, I want you to know I was more than fond of you, and I believe you're aware of that." The auburn-haired beauty nodded in the affirmative. "I would have waited as long as it took to be part of your life."

"I understand, Toby. Now that we're opening up to one another, I admit I was well on my way to falling in love with you. And I, too, would have waited until we could be together. But now, that has all changed." Then with her eyes glistening, she whispered into Toby's ear.

Toby said, "I want you to have this as a token of my feelings for you." The sailor pulled a quarter-sized medallion and necklace from his pocket. I received this coin from King George VI when he knighted me. I have kept it to myself ever since; now it is yours." Watching the smiling face of Toby Greene, Carol dipped her head as he slipped the medallion over her auburn hair and around her neck. The sailor looked into the woman's eyes, and a tear ran down her cheek.

She reached up with both hands on his cheeks, softly kissed him on his lips, then said, “You will always be my Shining Knight in Armor.” They hugged, then the Lieutenant said, “Fireman Greene, it’s time for you to disembark, and thank you.”

Nurse Darcy escorted the sailor to the gangway, where an orderly took over his assistance into a seat on a blue bus. Carol Darcy watched the bus leave, taking away the only man, other than her father, that she ever loved.

****

Two and a half weeks later, the passenger liner, decked out in a wartime paint scheme, pulled into Pearl Harbor. Men having transferred to units in Hawaii disembarked, and wounded men, followed by transferees, boarded for San Diego, California. Shortly after, the last man boarded, the hatch sealed, and the ship prepared to get underway.

Twenty days later, after running a track that took them outside normal shipping lines and constantly altered zigzag moves, the ship docked at the 32nd Street Naval Station. A seemingly unending line of military ambulances waited at the head of the berth to take the wounded to their respective service hospitals. Toby stood at the end of the line, his injuries almost fully healed. At the Balboa Naval Hospital, an orderly had Toby take a seat in a wheelchair, and the sailor held his meager possessions in the cloth bag on his lap. The orderly wheeled Toby to a beleaguered admitting clerk, who took Toby’s medical records and assigned him to a wounded ward and bed, then dismissed him. The orderly wheeled him through the busy maze of the huge hospital to his bed. Toby changed into the gown and crawled into bed, ready to sleep while he could.

A nurse softly woke the sailor, “Are you Toby Greene?”

“Yes, ma’am.”

“Please, call me Nurse Hopkins, or when there are no officers about, Peggy will be fine; I dislike ma’am.”

“Certainly, I understand.”

“Tell me, why are you here?” she asked while scanning his chart.

Toby went through the story, and Nurse Hopkins said, "You have had a tough time from the looks of your record. Is there anything I can do for you?"

"Yes, there is. I need to use the head, and I'm very steady on my feet; please don't put me in a wheelchair; save it for a wounded man or woman who needs it."

"We can do that, but you understand I can't allow you to wander around the hospital alone."

"I understand, and your company is welcome."

As the two walked toward the end of the ward, Toby asked, "What's the chance of finding an Exchange and maybe a phone booth?"

"We have a ship's store here and a phone bank exchange not far away. I would imagine you would like to call home."

"Thank you, but all in good time; I know you have other injured men to help."

"You appear familiar with our operations; where were you before coming to Balboa?"

"On the USS Solace, I woke up there following a few surgeries and became familiar with all the fine work Navy Nurses do for the injured and sick. You may not know it, but I can spot a nurse in a crowd."

Nurse Hopkins seriously looked at Toby, "And how can you do that?"

"Nurses always have a smile on their faces and a golden orb floating over their heads."

"You're such a character; I'm going to have to watch myself around you. Here is the head; I'll be right here when you're finished."

Toby finished his business and washed his hands, then exited the head to find Nurse Hopkins standing with two other nurses in a three-way conversation. Peggy Hopkins said to her friends, "My sailor's here, gotta go."

Later in the evening, after the busy hospital settled down for the night, Toby asked his evening nurse to take him to the phone bank. Needless to say, the family received the call with glee, and everyone had a chance to talk and ask questions. First, of course, Toby had to promise a full account of his acts when he arrived but assured them he was safe and would head home as soon as possible.

Toby located the XO, who made a couple of calls unbeknown to the Fireman. "I have some news for you, Toby. You will receive a notice of promotion to Machinist's Mate Second class, congratulations."

"Thank you, sir; I'd forgotten all about that with all we have been through."

"I don't doubt that."

"Any word on your situation?"

"Yes, I'm on a train heading back home to find a job for a one-armed man. But I couldn't have had a better ride; I doubt I'll have any problems."

"I'd bet on it." Toby handed the officer a piece of paper, "Here is my home address and phone number; feel free to call any time. When this is over, call me, and let's see if we can get together."

"I'd like that, you have become a good friend, Toby, and it's Mike Carvour; you may as well get used to dropping XO or Lieutenant."

"Thanks, Mike; keep in touch; I have faith in a lot of power."

"I don't doubt that in the least."

Toby spent his free time getting his newly issued uniforms ready for duty and new Second Class Petty Officer 'crows' sewn on his jumpers.

Doctor Harold Andes stopped by his bed, and a new, much younger Doctor watched and listened. "Fireman Greene? I'm sorry, it's now Petty Officer Greene and congratulations on the promotion."

"Thank you, sir."

"I have a couple of envelopes for you; the large one is your medical records and sufficient information, including your promotion, for your next duty station to recover a full copy of your permanent record. In addition, this envelope contains your tickets from Santa Fe to Norfolk to begin your thirty days' leave and your transfer to your next assignment, along with tickets for that move. How are you feeling today?"

"I'm feeling as good as I've ever been."

"No pains or soreness or problems with your shoulder?"

“None at all, sir.”

“Do you mind if we have a look at your shoulder?”

“No, sir.” Toby removed his shirt, and the two Doctors examined his scar and the healing progress, commenting on the wound in medical terms that Toby didn’t understand.

“Well, Petty Officer, you look as if you are ready to return to full duty. Good luck with your next assignment, and take advantage of your upcoming leave to get as much rest as possible.”

“Thank you again, sir; I will do just that.”

Reading the ticket information, Toby learned he still had time to get to the train station with time to spare. Nurse Hopkins helped him get ready, and Toby said his goodbyes to the thoughtful nurse. An orderly grabbed his bag while Nurse Hopkins insisted, he rides to the front door in a wheelchair, and the sailor complied with the rules once again.

Toby walked into the Santa Fe Terminal, got his seabag checked in, grabbed a magazine, and boarded the Chieftain.

USS A.J. DEFOE (DD-535)

CHAPTER FIFTEEN

Santa Fe's Chieftain, the current top series of diesel locomotives, had the warm painted colors of an American Chief. Toby moved through the car to an open aisle seat and sat on the soft, comfortable cushion. The sailor looked out the window at the last moment, passengers hurrying to get aboard before the big train departed. As he looked over the other passengers, he saw sailors. Most of them were recent graduates of boot camp, trying to appear salty. A number of Marine buck privates from the Marine Corps Training Depot sat scattered around the car, like the boot sailors, on their way to their first assignment or home for leave before heading out. Then there were the true old salts. A few Seamen and Firemen sat among the younger men with some time under their belts, and a mix of Third-, Second-, and First Class Petty Officers and two Chief Petty Officers were also present.

The experienced fleet sailors stood out with ribbons denoting campaigns and participating in major events. Toby spotted only two Purple Hearts and Bronze Stars, one set belonging to a Marine Sergeant, the other on a First Class Corpsman. Toby made the third man in the car with the award, except Toby also wore a small bronze star on his Purple Heart ribbon to denote a second award.

Three different ribbons on Toby's right chest stood out. Only he, of all aboard, served in the Royal Navy; there was no award for his battle wounds received in combat, as the R.N. did not have such a device. However, these three ribbons drew the attention of a Marine Staff Sergeant, who wore his chest full of awards and a red with yellow M.P. letters on the brassard wrapped around his left arm.

"Hi, Petty Officer. Do you have a minute to chat?"

"You bet, Sergeant, this train just got underway, and it will be a while before we stop again; what's on your mind?"

The big Marine shooed a young boot from his seat next to the sailor. "I'm not a stickler on ribbon alignment, or even if a pair of ribbons reversed. I leave that to the boot Second Lieutenants who have to make their mark. But, out of my curiosity, I have to ask about the three ribbons on your right chest. I know that's the location for foreign awards, and I wondered what they may be if you care to talk about them?"

"I get that a lot; I'd take them off, but the tailor sewed them to my uniform."

"I've never seen ribbons of that nature before," the Marine pressed.

"I picked them up in combat serving in the Royal Navy."

"Let's see, a DSO, that's a biggie in the Brit forces, usually an officer's award. Were you an officer?"

"No, I was a Stoker; I worked on a destroyer in the after-engine room."

"You're making me even more curious," the Sergeant teased.

"If you want to know, The King of England awarded one to me for downing two Nazi planes and damaging a third, and in doing so, helped save a cargo ship and its crew while manning a twenty-millimeter cannon."

"Now, there you go. I was just getting to like you, and you stiffed me," the slightly irate Marine growled.

"Let me show you something." Toby pulled out his wallet and handed the Marine a folded paper.

The Sergeant, Staff Sergeant Tommy Fontaine, read a copy of the letter from Captain Merrifield. He checked the seal at the top and the signature at the bottom. He had seen the signature before and knew it to be an original.

"I owe you an apology, Petty Officer Greene; congratulations on those awards. I believe your statement on how you got them is also accurate?"

"It is. And as icing on the cake, my grandfather-in-law is Admiral Sir Brian de Lacy, First Sea Lord of the R.N."

"The hell you say?"

"No lies, I promise."

"Tell me, what is the King like?"

Toby chuckled, "Take all his stuffed shirts away, and His Majesty is as down-home as you or I."

"No!!"

"As I sit here, I would not admit saying that to anyone, and probably you shouldn't either."

"I won't; besides, nobody would believe me. So I'd better get on with my rounds and find a boot to harass," he laughed. "Be careful, Petty Officer Greene, maybe we will meet again sometime in the future, and you can tell me how all this came about."

"When this is over, we plan to start a farm in Iowa; that's where you'll find me."

The Chieftain pulled into Norfolk on time, and Toby looked out the window. At the back of a crowd, he saw the most beautiful and exciting sight he could imagine, Amanda, as radiant as the sun, stretching up on her toes in a small bounce to see over the heads of passengers and waiting families.

Amanda, the Greenes, and Toby clashed in hugs and delicious kisses from his love. Then, in one moment of recovery from Amanda's intensity, Toby saw Sergeant Fontaine watching him and Amanda. When he noticed Toby spotted him, he gave the sailor a thumbs up, then was moved along by the crowd.

Toby picked up his seabag, and his father said, "That looks like its brand new."

"Toby," his mother asked, "Where are your other bags? You usually have a couple. You didn't leave them on the train, did you?"

Toby's face took on a deadly serious gaze, then only said, "Iron Bottom Sound."

The Greenes looked at their son, faces full of questions. Then, Toby added, "Not now, maybe later."

The sailor's face and tone of voice said to leave it alone. Then they piled into the family car for the ride home.

Amanda didn't miss the meaning of Toby's words and demeanor and sensed her husband had been through a tragic event.

She held him tightly to her bosom, *her mind went to work; 'his sudden lack of mail, clipped phone calls, new uniform and seabag, and now his behavior. Then, like a thunderbolt, it hit her; Toby's ship; the Japanese sank it.'*

Amanda tried to mother Toby without his knowledge, and she almost felt helpless with his pent-up torture. Amanda had seen it before, in her parents.

Toby's first act the next day was to check into the Veterans Hospital, which took in overflow patients from the war zones. After examining the sailor's wounds, they told him to go home and that they would contact him in three or four days. Three blissful days with his wife went too fast. Toby returned to the hospital; a board member said, "You have received serious wounds, and the board is inclined to grant you a medical discharge."

"No, sir, I don't want a medical; my job is in the fleet, fighting for my country. I am capable and willing to leave today if needed. I want to be assigned a destroyer and sent back to the Pacific; that's where I belong."

"And if we refuse your demands?"

"I have powerful contacts in England and will use them to reinstate me in the R.N. and fight the enemy there."

Taken back by the intensity of the sailor's determination, the board member excused himself and said he would be right back.

Minutes later, the man reappeared, "Did you say R.N.? What's that?"

"The Royal Navy, sir."

"You served in the Royal Navy?"

"Yes, until America entered the war. Then I was integrated into our Navy."

"I see; follow me."

A panel of Doctors ran Toby through a series of physical agility and endurance tests to determine his dexterity. Two hours later, the board, surprised and impressed, told Toby he had come within ninety-eight percent of ability compared to recruit training standards for entry into the Navy. His determination succeeded.

"A detailer will contact you for your next assignment, which will become effective following your thirty-day survivor's leave, which begins today."

"Thank you, sir; I will do my best to justify your decision."

"I have no doubt about that; good luck."

Toby's survivor's leave began a time of rekindling his and Amanda's deep commitment to one another into an inseparable bond. Unfortunately, their third day of family activities with the Greenes was interrupted by a long-distance phone call from the British Consulate in Washington.

"This is Thomas Greene speaking; how may I help you?"

"I am Edward Wood, British Ambassador to the United States. Is the Lady Amanda de Greene available?"

"Most certainly, sir, if you could hold for a second."

"Absolutely, thank you."

Holding his hand on the mouthpiece, "Nancy, will you call Amanda; the British Ambassador wants to speak to her?"

Nancy returned less than a minute with Amanda with a worried look.

"This is the Lady de Greene; how may I help you, Viscount Halifax?"

"Ah yes, my Lady. Your grandfather and I want to assure you he is quite well and has decided to activate his retirement. He has completed his close-out of Naval Service, and I must say, we are going to miss his leadership and friendship. Your grandfather and I have long been friends, and I know no better gentleman than he.

He has asked that I inform you he has taken passage on the RMS Mauretania, a troopship converted liner en route to the Norfolk Naval docks. Due to a weather front and zigzagging, his arrival time is in flux, but the Norfolk Harbor control can tell you when and which pier the ship will dock. Our best guess is in a fortnight."

"Thank you, Viscount Halifax; we can take it from here."

"My dear, I've known you since you were a child, and here you are, a married woman and sounding very much like an American."

"I know, the people and ways here are easier to assume than I believed. I've sent photos to the ladies I used to run around with, and they couldn't believe me running a farm tractor and wearing bib-overalls."

"My word, I would say not. And if you hadn't told me, I wouldn't have believed it myself. We are happy for you; you always liked the old American west and farming. It fits you. If you are ever in Washington, please accept my offer to stop by for a visit; my Lady and I look forward to seeing you and meeting your husband; I understand Sir Tobias is in favor of His Majesty."

"Yes, he is, and grandpa too."

"Good, I must return to the state's business; it never ends; stay safe and have Sir Brian call me when he arrives."

"I will, and God save the King."

"God save the King," he replied, then the line went dead.

"Is everything all right, my dear?" asked Nancy

"Yes," her daughter-in-law answered. "We, Toby and I, asked grampa to join us here, in America, to live. He's all alone now that we have married and moved here."

"Isn't that what you wanted?"

"Yes, we expected to be on our farm by then, and we haven't purchased the land, and there is no house," Amanda said.

"And we are in Virginia. And the trouble is what?"

"Where will we, and Grandpa live?"

"Amanda dear, think a little; we still have an extra ample-size bedroom available. Tom and I look forward to having him as part of our family. Then when Toby is home for good, we'll work on getting the farm and a fine farmhouse." Nancy promised. "We must stick together; after all, we are the last of our generation and must help prepare for the next, beginning with your firstborn."

Amanda's shyness slipped through, and although she had a slight hint of a smile, the rose color began to creep up her neck.

"We are to contact the Norfolk Naval Harbor Control or authority if that's what they call them, and we can find out where and when the ship, the RMS Mauretania, will dock."

"How much time do we have?" Tom asked.

"At least a fortnight; we should probably call them after next Monday," Amanda said.

The next day Amanda and Toby took a train to Niagara Falls for a belated missed honeymoon. For Amanda, she was almost like a child, being at the dream center of honeymoons. Toby purchased as much film as possible, due to the war, color film wasn't available, but he had plenty of black and white.

They returned home, Amanda a smiling and content newlywed. But unfortunately, Toby had a message that he needed to appear at the hospital for transfer information.

Toby returned home with his new orders. However, Amanda and Toby's mother showed signs of concern and nervousness with Toby coming close to shipping out.

"Where is the Navy sending you, Toby?" Amanda inquired.

"I am headed back to Bath, Maine for a new construction Fletcher destroyer, the *USS A.J. DEFOE (DD-535).*"

Nancy worked her way into a frenzy over Toby returning to the war. It took Amanda, Tom, and Toby an hour to get the woman settled down and accept Toby would survive and get back home safely.

Two days later, Nancy scanned the new General Electric refrigerator. Small magnets held handwritten notes requiring attention. *'Today, we must contact the Norfolk Harbor people about Amanda's grandfather,'* she thought. Taking the message from the door of the frig, Nancy set it in the middle of the kitchen table as a reminder.

During breakfast, the inquiry became the center of the table conversation. Finally, Tom pocketed the slip of paper and agreed to call the naval base after the business hours began.

Later, as the hands of the Kit-Cat clock approached ten-forty-five, the black dining room phone pierced the quiet of the house with its stark bell. "Greene residence," Nancy announced.

"Tom here, the RMS Mauretania will arrive tomorrow, and I have the dock location. We will need to be there by eleven o'clock."

"That's wonderful; Amanda will be so thrilled, and I'm looking forward to having such an important man in our home."

"I bet; I shall be home at my regular time; how are our honeymooners doing?"

"From what I hear, the same as we after our wedding."

"Mother, you shouldn't be eavesdropping on our son."

Almost whispering, Nancy told her husband, "I don't eavesdrop; I can't help it that your son is a chip off your block."

"What are you implying, dear?"

"We may want to replace their mattress with something softer and less squeaky. And I'm not implying Toby and Amanda are a passionate couple. But, I admit, we are just as good, and they come by it naturally."

"You're so naughty."

"Complaining?"

"Bragging, see later, love you."

"Don't overdo yourself; you never know; you might need the energy tonight." Nancy heard her husband chuckle as he hung up. Nancy Greene smiled as she softly replaced the phone in its cradle.

The following day, Nancy stayed home, making last-minute preparations while Tom, Amanda, and Toby drove to the Norfolk Navy base.

Tom and the newlyweds stood at the head of the wharf as the seven-hundred-seventy-two foot long, thirty-five-thousand ton ship was pushed into position by two Navy fleet tugs. The forty minutes needed to secure the vessel and open the hull access hatch seemed much longer; finally, the passenger began filing out.

Those to leave first were war brides, many U.S. Military families leaving behind the heavily damaged island nation. A number of the wives were in various stages of pregnancy and assisted by nurses or orderlies. One man stood tall and proud, having been the most powerful Admiral in the R.N. Once the passengers and ambulatory injured disembarked, the medical staff began taking stretcher cases off the ship to waiting ambulances.

Amanda reached her beloved grandfather first, wrapping herself around her only family member remaining. Then, the Admiral broke into a new smile as he hugged Toby, "It's wonderful to see you again, my boy."

"Grandpa, meet my father, Thomas Greene."

The two men exchanged initial greetings, and the Admiral added, "I am indebted to you and your wife for inviting me into your home; I'll try not to be a bore," he said, smiling and jesting.

"There is no debt between family members here. On the contrary, we honor your presence and welcome you to our home. We are of English descent, and therefore we are indeed family," Thomas explained.

Brian Lacy looked at his granddaughter's father-in-law, "I believe we are going to become the best of friends, as well."

"It's going to take time for your luggage to find its way to the right holding area. I have taken the opportunity to arrange for it to be secured until we retrieve it. I work not far from here, and I'll have everything delivered to my business and brought home tomorrow if you approve?"

"That will be quite satisfactory, Tom. Thank you for your thoughtfulness."

The two older gentlemen sat in the front seat of the Buick, chattering like magpies, allowing the lovebirds the comfort of the spacious rear seat. The Admiral commented on the spacious and scenic drive to Greene's home.

"America has vast open lands once away from the eastern cities; I think you will enjoy it," Tom said.

It took the remainder of the day to get the Admiral set in, and both Amanda and Toby were delighted to see the Admiral and Toby's parents rapidly becoming friends.

The days continued to march on, bringing Toby's departure closer. Along with that, tensions increased in Nancy and Amanda at his likelihood of seeing combat again.

****

Departure day arrived, and the family gathered on the train platform as they bid farewell to their loved one. Nancy held Toby as desperately as Amanda. She showered her son with kisses, all the while praying for his safe return.

Tom shook hands with his son, now a hero; the older man grasped his son and said, "God be with you, my son. Come home to us."

"I will, Dad, and hopefully permanently."

Then, the new member of the family, Admiral Sir Brian de Lacy, bear-hugged the smaller man, then held him at arm's length. "Toby, in the short days I have been here, it is readily clear I have never come across a family with greater expressions of love than I've seen here. So, have fair winds and following seas, my boy, and hurry home."

"Thank you, and thank you for coming to be with us. You have no idea how happy Amanda, my parents, and I are that you're part of us."

"Most heart-warming, my boy. Now, pay special attention to your wife."

Toby grasped Amanda's hand and walked out of earshot of the others. He wrapped his arms around her, and she locked her hands behind his head, her fingers looping in his short hair. "Amanda," he whispered, "I want you to know I'm doing what I must, and no knight would do less. I'm leaving you my heart; keep it warm and comfortable alongside yours. I have always thought of you daily; you are my anchor and will continue to do so. I love you and already miss you."

"Hurry home to me, my love; we'll have plenty of nights to recover and enjoy one another over and over again."

Amanda and Toby worked to keep a straight face as the others wept. Then, a final deep kiss of promise, and they parted.

"ALL ABOARD!" It was time.

FLETCHER CLASS DESTROYER

CHAPTER SIXTEEN

The train's speed fell to a crawl as it slowed down, nearing a new brick railroad station. As far as cities go, Bath, Maine, would classify as a town. But 'Bath Iron Works' shipbuilding on the Kennebec River is a star in the northeastern sky. BIW began shipbuilding in about 1884.

The passenger train halted with a slight bump of the car couplings readjusting themselves. Sailors stepped down onto the platform from both ends of every car, then migrated to the luggage car. A pair of conductors began calling out the name of a seabag and passing out the sliding door. Surprisingly, the process proceeded along quickly with the disciplined men. A line of blue Navy busses, each bearing a sign of the ship at which they would stop. Toby spotted the bus with *DEFOE* the third from the bottom. His bag and a dozen others landed in the last two rows of seats. The shipbuilders weren't far from the train depot, and after an eight or ten-minute ride, the bus driver began stopping and called the name of ships for the sailors.

In nineteen-forty, the Navy released contracts for hundred-seventy-five new class destroyers, called the Fletcher, while there were still unbuilt Gleaves class cans under contract. Bath Iron Works was the first shipyard to launch and commission into the Navy Fletcher destroyers. The first two were the *USS NICHOLAS*

DD-449 and *the USS O'BANNON DD-450,* sister ships built side-by-side in the same drydock.

****

Toby hoisted his seabag over his left shoulder, keeping his right available for saluting any officer that suddenly appeared before him. As the sailor marched past the bow of the tethered ship; he looked for hull number 535. He found a small representation in white paint instead of the normally large numbers. The vessel sported a camouflage paint scheme, with small numbers to avoid defeating the camouflage.

The sun had set, and the gangway had weak, yellowish waterproof-covered lights along one side. At the quarterdeck, Toby set the seabag down, rendered the required salute to the OOD, and asked, "Permission to come aboard, sir?"

"Granted, are you reporting aboard for duty?"

"Yes, sir," then Toby turned his orders over to the Officer.

After checking the sailor's date, destination, name, and rank, the OOD told the Bo'sun to call the X-Division duty Petty Officer to the quarterdeck. Then he eyeballed Toby's ribbons, taking particular note of the Purple Heart with star, the Bronze Star with V, and the three unknown ribbons on his right breast. He said nothing.

A couple of minutes later, a Petty Officer walked up to the OOD and saluted. "Have this man signed in and a bunk until assigned to his proper division."

"Aye, sir. Follow me."

"I'm Tom Shanks, Yeoman Third. We'll get you a bunk assigned. I wouldn't unpack your bag until you get to your division bunk, which will likely happen tomorrow after quarters. Once we drop off your seabag, we'll go to the Admin Office and finish signing you in."

"Sounds like a plan. And my name is Tobias Greene, but I go by Toby."

"Did you just get transferred from another ship?"

"In a roundabout way, I was on the *MANNING DD-452* at Guadalcanal."

"*MANNING*? I'm unfamiliar with her; what's her class?"

"She was a Gleaves."

"Was?"

"Yeah, she's on Iron Bottom Sound now."

"Oh, sorry, I didn't know."

"That's okay; I wouldn't expect everyone on the east coast to know what's happening half a world away."

"You're right about that. I've been here since I enlisted; where do you call home?"

"Virginia, I thought my accent would give me away," he laughed, "How about you?"

"The Bronx, New York."

"That's a big city; I prefer smaller towns, myself."

The chit-chat continued until they arrived at the Administration office. The checking-in duty Yeoman confirmed the instructions Shanks gave him and told Toby, "We hold quarters on the opposite side of the office on the weather deck. The Uniform is dungarees and a blue hat."

"Thanks; which head and showers do we use? I need to get cleaned up before I can relax."

Tom Shanks said, "It's on the port side, frame sixty, first platform. It's right at Officer's Country, so wear clothes."

"Okay, thanks again." Following his shower, he asked Shanks where he should be for the fire drill.

"Stay here in the Admin office since you're not assigned a billet yet."

Sure enough, the daily fire drill went off at nineteen hundred hours. It had been the norm since he enlisted. Following the fire drill, the evening movie set up on the crew's mess deck. The fantail had more room; however, the yard's work and lights made for poor viewing.

Several men sat around waiting for the movie to begin. One man, a particularly loud and obnoxious individual, noted Toby's new clothing.

Toby answered the question, "Matter of fact, I lost my seabag, and everything I have is new."

"Lost it?" the big mouth laughed. "How the hell do you lose your seabag? That's kind of irresponsible, isn't it?"

Toby turned and looked the man in the eye, "My ship took a torpedo, and the bag went down to Iron Bottom Sound with only a few of my shipmates and me surviving."

The big mouth shrank back in shame, "Sorry, Mac, I was out of line."

With resignation in his voice, Toby muttered, "Forget it; it's over."

That pretty much broke up the bull session. After that, Toby decided he wasn't in a movie mood and headed for his bunk. The sailor felt bad for losing his temper, but it did relieve his tension. Greene locked his wallet in his locker and hung his clothes on the bunk chains. He had never lost any valuables, but it happened now and then on all ships. Not all sailors are 'good buddies.'

Toby learned early in life he could go to the Lord in prayer and even conversation, which he often did. He believed with his entire being his survival in the sinking was divine intervention, and God had plans for him. The sailor lost his Bible with the *MANNING*, and he replaced it with a 1611 KJV, Schofield Bible.

Morning came with the 1MC blaring, "Reveille, reveille, all hands heave out and trice up bunks. Give the ship a clean sweep down fore and aft, empty all trash receptacles on the pier."

The new crew began a new day. Following the cleanup and breakfast, the crew went to quarters, where the Officers and Chiefs filled everyone in on the Plan-of-the-Day.

The Chief went over the roster of new arrivals. When he came to Greene's name, he called out, "Greene."

"Here, Chief," he raised his hand.

"You'll be going to M-Division; they will assign you a duty billet."

"Aye, Chief."

After the release from quarters, Toby received his papers and gathered his seabag and gear. A messenger took him to the Engineering Office a short distance away on the first deck, starboard side, frame sixty-one.

Chief Machinist's Mate Jerry Niemeyer looked the new Petty Officer over and consulted his wheel book. "How about the after-engine room? We need a Second Class down there."

"That will be fine, Chief; that's where I worked on my last ship."

'What's her name?"

"The *MANNING,* a Gleaves can, she was built right here; I went aboard her a couple of berths up the line."

The Chief glanced at the overhead, "The *MANNING*, I heard something about her a couple of weeks ago; she ran into trouble in the Slot, off Guadalcanal, didn't she?"

Toby's eyes glistened, and he looked down, "Yes, Chief, she took a fish and cut in half. I lost a lot of buddies that night."

"Can I ask how many Snipes made it out?"

Toby didn't answer right away, then murmured, "Just me."

Chief Niemeyer took a deep breath, "Damn, I'm sorry. You going to be, okay?"

"Yeah, I guess it's still a bit sensitive."

"I'm sorry for your loss, and if you ever want to talk, I'll be available."

"Thanks, Chief, I appreciate it."

"If you want to wait a day or so before heading to the hole, that will be all right."

"Thanks, Chief; I have to get back into the program. I'll have my whole life to reconcile with it. And right now, I have a job to do."

"I watched the yard build this ship," the Chief said. "She is tough, and our initial runs showed she is fast; we hit thirty-eight and a half knots. So come on, let's get you a bunk and stow your gear, then I'll introduce you to your new home. Speaking of home, where is yours?"

"West of Norfolk," Toby responded.

"Good, we'll probably be in and out of there for some training, and you can get some family time in."

Chief Niemeyer led the way to the first deck and aft the fifty-five mount, where a hatch sat open. This section of Snipes included all the Machinist's Mates, except Chiefs, in one compartment.

"Petty Officer Greene, this is MM1 Dan Seagram; he's the compartment Police Petty Officer; and will get you set up in a bunk."

"Welcome aboard; where did they put you?"

"After engine."

"The easy space. You'll have a good MM1 to work for; he watches out for his men. Unfortunately, we have only four bunks open." Seagram took him around, showing the four. Toby selected the bunk at the centerline of the ship and closest to the hatch. The sailor didn't explain why he took the lower bunk. Most men take the middle of three bunks, as they're easier to get in and out. One of Toby's primary reasons for picking the lower bunk had to do with heat. Heat rises; thus, the bunk only inches off the deck will be cooler. When they get to the South Pacific, the lower bunks are best.

The two men dropped down the vertical ladder to the engine room and found themselves facing the throttle board with all its gauges and hand wheels. A sailor had his head in a small enclosed space, talking into a black Navy ship's telephone.

When the Petty Officer hung up and turned around, the Chief introduced Toby to MM1 Michael Day, the space supervisor. "Welcome aboard, Greene; we can use another Second Class aboard. You get a bunk and locker yet?"

"All taken care of; the Chief was a great help."

"Yeah, he's good with the men. He isn't afraid of getting his hands dirty. Sometimes I think he'd trade the paperwork for tearing into a pump any time."

"It would be a big job filling his shoes," Toby noted.

"For sure, so, where do you call home?"

"I was born and raised in a small town west of Norfolk. Not quite farm country, but close to it," the sailor explained.

Day said, "I hail from LA. I hope we get stationed at Long Beach; it'll be close to home."

"I see you're married. Have a family?"

"Not that I'm aware, but you can never tell."

"The Skipper is a big family-oriented man. He'll do everything he can to ensure every man aboard will get home. He is a full Commander, Dale C. Cummings, USN. I think you will find him a good leader; we do."

"That's good to know; we'll need a lot of men of that caliber in this war."

"What was your last ship?"

Toby went through the questions and answers on his last ship, leaving the men listening in silence. Greene avoided his RN duty and the knight's story.

Mike Day placed Toby in charge of the lower level and all the pumps. He took him to a small walkway and down some steps to another walkway which took him to the forest of pumps.

Greene passed the remainder of the day speaking with the men on the lower level. He listened to their points of view and more intently to their explanations of the machinery. All the machinery was in an operational status, as it should be with a new plant.

An hour of shop talk provided Toby with a good baseline of each man's abilities. Then he said to the lot of them, "Will each of you give me the location of the loop seal, the machinery connected to it, and its function?"

All the men came up with variations of the same answer; its use and purpose are to stop the loss of vacuum in the main condenser.

"That's partly true. Sometimes it will stop the loss of vacuum. Are there any other problems that could cause the loss of the vacuum? It's in the manuals. Review the material, and we'll pick this up after we shut down the plant after our next outing. I want you to understand something. I'm not doing this to pick on anyone; this is a serious business. This machinery costs millions of dollars and losing anything more than a pump will put us out of commission. That could cost men their lives. Nobody wants that. Work together, learn how to run the plant efficiently, and protect it from casualties; it will save your lives.

And if you're wondering about me, I'm simple. I worked in the shipbuilding business at Newport News. I have helped build and rebuild Wicks', Clemson's, and Gleaves's cans, all in the engine rooms. With proper care and operation, these engines will last the lifetime of the ship." The sailor looked around the lower level and added, "Except when a torpedo comes through the hull."

Lunchtime called to the crew, and Toby joined Harold MacArthur, the upper-level Second Class, for lunch. The two men traded stories and information on plants. Greene asked MacArthur to show him several valves that seemed to get located in different places within the same class of ships; it's just a part of shipbuilding.

MacArthur followed Greene down the ladder, and no sooner than getting to the front of the throttle board, the 1MC growled: "Now prepare the ship for getting underway."

Day yelled to everyone to "Get rid of the cleaning gear, check for spilled oil, and check the oil levels in all steam pumps and the main sump."

The men went about their duties, with petty officers supervising the sequence and timing of events. Meanwhile, Mike Day prepared the steaming watch, putting Greene under him as in training for the underway Top Watch.

In his rounds, Day located Toby on the lower level, "Toby, you're with me for qualifications as underway Top Watch, on the eight to twelve, we'll talk more later."

"Okay," Toby acknowledged.

The plants were up to temperature and pressure by sixteen hundred, and no unplanned leaks appeared from any systems. The 1MC broadcast, "Now set the Special Sea and Anchor Detail." There was practically no running around by the crew, as they already stood by their stations to get underway.

"Shift colors" came across the loudspeakers, followed by a long blast from the ship's whistle, signaling she was underway.

The Special Sea and Anchor Detail remained on station during the long, slow trek from Bath to the open Ocean. Once beyond the shores of Maine, Captain Cummings made his initial remarks. "This is the Captain. We are heading for the naval station at Norfolk, where we'll be taking on a training load of ammunition for all weapons. The next few weeks will include intensive training in all departments and engineering spaces. Once we conclude that phase, we will join a convoy of ships for passage to the Pacific Ocean. Our training port will, of course, be the 32nd Street Naval Station. We will train at every opportunity between now and deployment. I know training can become a dull experience, and that is when we have to train harder. When we get to the war, there will be no time for training; each of us had better be experts in our fields and duties; if not, the Japanese have a way of dealing with the incompetent. Training never stops; it is only put on hold while we're on the line. We will be going through a lot in the coming weeks, and it is all geared to bring our ship and you home safely. While in Norfolk, I want all hands to take liberty to the max; there is no telling what liberty lies in the future. Captain out."

With Nazi submarines patrolling the eastern seaboard, the convoy commander, with Navy Intelligence input, took the convoy almost six hundred miles off the coast before swinging south. Fifty-six hours later, the newly added destroyers broke away and turned west toward Norfolk.

Mike Day took Toby aside in the after-engine room and asked, "Didn't you say that you live somewhere around Norfolk?"

"Yes, about a few miles west of the city," Toby confirmed.

"We have arranged for you to take three days off after replenishing supplies, ammo, and fuel."

"Wow, that's great; I hope it won't create a problem."

Day explained, "It's all been taken care of; just leave an address and phone number where we can reach you if necessary."

"No problem, I'll have it ready for you in a couple of minutes."

"Toby, keep it under your hat, too."

"Understood."

Upon entry to the Norfolk Naval complex, the *DEFOE* received directions to barges filled with supplies and topped with their hull number. The ship moored to the barges, and a pair of gangways set between them, allowing the men to walk aboard the barges on one gangway, pick up a crate of supplies, and step aboard the ship on the other gangway. The two gangways sped up the loading considerably. At the same time, oil lighters came alongside the opposite side of the vessel and topped off the fuel tanks.

Seventeen hundred bells rang, telling the tired crew that supper awaited in the galley. Toby cleaned up and met Day and the Chief at the after-engine room hatch. The Chief led the way to the quarterdeck at the fifty-five mount. There he talked with the OOD, another Chief, and returned to Day and Toby after a couple of minutes.

"You gave Mike your address and phone number?"

"Yes, Chief."

“Good, the boat at the bottom of the ladder will take you to the main landing. A bus runs every ten minutes. There is a phone bank at the Exchange, and it’s open until twenty-one hundred. Be back in seventy-two or less hours. The bus from the main gate will drop you off at our berth; all you have to do is give him your ship’s name.”

“Chief, not to look a gift horse in the moth, but can you tell me why the special favor?”

“Remember I told you the Captain was a family man?”

“Yes.”

“This is with the complements of Captain Cummings, now get.”

“Aye, Chief, see you in three.”

20MM GUN AND GUNNER

CHAPTER SEVENTEEN

Toby didn't need Day to tell him twice. He saluted the OOD and descended the ladder to the waiting boat. Two other resident sailors followed shortly, and the boat shoved off. The men hadn't known one another before their boat ride, but they set the tone for a friendly future.

The base bus dropped the sailor off at the Exchange, where Toby called home. He agreed to meet his folks and Amanda at the main gate. Greene hopped the base bus for the ride to the entrance.

Twenty minutes later, the Buick pulled up, and the excited Lady, dressed like a farmer's wife, rushed to her husband, planting a deep kiss on his lips, caring less if anyone noticed. The few sailors waiting for rides took notice with a touch of envy. Toby's two new friends watched, their mouths open.

Once the sailor detached himself from the delicious Amanda de Greene, Toby said, "Guys, this is my wonderful wife, Amanda, also known as the beautiful Lady Amanda de Greene, from England.

Never shy about boosting Toby's esteem, Amanda put on her official English face and voice, then said, "Gentlemen," in the sexiest, seductive voice she could muster, "It's finally nice to meet some of Toby's shipmates. I'm sure we could all fit into the carriage if you need a ride."

Amanda's voice and accent impacted the sailors more than the woman anticipated. "Oh, thank you, ma'am; we have rides en route, but thank you for your kind invitation." While Toby thought, *'Amanda, what are you thinking?'*

Nancy and Tom sat in the front seat, trying not to bust out laughing. Then, after Toby put his bag in the trunk, they piled into the rear seat.

Laughing, Nancy said, "Amanda, my dear, you're a hoot to be around."

Tom pulled the Buick away from the gate and headed for home. In the back seat, the sassy Amanda rested her head on Toby's shoulder and whispered into his ear, "Remember what I told you at the train station?"

He nodded and muttered, "Yeah," happy the sun had set so the red creeping up his neck wasn't visible.

"Good, my dear," the excited woman whispered again, "When we turn in, I'm treating you to a slow tantalizing strip show that isn't going to be a tease, and what I told you is coming will keep you from too much sleep for three days."

Toby knew he had to match her passion and said to her, "Do you have your screaming pillow?"

"You bet."

"Good, you're going to need it, and prepare for a lot of thrashing."

"Is that a threat, Mr. Greene?"

"No, sweetheart, a promise." Amanda curled up alongside her husband for the rest of the ride; an occasional tremor coursed through her as she fantasized about her coming evening. Toby held his wife and smiled.

The two sailors Toby befriended watched the big vehicle pull away. Wayne Hanson said, "That boy has himself one handful of a gorgeous wife there. And an English aristocrat to boot, how did he wrangle that?"

"I don't know, but he must have connections; those folks are a tight group and hard to get into."

Amanda had whipped herself into the height of sexual desire, and now Toby was stroking her thigh. Then, finally, the bright-eyed woman with flared nostrils repositioned her head and whispered, "Take it easy, dear; you have me afire already. If you don't, I'll unbutton those thirteen buttons and take you right here, even if it embarrasses your parents."

"Okay, only until I get you into the bedroom." He whispered to her.

"You'll enjoy it and everything that follows."

"I always do, and so do you."

"You better believe it, Hubby, and as I said, don't plan on a lot of sleep."

Toby turned to his love, "Amanda de Greene, your grandpa would blush if he knew his granddaughter behaved so naughty."

"No, he wouldn't; when I was a teenager, I remember many nights I heard grand times from their bedroom. He may be strait-laced, but he is no prude. He often told me when I married to make sure I pleased my husband in every way he wished and to enjoy him as much as a woman could. My grandfather is a very wise man."

Amanda's grandfather met the family when they arrived home. He welcomed Toby as a second father. The Admiral had proved he could contribute to the household budget and provided a rich level of information and history at the collegiate levels.

The house was dark by eleven o'clock. The newlywed's frolic continued past midnight; sleep finally overcame the lovers' tangled weave of arms and legs.

The family spent their days together; the camaraderie which developed solidified the new family structure. Finally, Amanda announced she would be taking courses of instruction in farming, then pass on the information to Grandpa since he was working.

The days seemed short for the family, and the nights shorter for Amanda and Toby. The two lay wrapped around one another, catching their breaths from the exertion of quiet but intense lovemaking.

Toby said softly, "We have made it a point to enjoy one another since our marriage, and there are still only two of us. But you know that's going to change one of these days."

"Yes, Darling. We haven't deliberately pushed or avoided that consequence, and I haven't said what is on my mind."

"Tell me; we do everything together, and all the decisions one makes directly impact the lives of us both." Then Toby opened the door. "You know, our actions will catch up with us sooner or later, and you will become pregnant."

"I know, and how do you feel about us having a baby?"

"I never thought of myself as a father until after we were married. Now the reality of the possibility feels like it is our destiny, and I'm beginning to embrace the idea of a handsome son or an adorable daughter. When we have a daughter, you will give her your beauty and charm."

"Toby, I am content to have a child when God grants us the honor."

"I have no doubts that He already has plans for us and any angels he may send our way. We must lay our children's paths at His feet, and he will direct them perfectly," Toby said. "There is something important I need to discuss with you."

Amanda's breath caught in her throat, "Are you all right?"

"Yes, I'm very well. I hate to bring this up, but we cannot avoid it any longer. I love you more than I can express. And because of that love, I need to talk with you about the future. We know I'm going into harm's way, and the future is an impenetrable veil for us all.

Understanding that, we must realize there is a slim possibility I may not come home."

Toby could feel Amanda stiffen, her breathing still. Then she gasped, "No, I won't accept that; it won't happen."

"I believe we have a mission, but we cannot predict the future. That is why, if it happens, mourn for whatever time you must. But not over a year. You must go on; you have a life, and wearing black is not your color. Remember, God doesn't close a door without opening another; we learned that in Sunday school. It is especially true with children; they will have their mother's love and nurturing. But to develop properly, it takes two parents, and a good father figure won't try to replace me; he will take the lead in setting guidance and protection."

"Oh, Toby, no, I couldn't bear losing you."

"Sometimes we have no choice, and all this is only a plan if things go astray. But, if I come home, we will have everything to celebrate, and we will."

The sailor felt her tears falling on his chest, and he wrapped his arms around her, holding her tightly and unwilling to let go.

The intensity of the discussion refused to allow any sleep, with their determination to spend every second together.

Three days can seem like an eternity under the right circumstances. Then again, for the Greenes, it came and went like a flash. True to Amanda's prediction, sleep was at a premium; however, the lovebirds rejoiced every second.

The Greene family crawled into the freshly cleaned Buick as the Admiral watched and prayed for Toby's safety. Tom headed for the Naval Station when the thick clouds opened up the faucet and rain poured to the ground. Tom looked at Nancy, and all she could do was giggle in a teenage fashion.

Amanda and Toby held onto one another in the rear seat, not wanting to part. The two spoke at a low volume when mentioning their activities, causing Nancy to giggle to herself, remembering when she and Tom did the same thing. Little was said otherwise; neither trusted their emotions at that point.

At the base, a dirt parking lot on one side of the gate sat empty, except for the Buick. Nancy had moved next to Tom, needing to hold onto her rock. In the rear seat, soft kisses and light caresses made their final pass on this deployment in the rear.

A guard became suspicious when nobody exited the black vehicle and headed toward it, his hand not far from the weapon at his side. Then a slender, crowd-stopping lady stepped out, followed by a sailor. Finally, Amanda wrapped herself around her Toby, in true Amanda fashion, giving him his kiss of better things to come.

Then she whispered, "Thank you for the three wonderful and exciting nights ever. I'm already looking forward to your homecoming. I love you and will always be here for you." She ducked into the car with a quick kiss, not wanting Toby to see the forming tears.

Toby kissed his mother, who said, "Come home safe to us; we need you here." And she, too, turned away with wet eyes.

Tom shook his son's hand, pride shining on his face for his son. "Take care, Toby, and try to write your mother a little more often. We pray for you daily, and God somehow lets us know you are safe."

Then he, too, had to crawl back into the car. The engine turned over, then purred, until Tom drove away, the tires crunching on the hard dirt and pebbles.

The sentry checked Toby's ID and bag, then remarked, "You have a nice family Petty Officer."

"Thanks, I'm very lucky, no doubt about it. If there isn't anything else, I'd better get back to my ship."

"No, go ahead, and wherever you're headed, 'Fair winds and Following Seas."

"Thanks," the sailor grabbed his duffle bag and half marched onto the pier. He found the ship moored to the dock, two ships down; her bow pointed toward the channel to the sea.

Once aboard, Toby only had a few steps to the hatch leading to the Engineer's berthing. He changed into dungarees, stowed his gear, and headed for the engine room. He found Mike Day on a large gray toolbox, exactly like the one on the *MANNING.*

"Mike, my family, and I want to thank you for the days off. I figure you, the Captain, and the Chiefs have a good policy, and I hope it repays you the rewards your work deserves.

"Thanks; we believe a happy crew is productive and proactive. There are two ways to exercise leadership: push and use whatever means or force necessary to get the job done; this method rarely doles out kudos, rewards, or even a 'well done.'" The second is to lead, first by example, be reasonable, yet ensure every man knows their job and actions are right. They must know the mission, and they will accept the risks. Ensure the men know their security and well-being are next in line before yours. I make the men first, whenever possible. The rewards the men give in return are far better than pushing or forcing."

"That's an excellent policy; the Navy should adapt it fleet-wide."

"That is what leadership is all about, and we exercise it as 'Petty Officer's business."

The 1MC interrupted the conversation, "Now hear this; all liberty is canceled; prepare the ship to get underway."

Toby and Day looked at one another with raised eyebrows. "Looks like something is up," Mike Day said. "Toby, check the oil level in the main lube-oil sump and light off the electric lube-oil pump while I get permission to start jacking the engine over."

"On it," Toby called as he headed for the lower level. The Second Class Petty Officer worked his way to the main sump oil level indicator. Seeing it at the full mark, the sailor checked the standby strainer, shifted them, and checked the now standby strainer for any debris, rags, or sediment. Toby checked the pump's suction and discharge valves, ensuring they were open, then pushed the green start button on the controller. The big electrical motor kicked over and settled down into a steady hum. Toby checked the pump's gauges and watched them for a minute, then, seeing the normal and smooth oil flow, checked the packing gland of the pump. It showed a slow weep, indicating no issues.

Toby turned to head for the throttle board and almost ran into a new Fireman. "I wanted to see the proper procedure for lighting off the pump."

"Well, since you're here, tell me, why is it important to check the suction and discharge valves before starting the pump?"

"To make certain they are open?"

"What would happen if they were closed and the pump started?"

The youngster thought for a minute, then said, "No pressure."

"Do you know what type of pump we have for lube oil pumps?"

"No."

"What's your name?"

"Charles Daniels."

"Look, Charles, right now; we have been alerted to start lighting off the plant. But I don't want you starting any machinery until you have fully trained on them. It could cause a world of trouble and damage if you do, Okay?"

"Sure, thanks."

"We'll get together and get you trained as soon as possible; then, you will understand why we have certain rules." Then, Toby reported everything to Day at the throttle board.

"Go ahead and check and start the electric circ pump and check the condenser for leaks. Then, get the condensate pump and the feed booster pump recirculating, and charge the loop seal."

"Will do."

Toby began the lighting off sequence for the pumps when Fireman First Jack Diamond arrived to take over the job. Toby explained what he had accomplished up to that point, then headed for the throttle board.

The complex thirty-thousand horsepower plant began showing signs of life a half hour later. In the forward engine room, men performed the same work to ready their plant for duty. Crewman worked in the two boiler rooms to increase the temperature and pressure in the six-hundred-pound boilers at pre-determined rates to ensure no leaks or damage would occur. In each engine room, the turbo generators and their associated equipment received the same level of care as the main engines. The electrical generators had long established themselves as the most reliable equipment aboard ships.

Finally, the plant came up to pressure and temperature for full operations. Each engine room received a call from their boiler rooms for feed water.

In the after-engine room, Day called Toby, who returned to the lower level to supervise the operations there.

"Jack, crack the discharge valve on the feed pump and switch from recirc to feed at seven hundred fifty PSI." A couple of minutes later, the boiler room reported full feed pump pressure.

Mike Day said to the throttleman, Fireman First Oran Douglas. "Tell Main Control the boilers have full feedwater pressure, and we are ready to secure the jacking gear at their command."

Three minutes later, the orders came through, "Secure the jacking gear, open the Guarding Valve and spin main engines as needed."

Day and the messenger ran to the rear of the deduction gear and completed their tasks. Day waved at Douglas, who began the spin on the engine to keep the turbines from warping.

The sailors could sense the life-like eagerness of the engines. The turbines and reduction gears sat like coiled cheetahs, ready to burst into full power and drive the three-bladed propellers into action, stirring up the muddy bottom and leaping for the rolling sea.

The Engine Order Telegraph, EOT, clanged, calling for one-third, and the exact RPMs showed up on the annunciator. Douglas complied with the order, and the ship moved in response.

The messenger wrote every order in the 'Bell Book,' the official orders the engine room receives to operate the engine.

On the bridge, Captain Cummings stood aside as the Harbor Pilot took the ship to the harbor mouth, gliding around sand bars, minefields, and torpedo nets. Once clear of hazardous obstructions, the pilot turned control over to the Captain. He thanked the Captain for help and headed for his speed boat, motoring alongside the destroyer.

Three destroyers in the small force turned south to rendezvous with a fast task force. After leaving Norfolk behind, the Captain came on the 1MC.

"This is the Captain. We will join two heavy and two light cruisers, six other destroyers, and an oiler fifty miles east of Cuba. Then, after topping off all ship's fuel bunkers, we will head for the Panama Canal and the Pacific Ocean. That's all for now."

The task force commander sent his movement orders to all the ships after the final refueling. The *DEFOE* fell in according to the Admirals plan. The op-ord called for a transit speed of twenty knots, with those vessels equipped with cruising turbines, to engage them for the economy.

Darkness had descended on the task force, and all the ships went to darken ship, turning into ghosts on the waters. Then, at the canal, the vessels entered one at a time. Thirty-six hours later, the task force turned their bows toward San Diego.

The three weeks spent in San Diego resulted in the intense training the ships and men would need to survive the war. The *DEFOE* and the other two destroyers from Norfolk trained together. The crews of all three destroyers went through every drill they required. Not once, but as many times as needed until every man got it correct three consecutive times. At night, the engineers went through their casualty control drills repeatedly until they made three successive error-free runs.

The last week included a live fire exercise. Every gun and gunner had to pass with a minimum score, including Toby, who once again showed he was an excellent shot. The engine room crew learned of Toby's marksmanship and kills, bringing forth a mountain of questions

Every now and then, the Navy must hold personnel inspections to remind the sailors to maintain a clean environment and personal appearance. Inspections include Material Inspection, where the Captain or XO inspects the spaces, sometimes with white gloves, to find dirt.

The last requirement was a scheduled personnel inspection to ensure the men had the appropriate and clean uniform with all the required ranks, rates, awards as directed, and other authorized specialty identifiers and polished shoes. In addition, clean personal hygiene is required. Finally, all awards would consist of medals.

Toby's foreign medals went down with the *MANNING,* but the Admiral helped replace them with a new set, which Admiral Dunsworth, the current First Sea Lord, authorized. He is a close friend of Admiral de Lacy, having served together on several occasions.

The Captain approached the engineer's formation; the Chief Engineer called the men to attention. Captain Cummings stopped at each man, looked him over, and if the man had an issue, a yeoman made a note of it. Any problems would be typed up later and delivered to the Chief Engineer, then down the chain of command to the Division Officers for attention.

Toby stood out among the sailors, having the only foreign awards and two Purple Hearts. He also wore a Bronze Star with V, as did the Captain.

Captain Cummings looked the sailor over, finding no issues. "Is this the man?" he inquired of the XO.

"Yes, sir."

Captain Cummings looked closer at the English awards, then asked, "What are these decorations for?"

Although Toby was sure the Captain had reviewed his service record, he explained the three foreign medals.

The Captain surprised Toby, saying, "You never mentioned the five confirmed enemy aircraft kills and damage to a sixth. That's a remarkable feat Petty Officer, especially for an engineer. It makes you an Ace. Someday, I would like to hear the story.

Toby became concerned the Captain was about to expose his knighthood. In a whisper, the Skipper leaned closer and said, "I read in your service record that the information you previously requested was confidential. I agree with your assessment and approve its classification. Another story I would find interesting.

“I also wish to congratulate you on your international accomplishments; you could no doubt find a diplomatic career after the war.” The Captain straightened up again and, in a normal voice, said, “Congratulations on bagging those bad guys; well done.”

“Thank you, sir.” The Captain moved on to the next man. The XO, Lieutenant Robert J. Owens, mouthed his congratulations as he passed. To which Toby smiled and nodded.

Later, the Division Officer had Toby walk to the stern with him. “What I’m going to tell you is no secret, but an unwritten order of silence about the subjects remains in effect.”

“It is a fact that a lot of whites aren’t fond of black people, and it’s no secret. However, a large number of whites don’t know that Native Americans are in the same predicament. The Captain’s father is a full-blooded Cherokee Chieftain, and his mother is a white woman who fell hopelessly in love with the Chief.

Without the skin color or texture of the Cherokee, Captain Cummings was teased by the local kids at the reservation school. The boys accused him of being an outsider and shunned him at every opportunity. Not even the girls would make friends with him. So when he received an appointment to the Naval Academy, Captain Cummings took his mother’s maiden name and left. The sixth sense from his father has stood him above most people, and if he says anything like he is feeling a certain way, pay attention; it may save your life.”

COMBAT TASK FORCE

CHAPTER EIGHTEEN

The battleship-cruiser-destroyer task force and convoy took up a zig-zag course to foil submarine setups as the convoy headed for Pearl Harbor in the Territory of Hawaii.

Questions and rumors began to float around the decks regarding the attack as reported back home. In addition, others, mostly the younger men, seemed concerned about the availability of Hula girls.

Younger sailors, new to the Navy and combat, thought they had mastered the drills covering all possibilities. Chief Niemeyer snorted; "you young landlubbers are jest beginnin to learn. Petty Officer Day, nightly casualty drills until every swinging johnson down here is a hundred percent qualified before you end training."

"Aye, Chief. Mac, you and Toby begin walking two men at a time through every drill, then run them through under pressure. Once all hands have been through, we'll start each watch running drills on the sixteen-to-twenty, twenty-to-twenty-four, and twenty-four-hundred-to-zero-four hundred watches. I'll have a drill schedule made up by sixteen hundred."

Daniels approached Toby, "Why's he being so tough on us?"

Toby looked at the youngster, "Charles, tell me, does 2160STP mix with condensate to lube the main air ejector?"

The seventeen-year-old said with a cocky smile, "It sure does; otherwise, the ejector couldn't get water out of the bilges."

By this time, a pair of Firemen First Class stood smiling and listening to Daniels dig himself into a deeper hole.

"Douglas, would you care to straighten young Daniels out before he destroys the engine room or sinks us?" Daniel's smug smile disappeared as it dawned on him that he had screwed the pooch on that answer.

"I don't know where you came up with that answer, but first of all, we use 2190TEP oil in the main engine and pumps, and oil and water do not mix. Second, there are no moving parts in the air ejectors, which remove air from the condensers, hence no need for lubrication. And lastly, papoose, there are no ejectors in the bilges; those are eductor's to quickly remove copious amounts of water rapidly and use the firemain for power."

"What have you learned from all this?" Toby asked.

"I should know what I'm talking about before I speak."

"A good start. We have plenty of resources available for you to learn from, Use them, and if you don't know the answer to a question, ask anyone, don't try to bluff it."

The sailor tried to write Amanda and his folks a couple of times a week. But, with the watches set for four hours out of eight and supervising in the engine room, little developed to explain in writing. He wrote to keep the family assured he had not been injured and remained safe. Too much of anything else stood a chance of inviting sensors to black it out.

The famous shores of Hawaii loomed out of the ocean as the convoy approached the islands. Throughout the ship, men talked about islanders' friendliness, dances, and culture. Those men who had been to the islands before had girlfriends, and others knew local families who would welcome them back. Some, like Toby, had seen the worst December 7 damage. Two battleships sunk into the mud, now refloated, and looked like ants were crawling all over the monster ships, rebuilding them into fighting dreadnaughts.

Army and Navy aircraft now shared the Ford Island NAS, flying constant combat air patrols over Pearl Harbor against another enemy attack. In addition, the islands had become fortresses of antiaircraft batteries and gun emplacements set in place to take any enemy ships under fire if they wandered within range.

As the ship passed the sunken hulk of Arizona, the 1MC blared, "Attention to port, *USS ARIZONA*, hand salute…to." An honor to the fourteen hundred sailors entombed within the hull.

The *DEFOE* moored pierside, with the other two destroyers at the destroyer piers in the Southeast Loch; the new Fletcher's looked mean and lean. Their five-mounted five-inch guns could accurately send fifty-four-pound high-explosive or armor-piercing rounds out to eighteen-thousand yards or ten miles. Each ship carried two torpedo launchers behind each stack, loaded with five-Mk 15 torpedoes. Antiaircraft weapons on the new original ships consisted of a single one-inch/ seventy-five caliber four-barreled mount, the so-called 'Chicago Piano,' and two stern roll-off depth charge racks.

The Fletcher's power plant could propel them at thirty-seven to thirty-eight knots, or about forty-two and a half to forty-three and a half MPH.

Those ships nested pierside connected to shore power and shut down their plants for little maintenance. The Snipes securing the boilers and engines always made it to the showers after most liberty sailors departed down the gangways. Most Snipes knew the engineer's motto; 'Plant first, then men.' One general complaint was cold water showers.

Harold (Harry) MacArthur and Charlie Nester approached Toby, "Toby," Harry began, "Charlie and I want to go on a tour where we can get some good photos of Hawaii to send home. We thought you could help us with cameras and film, and since you have been here before, maybe some good scenes."

"You bet; I didn't have any plans, and this sounds good. Let me grab my camera rig; it has holders for film rolls, making it easier to keep track of them."

"Where can we pick up a decent camera, and what else do we need?"

"I'd recommend the Exchange; when I went into town, the scammers wanted high prices for low-quality and obsolete products. Their primary targets are the first-time, wide-eyed servicemen, just like those on the strip in San Diego with diamond rings."

"The San Diego city fathers should run the scammers out of town; they give crooks a bad name," Charlie said.

It didn't take long for the three to make the Exchange, where they bee-lined it to the camera sales. First, the two new Exchange shoppers found thirty-five millimeter Cannon cameras similar to Toby's and black-and-white film. Next, the Second Class Petty Officer spotted a strap and molded camera cover that would hold his camera and four canisters of film.

MacArthur asked, "Ma'am, do you know of any island tours?"

Mable St. Johns, a Navy wife, smiled, "Yes, In October of 1941, President Roosevelt started putting together with the help of Hawaiian citizens, local organizations, the Army and Navy Club in conjunction with many churches, the YMCA, and YWCA to form the Hawaii USO. They have many wonderful recreational events, including tours of the island. Here is a map; they are only a short walk away."

"Thank you; your help saved us from getting lost looking for a tour."

"That's why we are here; just ask."

The three sailors purchased tour tickets at the USO and had an hour to kill. So they found a canteen in the USO building and sat down to the best homemade meal since joining the Navy. The tour was as advertised, with the sailors expending all their film on the outing, including plenty of one another.

The remainder of the two-and-a-half weeks saw the men working or cleaning their spaces and enjoying liberty, much of it at the USO or other organizations.

Petty Officer Day had the men finish cleaning, then repainting those spots as needed. By that time, it was busy work, but the space remained relatively cool, and the men didn't mind, many of whom had ran out of money.

The 'clang' of feet hitting the deck plate at the bottom of the ladder announced the arrival of the XO, Lt. Robert Owens, Chief Engineer, Lieutenant Norman Eisner, USN, and the M-Division Officer, Ensign Jerry Throckmorton.

The three men at the throttle board snapped to attention at Day's command. "Carry on," said the XO. The three officers quickly looked around the upper level; then the XO turned to Day, "You have a squared away engine room, Petty Officer; well done."

“Thank you, sir; how may I help you?”

“Is Petty Officer Greene around?”

“Yes, sir, he is on the lower level; I’ll have him up in a second.”

Day quickly located the sailor near the auxiliary condensate pump. “Toby, what did you do? The XO, Chief Engineer, and Division Officers are at the throttle board, asking for you.”

“Nothing, but I can guess.”

“What’s that?”

“They will want me to back up one of the gunners.”

“You were a gunner?”

“I have always been a Snipe; we were called Stokers in the RN, MMs here. But the Brits found out I could shoot, and I wound up on a twenty, and ever since, every ship I have been on wants me to be a backup gunner.”

“That’s not too bad,” Day said.

“Tell that to my Purple Hearts.”

The men hurried to the throttle board, where Toby came to attention, “Petty Officer Greene reporting as ordered, sir.”

Day left the four to talk about their business and ambled over to the generator flat. MacArthur, watching the proceeding from the generator, asked, “What’s going on, Mike?”

“I’m not sure; the XO, Chief Engineer, and Division Officers came down wanting to talk with Greene. I hope he isn’t in trouble, or worse; something happened at home.”

Lieutenant Owens addressed the sailor, “Petty Officer Greene, we review every man’s personnel file as part of our administrative duties and to ensure every man is doing their proper job. Once in a while, we come across information that a man has additional attributes that may become invaluable. Your file is particularly interesting; aside from your personal achievements, your expertise with the twenty-millimeter gun stood out. All of our gunner billets are full, but you give us the advantage of having an outstanding gunner in the event one of the assigned men goes down. The Captain and I are not ordering you to make yourself available; even though it is our prerogative, we are asking if you would consider the proposition. We know you have been wounded three times in combat, Petty Officer Greene. Your record does not indicate such activity because the UK does not have an equivalent to the Purple Heart, but we suspect the same thing happened to you while on duty in the RN."

"Yes, sir, it did."

"The Captain and I thank you for your service on the guns and in the engine room. You are a rare individual, and we are glad you are here. If you would, let Mr. Throckmorton know if you'd consider acting as a backup gunner."

"I see," the sailor said. "As you probably saw, I had the opportunity to take a medical discharge following my injuries in the *MANNING's* torpedoing but elected to stay in the Navy. Although I don't regret that decision, I came to fight my country's enemies, and that is what I will do, including fulfilling the role of a backup gunner."

"Captain Cummings said you would volunteer. Your character confirms one of the reasons you received that classified honor. Thank you."

"Thank you, sir."

"Tell me, in your experience, what do you think a good tactic would help us when a fighter attacks?"

"Sir, having no training in combat ship handling, I can only suggest a couple of maneuvers. When the enemy attacks from the rear or front, he will tap his rudder, giving him a swaying effect and allowing his machine gun stream to sweep back and forth on deck. If we duplicate his maneuver by swinging our rudder as he swings his, we might mess up his planned attack and, at the same time, unmask additional AA guns against him. One other possibility could work, once the fighter sets up to shoot, you only have seconds to do an emergency back down, just for a couple of seconds, then flank ahead. It could cause him to overshoot his burst. Then there is one other thing to think about; if the enemy is attacking astern, have the Boilermen change the fuel-air ratio to create a smoke barrage for only five seconds; it could cause the pilot to flinch."

"I like your thinking; I'll pass it on to the Captain for consideration."

"Aye, sir."

Mr. Throckmorton watched, confused by the cryptic sentences from the XO, then followed the two senior Officers up the ladder.

After the Officers departed, the engine room crew not on watch crowded around him with the usual questions. The sailor had been basking in the delight of not having to man the big twenty. And, if they were lucky, he still wouldn't.

The ships refueled and replenished a few days later, then turned their bows toward the southwest and the war.

The days seemed to linger in Virginia as the family set into a routine. Then, the Admiral began putting together the initial pages of his memoirs. Amanda worked at the local war production plant for three weeks; then, one morning woke up feeling ill. Fearing some malady, she made an appointment with the family Doctor. Nancy took it upon herself to drive her daughter-in-law to her appointment, suspecting what Amanda's issue could be. However, she didn't want to deprive the young Lady of the excitement of announcing she was pregnant.

As expected, Amanda rushed from the examination room, leaving two nurses behind bearing broad smiles and throwing her arms around Nancy. "Mum, we're going to have a baby," she squealed.

"Nancy hugged her beautiful adopted daughter and said excitedly, "Oh Amanda dear, Toby will be beside himself, as will Tom. He has always wanted either a grandson or daughter to spoil."

"And I know you are just as happy about spoiling the baby."

"Certainly, it's the first for us, too," she giggled in delight.

"Yes, and I fear Grandpa will be the worst; he tried his best to spoil me and succeeded, as you see," the bubbling mother-to-be, blared in her excitement.

Nancy turned serious and looked Amanda in her eyes. "Your Grandfather is a fine gentleman and giant of gentleness. Nobody could have raised you any better; you are heads above anyone I know in everything you are and do. Toby is the luckiest man alive to have you at his side, and so are we; you are the daughter we always wanted."

"Oh, thank you, Mum, you have made me the happiest woman alive."

"Enough of this; we need to put something together for this evening to surprise Tom, and you must find a way to tell your husband."

Amanda thought about her newfound world, and an impish smile crossed her face, *'The old bags and nags in London's single ladies group will flutter like crippled Starlings trying to outdo her new life. I'm so happy to be a world away from their negative, critical outlooks of other women. I'd bet a pound the photographs I sent will give them plenty to gossip over, and I have no doubt one or more will hunt for an unsuspecting colonial to bag.'*

"Oh, Mum, I wasn't thinking. With grandpa, me, and now a new baby coming, this will put a burden on you; I'll start looking for a flat that can accommodate us this week."

With a never-heard explanative, Nancy blurted, "The hell you will, we wouldn't think of it. Thomas and I would both be heartbroken if you left. You are our daughter-in-law, and we see you as our daughter. Besides, you will need someone to take care of your precious bundle while you work, which is my job. Not to mention that your husband would put his foot down with a thump. We are family; we live together, work together, and play together.

Amanda wrapped her arms around her adoptive mother, who was on the verge of crying. "I have never felt so loved, not only by you but everyone here. Toby is right; the family is the greatest of unions, and no man, or woman, is an island."

That evening, the Lady wrote Toby the longest and best letter she had ever penned.

****

The *DEFOE* and the rest of the fast convoy turned their clocks back at zero-one-hundred as they sailed from one time zone into the next, making the midnight to zero-four-hundred a five-hour watch. And each day brought them closer to an increasing possibility of enemy contact. So it didn't take much to convince the lookouts to sharpen their search efforts.

At twenty knots, the speed-induced noise drowned out any chance of hearing a submarine. Finally, however, one sonarman listened for the screws of a torpedo to see if the technician could detect a weapon.

Toby, now qualified as an underway Top Watch, had his team of watchstanders well-trained. Then he devised a program where each watchstander stood an extra watch with a qualified man until he qualified for that watch, such as the throttles. Toby's goal included each man completing the qualifications for all the watch stations by the time they arrived in the war zone. With that accomplished, any member of the team could stand at all watch stations, making the team self-reliant. A side benefit of the program prepared each man to perform better on promotional exams.

Toby's watch consisted of Fireman First Charlie Nester, from Niles, Michigan, on the throttles. FM/1st Steward Ryan, a native of Wichita Falls, sat on the pumps on the lower level with Messenger of the Watch, Fireman Second Class David Dymond, from Casper, Wyoming. Toby's goal to develop a fully qualified engine room watch included training all the Firemen on each aspect of the startup, operational, and shutdown of each piece of machinery and how they interact with the rest of the engine, and auxiliary components began to take effect.

FM/2d Dymond had successfully mastered the full operational requirements to operate and maintain the turbo-generator.

Charlie Nester became bored living in his sleepy little hometown of Niles, Michigan. Niles sits north, a little east, and in a different time zone from South Bend, Indiana. His option for meaningful work would come from the Packard factory in South Bend. So instead, he opted for running the throttles of a twenty-one-hundred-ton Greyhound.

Steward wanted to get away from a life surrounded by and guided by the oil industry, which thrived in the Texas County around his home. So, Steward joined the Navy to get away and now works on a sea-going machine whose life's blood is oil and derivatives.

The heat of the daily tropical zone sun raised the ship's interior temperature to uncomfortable levels, making sleep all but impossible. Men began sleeping on the weather decks when no rain threatened.

Toby made his third crossing of the equator, and his records reflected him as a Trusty Shellback. After the fun in the sun, the convoy continued to Bora-Bora for refueling before steaming to the Big Bay on Espiritu Santo. The convoy commander had planned a zig-zag course designed to thwart enemy submarines from setting up a torpedo attack.

Eleven days later, the convoy picked up harbor pilots and entered Big Bay, where they moored or anchored according to a previously planned system.

"This is the Captain," came over the 1MC. "Our training has ended; any call to General Quarters will be a no-drill call for the remainder of our tour of duty. The XO has informed me of darkened ship violations. Violation of darkened ship policy will not happen again. Any violator will face a court marshal and the strictest penalty we can impose. I will not allow any man to endanger this ship by violating safety protocols; remember, the enemy can see the flare of a match or lighter miles away. If their lookouts can see us, they can sink us. Captain out."

The new Fletcher was tied to a buoy with two other destroyers when the 1MC announced, "*DEFOE*, departing." The Main Control Officer of the Watch, called all four main spaces and said, "Maintain the steaming watch with the engines on the jacking gear, with the Guarding valves chained and locked. Police your areas, remove or secure all movable objects, and prepare to get the ship underway."

MM1 Day called Fireman Dymond, "Take the box of salt tablets to all the men; if they haven't taken any in the past four hours, have them take two with as much water as they can handle. We have no idea how long the high temperatures and humidity will remain with us, but I would bet a 'fin' we'll stay hot and sweaty for the foreseeable future. So, we must keep our electrolytes in balance."

FM/1st Nester yelled, "Disengage the jacking gear, open the Guarding valve, and prepare to get underway."

IJN B-1 CLASS SUBMARINE

CHAPTER NINETEEN

Commander Dale C. Cummings, the CO, was born in San Diego in August of 1910 to a Native-American enlisted family; his father, a Chief Petty Officer and Medal of Honor recipient in the First World War, paved the way for Dale's admission to the Naval Academy, where he ended in the upper third of his class. The Captain's first ship hauled coal to other coal-burning ships. Then, Captain Cummings served on a repair ship in the Mediterranean Sea after his time on the collier. His next service required him to serve on a Sims Class destroyer until he transferred to two Clemson class destroyers before accepting the lead position on the *DEFOE.*

XO Robert J. Owens, USN, also a San Diego native and lifelong friend of Dale Cummings, was born on 18 March 1911. Lieutenant Owens, unlike the CO, was a confirmed and happily married man. His wife, MaryAnn, also a Navy Brat, presented him with twin children, Lyle and Regina. The younger Owens' have announced they intend to pursue Navy careers like the father and Godfather, Captain Dale Cummings. The Lieutenant is on the list for the next CO course in Pearl Harbor, after which XO Owens promotion to Lieutenant Commander will put him in line for his first command.

****

The convoy steamed from Big Bay and formed up as they exited the broad mouth of the protected bay. One of the dozen destroyers, the *DEFOE*, fell into her assigned position on the starboard after-quarter of the convoy.

"OOD, have the lookouts relieved every two hours, we're entering the enemy's backyard, and you know there are submarines out there that will take exception to our presence.'

"Aye, sir, talker, did you hear the order?"

"Aye, sir, I did."

"All lookouts will stand two-hour watch and add special attention to ASW protocols" the OOD ordered.

"Aye, sir."

Turning to the Captain, the OOD suggested, "Sir, our transit speed is set for twelve knots, and the sea is calm; how do you feel about having sound keep an ear underwater?"

"Good idea, Mr. Bellows, make it so."

"Aye, sir," the OOD said with a smile.

The engineers in the four main spaces settled into a steady steaming speed governed by the slowest ship. In the after-engine room, Toby Greene moved watchstanders around, bringing novice operators in control under the supervision of the regular watchstanders. The Second Class Petty Officer's training plan was now in full bloom.

****

Three hours out of Vanuatu, the convoy entered the patrol sector of a B-1 submarine under the Command of Commander Daichi Matsuo of the Imperial Japanese Navy. Captain Matsuo graduated third in his academy class with honors in mathematics and proved his worth as an excellent submariner.

The thirty-nine-year-old Officer enjoyed the backing and loyalty of his officers and men. But, in the eyes of those dedicated to dying for the Emperor for any purpose, Captain Matsuo lacked the drive to ask his men to die for the Emperor, no matter how trivial the issue. Moreover, the Captain was a realist; in his mind, dead officers and men make poor fighters. Hence, the senseless charge into death's teeth; says you are fearless, not intelligent.

Therefore, a man who could honor the Emperor could be pleased with the officer or even an enlisted man who could devise a way to defeat the enemy and live to repeat the victory many times.

Having spent a year with German U-boats in 1939, Captain Matsuo gained experience and appreciation for precision attacks. Furthermore, the excellence in material construction and maintenance of German war products impressed the officer with the desire to apply German techniques whenever possible. As a result, their B-1 performance became the standard for others in their class to achieve.

The Captain watched the slow approach of the Allied convoy and positioned his boat into the most favorable torpedo solution position to ensure a hit. He placed his target in the strongest light by placing the sinking sun behind him to blind his scope and shadow, the very situation cargo and oiler captains fear the most.

Captain Matsuo needed one more reading on the convoy's course and speed to complete his fire trajectory. The Torpedo Officer awaited the numbers to pass onto the torpedo room and the Type 95 torpedo, the finest submarine-fired torpedo in the world at the time.

Turning to the OOD, Matsuo ordered, "Bring us to periscope depth for our final readings,"

The OOD repeated the order, and a Chief Petty Officer on the air control valves gave the ballast tanks a short blast of compressed air, bringing the sub up to the prescribed depth.

"Raise the scope to the deck." The hydraulic system whined softly, pushing the long slender tube upward. As soon as the controls and handles emerged, the Captain dropped down to the platform to look through the lens.

****

Another Fletcher picked up a blip on their sound gear and sent an alarm to the convoy command ship, which in turn sent the convoy to General Quarters. The *DEFOE*'s bridge quickly sounded General Quarters, ASW alert, and directed the main battery toward the coordinates provided by the cruiser.

“OOD, have the talker fill in the sound crew. We are to maintain the convoy’s security; the cruiser has deployed two escorts to investigate.”

****

Commander Matsuo called out the course and speed while the Torpedo Officer sent it to the torpedo room, where an officer set the ton-and-a-half torpedo’s guidance.

The Captain noted the alerted destroyers but maintained his iron-like stature, and at the proper time, he calmly called out, “Hatsubai.” A Torpedoman launched the black torpedo ahead of a cloud of compressed air bubbles, sending a recoil tremble through the boat.

Before leaving its tube, the turbine engine rapidly accelerated the fish to its full unheard-of speed of fifty-one knots, its counter-rotating propellers screaming at a high pitch, which alerted every sound system in the escort force.

Finally, the Captain turned the scope toward two-eight-seven degrees, the course the boat’s sound man frantically yelled a warning about a charging destroyer. One look was all the Captain needed; he saw the knife edge of a bow, with white frothing waves curling back on both sides of the cutting bar. A quick estimate made the destroyer’s speed at thirty knots. “DIVE! DIVE TO ONE-TWO-FIVE METERS, EMERGENCY DIVE. At seventy-five meters, turn to zero-five-zero, port motor half astern, starboard motor emergency flank ahead. Seal the boat, standby for a depth charge attack.”

The crew rushed to follow the life-saving orders, unsure if they would be enough. The B-1 for all the allocates for suburb operations turned excruciatingly slow. Finally, at seventy-five meters, the boat heeled to port like a plane in a bank. The thumping of the Benson’s screws gave the soundman a headache.

****

Sixteen-hundred-thirty tons of steel ship driving through the sea at thirty knots, and one rudder cannot turn to the same course as the sub did when the surface ship passed over the diving point and heard the B-1 turned to port. Before the fast destroyer could maneuver, their soundmen lost contact with the submarine.

****

Sweat had started running down the bodies of the Japanese submariners, and ran down the Captain's face in rivulets. He had looked into the eyes of death, and it shook his soul. No fresh air had been available for over twelve hours, and with the sub-sealed, the men only had the stale-tasting air sealed with them in each compartment.

"Where is that destroyer," inquired the Captain.

The soundman said, "He went over us and is about two kilometers east of us and appears to be searching, sir."

"Diving Officer, come to zero-five-zero true, and maintain silent mode, but secure from sealing the boat. Set speed to three knots; it is time to disappear. OOD, find out the condition of our batteries."

The two men responded and began following their orders.

"Captain," the OOD called to his leader. "Engineering says we have thirty-two percent battery power remaining."

"Navigator, is there anywhere we can sit until full darkness?"

"No, sir, our charts show we are in the Coral Sea, and the closest area we could set down is two hundred kilometers on course three-four-six degrees. The water under the keel now is over forty-four-hundred meters."

"Well, that certainly isn't an option." He murmured. The Captain's mind rolled around the numbers on distance and remaining battery charge without an acceptable solution. "OOD in one hour, bring us to one hundred meters depth, then begin a slow rise to periscope depth. Sound, any signs of our watchdogs?"

"No, Captain, it sounds like they faded to the northwest to catch their convoy."

"Keep a sharp ear out for any signs of the Americans, especially on our slow ascent."

"Yes, Honorable Captain."

"OOD, I will be in my quarters if needed."

"Yes, sir."

Captain Matsuo formulated a dispatch for Rabaul, outlining the failed attack due to enemy escort action. He added all the information on the convoy and escort ships, along with their last known course. Then the exhausted man immediately fell asleep in his Spartan quarters.

"Captain, we approach periscope depth; there are no sounds of other vessels in the area," the messenger quietly said to the sleeping form. "Captain, please wake up," repeated the messenger, this time with results.

The groggy voice of Matsuo croaked out, "Did I hear that we are approaching periscope depth?"

"Hai."

"I wanted only to sleep an hour," he turned on his small overhead light to glance at his watch. "Why was I allowed to sleep over two hours?" his voice tinged with anger.

"Sir, the Executive Officer, ordered the alteration in the night orders and said he would take your anger, but wanted to remind you a tired Captain could make a dangerous mistake, and the extra hour of rest gives you an extra four hours of control time with a clear mind."

"Ooh, our XO is quite logical, and I must admit, just as correct. Thank you, Seaman, you did well."

After splashing fresh water into his face and donning a clean shirt, the commander headed for the bridge. When he arrived, a cup of tea and light pastries awaited him.

"What is this? Is someone attempting to curry favor from the Captain?" he growled.

The XO stepped up, "Happy Birthday, Captain; the men wished to express their gratitude for your excellent leadership."

The humbled Captain gave a quick bow toward the crew of the bridge, "Thank you for the honor and your loyalty." The Captain failed to hide his affection for his men with a staunch attitude. "Now, sound, can you hear any vessels about us?"

"No, honorable Captain."

"Very well, OOD, bring us to periscope depth and slowly raise the periscope."

"Hai, lookouts to the bridge."

The scope's low hydraulic whine betrayed its slow movement. Captain Matsuo dropped to the deck to look through the eyepiece as soon as it appeared. The short man followed the upward pace of the tube, moving in a constant circle, watching for any shadow which may reveal a ship's hull. But, instead, only blackness greeted the Captain.

"OOD, surface the boat." The equally black submarine seemed to materialize from the deep, water quickly draining from the decks and running out the scuppers. A Radioman immediately transmitted the attack message to their base in Rabaul. Additional information suggested the Allies may have developed a method of detecting the presence of a submarine quicker than previously believed, based on the fact the sub was lying in wait.

After ensuring the boat was alone, the diesel engines started charging the low batteries and providing propulsion. Then the surface routine of cleaning the vessel and exercising the men in groups on the afterdeck began.

****

The convoy continued its twelve-knot pace toward the Solomon Islands. Prior to May of 1942, the island chain and New Georgia Sound came under the UK control of the Australians. The Royal Australian Air Force built two seaplane bases, one at Tulagi and the other at the twin islets, Tanambogo and Gavutu, and a causeway joined them. The islets lay a mile and three-quarters miles east of Tulagi. Japan captured the Solomon Islands and seaplane bases in their expansion of conquests in May of 1942.

The relentless rays of the sun and ambient air temperature increased as the convoy neared the island of San Christobal at the lower end of the Solomons. Berthing compartments became ovens, and the deck could burn an unprotected hand.

"Navigator, what's our distance from the Equator?" asked the OOD.

"Roughly eight hundred miles due south."

"That explains the rise in the temperatures."

"Is this your first trip out here in the vast South Pacific and the famed South China Sea?" the Navigator asked.

"I'm afraid it is, Tom; how about you?" Ltjg Michael Hines asked.

"This is my second trip, and it hasn't changed at all."

“Captain Cummings, this message just came in.” the signal messenger said.

The CO read the message twice, then picked up the 1MC mike. “This is the Captain; When we reach Assembly Area X-Ray; we will take a defensive posture against air, surface, or subsurface activity. Our primary concern will be enemy air attacks. Evening, night, and dawn will bring the threat of submarine intrusions. The Japanese seem to prefer night attacks. Therefore, we must prepare for contacts in any of the three environments. That is all.”

The *DEFOE* quietly hissed through the black water at ten knots. Meanwhile, the Sound technicians scoured Iron Bottom Sound at the southeast passage by Savo Island with the sonar suite in full operation. The men listened; their faces twisted into questioning frowns. The new radars reached several miles searching for ships or aircraft trying to sneak into Assembly Areas Yoke or X-Ray.

The night remained quiet on the waters, but Marines and IJA units ashore clashed in bitter combat. Then, by zero-seven-hundred, another message came to the bridge:

All air defense units:

An air attack is expected to arrive at approximately zero-nine-hundred.

Expect G4M Torp/Bomb; D3A, B5N, Possibly Ki-43, and A6M escorts. Good Luck.

Nightmare
Mirage

Cover Tassafronga to FLA Is. (C-line).
From Savo to C-line. Additional assets en route.

Cactus 2 sends.

“Messenger, respond to message, Nightmare copy.”
“Aye, sir.”

"Messenger, show this to the OOD, and he will enter it into the log, then take it to the Navigator in Ops; tell him to draw up a track which will put us northeast of Tassafronga by zero-eight-thirty. Then return here for another message for signal."

"Aye, sir."

After the messenger left, Captain Cummings wrote a short message to their partner, a Gleaves destroyer.

To: Mirage
Fr: Nightmare

I'm sending track for AA defense orders from Cac-2. We will be NE of Tassafronga for air defense at zero-eight-thirty. Set 1700 yds for maneuver room. Watch for bloodsuckers popping over Florida and Cactus. Careful.

Nightmare sends.

Zero-eight-hundred found the destroyers in position northeast of Tassafronga Point, their crews primed and ready for the expected air assault. Both ships continued an ASW passive posture, listening for any man-made sounds that would reveal a submarine presence. Finally, zero-nine-hundred arrived, and the skies had a few puffballs of clouds to the east, but other than that, the sun showed brightly in a clear blue sky.

"Bridge, radar, we hold an air contact of many aircraft, bearing three-zero-nine degrees, course one-three-zero, speed one-nine-five, distance seventeen miles, altitude estimated at five-zero-zero-zero feet."

"Bridge, aye," the talker relayed the message to the OOD. When the Officer of the Deck turned to the Captain, he nodded acknowledgment.

The OOD said, "1MC." The Bo'sun flipped on the 1MC switch and handed the mike to the officer. "Now hear this, enemy aircraft at seventeen miles, bearing three-zero-nine, five-thousand, all guns prepare to fire on command."

Captain Cummings flipped on the TBS, "Mirage, Nightmare…," and alerted the Gleaves.

The first aircraft seen had white paint with 'red meatballs' on the bottom of both wings, 'IJN Zeros.' Behind them was a squadron of Ki-43 'Oscars', then a thousand feet higher, four flights of three G4M "Betty" torpedo/bombers in each flight, one of which carried torpedoes, and the tail-end flight consisted of six D3A 'Val' dive bombers.

The early warning from an Australian Coastwatcher gave the cargo ships time to roll up their supply landings and weigh their anchors. The last freighter cleared Assembly Area X-Ray at zero-eight-hundred and headed for Lengo Channel an hour before the arrival of the air assault.

The timely warning allowed all available Marine and Navy fighters to lift off Henderson Field and position themselves to attack the Japanese force. In addition, six destroyers scattered in the lower section of the New Georgia Sound to make themselves difficult targets.

The light construction of enemy aircraft, including no armor protecting the crews and fuel tanks, made them vulnerable to antiaircraft fire from the destroyers; hopefully helping the less maneuverable American fighters overcome their adversaries.

The Zeros and Oscars broke up, with two flights heading for Assembly Area X-Ray, along with the majority of bombers and three Vals. The main battery of the Gleaves and *DEFOE* gave off sharp cracks as they pumped fifty-four-pound AA Common shells skyward. The forty-millimeter cannons sounded like a small kettle drum with its 'Pom-Pom' sounding reports.

A secondary explosion caught the attention of several men topside, and they looked skyward to see a G4M spiraling down in flames, pieces flying from the wings and fuselage. As the bomber began to corkscrew in, a Wildcat pilot buzzed the ship. The pilot wasn't happy. First, he pointed at his perforated rudder, then flipped the gunners his middle finger as he flew by the bridge.

Puffy gray-bottomed clouds moved into the area, obscuring parts of the sky. The attack lifted eight minutes after it began. The Gleaves took a strafing by one Oscar, injuring seven men. The gunners started to breathe normally when the messenger jumped at the near scream in his ears.

"BRIDGE, RADAR, A PLANE IS DIVING THROUGH THE CLOUDS OFF THE PORT QUARTER."

“All ahead emergency flank, come port to zero-one zero, sharply, watch the clinometer.” The Captain called. The ship heeled to starboard, catching several men by surprise.

Guns slewed toward the cloud bank, and men waited. Finally, a Zero popped through the clouds; his seven-point-seven-millimeter machine guns began spitting bullets at the ship. As he closed the destroyer, the pilot opened fire with his two twenty-millimeter wing cannons and began pumping out armor-piercing and explosive shells.

Just before the pilot pulled up, his lighter bullets shot up the starboard stern twenty mount, taking out the three-man crew. Two armor-piercing twenty-millimeter rounds punched into the forward engine room, wounding two men with splinters; the rest had taken cover beneath machinery.

The ship’s phone in the after-engine room boomed out its “Oooga!” Day grabbed it before the second ring.

Day couldn’t get out his words because the OOD yelled, “Get Greene to the starboard stern twenty, gunners down.”

IJA Ki-43 'OSCAR'

CHAPTER TWENTY

Petty Officer Day yelled for Toby over the plant's operational noise, "Greene, they need you on the after-twenty; the gunners there are down, and they need that gun in action."

"On my way," returned the sailor as he dashed for the base of the port side ladder. Unfortunately, Tobias Greene was about to be thrown into the mix again, contrary to his better judgment. Seconds later, Toby secured the hatch and made his way aft, grabbing a helmet from a helmet stack aft the after deckhouse. He rounded the fifty-five mount, and the port loader pointed to the starboard Twenty. As he approached the weapon, it appeared undamaged and still had a magazine attached.

Toby yelled to the port talker, "See if you can get me a loader and talker," then he checked an inert body on the deck. The young talker had taken a round to the side of his head, probably killing him instantly. The gunner and loader were missing; Toby figured other crewmen had taken them to the sick bay. Greene completed a fast check of the gun, and lastly, he pulled the magazine, finding it almost full. The sailor strapped himself in and began looking for enemy planes.

The replacement gunner spotted a Val start a dive on another destroyer, and Toby set his sights twice the length of the plane ahead of it. In the one-second burst, the tracers passed in front of the bomber, causing Toby to reduce his lead. Then the shells began tearing into the lightly built aircraft. The recoil of the twenty threw Toby's aim off the distant bomber, and two rounds went under the cockpit, hitting the five-hundred-fifty-pound bomb, which detonated with a resounding report. Shrapnel from the blast rained onto three ships, causing minor damage and no casualties.

A second, Val pulled out of his dive, already having released his bomb toward *DEFOE's* partner. Fortunately, the quick destroyer's twisting and turning caused a miss; however, the blast caused underwater damage, which would take a shipyard to repair. After dropping his weapon, the pilot reversed his climb and dove for the water and would have managed to escape with the unexpected maneuver if he hadn't flown past the *DEFOE's* stern at a hundred-foot altitude. Toby watched as the Val started dropping toward the water again, and the sailor fired. That range is point-blank for the cannon, and its shells made quick work of the light aircraft.

The attack lasted only a few minutes, and the attackers turned northwest to run the gauntlet of Cactus interceptors waiting for them.

Sometime during the clash, a loader and talker appeared without Greene's notice. The men began clearing the brass and blood from the deck as the Gunnery Officer climbed into the gun tub.

Holding out his hand, Lieutenant Mason O. Lee said, "Congratulations on downing those two bandits. Sorry I haven't been able to meet you before now, but your expertise precedes you, good work. Captain Cumming wants you to stay with the gun until we get a replacement, which might be a couple of days."

"No problem, sir. I told the Captain I am at his service."

"I know you had to man the gun under fire, and with the attack over, you need to put on a life jacket."

"Yes, sir, that's my first order of business after I hit the head."

"I can agree with that," then the officer climbed out of the tub. Then he turned and said, "Petty Officer Greene, I want to thank you for your dedication to the ship and your shipmates."

"Thank you again, sir. I believe we either fight together or get away from the sinking ship. Having done that, I intend to fight with all I have to stay afloat."

"Good point. Can I use that in encouraging the division?"

"Certainly, anything to help."

Lieutenant Lee reported to the XO and Captain on the bridge. "Sir, that sailor should be decorated for his performance; those two planes bring him up to five confirmed kills and one damaged, I believe. It clearly makes him an Ace, and I thought he earned it."

Captain Cumming answered, "I plan on putting him in for his second Bronze Star if he accepts it."

"I've made some discrete inquires on our Machinist's Mate. First, do you know he suffered a war-ending wound on his last ship before it sank? Second, he is seriously connected and could live in safety and luxury in England, but he turned it down to serve in the Navy, yet is reluctant to be recognized. He is a bit of an enigma."

The Lieutenant commented, "Whatever he is, there is no doubt he is one hell of a shot."

"That he is," the Captain said. "What's the damage report?"

Lieutenant Lee replied, "No damage to the gun or ship, but we lost the talker. The gunner and loader were wounded, but not seriously, and replaced."

"That's better than I expected."

"Aye, Captain," the XO said.

Then the Skipper ordered, "Let's get the ship and men to modified Condition One and get the galley working."

"Yes, sir." The XO said.

The Signal messenger handed the Captain a flimsy. After initialing the thin paper, Captain Cummings read it twice, then called for the 1MC.

"This is the Captain. We have been relieved of convoy escort and protection and reassigned to hunt the 'Tokyo Express.' For new South Pacific sailors, Naval Intelligence has developed information the enemy is sneaking supplies, ammunition, and soldiers into Guadalcanal during night hours; we and our partner, the *USS RICE,* will be hunting these vessels and barges. Our job, stop them. Our action will occur during the night hours. Therefore, the supervisors will review all known material on Japanese night operations for lookouts and sound. We will also be a tripwire for spotting air assaults headed toward Cactus and any surface forces doing the same. I won't try to sugar-coat our assignment. We are going into harm's way to help our Marines on Guadalcanal, and we will find ourselves out-gunned and in a two to four or more disadvantage in ships. We will put out a hundred percent during the day and hundred-and-twenty percent at night. Everyone on duty at night will be lookouts as well. When not at Condition One, everyone is to get as much rest as possible, and there will be times rest will become a premium. Ship's work will be placed on hold, rest, and full concentration on watchstanding are the orders. That is all."

Toby sat on the toolbox glancing at the gauges every few minutes. Fireman First Charlie Nester, on the throttles, listened to the chatter on the 2VJ sound-powered net. Then Charlie turned to Toby, "Did you really shoot down two planes?"

"Yes, but I'm not in the mood to talk about it. I did my job, nothing more."

"Oh, sure, Toby, I didn't mean to step on your toes."

"It's not you, Charlie. I don't care for people celebrating my killing people; it's barbaric. I know it's my job, but I still don't have to like it."

"You're feeling like you're compromising your faith by violating God's law on killing men, aren't you?" Charlie asked.

"How did you know? I wasn't aware you were a Christian."

"I am, and like you, I don't like killing; no Christian does," Charlie said.

"How do you reconcile it then?"

"When God laid down His commandment "THOU SHALT NOT KILL," he meant for no person to kill another for any reason. That is murder. He also said the people were to kill the offender if they met specific requirements. The offender was to suffer death at the hands of the government, not individuals. It is the government's responsibility to take human life because no government is in power except by the authority of God. God has ordered armies into war to kill. By doing so, we are part of the government; therefore, taking the life of the enemy is within God's framework and not a sin."

"Wow! that's quite profound; how did you come by that?" Toby asked.

"I felt the same as you, so I sought the counsel of my Pastor. He laid it all out for me and how it comes together in the Bible. Since then, I've been at peace with myself."

"What are those passages, and how are they linked?"

An hour later, the two men continued their conversation until the end of the watch. After being relieved, Toby dropped into the berthing compartment and pulled out his Bible to begin checking the chapters and verses. After another hour, Toby knew Charlie knew exactly what he was saying.

Following their orders, the two destroyers located the oiler southeast of Guadalcanal and filled the hungry Greyhound's tanks. Then, after completing the refueling evolution, the two destroyers steamed back to the New Georgia Sound by way of Nggela Channel. Finally, the two vessels sailed past Tulagi, the second landing sight of the Marines in Operation Watchtower. The troops recovered the Island and neighboring islands where Australia built seaplane bases that the Japanese had used.

As the destroyers passed south of Savo Island, the ship slowed to give those who wished the opportunity to give homage to and pray for the entombed men in the wrecks three thousand feet below them in Iron Bottom Sound. Among the respectful stood Tobias Greene. Toby had reconciled his concerns with killing the enemy; the relief of that burden felt like a ton lifted from his shoulders. His talks with Charlie also helped him overcome his sensitivity over the popularity of his score.

The gunners of the division broke out the black, red, and white paint and brushes, then painted three black crosses, two red and white Japanese miniature ensigns, and a hash mark for a damaged plane on the tub. One other item showed up, an Ace of Spades.

Lieutenant JG Carl Saunders, a recent replacement in the Supply Division, had transferred in at their last inport stop. His expertise lies in accounting. The only time he would appear was at the meal table; then, he would disappear and cuddle up with his mounds of reports, receipts, and other tools of his trade.

One meal after the busy attack, the officer asked Captain Cummings, "Sir, I was wondering about the legality of and cost of the paint and time to paint a scorecard on the after-twenty mount. Doesn't that usually appear near the bridge, if at all?"

The wardroom fell silent; the officers present stopped eating and talking among themselves to listen to the education program about to take place from the head of the table. Around the pantry corner and out of sight stood a Steward, drying dishes but listening intently. He was the pipeline to the rumor mill of the ship.

"Mr. Saunders, will you give us the definition of morale and how it affects the crew on a combat ship?" The Captain asked.

The question fell into the field of the supply officer, and he spat it out in perfection.

"Now, Mr. Saunders, do I, as Commanding Officer of this ship, have the authority to make minor modifications to what I consider a morale booster for the crew?"

"Certainly, sir."

"Thank you, Mr. Saunders, for keeping me abreast of the ship's morale regulations and my authority. I have a question for you."

"Yes, sir, what is it?"

"Does the display on the Twenty-millimeter gun tub offend you?"

The officer looked around the table, now somewhat suspicious. "No, sir."

Addressing the officers present, the Captain asked, "Is there any officer present who feels, in any way, slighted by the score icons on the after-twenty tub?"

Every officer, except the Supply Officer, shook their head and said, "No."

"Then," boomed the Captain, "I decree that the display of Petty Officer Greene's outstanding gunnery accomplishments is hereby authorized to improve the morale of the ship. End of issue."

The officers broke out, raising glasses of water and chanting, "Here, here," followed by smiles and laughter. The bean counter looked around in mild confusion, still befuddled by everything.

Captain Cummings stood to return to the bridge, and as he did, he leaned over to the XO, "Necessary ship's work can be restored during the morning hours. Holiday routine: rest near their guns in the afternoon, except during GQ."

"Aye, sir."

"Now knock off ship's work. Sweepers, sweepers, give the ship a clean sweep down fore and aft. Empty all trash cans and butt kits" blared out of the 1MC.

Men stood clear of the 1MC speakers; the volume had been turned up to ensure everyone within hearing distance could hear and understand the directives or information transmitted.

Mike Day had the 1200-1600 watch. He called the men to the throttle board. "As you heard, our operations are primarily in the night hours. He is giving us the afternoons off to rest. I know you can't get to the compartment right now; that is in the works. Find a place on deck to sleep or gather, but do not create a problem, and remember, a shipmate has to clean that area wherever you are. So, take care of it as if it's your cleaning station, and clean up after yourself. Time for lunch. Oh, you can always hide out down here."

Toby wandered back to the after-starboard twenty mount. He noted the oil tarp wrapped around the breech of the weapon and a tarp muzzle cover to ward off salt spray. He could see the fresh protective oil on the bare steel. The heavy-weight oil provided the best protection. While checking the exterior of the mount, Toby spotted the three black crosses and two red meatballs.

'I sometimes think these guys are a little off-center, comparing him to a fighter pilot. But they're good-hearted and mean well,' he thought to himself. Then he saw the large black Ace on the other side of the cutout entrance to the mount. Smiling, Toby shook his head.

Toby continued to look around, noting that the ready boxes were loaded with full magazines, and a full magazine was attached to the weapon.

Lieutenant Owens, the XO came around the fifty-five mount on his inspection rounds, and seeing Toby, he called up to him, "Petty Officer Greene, do you know something we don't?"

Looking over the side of the tub for the owner of the voice, he said, "Oh, no, sir. I was checking the twenty over; you never know when we'll need it."

"That's for sure; you're doing a great job, Petty Officer; we need more men like you."

"Thank you, sir," the slightly embarrassed sailor returned. The XO waved and continued his inspection tour.

Toby headed for the side of the tub when a glint of sunlight caught his attention. The Petty Officer cupped his eyes against the bright sunlight and saw two G4M torpedo/ bombers in a torpedo configuration skimming off the water. Shifting his eyes, he followed their track and guessed they popped over the ridge of an island mountain ring and dropped to attack altitude. An instant after seeing the sun's reflection, Toby grabbed the talker's sound-powered phone set. "Bridge, after starboard twenty, two G4M torpedo bombers on the water at green four-five."

"What? Say again," said a new unqualified trainee.

"There are two torpedo/bombers bearing zero-four-five degrees on the deck in a torpedo attack," Toby yelled.

The new youngster called the Bo'sun over and said, "Some clown is yelling about two torpedo/bombers coming out of zero-four-five degrees."

The Bo'sun took one look and yelled, "Air attack bearing zero-four-five degrees on the water."

Without hesitation, the OOD sang out, "Sound General Quarters, air attack bearing zero-four-five, repel air attack starboard quarter. All ahead flank, come to two-two-five smartly, mind the clinometer. Captain to the bridge."

The bridge exploded into a frenzy of activity; each man, save one, knew exactly what he had to do. The alarm sounded while the Helm spun the wheel, and the Lee-Helm rang up flank speed, twenty-five knots. Throughout the ship, men mirrored the activity of the bridge, and in under a minute, the slam of hatches began reports of "Manned and ready."

At the after-starboard twenty mount, Petty Officer Green yanked the covers off the weapon, strapped himself in, and swung the big gun toward the bombers. As the ship began its turn, the bombers came into view again, and Toby lined up his lead and depressed the trigger. The big cannon roared out three-quarter-inch shells at over three-hundred-fifty rounds per minute. The projectiles whistled toward their target at twenty-seven hundred feet per second.

Thirty seconds later, the two forward five-inch guns opened fire, sending fifty-four-pound shells toward the bombers at twenty-six hundred feet per second. The twin forty-millimeter twin cannons followed them. From the first glimpse of the planes to guns firing at them was registered in seconds, and by the end of eighty seconds, all forward-firing guns burst into action.

The aircraft quickly disappeared from the Machinist's Mates view, and he released the trigger. Toby heard the order over the

1MC to open fire; then fear gripped his soul; he'd fired without proper authorization and knew he was in serious trouble.

He thought, *'Well, I'm in for it now; goodbye stripes if I'm lucky. But, on the other hand, it's better than being torpedoed; I don't want to do that again.'*

The ship's turn and unexpectedly vicious response to their attempt to sneak up on the Americans foiled their planned attack. Toby found them about three miles from the stern of the ship, and they turned toward the two destroyers as he watched and waited. The Virginian swung the cannon toward the approaching aircraft.

Toby reviewed his moves in his mind. *'Rest the center of the sight at the top of the cockpit, and begin firing at a thousand yards. Watch the tracers, and adjust as needed,'*

The two aircraft throttled back to launch speed. The talker called out, "Fire at will."

Toby checked his sight and depressed the trigger. Tracers flew over the top of the cockpit, and the sailor raised the handles a millimeter, bringing the line of shells into the cockpit. The weapon's recoil moved it enough to spray rounds throughout the cockpit, killing the pilot, co-pilot, and crew members through the craft. The pilot's remains fell forward, pushing the column before him, causing the plane to nose into the sea. The twin-engine plane flipped over, causing the two externally mounted seventeen-point-seven torpedoes to break away. Both weapons broke up on impact with the ocean and sunk into the seabed.

The second plane bored in until the fifty-four and fifty-five mounts put up geysers in front of him, which stalled one engine and crashed the plane into the ship's wake without launching his torpedoes.

With the threat gone, the firing ceased. Toby looked around, watching the sailors celebrate life. It was a weird picture for the Virginian; he could see lips moving but only heard ringing in his ears. The rapid onset of the fight didn't give Toby time to stuff anything in his ears to protect them. He did find a life jacket and put it on, along with a helmet, to escape another chewing out by a Gunnery Officer. His first order of business was to go to sick bay and check his ears. The Doctor wrote, 'No eardrum damage, ringing should stop in a day or two,' then gave him a couple of packages of earplugs.

Operations on the ship returned to the normal wartime modified Condition One routine; this brought up the legal questions of the attack, the warning, and resulting actions. Most importantly, who fired the first rounds and by what authority?

The Captain stepped over to the OOD and asked him to recite the timeline of the events. The two officers moved to the small foldup desk holding the daily log. The log showed the starting time with an anonymous warning of two G4M bombers inbound at sea level from zero-four-five. Then the Quartermaster confirmed the report and called for General Quarters. The next line states the Captain took the conn, and the following events were known to the Captain.

"Very well, Mr. Bellows; please call the XO to the bridge."

"Aye, sir."

The XO arrived seconds later, "I was in Operations; they were trying to piece together what happened and how those aircraft got in as close as they did."

"We're on the same track. We have some serious issues to resolve first; then, we can find out how these planes managed to get so close. Now, we need to identify the person who gave the warning and how it was given; third, who gave the order to fire, and that authority. And lastly, who opened fire first, and under what authority? So, you know what the armchair experts will be looking at."

"Aye, sir, those came to me while in the Ops center."

"When you finish your investigation, write it up, and we will have to name names. Supporting information about who shot first is important. Why John Doe shot first will become critical to two people, the one who shot first and me."

"I understand, sir."

IJN MOMI CLASS DESTROYER

CHAPTER TWENTY-ONE

An hour and a half after his talk with the Captain, XO Owens had his answers. Sitting at his miniature version of a folding wall-mounted desk, he typed his report in the Navy format. Then, after reading through it twice and making two corrections, he placed a carbon copy in his safe, folded and placed the original in an envelope, and headed for the bridge.

Captain Cummings, like the XO, read through the report twice. He wasn't surprised at the XO's findings; he had a feeling the Machinist's Mate would somehow be involved.

"Bob, I only see one point of issue. Although Petty Officer Greene was firing at the second plane, the forward five-inch guns took it down. Therefore, I will credit the first Betty to Greene and the forward main battery to the second plane."

"That's fair to me, and knowing Petty Officer Greene would probably say both should go to the forward guns," said the XO.

"The man is seriously shy of distinction," the Captain noted; "However, I'm putting him in for the Silver Star."

"I think he deserves it, sir," the XO put in.

"It's apparent those torpedo bombers sought to pop over the Florida Islands, then drop to the wavetops and launch their torpedoes before we could respond. Looking at the facts, they would have had a high chance of success had it not been for Petty Officer Greene. His alarm saved the ship. As for opening fire before authorization, I find no fault in his act; he was trying to save the ship. There is, however, a weakness in the bridge and lookouts. Talkers in training must not be left unattended in the combat zone. I know we only lost seconds, but in modern warfare, lost seconds can be fatal.

The Quartermaster wisely sounded the verbal alarm after verifying the threat. Instead, we would have lost less time if he had sounded the alarm first. But, again, I'm not finding fault; thinking of a quicker response. Look into ways to shave seconds from sighting to alert; maybe we can do better."

"Aye, sir, we must do better; this will be an excellent training vehicle," the XO said.

With the sudden attack by the bomber in the past, the two destroyers continued their Tokyo Express patrol with a heightened sense of readiness. The ships steamed to the northwestern end of their patrol sector, and with no returns on the sound or radar, they backtracked to the Russell Islands between Nggatokae Island and Guadalcanal.

"Mr. Hines, You were on watch when I presented a bushwack location to the wardroom. Did anyone fill you in on the plan?"

"Mr. Bellows mentioned it in passing, but there were no details, Captain."

"Okay, Captain Bernstein of the *RICE* and I talked with another Fletcher driver, and he filled us in on these two small bays sitting between Marulaon and Hanawisi islets. We can anchor a short distance into the bays or even both in one bay if we wish, and our radar is high enough to see over the land to watch for Express traffic."

"What about the depth?"

"The reef falls steeply twenty feet from the beach onto a sloping floor, reaching about three hundred feet in the center of the bays."

"That makes it a perfect hunting location, Captain."

"Yeah, Jerry Hanson said he learned about it when he found a pair of IJN cans set up in the bay to the west. Unfortunately for the enemy, he slipped up behind 'em and boxed their ears."

"It sounds like a good deal. Are we going to try it out?"

"That's what I'm thinking."

Without warning, the hair on Captain Cummings neck raised like those on the back of an alerted cat. The Cherokee in Cummings sent him a sign, 'DANGER.' The man in charge stepped onto the bridge's port wing as if to sniff the night air for the scent of an enemy. Nothing, yet his body tingled with the feeling the ship cruised into mortal danger.

The Captain returned to the bridge, "OOD silently, send the ship to General Quarters ASW."

Lieutenant JG Michael Hines called the talker and Bo'sun to meet with him, then gave the sailors their orders. Men scrambled to prepare the ship for depth charge attacks, while those in the main battery handling rooms and mounts prepared to take on a surfaced enemy sub. In less than a minute, the ship, already at condition one, called in the manned and ready reports. Captain Cummings saying nothing, nodded as the ends of his lips curled into a proud smile.

He picked up the low-powered TBS, "Nightmare, Mirage, have gone to GQ-ASW, sense trouble."

"Confirmed."

The two patrol destroyers reached the southeastern end of their patrol area, and the OOD ordered the planned turn to port, with the *RICE* a thousand yards to their port side, turning with them. The maneuver placed the *GLEAVES* in the lead.

Three Seaman had the same thoughts, *'The Captains gone around the bend. There is nothing out there except fish.'*

Captain Cumming flipped up the switch to connect the bridge to Ops. "Radar, bridge, are you seeing anything out there?"

Bridge, radar, we're only seeing the islands of Nggatokae and the small Mbulo to our port, but if there is a reef hugger, he's lost in the clutter."

Next, the Captain flipped the Fire Control Director switch, "Fire Control, bridge, anything out there?"

"Bridge, Fire Control, we're picking up intermittent returns on a possible surface contact, but they must be right next to the reef."

Everyone, with and some without binoculars, began scanning the black shoreline, only visible because they blackout the stars on the horizon. Those with binoculars watched as a bow wave appeared, and the ship making it had to be at the edge of the reef as it headed between Nggatokae and Mbulo.

"OOD," the Captain called out, "Surface action to port, four Star Shells between Mbulo and Nggatokae."

Seconds later mounts fifty-three and fifty-four blasted the four Stars Shells on their way with flashless powder.

"Signal, tell Mirage what we're doing, and have her reposition in our wake at five hundred yards."

"Talker, check with sound; are there any sounds of submarine activity?"

"Aye, sir."

"Sir, sound reports no man-made sounds towards the Slot, but the waves and surf could be hiding a contact."

"Very well."

"Port and top lookout report three destroyers, each towing a barge bearing two-six-four, course one-seven-zero, speed eighteen knots," reported the talker.

"Very well."

Flipping the switch to the Mark 37 director, "Fire Control, can you get a fix on those three cans the stars have lit?"

"Still intermittent, but we may have enough to get their attention."

"Do it."

"All hands stand clear main battery," blasted over the 1MC. A second later, the first of the three-salvo bombardment from the five guns headed for their targets.

"Captain," Mr. Hines called out, "The three destroyers are Momi class, with three four-point-seven main battery, two twin twenty-one-inch torpedo launchers, and a speed of thirty-six knots."

"Very well."

"OOD, slow to eighteen knots; maintain your course."

"Aye, sir."

With the *DEFOE* matching the speed of the short convoy, the American destroyers remained in a position to attack the enemy as they became visible at the southeastern edge of Mbulo.

"OOD, have Gunnery watch the southeastern edge of Mbulo; when the second destroyer appears, open fire, three rounds of common per tube, and order the secondary battery to open fire when they have a clear shot, then signal Mirage to copy."

"Aye, sir," and he had the talker send the orders to Fire Control.

On cue, the Fletcher and Gleaves opened fire, sending thirty, five-inch diameter high explosive shells into the convoy, which could only advance on their course or turn. Unfortunately, neither of these could be a viable solution for the enemy.

The fifty-one-mount fired one round to check the accuracy of the initial settings, and the shot landed past the first ship. Immediate corrections set the point of impact correctly, and all five gun mounts opened fire, followed by those from Mirage. Several rounds were on target, ripping into the destroyer and bringing her into a floating, flaming wreck, drifting slowly with the barge still secured to her burning hulk.

Upon seeing the lead ship's almost instant destruction, the second destroyer cut loose its supply-loaded barge and began speeding as it came around the island.

"Captain, that destroyer has broken away and looks to be charging us, possibly with the intent to ram Mirage or us," the OOD warned.

Mr. Hines turned to look at the Captain as he calmly said, "So it would appear."

The fearless Japanese Captain ordered its single four-point-seven forward gun to open fire on the American destroyers. One round from the gun struck the after-deckhouse of the *DEFOE*, gutting the space and injuring eight men. Another round ricocheted off the bullnose of the *RICE* and exploded as it hit the water, with shrapnel puncturing the bow several times, injuring four men.

The enemy destroyer came into view; her bow pointed at the *DEFOE.* Captain Cummings yelled loud enough for everyone on the bridge to hear, "Helm, don't let that bastard ram us."

"Aye, sir," the helm grunted as he spun the wheel first to port and, two seconds later, reversed the turn to starboard, returning to the ship's original course, expertly moving the destroyer eleven feet out of ramming danger.

Petty Officer Toby Greene saw the enemy vessel appearing from the forward of his ship and opened fire with the big cannon.

The shells laced the Momi at point-blank range, causing chaos and havoc on the sailors across the decks of the enemy destroyer, putting several men down. The two ships completed their pass a second later, and the Japanese four-point-seven and American five-inch guns traded fire. Unfortunately, due to the rapidly changing angles, none of the shells hit home. However, the after mounts scored two hits in the Momi's after turret, putting it out of commission. The Japanese destroyer design came from the end of WWI, with top speeds of thirty-six knots and a powerful main battery of four-point-seven inches. The vessels held an obsolete classification but remained dangerous adversaries to misjudged or poor use of fighting techniques. Bold IJN Officers often looked for opportunities to exploit an enemy's strict adherence to the Allies' WWI tactics and more often came away victorious.

The two remaining IJN destroyers used the confusion created by the unexpected charge of the second destroyer to make their escape good. When the Samurai-like offensive broke up the coordination of the two Americans, Mirage and Nightmare turned their attention to the barges of supplies and men, sending them to the bottom with five-inch gunfire.

Secondary explosions on two barges indicated loads of munitions. About thirty soldiers floated on the surface with the help of life jackets. Under the yells from those believed to be officers, half a dozen men who indicated they wanted to surrender recanted. The sailors at the ship's rails turned away. One Seaman commented, "They may make it to one of the islands, but nobody took the odds."

With the action for the night over, Captain Cummings stepped into his sea cabin; he was not a happy man. The enemy destroyer's Captain had outfoxed the bridge personnel, including himself. The only saving grace was the destruction of one destroyer and the three barges and their cargo. Nevertheless, Cummings admired the Japanese Commander's courage, determination, devotion to his duty, and fearlessness in the face of certain death.

The Captain wearily thought, *'This is going to be a long war.'*

In his after-action report, Captain Cummings added, 'The Japanese Commander,' he commented, 'Could have been crazy or wanted to die in battle, but it was not an act of desperation. He had plenty of room and existing confusion to escape to the south. I have concluded the Commander of that destroyer is a fearless adversary, quick to assess the situation accurately, and took a calculated risk to use the events to break up our attack and escape. Undoubtedly, the Captain of the enemy vessel is a cold, calculating tactician.

Captain Cumming made several notes from his report to form a plan of action if they came under another Samurai attack.

The two American destroyers returned to the northern edge of Pavuvu Island and the two bays between Marulaon and Hanawisi Islands.

The Captains of both destroyers saw the wisdom in Captain Hansen's plans. Captain Cummings pulled the black handset to the TBS and called Captain Bernstein, "Mirage, Nightmare."

"Mirage one here."

"The two small bays to our port are perfect for us and have less chance of someone sneaking up behind us."

"Agreed, I was looking at that on my map. What are your plans?" Mirage asked.

"Our radar should give us ten or more miles advanced warning of approaching ships. It will be too late when they become aware of us. You take the west bay; it will give you the first shot on any bad guys. We'll be right next door, where we can keep an eye on the inlet from the east. Entry by an IJN can is unlikely, but we can't chance to ignore it," Cummings warned.

"Thanks for the confidence."

"The best learning tool is doing. If an Express comes by, as they most likely will, to hug the coastline, thus foiling the radar. That should put them within torpedo range and give us a good setup. You target the number two ship, and we'll do the same for number one. We will coordinate our launches. I suggest a simple pattern of letters and numbers using the TBS. The radio operators on the enemy ships won't make heads or tails of it for several minutes, if at all. Example: 'Nightmare, 3c.'

That will tell me three IJN DDs, with or without barges coming into range. By then, we should have them on our radar as well, and we can complete the targeting assessment of number two can. When the targets enter the fire zone, you will call: 'Mirage x seconds to f.' That sets the attack into motion. We fire the fish simultaneously and hit or miss; we open with the main battery at the end of the fish's timed run."

"I like it, brevity on the TBS and a clear attack plan. So, let's go for it. What do you say about using a secondary, normally unused frequency on the TBS?" Captain Bernstein asked.

"Good idea, Let's let the radio folks set that up, and they can tell us what they developed."

"Sounds good; we will get our men on the line if we're finished."

"Nightmare, out."

Each Destroyer took their designated bay and turned around to face the Slot. Their radar antennas stood just over the low hills of the islands to scan three-hundred-sixty degrees. First, the Torpedo Officers had the Chief's detail men check the torpedoes, and another group examined the launch tubes, ensuring the system worked to perfection. All ten Mark 15 fish passed their examinations on each ship. Next, the men in the five-inch mount handling rooms set high explosive shells in their hoists for the expected surface action. Then, the waiting began.

The rest of the night failed to produce any enemy contact. The ships waited until zero-eight-hundred, with the Captains debating the pros and cons of sitting out the day in the small bays. Proverbial wisdom would put the vessels to sea for maneuvering room if attacked.

"Jerry Hanson said he took the path of the unexpected. Attack when proverbial wisdom says to fall back. Or to do the unexpected at every turn."

"If we put to sea, we leave a wake which points directly at us. But, on the other hand, a pilot looking for enemy interceptors may rely on the wake to indicate a ship, and if we are static, the lookouts may not notice us in these small inlets."

"It may come down to explaining why, no matter what we do," Captain Bernstein noted.

"That is what will probably happen," Captain Cunnings agreed. If we sit, we can always get ready if a strike is detected and prepare for maximum speed if needed. They will unlikely be looking for two small ships in narrow coves after a mauling by

Wildcats, P-39s, and AA fire. I keep hearing Hanson's words, 'Do the unexpected.' Therefore, I'm in for sitting tight."

After two minutes of silence, the TBS came alive, "Sitting tight, we are."

Turning to the OOD, listening intently to the conversation, Captain Cummings said, "If you have a question or comment, I need to hear it now."

"Permission to speak freely, sir?"

"Certainly, these men are now in harm's way, based on my decision. If there is a better way to handle it, now is the time to speak up, any of you," he waved his hand toward the sailors.

"Sir, if we are spotted, we'll be sitting ducks; how can you justify this decision?"

"Valid question, OOD." Turning to the bridge crew, "How about you, men? The OOD has made the essential question of the moment; this is an open discussion, and your input is important to me and may persuade me to change the course I've taken."

"Sir," the GQ Bo'sun spoke up. "Are there any percentages of survival available?"

"Another excellent question. Let me answer Mr. Bello's question first," the Captain said.

"As you all heard in my discussion with Captain Bernstein, it is a damn or be damned situation. I laid out my explanation from both sides, but to be a little clearer on the subject, let me add this. There are senior officers throughout the Navy who are operating within the framework of World War One. Today we struggle with a nation having a superior number of ships and aircraft not far from here. We are holding our own, but that is all. And that is due to individual commanders who must make difficult decisions daily. You have all seen it right here on this bridge.

I don't know if you are up on the last war, which ended about the time many aboard this ship were born. In the First World War, Japan was an Ally. As such, the Japanese trained and fought with us and learned our strategy and, more importantly, our tactics. Our senior command officers continue to use those tactics today, giving the Japanese the upper hand. The Japanese refused to abide by the Washington Naval Treaty of 1922, giving them a head start in developing and building new warships. We are playing catchup.

Captain Hanson's techniques have proven successful, and I believe they would benefit us.

As for percentages of survival, nobody with any common sense would place their character, mental faculty, or reputation on assessing ratios. There are way too many unknown factors that could turn assumed victory into disaster. I direct your attention to the Battle of Midway; it makes no sense, the Japanese had us out-gunned and had the advantage of surprise in the attack on the island, yet they lost four of their front-line carriers to our one. All I can say is do your job to the best of your ability and place it all at the feet of God. Any other questions or suggestions? Then, I have one last question for you; Do we play the game by their rules or ours?"

The sailors raised their fists and said, "We fight to win."

"Boat's, the 1MC, if you will. Men, this is the Captain."

IJN MITSUBISHI G4M 'BETTY'

CHAPTER TWENTY-TWO

Before Captain Cummings could address the crew, a messenger handed him a flimsy from radio: "Belay my last," the Captain said, then hung the mike on its hook. He opened the message; it was from Cactus:

Nightmare, Mirage
Cactus 2

Rec. After-action rpt.
Proceed to Tulagi for battle damage assessment.
Relief en route.

Cactus 2 sends.

The Captain initialed and handed the message to the OOD, "It would appear that a higher power has changed our plans. Confirm Mirage received this message and set a course to Tulagi at twenty-five knots."

"Aye, Captain," Mr. Bellows responded, hiding his pleasure at not teasing fate.

"What do you think about the after-deckhouse? That shell did a lot of damage."

"There's little doubt a tender might handle it; if not, it will take a shipyard."

"Aye, sir."

Two and a half hours later, the two ships arrived at Tulagi. A motorboat with three Material Officers boarded the *DEFOE*. They took one look at the after-deckhouse and ordered Captain Cummings to rendezvous with the tanker southeast of Guadalcanal and head for Noumea, where a tender would determine if the damage required a shipyard.

Following the rendezvous with the oiler, the two American destroyers headed south for the thousand-mile voyage to Noumea, capital of New Caledonia, in the New Hebrides Islands. After a zigzag run of fourteen knots escorting cargo ships, the cans entered Moselle Bay four days later. The destroyer tender ordered them moored to their port side. Their team of seasoned Repair Officers wasted no time recommending the *DEFOE* to the shipyards in Brisbane. The damage included watertight bulkheads and the handing room for the fifty-three mount. The estimated repair time ran from five to eight weeks.

In the after-engine room, Mike Day called his Second Class Petty Officers to the throttle board. "I just got word we'll be in the Brisbane yards for up to eight weeks at the maximum. After the plant cools, examine all the finger, main and auxiliary condenser zincs. Get back to me as soon as you can; we'll use it as an indication of the erosion to the stern zincs. Next, check the oil in all the steam-driven pumps, and look at the hours of operation, color, clarity, and contamination. We may have enough time on that oil to either run it through the oil purifier or replace it. When that is complete, Those men not active in the zinc detail will begin repairs to the valves on the repair list."

"That will keep the guys out of trouble for a while," MacArthur said.

The next morning both destroyers set sail for Brisbane, nine-hundred miles west-southwest, on a course of two-two-four degrees. It took almost two days with the precautionary zigzag antisubmarine track. Finally, the harbor pilots took the ships to the repair docks and tucked them away in a dead-end mooring location. There, dock workers and sailors worked together to rig shore power to the vessels, and the plants shut down.

Three Firemen from the number two engine room cornered Toby. Nick Riccati, Abe Holstein, and Andy Gables crowded around the gunner, Abe asking, "Would you mind tagging along with us on liberty?"

Toby thought about the strange request because he had a reputation for not drinking alcohol. "Sure, with one exception."

"Okay," Nick said, "How much do you want?"

"Naw, I don't want any of your money. But I want you to remember you asked me to do this; if you give me any trouble, especially take a swing at me, I'll bust your head, and the other two can haul you back to the ship."

"Aww, man, why are ya so hard?" Andy asked.

"You three have a reputation for getting drunk, then wanting to fight. I could fight with one of you, and the other two would still have to bring you back. But the chance of the other two coming to your rescue outnumbers me three to one. So, to level the playing field, I'm going to borrow a shillelagh from an Irishman I know so that you'll know I mean business. And mind you, if I have to use it, you will never forget your headache. Take it or leave it."

The three friends babbled back and forth, then Nick said, "Okay, you're on."

When the four left the engine room, they headed for the berthing compartment to get their shower gear. When finished with his shower, Toby dressed and pulled out a 'Billie club,' he carried while in the RN Shore Police, in lieu of a gun. Greene carefully concealed the weapon, and only a search would reveal its presence.

Each man passed inspection and headed into Brisbane for the evening to enjoy beer and relax. The three sailors were no strangers to Brizzy, Brisbane's nickname. Upon entering the pub, the owner approached them with the intent of barring their presence because their last visit resulted in a fight.

"Sir, I am here to ensure these men enjoy themselves, do not pester other patrons, and will not get rowdy, and I will not be drinking alcohol. They will be almost gentlemen this evening, and we'll leave by twenty hundred hours."

"All right, mate, what do ya want to drink?"

"A cola or root beer, if you have any."

"Have a seat at that table; it will give you a clear view of the hall. By the way, have we met before?"

“Not here; I’ve been to Brisbane a while back, but not in your establishment.”

“I’ve seen you somewhere, or a picture of you, it’ll come to me.”

Twenty minutes later, the owner stopped by with another cola, “I know who ya are. I was in London when the King knighted you.”

“Were you at the ceremony?”

“No, but they had an excellent photo of ya in one of the tabloids. Welcome to the Northend Pub.”

“Thank you, sir, but I must ask for a favor.”

“Anything Sir Tobias.”

“These men know nothing of my knighthood, and for security purposes, we must keep it that way; men’s lives and mine depend on that silence.”

“I understand; how shall I call ya?”

Smiling, The knight said, “how about Toby?”

“Toby, it is, and ya will always be welcome here.”

“Thank you, sir.”

“It’s Dan, but everyone calls me D-Dan.”

“Thanks, D-Dan.”

An hour later, three bar girls joined the American sailors. They enjoyed the new company and spoke loudly to hear one another over nearby loud conversations and music.

Toby walked to the bar for a refill on his cola. He asked D-Dan, “Is that bunch getting too loud for you?”

After looking around the bar, D-Dan said, “Naw, they’re having a good time and no louder than the rest of the crowd. The sailors are much better behaved than a year ago when they were on a different ship and pretty rowdy. But now, either they have matured, or maybe they don’t want to piss ya off.”

Toby replied, “I hope it’s the former; if not, they know the penalty for not playing nice.”

“That’s right, ya served in the RN, and they don’t tolerate cheekiness or fighting. But it’s good to see a shipmate care for his buddies. I’ve seen it different when rival ships are in port at the same time.”

Toby checked his watch, “It won’t last too much longer; I will have to head them back to the ship before curfew begins.”

"You're a good mate, Toby. If ya need any help, I'll be here for ya."

"Thanks, you run a good place for their level of fun, and I wouldn't want to see them unwanted."

"That's no problem, as long as they don't start fights or throw things; it's getting too expensive to replace these mirrors, windows, chairs, and tables."

"I'm not surprised at the high cost of replacements, with the war and all. But, as far as they are concerned, I promised them one hell of a headache for not playing nice."

"Good on ya, Toby."

Thirty minutes later, "Come on, mates, curfew is almost upon us; time to head back," The gunner announced.

Andy stood, and the beginnings of obnoxious slurs started to form when Nick poked him in the arm, "Knock it off, Andy. Remember we promised Toby we'd behave. After all, he's giving us his time so we can have fun. Besides, I'm too drunk to carry your lame ass back to the ship. But, most of all, remember the penalty for giving him crap, and they didn't give him three Purple Hearts for cowardness, either."

"Yeah, you're right; sorry, Toby."

"Come on, Andy, let's get you back," Toby chuckled. The walk and fresh air helped the sailors shake the cobwebs from their heads. At one point, a pair of Navy Shore Patrolmen stopped the group. Toby stepped up and identified himself. The issue with the SPs was the men's intoxication.

Toby explained he was with them to ensure there was no trouble, and he was escorting them to their ship.

One of the SPs looked Toby's ribbons over, then questioned the three other decorations on his right breast. Toby showed them the letter from Captain Merrifield, which satisfied the SPs, and Toby shepherded his men to the Fleet Landing.

At the landing, the four met sailors from the *RICE*, and the war stories and laughter continued. The crews from the two destroyers had worked together since San Diego months earlier. An air kinsmanship had developed from interdependence in combat, and numerous friendships ensued.

Two motor whaleboats moored at the pier, and the coxswains called out the names of their ships. The men piled aboard for the short trip across the narrow end of the bay. Once aboard the *DEFOE*, Toby returned his Billie club to its holder. He wondered why he never took it aboard the *MANNING*, then felt thankful that he hadn't. The sailor hit the sack early, already short on sleep.

The next morning, Quarters sent the men aft the fifty-five mount,

The Division Officer and Chiefs went through the requirements of the evolution. After rendering honors to the colors at zero-eight-hundred, the Division senior Chief dismissed the men with orders to lay to the spaces.

At ten-fifteen, Mike Day went to the compartment, where he picked up the mail for the men. Then, he redistributed it in the engine room. Three men and Toby received a mittful of letters. The sailor began with the earliest dated letter and read through them for any important information. He planned on going through them in detail after work. He read one letter, stopped, and reread the letter, then stood, stunned into silence.

"Hey, Toby, are you Okay?" Mike asked.

"Yeah, but no. My wife says she and the baby are doing fine. We don't have any children."

A huge smile crossed Day's face, "Congratulations, Daddy. When is the happy day coming, or don't you know yet?"

"She says our baby will come sometime in September." Toby suddenly needed to sit down. "Amanda is going to have a baby," the astonished sailor mumbled. "Wow, that's almost five months from now. It has taken that long for the mail to get out here to us."

"Don't forget, Toby," Day offered, "We have had a hard steaming schedule since we got here. Anyway, don't forget me when you get the cigars, and I'm not choosy."

"Okay, Mike." The sailor couldn't read any more letters due to the shock of his impending fatherhood.

A few short weeks later, the efficient Australian shipyard had the fabricated after-deckhouse manufactured and installed. The bulkheads and decks were repaired, along with the ammunition hoist. No *DEFOE* machinery appeared on the repair board, and the Navy certified her ready for duty.

The time for the *DEFOE* and the *RICE* to return to the war had arrived. The destroyers blew their whistles, announcing their underway status, and harbor tugs and pilots guided the two destroyers through the minefields and torpedo nets and into the outer edge of Morton Bay. The two pilots disembarked, and the men-of-war turned to join a convoy's escort force heading for Guadalcanal.

As the convoy passed Vanuatu, five additional cargo ships and two additional destroyers joined their convoy. The maximum speed of the convoy came down to twelve knots. Those escorts equipped with sonar suites listened for any telltales of the enemy, especially the high pitch whine of torpedoes. Their irregular zigzag pattern added miles to the trip, but not zigzagging invited disaster for any ship.

Tension crept into the crews with the convoy closing on the Solomon Islands. Finally, Captain Cummings ordered the ship to assume war condition one, all guns manned, with relieves every twelve hours. The lookouts remained on four and eight, four hours on watch and eight hours off.

Toby received orders to man the stern twenty-millimeter gun. Rumors bounced around that the Machinist's Mate had a permanent posting. But, permanent or not, Tobias Greene maintained a deadly attitude about his duties. The splinter shield sported three German crosses, three red and white Japanese ensigns, and a hash mark. On the other side, the red lips remained until an unknown sailor painted a stork next to the lips. When the gunner saw it, he smiled and shook his head. Unbeknown to the gunner, those men who saw Toby in action felt safer with him on the weapon.

Two young sailors marveled at the scorecard, thinking only planes had that right. The youngsters questioned why it was there until a Petty Officer enlightened them.

One exclaimed, "Wow, wait until I write and tell the folks about that; the whole family will want to know about it."

Boatswain's Mate third class warned both boots, "I wouldn't do that if I were you. First, the mail censor will either black it out or have a word with you about security. Your family would be lucky if the FBI didn't begin an espionage investigation because you forwarded secure information to them."

The color drained from the faces of the two young sailors, and both promised to say nothing. Later, the Petty Officer watched as the two seventeen-year-olds took photos of the mount markings.

The mountains of Guadalcanal peeked over the horizon, and the Gunnery Officer and Chief reminded the gunners of the importance of target identification before firing on it. Each gunner was questioned and interviewed to ensure. Allied and American aircraft and pilots remained safe around and over the escorts.

The closer the convoy approached, the monitoring of Japanese air frequencies intensified. The duty radio operator assigned to monitor the frequencies reported picking up long-range transmissions, possibly due to frequency skipping. He could make out the word Buin, the home of a major airfield on Bougainville. There were no indications of enemy aircraft in the vicinity. The morning raid on Guadalcanal had struck an hour earlier.

The convoy split south of San Cristobal Island, with half sailing on the north side of the large island; the rest of the convoy vessels entered Lengo Channel with several ships seeking cover unto overhead trees in Purvis Bay and other inlets aligned with Assembly Area Yoke at Tulagi. The remainder continued to Assembly Area X-Ray off Lungga Point. Cactus Control assumed control of the two destroyers and placed them on ASW patrol.

Captain Cummings called to the OOD, "We'll begin running ASW patrol in the lower Sound; tell Mirage to take the north side, two miles from the islands, and we will do the same along Guadalcanal. Turn to one-eight-zero, then at two miles from the coast. Follow the coastline. Speed ten knots. And maintain the antiaircraft condition."

"Aye, sir."

The daily rains began moving in, which would help the antiaircraft watches. The shower was warm but much better than the sweltering sun, and it helped cool off the ship's metal skin, thus the interior compartments and engineering spaces.

On day two of their arrival, Cactus 2 ordered the cans to antiaircraft duty off Lungga Point and Henderson field. Most of the cargo ships had already departed and sailed well southeast of Guadalcanal. Several freighters were still wrapping up their unloading rigs and estimated getting underway as soon as possible, no longer than thirty minutes.

Radar identified a large formation of planes twenty minutes northwest of Cape Esperance heading toward Assembly Area X-Ray and Henderson Field. The CAF (Cactus Air Force) launched Wildcat fighters, P-39 and P-400 Airacobras, one leaving the ground every thirty seconds. First, the Marine and Navy Wildcats would take the fight to the Japanese escort fighters, usually Zeros, Zekes, and Ki-43 'Oscars,' which may be in the mix. Then, the P-39s and 400s would go after the bombers.

While under the thick clouds and rain, machine gun fire rattled across the sky over Iron Bottom Sound. Then a lookout reported a white Japanese plane had fallen through the clouds and spun into the water.

"Top lookout, bridge, did you get an identification of the downed plane?"

"Bridge, top lookout, it was a white Val with red meatballs on the tops and bottoms of the wings, no parachutes observed."

"Bridge, aye."

"All lookouts, pay special attention to torpedo planes just above the water; they may try to come in under the weather."

A single destroyer escort patrolled the south entrance to Iron Bottom Sound near Savo Island as a tripwire for low-flying torpedo aircraft. The TBS lit up with a warning that three G4M Betty planes were in a torpedo configuration southeast of the small destroyer. The ship's guns barked in the background as the TBS transmitted.

Two Vals pushed over into their dive through a hole in the clouds. Toby spotted one already in a power dive toward a freighter late getting underway. When the plane entered his range, Toby fired a quick burst for ranging. He adjusted his lead and fired for effect. The aircraft continued in its dive at the maximum distance for the cannon, but several pieces of the plane blew off from shell impact and fluttered toward the water. A heavy bomb detached from the swing carriage and screamed toward the cargo vessel. Fortunately, the bomb hit the water over fifty feet from the ship and exploded on contact. The cargo ship steamed on as if there was no or little damage.

Toby scanned the action and saw the black puffs of five-inch AA Common shells slice off the wing of a Betty, and it spun into the water, sinking rapidly out of sight.

Two five-inch guns sent fifty-four-pound high explosive shells into the water in front of another Betty, each shooting geysers into the air, but the plane went through the water without hesitation. Toby sent a ranging shot toward the aircraft, made the appropriate adjustments, and then held the firing lever down. Three-quarter inch armor piercing, high explosive, and tracer rounds began chewing up the starboard engine, causing it to seize. The plane rolled, exposing the port engine to the bullet stream, and it fell from the nacelle. The roll also revealed two torpedoes on their racks, and the gunner, spotter, and loader watched as the tracers began chewing up the weapons. A torpedo warhead detonated, causing the second torpedo to have a sympathetic detonation, turning the entire bomber and crew into pieces no larger than a fist that covered over three hundred square feet of water, and the *DEFOE* took a couple of pieces, with no injuries. Another meatball for the splinter shield.

The Army Air Corps fighter/bombers mixed in with the enemy aircraft as the furball descended to the deck, and the cease-fire order went out.

IJN D3A 'VAL' DIVE BOMBER

CHAPTER TWENTY-THREE

Despite the cease-fire order, the battle continued to roar overhead. Fighters would burst from the thick clouds, find their target, then the rattle of gunfire ricocheted from the surrounding mountains, and the aircraft climbed back into the safety of the billowing swirls of mist. Here and there, a plane would spiral or dive from the overcast on terminal plunges.

One blue and gray Wildcat popped from the base of the clouds and flew over the ship streaming black oily smoke from a ruptured oil tank. With his canopy slid back for rapid escape, the pilot dropped to the water's surface near its stalling speed. He cut the tortured engine and pulled back slightly on the stick, bringing the nose up and causing the tail to lower into the water, acting like a brake. The stubby fighter pancaked on top of the calm water in a splash. With the forward movement suddenly stopped, the pilot released his straps, climbed out of the cockpit, walked the length of the short wing, and stepped into the water as the plane made its final dive.

Captain Cummings watched the planes overflight and called out, "All ahead full, call out Search and Rescue, aircraft ditching." The alarm activated several deckhands, engineers, and medical personnel. A motor whaleboat swung out on its davits with a Coxswain, engineer, and rescue crew aboard.

"All back one-third," ordered the Captain as he gauged the decreasing distance to the waiting pilot. Then, when the ship's speed dropped to five knots, he called, "All stop, away the motor whaleboat." The engineer started the diesel engine before the boat entered the water, so the turning propeller could immediately power the boat away from the ship's side to prevent contacting the vessel from the pressure of the turbulent bow wake

Meanwhile, Mirage moved into a covering position to ward off enemy intruders.

The whaleboat carefully approached the pilot, who signaled he was uninjured. Then, the boat's crew hoisted the soaked flyer into the motor whaleboat and wrapped a blanket around him to help ward off chills as the Coxswain rang the bell for maximum speed. The engineer, hearing the bells, opened the throttle to its stop, and the boat turned back to the destroyer. All the passengers remained in the whaleboat until it was hoisted and locked into its carriage.

Then a short ladder allowed the passenger to descend to the deck, walk to the sick bay for a check-over, and be taken to the officer's showers a short distance from the wardroom. When he finished washing the saltwater from him, he dressed and retrieved any property from his clothes, which a sailor whisked to the laundry for washing and drying. Meanwhile, the XO invited the flyer, a Lieutenant and XO of his squadron, for hot food and coffee in the corner of the wardroom. An hour later, the pilot had his clothes on but was stuck with wet shoes.

The Lieutenant couldn't thank the officers and crew enough. He would be a guest until the ship's boat returned him to the pier at Lungga Point, where a jeep would return him to his squadron. Up til then, the officer only worked ashore or carriers, and he came to appreciate the hard-working destroyer navy.

With the attack over, those ships damaged in the fighting had time to make what repairs they could and lick their wounds. Two freighters caught in the attack had extinguished fires started by enemy action. The cargo ship with the near miss reported minor flooding under control. Smoke rose from still-burning aircraft remains at Henderson Field and lingered here and there over Iron Bottom Sound, where planes went down.

Petty Officer Greene headed for the engine room to take his watch and make himself scarce, avoiding celebrations on his latest success. He was tired, tired of the war, tired of killing men. Toby

Greene just wanted to go home, where he could forget the insanity of war.

Mike Day picked up the clipboard, signed in the box at the bottom, and then timed and dated it.

"Other than switching and cleaning the main and auxiliary lube oil strainers, everything is as when you left for the fight."

The EOT bell rang, and the RPM repeater came up for twenty-five knots. Nick Riccati, the throttleman, answered the bell and brought the engine speed up to twenty-five knots.

"Any info on what's happening up there?" Toby asked Nick.

"The bridge reports we have a sound contact on a sub."

"Okay, let me know if anything comes of it; I'm gonna look around," Greene said.

"Will do."

As the gunner checked with the men on watch and the machinery, he thought, *'This end of the New Georgia Sound seems as busy as ever, with the Japanese intending to drive the Allies out of the Solomon Islands.'*

Toby spent time writing names on paper, trying to find the perfect name for the coming baby. His thoughts filled with a hundred ideas of what will I do 'if'? Sir Tobias shook his head and commanded the evil thoughts to leave. Finally, he felt better and folded the paper and placed it in his wallet.

Sleep had become a premium, so when he reached the berthing compartment, he wasted no time climbing into his rack and falling asleep. Once he got to REM sleep, the dreams came. He only vaguely recalled two dreams, but a third dream seemed like a nightmare; Toby would never forget it; his most vivid scene was looking at an open casket, with Amanda lying in it, as if she were asleep.

The sailor instantly awoke, and his head bumped into the bottom of the bunk above him. He felt drenched in sweat and felt his entire body shaking in terror. Toby dressed and worked his way to the main deck to get fresh air. Then he felt cold as the warm tropical air drifted across his wet shirt.

Toby sat on a 'bitt' (A pair of large steel drum-like posts for wrapping and securing mooring lines), trying to figure out if there was a message in the horrible nightmare. Toby looked at his watch and saw he had been asleep for about two hours. Still tired, the sailor returned to his bunk without answers and laid down again. Finally, the 1MC woke Toby from a sound sleep.

Then he recalled the nightmare but nothing else. The Machinist's Mate crawled out of his bunk, dressed, and headed for his General Quarters station. The sailor checked the weapon closely, noting the fresh coat of protective gun oil. From zero-five-hundred, the crew in sound hunted for signs of submarines. By zero-six-hundred, the danger period expired, and the regular watch gunner replaced the sailor. Then he headed for breakfast, the nightmare receding in his memory.

Following breakfast, Toby joined the other engineers heading for the holes. The men gathered around the throttle board for information on the day's events. They were in the war zone, and the immediate orders were to get ready to fight.

Morning rain clouds began gathering at first light and now looked like they were about to open up. "Bridge, sound, we have identified a submerged contact bearing zero-four-nine, paralleling us on course zero-four-eight. Contact is identified as a submarine at two-eight zero-zero yards, estimated at a shallow depth," the talker said.

"OOD," the Captain called, "Set K-guns and stern racks to one hundred feet. Bo' sun, sound General Quarters, ASW alert, prepare for surface action on a suspected submarine. Tell Main Control to standby for multiple bells and light off the superheaters."

The orders brought a sense of urgency to the crew as they rushed to switch from antiaircraft defense to ASW offense. Twenty seconds later, the ship reported manned and ready for ASW. Captain Cumming offered a small smile in the comfort of knowing he commanded a first-rate crew of sailors.

Operations plotted the submarine's movements and forwarded the recommended attack profile to the bridge. Mr. Bellows looked toward the Skipper, nodded approval as he watched each man, and listened carefully to each report and order.

"Helm come to zero-four-niner, flank speed, twenty-five knots. Talker to Gunnery, stand by to roll the depth charges, and prepare to fire the K-guns to a hundred yards."

The Captain's orders were acknowledged, and the talker sent the information to the designated recipients. In the main engineering spaces, the check men closely watched the boiler water levels; the burner men installed the large orifice tips for maximum output of the boilers. Other sailors monitored the operation of the pumps, lube oil coolers, forced draft blowers, and a variety of gauges to keep the operations safe.

In the engine rooms, the men on watch checked oil levels, pressures, and temperatures on several pumps, turbo-generators, and main engines. Everyone eyed a forest of gauges that indicated output pressures and temperatures of the boiler water.

The hunt was on; the Fletcher, in her natural element, charged in to hunt an enemy submarine, hot on its scent and a bone in her teeth.

****

Three-hundred-fifty-six feet of the Japanese B1 diesel-electric submarine cruised parallel to the two American destroyers at periscope depth. Captain Daiki Fukushima and ninety-three officers and men guided the sub to the attack point the Captain planned. Submarines are not fast boats, as a rule. However, the B1 was one of the fastest in the world, with a surface speed of twenty-three knots and a submerged speed of eight knots. Moreover, Captain Fukushima, a Japanese Naval Academy, and Submarine School graduate, had proven himself as a driven man destined for flag rank.

The Captain's mannerisms seemed to change as he suddenly stood up from the periscope. The two destroyers steamed at the edge of a convoy in one second. Then, in the next second, with no indication of discovery, the two ships belched dark brown smoke from their stacks, lunged ahead, and turned directly toward the Captain's eyes.

"Somehow, the Americans know where we are, DIVE, DIVE, take us to a hundred meters, turn right five degrees to three-five-five degrees. Then, run for a hundred meters, and come left to three-one-zero degrees. All quiet throughout the boat; seal all watertight doors."

Those men involved repeated the orders for clarity and began carrying them out. The boat glided silently through the black sea at almost nine knots as it headed deeper into the abyss. As they reached three-hundred-thirty feet, the B1 turned left as depth charges burst over and behind her. Then the wall of millions of bursting bubbles shrouded the boat's turn, and she disappeared from the American's sound equipment.

****

"Bridge, sound, sorry sir; we lost him in the mass of bubbles."

"Bridge, aye," the talker told the OOD.

"Very well."

The destroyers searched for an hour, then returned to their patrol. Captain Cummins prepared his contact report for Cactus. Then he ordered the modified condition one while they could. It wouldn't be long, and he expected the daily air raid from the north.

Captain Cummins stepped into his tiny cabin and washed his face in the equally small sink. A quick sponge bath and shave felt like a million dollars to the tired, hungry officer. He called the galley, and the Steward said he would be up in five minutes. True to his word, Stewards Mate First Class Archie Washington knocked on the door to the sea cabin. Suspecting the knock came from a laden man, the Captain hurried to the door and relieved Washington from part of his load. After a few words, the Captain thanked the man he held in respect and turned to enjoy one of the perks of being the commander.

While he ate, the Skipper's mind ran through part of the responsibilities he carried. He recalled seeing and hearing the tone of the crew; although remaining sharp and seemingly alert, their dark eyes told him the men were weary and needed a shot in the arm.

After returning to the bridge, Captain had the OOD call the Supply Officer to the bridge. "Mike, do we have any steaks aboard?"

"Yes, sir, I was saving them for a holiday."

"The men are showing signs of fatigue, and I thought a good meal would help bring them around. What do you think of a steak dinner with full trimmings?'

"Let me see what our storage spaces hold; I'll get back to you as soon as I can put something together."

“Sounds good enough for me; you always put together a great meal.”

“Thank you, Captain; I appreciate your approval.”

A messenger from radio approached the Captain, “For you, sir.”

Thanking the Seaman, the Captain opened the message and initialed his acknowledgment.

Nightmare, Mirage

Request we set up bushwack as discussed.

AB sends

Captain Cummings reread the message out of habit. *‘So, the young Captain wants to ambush the bad guys,’* reasoned the Captain.

As the SOPA, Captain Cummings’ responsibilities extended to the *RICE* and the *DEFOE.* As a result, the Skipper’s mind began filtering through the issues the two destroyers faced.

“This might work; I haven’t heard of such activity since we entered the theater.” He mumbled to himself. The Captain looked over the map showing the area from Pavuvu to the Florida islands.

If we set up the ambush and have good weather, the radar should pick up the Express at least twenty-five miles to the northwest. We would have surprised and concentrated torpedoes and guns to stop them. On the other hand, if we patrol, we would still spot them, assuming the radar is working, or we could pass one another in the night.

If we are out of position, or the enemy is off the shoreline as they have been in the past, we might miss them in the clutter of island return.

With the pro and con issue like this, I have to say the ambush is the way to go.

The other side of the equation considered history, and that says the Japanese routinely steam along the interior edge of the islands as far as Vangunu, then dash for Guadalcanal’s northwestern shorelines.

The SOPA had to make a decision. He supported the idea in the earlier discussion on the ambush. *'Well,'* he thought, *'The worst I could face is a court-martial.'* Then he added, *'and time in Leavenworth.'*

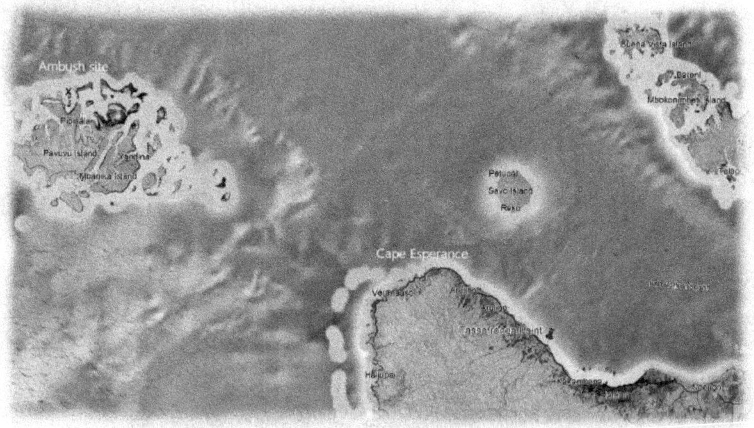

AREA OF OPERATION

"Messenger, send this answer to Mirage."

Mirage, Nightmare

We will set up after dusk ASW.

DC sends.

"Aye, sir," Then he was gone.

"OOD, call for the XO, Gunnery, and Navigator with his map of Pavuvu to the bridge."

"Aye, Captain"

When the key players arrived, Captain Cumming laid out his plan for the night operation. "What do you think? Be specific, gentlemen."

After several minutes of discussion, the XO said, "We're in agreement; this is one of the best natural ambush sites we have seen."

Captain Cummings asked the Navigator, "Do you have any information regarding the depth of the water between the islands and its contour?"

"I'm unaware of any specific information. After we talked, I had a copy of Captain Hanson's report sent to me, and he determined the water depth between the islands we're looking to exceed two-hundred-fifty feet. Neither ship in that operation had problems staying centered. The contour of these islands is a rapid drop-off a short distance from the water's edge. Remember, volcanic action made these islands centuries ago."

"Then you believe we have a better than fifty-fifty chance of clearing the bottom in the center?"

"With no problem, sir."

"You're a good Navigator, Tom; I trust your opinion."

"One last item, I suggest dropping the anchor in there. We have no data on wind or water currents."

"I'll put it in the mix, Tom. Take this down. Mirage, take point AS 1 between Marulaon and the center islet. We will take AS 2 between Hanawisi and the center islet. Put the information we had and your recommendation from our discussion into a message and send it to Mirage immediately."

"Aye, Captain."

"OOD, have radio establish a connection with Mirage on an unused TBS frequency and work out a voice connection between us using low power.

"Aye, sir."

The Supply Officer, Lieutenant David Whistler, requested to see the Captain. "What do you have, Dave?"

"Dinner will consist of Steak, mashed spuds with gravy, green beans, and corn. Desert is an Upside-Down cake."

"Good job, Dave. See if you can figure out a way to compensate the galley cooks, Stewards, and mess cooks with some extra time off when we get in port; they deserve it."

"Thank you, Captain," The Supply Officer left with a smile on his face. The food preparation gang will be busy but happy with their extra time off."

"Bridge, radar, we're holding a large return from aircraft bearing two-nine-eight degrees, course one-one-eight degrees, distance three-zero miles, speed one-niner-five miles an hour.

Estimate overhead in nine minutes. Same information for Cactus, except estimate time overhead Cactus thirty-three minutes."

"Bridge, aye," the talker passed on the information to the OOD, and the Captain listened intently.

The OOD turned toward the Captain, who said, Have radio post a warning report on a flash message to Cactus; everyone else will get it too, saving time, and send it in the clear."

"Aye, sir."

"Bo'sun, sound General Quarters, repel aircraft from two-niner-eight," the Captain ordered.

The alarm sent the crew scurrying to their combat stations. A minute and a half later, the ship was locked down, all guns locked and loaded.

"Standby to engage enemy aircraft at two-eight-niner degrees. We have reports of Vals, Bettys, B5Ns, Zeros, and Ki-43s."

The weapons turned to the incoming attackers, the spotters straining to provide any information on overt movements which could endanger the ship. The main battery opened fire, bursting blossoms of death above and below the attackers. Then as they passed overhead, the gunner got the range, but it seemed as if nothing touched the enemy aircraft. The pilots ignored the destroyer's efforts, continuing to fly toward Cactus.

An hour later, the aircraft made their return flight; however, they were further south and out of the range for the five-inch battery.

IJN FUBUKI CLASS DESTROYER

CHAPTER TWENTY-FOUR

The remainder of the day stayed on the quiet side, with the crew almost feeling like it could be a holiday. Then, finally, the evening began closing in, along with the dusk ASW evolution. The sound suite confirmed no submarines within the listening range. The crew settled into the night watches, with everyone on deck looking for details indicating a ship on the surface.

Upon arriving, the two destroyers turned their bows toward Pavuvu, entered the two small bays, and turned around to face the mouth and the Slot. Their communications were re-established, and the crew settled for the wait ahead.

The anchors dropped and surprisingly used only seventy-five feet of chain to reach the bottom. The bridge took the time to have the Bo'sun announce softly, "The smoking lamp is out on all weather decks; now darken ship, extinguish all lights on deck."

"This is the Captain," the Skipper's voice came over the 1MC. "If a Tokyo Express tries to make a run tonight, all indications are they will pass in front of us to get to Guadalcanal. We will launch a torpedo spread, then follow it up with a five-inch barrage. Listen carefully to the 1MC to give instructions on when to open fire. The main battery targets the bridge, enemy gun mounts, and engineering. Secondary fire from the forty and twenty-millimeter cannons will target the decks in anti-personnel attacks. Other than gun crews, all unnecessary personnel must stand clear of weather decks and take cover within the ship.

The Operations Center had the critical task of 'seeing' with the ship's radar and listening for submarines on and below the surface. The engineers kept the plant in full operation and the main engine on the jacking gear.

The New Georgia Sound, unofficially known as 'The Slot,' seemed eerily quiet, with two-foot calm swells slowly rolling across the black waters.

The clocks throughout the destroyer showed twenty-two-thirty-five when the radar operator alerted to a spike on the scope. The additional activities revealed themselves, and the operator alerted the duty Operations Officer.

"Pass the information to the bridge."

"Aye, sir."

"Bridge, radar, surface contact bearing three-zero-three degrees, course one-zero-three degrees, speed eighteen knots, four destroyer size vessels followed closely by smaller returns, indicative of towed barges. One larger return in trail position, possible cruiser size, distance seventeen miles."

"Bridge, Aye."

The talker read the report he wrote on a tablet to ensure accuracy to the OOD.

The deck officer turned to the Captain, who said, "I have the conn. OOD, confirm Mirage has the contact. Talker, tell Main Control to secure the jacking gear and spin engines as needed. Light off the superheaters and prepare for all bells. Weigh and secure the anchor. Then, to Gunnery, standby for surface action to port, and standby for torpedo attack to port."

The Machinist's Mates secured the motor and disengaged the jacking gear in the engine rooms. The Petty Officer waved at the throttleman, who removed the chain from the throttle valves while the top watch and messenger cracked open the drains. The throttleman cracked open guarding valve, allowing what little condensate might be there to travel to the drains with steam. After a few minutes of ear-splitting roaring drains, they were closed, sending the hot steam and any further condensate to the high-pressure drains. Everyone's ears suffered for a few minutes after the sailors closed the drain valves. Finally, the throttleman could spin the main engines to keep the turbines from warping.

Captain Cummings called out, "OOD, turn us to starboard enough to unmask our after tubes, then when ready, fire a five torpedo spread, target the lead destroyer."

"Aye, sir."

The orders went out, and the bow of the can began to turn to the right. Five consecutive coughs emanated from behind the after stack less than a minute later. The bridge crew watched as the five torpedoes leaped into the water almost next to the bridge at two-second intervals, their counter-rotating propellers already screaming. Four miles off the port bow, the Express destroyers steamed southeasterly, oblivious to the incoming death and destruction.

The five fish traveled at thirty MPH, the slower of two speeds available on the weapons due to the enemy's distance. The talker said to the OOD, "Sir, sound reports multiple torpedoes launched by Mirage." Captain Cummings acknowledged the report.

The torpedoes from both American ships would take seven minutes and almost fifty-four seconds to make the journey. When the travel time expired, no detonations occurred.

"We missed," the disappointed Captain on the *RYAN* mumbled.

Captain Cummings cautioned the crew to wait and have faith while he, too, suspected all the torpedoes had missed. Then, the Captain pulled the TBS handset and called their running mate, "Mirage, take the after two cans and barges; we will do the same with the first two; good luck and straight shooting."

"Copy, you too," came back the reply.

The waters in front of the American destroyers reflected the flare of a torpedo exploding at the stern of the lead destroyer. The blast of four-hundred-ninety-four pounds of TNT destroyed the rudder and both screws of the Mutsuki class destroyer and shredded the hull fifteen feet forward of the impact point.

Torpedo explosion number one signaled the commencement of the surface-to-surface gunfire from the American destroyers. The ship shook with the rapid fire of fifteen rounds at the enemy ships. Each five-inch shell took just over eight and a half seconds to reach the enemy destroyers.

With its propulsion capabilities destroyed, the lead IJN destroyer began to drift. Erratic, rapidly changing movements of the unguided vessel resulted in those shells being fired to land harmlessly into the sea.

The Captain ordered another volley with corrected figures, this time with good results. First, two shells started fierce fires in two torpedo-loaded launchers. Then, in the forward fire room, a five-inch shell detonated inside the firebox of a boiler, killing the engineers and shrapnel severing the keel. Fuel oil spewing from ruptured fuel lines fed the growing conflagration until the after half of the destroyer was fully engulfed.

Two torpedoes in each nest struck by American naval shells reached the spontaneous ignition point and exploded in a cataclysmic eruption never seen in the Sound since the volcanic age. The thousand-eighty-one pounds of explosives sheared the dying vessel into three sections, each quickly succumbing to the sea, and the remnants of the stern pulled the still tethered barge with it to the crushing bottom of The Slot. Those sailors who managed to get off the doomed warship made it for anything that floated.

In confusion, one Japanese destroyer succeeded in making good its escape, still towing a barge filled with soldiers. The IJN ship joined up with a light cruiser, which under orders, did not join the melee. The two American cans called to the occupants of the barges to abandon them, then finished each off by shell fire.

As the destroyers approached a large number of soldiers and sailors in the water, the Japanese rebuffed the rescue attempt. One officer shot a young soldier as he reached for a rescue rope. The Japanese took the object lesson to heart, and no other swimmer looked to a rescue.

Captain Cummings ordered the OOD to enter the officer's actions and their results into the log. Then the Captain ordered a half dozen life rings tossed overboard in a humanitarian gesture. Finally, the two patrolling destroyers turned away to the southeast, with many who witnessed the barbaric behavior of the officer vowing never to forget it.

The radio messenger appeared again with another message for the Captain.

To: Nightmare , Mirage

Fr: Cactus 2

Re: Orders

You will anchor Purvis upon relief, and a
battle damage team will assess the ship's damage.
Good work.

Cactus 2 sends.

Captain Cummins handed the OOD the message and said, "Make sure the XO is aware of this; he will have plenty of work ahead of him."

"Right away, sir. Messenger."

The young messenger appeared from the after part of the bridge, "Sir?"

"Take this to the XO in Ops, then after he reviews it, return the message here for filing."

"Yes, sir."

The Captain picked up the TBS handset, "Mirage, Nightmare."

"Mirage here."

"Did you receive the order reference tomorrow?"

"Received and filed."

"Very well, best news since we got out here."

"Roger that, Mirage, out."

"Bo'sun, the 1MC, please."

"This is the Captain. It's time to change our persona from pirates of the open sea to sailors of the United States Navy since we fly the flag and sail an American ship. Tomorrow brings our relief, and we will head for Tulagi when the reliefs take over. Captain out."

Following the Tokyo Express Patrol turnover, the *DEFOE* and *RICE* turned their bows toward Tulagi. In Purvis Bay, the two destroyers tied up to mooring posts under the protective cover of large trees. The natural covering provided the best camouflage against discovery by enemy aircraft.

The almost daily air raids from Japanese air bases in the northern Solomon Islands continued. Dogfights increased ferociously, with the nimble Zekes and Zeros having more performance than the stubby Wildcats and P-39s. Only the ruggedness and protection of the American planes and freedom of initiative and pilot training helped keep the American fighters near par. Meanwhile, the repeated attempts to resupply the enemy troops on Guadalcanal showed an increase in frequency, with dangerous success.

The first order of business, so far as the crew thought, was mail from home. As usual, Toby received a mittful of letters, and the sailor began opening the earliest post-dated letters first.

Gladly, Toby read that Amanda and their baby were doing good, with the baby now a bump for mom. According to Amanda, Grandpa expressed great joy at the prospect of a new family member and acting more like an expectant father.

Amanda mentioned her grandpa received a letter from the King, and His Majesty asked how we were doing and if you were keeping your head down.

In other good news, the family had located a five-hundred-acre farm with a 1940 two-story farmhouse with five bedrooms, a barn, and three additional outbuildings suitable for chickens and other fowl. In addition, the property included farm equipment, some old but in good condition, and a three-acre pond. The bank dragged its feet on the proposal until Grandpa and Amanda added their savings to the pot, which won the day. However, Grandpa insisted on fully evaluating the credibility of the land and buildings before the Greenes signed any papers.

Amanda wrote, 'Dad and Grandpa have hired experts Dad knows from work contacts, and they will travel to Iowa for the investigation. I will keep you appraised of anything I hear.'

Toby reread the letter and thought, *'I guess we will be going into farming.'*

As Mike Day walked toward the compartment, he noticed the deck crews acted as if they were preparing for sea. The word spread fast, and Mike Day sent a messenger to round up the engineers and had them muster in their spaces.

Day addressed the men, "I received word that we're preparing to get underway; our buddies on the *RICE* are doing the same, and we will get underway after dark. We're joining the escort screen for a carrier task force. That's all I know, so check every piece of machinery twice, and begin getting this plant ready to answer all bells. But I suspect we'll pull three types of duty, ASW screening, plane guard for the 'bird farm,' and carrier air defense."

Dave Dymond asked; I know about the ASW and Air defense, but I'm in the dark on this 'plane guard.'

"On plane guard duty, we sail about five-to-seven hundred yards behind the carrier; our job is to rescue any pilots or crewmen who can't land on the carrier and have to ditch their aircraft that might have battle damage, running out of fuel, hung ordinance, or a fouled deck from a wreck or other problem. You will have to prepare for a series of bells during the maneuver. No matter what, everyone must be on their toes; usually, lives will depend on it."

Fireman Nester turned to Toby, "A carrier? When Tojo hears there is a carrier in the area, he will have every plane he can get out to destroy her. That means you're going to be a busy man. Remember to play turtle, keep your head tucked in, and watch everything like a hoot owl. We don't want anything happening to our star Petty Officer."

Laughing, Toby said, "I'll take your advice on that; it can get pretty dicey up there at times."

Nester, on the throttles, cut in, "The *RICE* has cast off and is moving into the bay, and we have singled up our lines. So, you better get ready to disengage the jacking gear." Then he removed the safety chain from the guarding valve and throttles while men cracked open the drains on the engine.

Day and Toby quickly moved to the end of the reduction gears, and when Nester waved, Mike Day turned off the jacking gear motor. Then Toby disengaged the jacking gear. Day waved back to Nester, who began the spinning process.

Once the engine warmed up, Messenger Daniels secured the drains, stopping the banshee scream filling the engine room. The EOT (Engine Order Telegraph) rang at the throttles, and the Bo' sun on the bridge called out over the 1MC, "Shift colors." The *DEFOE* and their partner, the *RICE,* were once again headed into harm's way.

As the ships exited the east end of the Nggela Channel, they passed into the Indispensable Strait, where they turned southeast on course one-two-two and boosted their speed to twenty knots for the next hundred-sixty-five miles. Their first stop would be the oiler east of San Cristobal Island.

"This is the Captain," boomed over the 1MC. "We received orders to refuel and replenish our supplies, then join a carrier task force. Each of you knows your job and has performed admirably. Every man jack has helped set standards that are the envy of the fleet, and I have no doubt you will strive to better those standards. So, let's leave them with a positive impression that you are the true professionals I know that you are. Captain out."

Main Control called on the intercom, "Engage the cruising turbine."

Harold Mac Arthur said in the after-engine room, "Now that's one of the best, 'Go git'em speeches I've ever heard."

Day added, "The Captain is proud of this crew, and he is right; I've been around and served with four crews, none of which have come together as this one has. Captain Cummings is the best Skipper I've ever served under."

"I agree," claimed MacArthur, but I've only seen him face-to-face during inspections. And he has always seemed professional and good-natured."

Toby retained a low profile. He'd had more and longer contact with the Captain face-to-face than all the men in the engine room combined, and he agreed with Day's assessment.

The watch wore on with the plant smoothly operating in a boring manner. Top Watch, Petty Officer Greene, had the watchstanders review the previous forty-eight hours of operation logs showing the last readings, then compare them with the current records to highlight any abnormalities. The readings confirmed the manufacturer's expertise in design and operations.

Toby said, "Mike, I'm going to have a look around. Would you watch things up here for a few minutes?"

"You bet." The POIC (Petty Officer in Charge) of the space answered.

Toby stopped by and chatted with Steward Ryan about the pumps and their impending task, then headed for the upper level when a loud clang from the lower level and a jar knocked him off his feet.

The sailor dropped back to the lower level deck plates to check on Ryan, then said, "Stew, check the hull for any bulges and bilges for any flooding,"

"What was that? It sounded like it came from the port side."

"Unknown, but it sounded like it came from outside; check everything down here," then headed for the throttle board. Everyone there was on their feet, looking around. Then, finally, he yelled to Mike Day, "I'll check the port hull."

Day clicked the IC to Main Control. "Main Control, after-engine room, we had a loud clang with that jar, we are checking everything, and the plant is running normally."

"We heard and felt it too; the Chief Engineer is on his way."

"Copy that."

Toby yelled up toward Fireman Oran Douglas, who watched Toby and acted as an information relay for the growing collection of men near the throttle. "I found it, or rather a huge bulge in the hull at the lower level."

Douglas called for Day, and the Petty Officer was at his side in three steps, then he dropped alongside Toby. "The bulge looks like it could be twenty-five inches across and indented the hull several inches," Toby noted.

Day and Toby looked at one another and said together, "Torpedo." Then the color drained from Toby's face, making him look chalk white.

"Are you going to be all right, Toby?"

After a few seconds, the tough sailor said, "Yeah, I don't do well with torpedoes."

"I understand that; head up to the throttle board; the Chief Engineer is there, and fill him in on what you found."

Toby climbed up to the upper level, thinking, *'I know the power in those torpedoes, and this one was only feet away. I must have a guardian angel nearby because I wouldn't be here if that thing weren't a dud."*

The Chief Engineer turned to Toby, noting his strained features, and asked the same question Day asked.

"I'm fine, sir. I just don't like torpedoes."

"I know; tell me all you learned."

Toby described his find, and the Lieutenant agreed the torpedo had to have malfunctioned. Then he turned to the throttle man, "Tell Main Control we have been hit by an apparent dud torpedo and have them notify the bridge."

Seconds later, the general alarm sounded for ASW General Quarters. On the bridge, the Captain ordered a turn, notified the command vessel that they had a bulge from the fish with no leaks, and requested to begin pinging for the sub.

The Convoy Commander ordered a change in their zigzag track and dispatched the *DEFOE* and *RICE* to prosecute the submarine.

The two destroyers set up a search pattern and began actively searching for the submarine with their sonar pings.

The Executive Officer, Repair Division Officer, and First Class Shipfitter examined the damage. With no leakage, the Chief Engineer recommended the engine room crew keep an eye on it and report any leakage or other unforeseen problems.

As the repair inspectors left, the XO remained behind, "Petty Officer Greene, may I ask a question?"

"Certainly, sir."

"I know you survived a torpedoed ship, and I believe you are the only man aboard who has. Can you compare the damage from your former ship to the damage to ours?"

Toby thought for a moment, "Sir, our damage is minimal, which will become evident in a moment. The *Manning* was a Gleaves class destroyer that took a torpedo into the forward fire room. The structure at that point was much stronger than here in the after-engine room. In addition, the weight and supporting structure for the stacks above the main deck make the area capable of withstanding greater damage than below decks.

The torpedo's detonation released sufficient energy to blow the ship in two, with the starboard stringers holding tight. The forward motion of the *MANNING* forced water pressure to fold the forward end back along the starboard side of the stern, where I saw it.

If the torpedo that hit us exploded, there would be no survivors here, as on the *MANNING,* and I have no question the energy would completely sever this ship in half. Those Japanese torpedoes are ship killers; of that, I have no doubt."

"Thank you, Petty Officer Greene, you have helped me prepare my report for the Captain."

Mike Day, standing nearby the conversation, asked Toby, "Are you feeling better discussing the loss of the *MANNING*?"

"Come to think about it, yes, it's easier now; I guess time helps to heal the open wounds, as they say."

"That's a good sign you're coming to peace with it. Actually, it's a milestone, and if you ever want to talk, I'm always available."

"You aren't a shrink, are you? You sound like one, or are you speaking from experience?"

"Shrink? No, through it, yes. However, I did see a psychologist after my ship went down in the Atlantic."

"Were you Navy then?"

"No, Merchant Marine. I signed onto a freighter, and a U-boat got us within spitting distance of Liverpool."

"I remember something about that; I was aboard the *AMPTHILL* in Devon when that happened."

"That's right; you were in the RN. What do you think of the English ships?"

"The RN is among the oldest and largest Navies in the world. They have more experience in developing and building ships than anyone else. However, they are a bit backward in a couple of areas. When the Lend-Lease ships arrived for conversion, the first thing they did was gut the berthing of the enlisted men to switch from bunks to hammocks. Then they added an open bridge."

"How about the American ships in comparison?" Day pushed.

"The berthing's a lot better; hammocks make your back sore. The UK vessels provide a pint of ale after work," Toby explained.

"How did you like that?"

"I don't drink alcohol and gave mine to my buddies; it's a fast way to make friends."

"Wasn't the AMPTHILL an old four-piper?"

"Yes, she was old but fast; we had no trouble turning thirty-eight knots. But it rolled like a bowl, and both engines turned in the same direction, making for a dicey approach and maintaining the proper distance between the ships during refueling and underway resupply."

"I'll bet."

"Tell me, why did you stay in the Navy? You could be home with your family from what you have said and what I've seen?"

"That's a bit more difficult. I'm not so sure about the why, but regrets? I have none; I'm where I'm supposed to be. My duty is here; my exact job is two-fold, one I know and one I may learn about later. I know it may sound crazy, but there are other forces at work here."

"How do you know that? Are you clairvoyant?" Mike asked.

Toby thought for a moment, "A voice, and it was much stronger and clearer than I've ever heard. No hesitation or stumbling, unexplainably exact in its message and meaning. It was like a dream; then again, it wasn't. But the voice said, "I am He, I want you to go back, I have bidding of you," then, it was gone."

"You're sure the voice said, 'I am He?"

"Without a doubt."

Mike asked, "You are a Christian, aren't you?"

"Yes, I believe."

"Pay attention to the voice and do exactly what you are asked or told to do. Are you familiar with the words "I am?"

"I've heard them before, but right now, I couldn't tell you."

"Take a moment to review Moses' encounter with God on the mountain; you will find the answer there. Of course, we share more than working together, but that's another story. I'm glad to have you on our team, you're an important part of it, and we'll talk later."

It took better than an hour for the two cans to regain their positions in the convoy. Finally, Captain Cummings reported to the convoy commander, "Nightmare and Mirage are finishing up with their loss of the sub's trail.

The run-in with the sub convinced the convoy commander to initiate unscheduled and on-the-spot alterations to the zigzag timing and angles. As a result, the further south they steamed, the less likely encounters with enemy subs should occur. The unexpected move is the result of experienced seamanship. Fortunately, the convoy commander and every escort Captain refused to adhere to conventional wisdom willingly, so they wisely continued the unscheduled maneuvers.

Twenty-six miles from Moselle Bay, the Captain of an RO boat seven miles off the convoy track shot a pair of torpedoes into their midst. The sound suite of the *DEFOE* picked up the high-pitched whine of their counter-rotating screws well over an unheard-of distance of three miles.

"Bridge, sound, two propellers from high-speed torpedoes bearing two-five-eight, course zero-eight-two, speed four-five knots."

Captain Cumming grabbed the TBS and urgently called, "Torpedoes in the water from two-five-eight, recommend all ships emergency turn to two-five-five degrees."

The convoy commander responded, "All ships turn to two-five-five degrees now," then he selected three destroyers, one British and two Australian, to find and sink the submarine.

The remaining escorts kept the convoy together and guided them into Moselle bay.

USS DEFOE (DD-535)

CHAPTER TWENTY-FIVE

As the convoy approached Noumea, boats met them about five miles from the entrance to Moselle Bay for those ships destined to enter for commerce or military purposes. First, the two destroyers moored to the tender to evaluate the damage caused by the torpedo. Then, following the inspection and Shipfitter recommendations, the *DEFOE* would enter a floating drydock, where Shipfitters would cut out the indented plate and weld in a new sheet of Special Treated Steel in its place.

The dry docking allowed the engine room personnel to inspect the underwater valves, inlets, and stern zincs. In addition, the rudder, propeller shaft struts, and screws would receive a checking over.

When the tender and *DEFOE's* Shipfitters completed repairs and the new protective coating and paints dried, the destroyer re-entered the water, and a tug pulled her to a buoy. The following three days flew by with the crew replenishing the supplies. The final two days in the friendly port had been reserved for liberty and standing down. The engineering plant was lit off and checked over closely for any deviation from previous operational norms.

The time came, and the vessels steamed out of a paradise for the insect-ridden hellhole called Guadalcanal. *DEFOE* and *RICE* departed with other destroyers to sweep the area five miles around the entrance to Moselle bay. In addition, two French destroyers patrolled and searched from five to ten miles around the mouth of the bay for submarines. Once the area had been declared safe, the convoy of eight ships departed for Vanuatu to join a larger convoy bound for Guadalcanal.

Older cargo ships plodded along at twelve knots, giving the sound suites on the destroyers a chance to search for enemy submarines. The attack on the convoy before entering Noumea remained fresh in their minds, making everyone serious sub-hunters.

Two days later, at Vanuatu, the convoy vessels anchored as directed. Destroyers and cruisers acted as the aircraft defenses for their flock. The Big Bay at Vanuatu could contain two hundred ships if need be. The current number was well below that, but it still appeared congested.

A day and a half later, the larger convoy and escorts departed for the Solomon Islands. Two days later, the convoy pulled into Assembly areas Yoke and X-Ray and dropped anchors by zero-seven-hundred; unloading began immediately.

An hour later, Cactus alerted the convoy ships that an attack would materialize in an hour. Those vessels not unloading weighed anchors and headed for Lengo Channel and safety east of San Christobal. Those unloading secured their gear and followed the earlier cargo carriers to safe waters. Half a dozen destroyers steamed around Iron Bottom Sound, waiting to engage the aircraft.

Wildcat fighters from Henderson CAF group jumped the escorting Zeros and Ki-forty-three escorts while the P-39 and P-400s tore into the Bettys and Vals going after the destroyers.

Toby's spotter, Seaman Roy Ackerman, pointed to the starboard after quarter. "Look, a Val," the white navy dive bomber with bright red 'meatballs' on the top and bottom of both wings dove in a spiral toward the water.

"The pilot must have bailed out or dead," the young sailor guessed. "Look at that; the gunner is still blasting away at the fighter that's after him. What's he got for guns? He asked Toby.

"Gun, his has a single seven-point-seven machine gun."

"I heard about them in boot camp, but they didn't sound familiar."

The older sailor smiled, "Roy, have you ever heard of the Lee-Enfield rifle?"

"Yeah, another foreign gun I heard about but never paid that much attention to them; the best gun is the big fifty caliber 'Ma Duce."

"I always say what you use is not as important as knowing how to control its accuracy. You can have the biggest gun, but what good is it if you can't hit anything?

The Lee-Enfield is a British rifle developed in 1895 and is the main army weapon of the UK and many other nation's soldiers. The round is a .303 in the thirty-caliber family. The Japanese were Allies in World War I, and the British gave them many weapons chambered for the .303, including machine guns and a license to build them. However, after the permit met its demise, the Japanese signed the Tripartite Pact with Germany and Italy, becoming the Axis Powers. Nevertheless, Japan continued manufacturing the seven-point-seven ammunition family and weapons.

Despite its few drawbacks, the twenty-millimeter cannon is more powerful, has a greater range, and is harder hitting with explosive shells, armor-piercing rounds, and high-explosive-incendiary projectiles than the fifty caliber."

"Wow, I didn't know that." The youngster replied.

Following daily air raids, Nightmare and Mirage received orders to continue their escort duties and join a quartet of cargo ships bound for Noumea. The trip turned out to be the proverbial milk run, with no contacts and quiet. Nobody complained. Two days later, the four freighters turned north toward Guadalcanal.

Toby and Mike Day sat drinking coffee and swapping stories in the after-engine room. "Mike, have you ever had the chance to visit any Australian cities?"

"Once, before the war. Most people are well-meaning, but as in all coastal cities, there are those who want to prove they are tougher than anyone else on the block. But, of course, alcohol didn't help the situation; it only removed what little common sense they had in the first place. However, I have to say, except for a few problem children, the population is good people."

"What do you think about visiting the sights in the cities the next time? We can probably get one or two other guys to join us."

"Sounds like a good plan; we'll need to pick up the film; I only have a roll of black and white," Mike said.

Toby looked at the main condenser vacuum, "We're getting closer to the Solomons; the seawater is warming up and increasing the pressure in the condenser."

Mike glanced at the large vacuum gauge, "Yeah, but it should settle at about twenty-eight-point-five inches."

At Assembly Area X-Ray, the freighters dropped anchor in pre-designated locations. There the deck and boat crew lowered two medium-sized, flat-bottom landing boats. Next, the ship's teams went to work swinging pallets full of beans and bullets into the boats for transport to the beach. The air was thick with a sense of urgency; everyone knew or suspected an air attack lurked nearby or was winging in their direction.

Wristwatches and clocks showed zero-nine-hundred, or close to it, and the general alarm went out to all commands, "Air raid, no drill.'

Toby strapped into the starboard twenty with the help of his loader. They checked the weapon, and then Toby jacked a fresh, greased round into the breech.

"Bridge, radio, Cactus 2 reports the enemy attack force split their force at the Russell Islands, a section turned into the Coral Sea, and south along Pavuvu and Guadalcanal. The other part, which looked like Nells or Betty bombers, took the north passage around Savo Island into Iron Bottom Sound; they used a zigzag flight pattern."

"Bridge, aye." The talker repeated the confusing report to the OOD and Captain.

The Captain said. "I'm not too fond of Tojo's flyboys changing their tactics. They probably did it because we were getting their range too quick for them and shooting down their aircraft: boats, 1MC. OOD, get this to Mirage. This is the Captain; we just received word that the enemy has split their attack force. Watch for the smaller aircraft coming over central Guadalcanal and the heavier bombers on the deck from the Florida or Tulagi areas. Captain out."

"Why would the Japanese high command send their heavier bomber in a roundabout maneuver like that?"

"I would say because the smaller planes have the lesser range, hence over the island. But, on the other hand, the larger bombers have a greater range, and with that track, they are already on the water for their torpedo attack."

"That makes good sense; you must give them a mark for ingenuity."

"I'm thinking," the Captain answered, "Let's make it a lead mark."

Each side of the ship watched the sky where it met the trees, and the water, where it met the shore for anything that moved.

Toby watched as the last seaplanes flew off the water from Tulagi and stayed low as they scooted to the east, out of fighter range. The sound of powerful aircraft engines growled as the CAF lifted from Henderson and climbed to a thousand feet. One flight of four aircraft circled to overfly Guadalcanal, looking for the incoming enemy from the south. They wanted to hit them before they reached the airfield. Another headed for Tulagi, doing the same as they hunted the twin-engine bombers.

Toby's spotter pointed toward due north, "On the water, four bombers inbound."

Toby yelled, "Call it into the bridge; use the proper format," Then he swung the big cannon toward the threat.

No sooner had the spotter made his report than all the five-inch guns began barking like excited dogs. The starboard quad forties quickly followed them. Toby tracked the aircraft with an experienced eye and steel determination to get them first. The forced draft blowers howled as they spooled up with a belch of the brown stack gas. Then the water behind the ship began boiling as the twelve-foot screws bit into the water, forcing a tall rooster tail to form. The stern squatted much like a race car in high acceleration.

Toby calmly placed the reticule on his sight over the cockpit of the lead bomber, then closed the trigger, sending a dozen shells toward the pilothouse. The heavy rounds bled off energy along the trajectory. When they reached the aircraft, twelve high explosive, armor-piercing, and incendiary shells crashed into the cockpit, turning the controls and three men into bloody trash. The dead bodies of the flight crew fell forward on the control wheels, sending the bomber into a short dive before the nose crumpled on contact with the sea.

The plane's speed forced the remains to cartwheel; the resulting centrifugal force detached the two torpedoes from their racks. Then each weapon skidded across the water, breaking up and sinking into the three thousand-foot depths.

The second bomber, another Betty, bored in, the pilot wanting to extract retribution for the death of his commander. The pilot, his mind screaming 'revenge,' put every ounce of concentration into aiming the torpedo beneath the gun tub responsible for the Lieutenant Commander's death. His mind and vision narrowed into tunnel vision at the American; he didn't hear his co-pilot screaming, nor feel the co-pilot attempt to pull the wheel back as the nose dropped to wave top altitude.

The American's hundred-twenty-seven-millimeter guns started firing into the water in front of the plane. The co-pilot stared at the aircraft commander, his eyes glued to his target, almost as if in a trance.

Two huge water columns shot up in front of the big bomber's engines, stalling them to silence. Then, with insufficient power, the plane pancaked at hundred-forty miles an hour. The impact ripped the thin aluminum from the bottom of the aircraft; then, the plane began coming apart. In a blink of an eye, the fat-looking plane disintegrated. A torpedo broke loose from its rack and jammed into the wreckage, dragging it to Iron Bottom Sound's bottom.

The raid began moving back to the northwest, with the Cactus Air Force and Japanese twisting and turning to gain an advantageous position.

Minutes after the sailor relaxed, Toby's fans crowded around him, yelling praises and congratulation on saving the ship. A can of red paint materialized with a brush, and the tub's scorecard picked up another miniature Japanese ensign, bringing cheers to the gunner as being the ship's unofficial 'Ace.'

By noon, orders arrived, directing Nightmare and Mirage to assume a defensive posture for Guadalcanal. Additionally, Cactus specified the two ships to patrol the entrance to the lower section of the New Georgia Sound from Cape Esperance to the northwestern cluster of the Florida Islands.

Captain Cummings and Bernstein had a quick meeting during which the subject of setting an ambush after dark on the northwest edge of Pavuvu Island reached another planning level. The commanders decided to sail under darkened ship's condition to the previously used ambush bays.

Once set up, each ship dropped an anchor to remain in the center of the bay, with the radar-tipped masts peeking over the islands' low hills. All main battery weapons held surface action high explosive rounds in the breeches. The main engines stood idle, the jacking gears engaged, and the boilers simmered like overgrown teapots. In all four main engineering spaces, mounts, and workspaces, the men sat around, swapping sea stories or other means to use the time wisely.

Fireman Nester was on the throttle watch in the after-engine room, which included the 2JV Engineering sound-powered phone circuit. The sailor answered a message on the phone circuit; after a few minutes of nonchalant moments, he asked the young messenger, Brad Norton, "Hey, Brad, have you ever seen a sea bat?"

"Sea bat?" Norton asked. "I've never heard of one; are they dangerous?"

Former enlisted Machinist's Mate, now the M-Division Officer, Ensign Simon Weiss, watched the interaction and smiled.

"Naw," Nester said, "But they hold the world's record for the most colorful South Pacific flying mammals."

"Really?" the now excited youngster asked.

"Yeah, I just heard they caught one, and it's in Main Control. So, if you want to see it, you better hurry and get up there because they have to release it soon," Nester urged.

The messenger turned to Mike Day, "Can I go up and see it?"

Petty Officer Day waved the youngster on his way, and Nester's voice followed him up the ladder, "You better hurry up."

Ensign Weiss chuckled, "You know he will never forget this experience."

Mike looked at the new officer, "How many kids did you send on the errands?"

"More than I can count, and none of them ever forgot it."

Mike responded, "I was thinking about a muffler bearing, but that kid is too sharp for that one."

"Yeah," Weiss added, "After this one, I doubt you could snag him on a bucket of vacuum."

"Probably not me, but I'd bet an officer could pull it off."

The Ensign laughed, "You trying to get me into trouble before my butter bars develop any green grass?"

The ship's service phone rang with its 'Oooga.'

"After engine room, Petty Officer Day, sir."

"He did? That would have been a sight. It's too bad you didn't have a camera on him. Thanks, see ya later." Mike sported a broad smile when he turned around, "Dan Seagram said the kid was the best candidate in years; he jumped two feet straight up when the broom made contact."

The response from the men indicated positive morale among the crew, the Ensign noted.

A rather sheepish Brad Norton quietly came down the ladder to his peer's clapping and good-natured ribbing.

"You guys got me good with that one; I'll say that. I'm not mad and can take a joke with the best of ya. But to be fair about it, things have a way of coming back." More laughter and joking filled the air.

Machinery hummed, and the low hiss of steam in movement only came from the turbine-powered pumps and the turbo-generator. Men found blowers to sit under or nearby, drawing warm, humid salt air into the space.

At nineteen-thirty, the twenty-to-twenty-four-hundred watch dropped into the space. As the sailors stepped onto the main deck, the off-going watch standers felt relief from the cooling night air.

The ships maintained a modified condition one, wartime setting, with the weapons half manned. The heat forced the resting sailors to sleep on the weather decks.

The watches throughout the ships changed again at twenty-three-thirty. A new day began at midnight.

"Bridge, radar, surface contact bearing three-zero-one degrees, course one-one-niner degrees, speed twenty knots, four destroyer size contacts with intermittent contacts between the vessels, suggesting barges. If they maintain their course, they will pass right in front of us."

"Bridge, aye," and the talker repeated the message to the OOD. Mr. Bellows turned to Captain Cummings, who nodded acknowledgment.

"Mr. Bellows, reset condition one, surface action at three-four-zero. Gunnery prepare for torpedo attack to port." The Captain pulled the handset of the TBS, "Mirage, Nightmare, surface contact three-four-zero, prepare for torpedo attack to port."

A whisper came from the earpiece; "We're ready to fire fish, then main battery at fish arrival."

"Copy that. You have the first shot, take the second can, and we'll target the first."

"Mirage copies."

"OOD," the Captain turned to Mr. Bellows, "Alert Engineering to standby for surface action and light off the superheaters.

When our sound hears Mirage's fish hit the water, disengage the jacking gear and spin as necessary. Weigh the anchor. When he comes into view, Gunnery may launch three torpedoes at the lead destroyer. Mr. Bellows began carrying out his orders like a maestro directing his orchestra. As Captain Cummings watched the OOD perform his duties, he thought, *'Mr. Bellows is ready for an XO's billet.'* He made a mental note to check on Bellows' other qualifications and, if he meets the requirements, to recommend him for the next XO candidate course.

Petty Officer Toby Greene strapped himself into the starboard stern twenty-millimeter cannon. His spotter and loader helped check the weapon and ammunition drum, then set up two replacement sixty-round drums on standby.

"Bridge, sound, torpedoes launched."

The bridge talker relayed the information to the OOD.

Mr. Bellows asked, "Did Gunnery receive it?"

Just then, three successive coughs from the forward torpedo tubes announced the launching of Nightmare's fish.

"Here we go," Mr. Bellows said, "Weigh anchor, secure Jacking gear, and standby to answer all bells."

A minute later, the talker called out, "Anchor in view, and Main Control says ready to answer all bells, and radar reports the first ship is coming into range. Fire Control reports they have the target locked and requests a five-degree turn to starboard to unmask the fifty-three mount."

The OOD called to the helm. "Helm, five degrees to starboard, five knots."

About four miles due north of Pavuvu island, a dull flash lit the bow of a Mutsuki class destroyer, and the blast from eight-hundred-twenty-five pounds of HBX ripped the ship's bow away and jammed the forward gun mount into a fixed position.

The three remaining Mutsuki's four-point-seven-inch Naval guns fired two rounds toward the *DEFOE.* Captain Cummings yelled, "ALL AHEAD, FLANK." Despite the commander's quick action, the distance between the ships was too short to matter. One round struck the after-torpedo tubes. Three of the Mk fifteen torpedoes flew overboard and sunk out of sight. Six men manning the tubes died outright. Shrapnel sprayed along the ship's exposed stern, wounding the gun crews in both the stern twenty millimeters mounts.

By then, the Fletcher sailed abeam the older Japanese destroyer. "Five rounds, all main battery, fire," called out the OOD. The ship shook from bow to stern from the broadsides sent toward the Mutsuki.

Rounds one thru three buried themselves into the forward bowels of the older destroyer, one into the forward magazine. Already breached by the torpedo explosion, casings lay split open, their powder strewn among live shells. Finally, a blinding blast beneath the forward gun mount threw the weapon and its crew overboard. One of the Japanese twenty-four-inch diameter Type 93 torpedoes in front of the bridge cooked off, cleaving the bridge away from the hull and killing all within the structure.

Two shells destroyed the forward fire room, bringing instant death to the engineers and breaking the ship's back. The remnants of the bow area quickly submerged beneath the calm waters, lifting the stern. The two remaining boilers continued to supply steam to the engines, turning the twin screws into buzz-saws when they cleared the water. With the lack of resistance on the propellers, the turbine RPMs spiked above their red line, and they disintegrated, destroying all the machinery and men in the engine rooms. The old destroyer dived into her gravesite, dragging the soldier-filled barge with her.

One of the three torpedoes fired by Mirage struck a barge towed by the second Mutsuki. A brief gun battle ensued, then the two remaining enemy destroyers broke away and turned northwest.

"Bridge, sound, torpedoes in the water from three-zero-one."

The rest was lost in the scramble to defend the Gleaves class ship. As the vessel turned away from the enemy, a three-ton ship-killer brushed the side of the *RICE,* not unlike the information-seeking brush of a shark against potential prey. The battle ended with a draw, yet declared a victory because the Americans turned back the Tokyo Express that night.

In the starboard stern twenty mount, the three men watched the battle progressing when a gigantic flash and thunderclap stunned the gunner and crew. Before they fell, holes appeared like magic in the splinter shielding tub. Because Toby manned the gun, he stood higher than the two other crewmen. Then, a quarter-sized chunk of metal blew into Toby's thigh, knocking him off his feet. But before he went down, smaller shrapnel ripped into his other leg, previously injured shoulder, and left forearm. The sailor catapulted from his straps, unconscious, to the deck.

PRESIDENT OF THE UNITED STATES

HIS MAJESTY KING GEORGE VI

CHAPTER TWENTY-SIX

A Corpsman made it to the stern twenty-millimeter gun tubs a minute after being summoned. The three men in the port tub had superficial wounds, and the Corpsman had other seamen apply direct pressure to the injuries until more help arrived. Then he rushed to the starboard. Looking at the splinter shield, he knew the wounds would be more severe. A quick check confirmed that the spotter and loader died in the attack. Next, he checked the gunner, lying in a heap alongside the splinter shield. He found his pulse and noted his breathing, though labored, was strong. Finally, the Corpsman found that the man suffered wounds to his back, legs, and left arm. He injected Toby with a quarter grain of morphine to relieve the agony gripping the man. Then he put an 'M' on his forehead to alert the Doctor about the medical injection.

After wrapping the sailor in very snug bandages, he supervised securing Toby into a wire-basket stretcher. Four men took the sailor to the wardroom for medical treatment while the Corpsman returned to addressing the other wounded men.

Lieutenant Jonathan Brewster, USN Medical Corps., had the wardroom ready for emergency surgeries. The medical team loaded Petty Officer Greene on the table, and the Doctor began treating his leg while a senior Corpsman worked on his forearm.

After an hour, Toby rested on the table as he began coming around. The Doctor administered pain medication, which allowed

Toby to become conscious without excessive pain.

"Petty Officer Greene, can you hear me?" the Doctor asked.

"I'm Doctor Brewster; you are on the *DEFOE;* do you remember what happened?"

Toby bearly heard the voice, and he struggled to wake up. Finally, after a few minutes, he opened his eyes, still groggy from the anesthetic.

"Can you hear me, Toby?"

In a shaky voice, the sailor almost mumbled, "I hear you; where am I?"

The conversation continued, with Toby coming around more with each passing minute. "I'm Doctor Brewster," the physician tested Toby's memory.

"Yes, you are; we met when you stopped by the engine room on a walkabout inspection."

The Doctor looked up at his Chief; "He's coming out of it now."

"Petty Officer Greene, you suffered a few wounds when an enemy shell hit the after torpedo tubes."

"I remember now, that was a whale of an explosion. How's my crew doing?"

"I'm sorry to tell you, but your friends didn't make it."

"God, I hate this war, all wars," Toby growled.

"And rightly so. May I call you Toby?"

"Sure."

"Toby, I had to do some work on you because of your injuries, and you will be transported back to the states for further treatment and, in all likelihood, medically discharged. Your body has absorbed all the injuries it can take, and it's time to go home. I understand you are married."

"Yes, sir."

"Family?"

"Our first baby is on the way."

"Good; I hope you will be home in time for the great addition."

"Doctor. Tell me what's going on; I can handle it."

"I've heard that about you. A quarter-sized piece of metal hit you in your knee joint. The damage, although not severe, required the use of stainless steel screws, and you lost some of your bone.

The end result may require additional surgery, and you will have a slight limp, which shouldn't incapacitate you, and it probably won't even be noticeable after full recovery. However, you can no longer meet the military's minimum standards, which will be permanent."

Toby lay quiet for a few moments, then said, "Sir, I can live with that. I'm tired of being shot at, blown up, and spending time in the hospital. Not that the latter was bad, just more than I wanted. I have a family back home, and we are planning to become farmers if this won't interfere."

"It shouldn't; farming's a tough life but probably one of the most rewarding. So where are you planning on breaking ground?"

"Iowa, sir."

"I've been there, it is a great state, and the people are the salt of the earth, and I think that is right down your ally."

"I'm glad to hear that our priority is to move to Des Moines or Ames and begin farming classes at Iowa State; my research shows it is the best farming college in the mid-west."

"I read an article in a medical journal that farming will become one of the world's most needed industries in the years to come. So let your wounds completely heal, and check into the Veterans Hospital in Des Moines; they can help guide you on the best path of farming.'

"Thank you, sir. And if you ever get to Des Moines, look us up."

"Since I'm single, you never know what might happen."

"Where will I go from here, Sir?"

"We are headed toward Tulagi, where you and the other wounded will go to the medical facility on the island. The medical folks there will provide treatment as needed. But they are mainly a triage center because of the volume of wounded from Guadalcanal. The Army Air Force is flying planeloads of men to the hospital ship in Noumea and Brisbane for necessary surgeries; after that, returning troop ships take the wounded back to the states. Your injuries are stable, so I expect you may go directly to a passenger ship to the states."

Toby didn't mention his last stay at the hospital ship because the dreams he occasionally has about Carol are unnerving enough.

Doctor Brewster brought the Captain up to speed on the injured men's condition. When he came to Petty Officer Greene and his disability, the Captain maintained an unreadable face, but Captain Cummings heart was saddened at the sailor's impending discharge. The Navy needed Greene and more people like him.

Doctor Brewster added, "Petty Officer Greene was lucky; he came within a hair of losing his leg, but he will have a new lease on mobility. He will, in all likelihood, have a minor limp. His other injuries should heal with no abnormal effect, but his military career is over."

The Captain said, "He is a remarkable young man. Did you know he served in the Royal Navy against the Germans and the Japanese? His actions and family ties got him knighted by King George of England, and he married Lady Amanda de Lacy, the granddaughter of Sir Brian de Lacy."

"I've heard that name but have no recollection of the man," Doctor Brewster said.

"Sir Brian de Lacy is the First Sea Lord of the RN."

With raised eyebrows, the Doctor replied, "Ohhhh."

The Captain added, "To top it off, the man is an 'Ace.'

"I thought he was a…," the confused Doctor checked his files, "A Machinist's Mate."

"He is, and he's one hell of a shot. Circumstances put him behind a twenty-millimeter cannon, and he shot down three Nazi aircraft and damaged another. One of those kills also saved a cargo ship and crew from a torpedo. If you ever saw him in his dress uniform, you'd see the English Conspicuous Gallantry Medal, Distinguished Service Medal, and Pacific Star Medal. The Purple Heart he will get for these wounds is his fourth award, and Greene is under consideration for the Silver Star."

"I had no idea." The stunned Doctor mumbled.

In one last item for the new Doctor, "Check the splinter shield at the stern starboard twenty mount; the crew painted Greenes' full combat record there."

"Captain, what do you know of his family?"

"Greene's wife is expecting a child, and now he might get there for that. His supervisor told me he has plans to become a farmer. Will his wounds stop that?"

"I doubt it, but he needs to give his injuries time to heal properly. He told me about his farming desires and said he and his wife planned to take college courses in agriculture. That will give him the time he needs to heal. Farming is hard work, but I wouldn't hesitate to bet on him becoming a successful farmer or in any endeavor."

"So would I, Doc, so would I."

Captain Cummings liked the young sailor, his courage, accomplishments, and loyalty. He decided to write his next of kin, telling them he was hurt but safe and coming home. At the end of the Doctor's report, the Captain called the Chief Engineer and gave him the news of losing Petty Officer Green. The Engineering Officers' feelings mirrored Captain Cummings'

Mike Day hung up the ship's service phone. He had a heavy heart as he told the messenger, "Go find everyone and have them meet here."

Fireman Norton saw the look on Day's face, and sensing a serious issue, he didn't say anything and left to notify the men.

Mike Day looked around and confirmed all the men assigned to the space were present, save one.

"If you haven't heard, the shell which took out the after torpedo tubes wounded MM2 Toby Greene. Toby will survive, but with his previous wounds, and those received today, they took their toll on Petty Officer Greene. So he will off-load at Tulagi with the other wounded men. Toby is going home to his wife and new baby, and the Doctor said he would lead a good normal life."

Day answered several questions from the crew; then, the men returned to their duties.

Three weeks later, the small battle in the Slot where Toby received his wounds only appeared in files that would become an obscure, minor encounter with the "Tokyo Express."

Half a world away, in a modest Des Moines, Iowa, framed home, the newly transplanted Greene family received a letter from Toby's Commanding Officer.

Amanda sat at the kitchen table, not wanting to open the letter she feared would someday darken their home. When Tom Greene came home from work, he held his daughter-in-law.

"Amanda, this letter is from Toby's Commanding Officer. If a death notice is issued, an officer or senior enlisted man and a clergyman make the notice in person.

Relieved, the tear-streaked woman opened the letter and quickly read through it, then tears returned. "Oh, Dad, Toby will be all right, but he was wounded again." The shaking woman read further, then said, "Oh, my. Toby is coming home for good. He suffered a wound that made him ineligible for military service."

Amanda had to stop to regain her composure at the bittersweet news. But, unfortunately, the Captain couldn't confirm which hospital would receive Toby.

Amanda took the time to answer Captain Cummings' letter. She thanked him for his kindness and for remembering Toby's family. The smiling woman ended her letter with an open invitation for the Captain to stop by if he got to the midwest and added their address.

Three days later, Amanda received an official letter notifying her that Toby would receive medical treatment at the US Navy's Balboa Hospital in San Diego, California.

Another letter arrived, containing information on contacting a coordinator for their reunion.

Thomas Greene sat with the bank president, who hired him in a vice president's position. The President had two sons in uniform and readily authorized Tom's leave.

Two days later, the Greenes leased a house in San Diego, not far from the hospital. Travel arrangements took another day, and the family flew to the city on the border. When they arrived, the house was short one bedroom. But, after a conversation between Natalie Longshaw, Grandpa's fiance, the issue quietly disappeared with nobody saying a word when Natalie moved in with the Admiral.

Toby arrived within two weeks and, following three physical and dexterity examinations, began an eight-week therapy schedule. The therapy required a two-month modified treatment to ensure he developed permanent dexterity in his left leg.

The family received an invitation to an awards ceremony for numerous sailors and Marines. Toby received orders to don his dress uniform. To his surprise, the uniform still fit perfectly.

Only one person sported English awards on their uniform, and his wife held his arm tightly with pride. Finally, the time came when Toby had to join other men to be recognized. Amanda felt him stand and leave her and almost jumped when another person sat next to her. However, she relaxed when her olfactory senses identified Nancy's light perfume.

The ceremony began with promotions and moved to civilian promotions. Then two men and three women received recognition for battle-related wounds and emergency action.

"Petty Officer Second Class Tobias Greene, front and center," Captain John Matthews ordered.

Toby stepped up, standing at attention; he didn't notice the movements at the podium.

"Ladies and gentlemen, we have a distinguished gentleman who will introduce the real Tobias Greene to you. Sir Brian de Lacy, Admiral, OG, DSO, CG, First Sea Lord of the United Kingdom, retired. Sir Brian," The First Sea Lord dressed in his full Admirals attire in honor of his unofficial adopted grandson.

"Thank you, Captain Matthews. Ladies and gentlemen, I'm honored to be with you today…."

Grandpa laid out Toby's career and accomplishments in fine detail, to the chagrin of the Petty Officer. However, his shyness and humbleness increased Amanda's love and respect for her husband.

When the Admiral finished, he called the Petty Officer to attention. Again changes occurred outside the gunner's view.

"Machinist's Mate Petty Officer Second Class Sir Tobias de Greene, Knight of the Relm, CG, DSO, Pacific Star, Attention to orders." *That voice, I've heard it before in England. Commander Michael Champs, the Captain of the AMPTHILL,'* Ran through Toby's brain. The sailor felt the first moisture of sweat on his forehead. Yet, again, the rustle of people changing places.

Then the unmistakable voice of Commander Dale Cummings, Captain of the *USS DEFOE DD-535*. Captain Cummings read the specifics of Toby's spotting the incoming G4M Betty torpedo planes and actions that saved the ship from a surprise torpedo attack. The Captain ended his verbal report, then stepped in front of Toby, wearing a genuine smile. "Will the Lady de Greene please step front and center?" Upon her arrival, the Commander said, "If you will, please pin this Silver Star on Petty Officer Greenes' left breast above those present."

Amanda's radiant beauty shined with her gracious smile and perfect white teeth, adding to the splendor of the event. Toby received another Purple Heart bronze star to add to the previous three.

The reception following the ceremonies was like an old home week. Amanda and Toby were at home with the Admiral and other naval officers. As to be expected, Toby fielded many questions asked about his exploits.

The afternoon finally ended when Amanda had to sit down in near exhaustion. She became the center of attention with the wives and officer's sweethearts not having known a genuine Lady until then.

The family took the next day off to pack and prepared for the Iowa flight. Toby received his medical discharge and orders to register with the VA hospital in Des Moines at his earliest convenience.

****

In late September, Brian Thomas Albert Greene came into the world as the latest in Norton's Greene ancestral line. His middle name, Albert, was given to him in honor of King George VI, who bears Albert as his name.

World War II raced toward new heights in viciousness and combat; with the Allies and Axis forces finding their opponents tough and resilient. At the same time, American and English ties drew together. King George traveled to Washington to consult President Roosevelt on the direction of the war effort.

When he arrived in Washington, he was stunned to learn of the young American's injuries and return to private life. Then he heard his knight lived in the midwest, where he and the Lady de Greene planned on farming. So the Monarch began planning a visit to mid-America, one of the few places he'd never visited.

As their meeting drew to a close, King George proposed a joint visit to spend a day with one of his favorite subjects if the President felt up to it. Always the gentleman, President Roosevelt brought his wife into the conversation. The King told the famous couple the story of Sir Tobias of America. The Roosevelts, particularly Eleanor, expressed excitement at such a visit, with Eleanor wanting to meet the First Sea Lord and his granddaughter.

The two statesmen elected to keep the short trip confidential, and four Secret Service Officers accompanied three of the most important people in the world on their flight to Des Moines. In addition, the head of the Presidential Protection Detail contacted the Des Moines Chief of Police, an old friend, for assistance in providing inconspicuous transportation for the high-level party. During the drive, King George described some of Toby's adventures and events to the President. The President and his wife looked forward to meeting these active and special people.

The secretive party of two vehicles pulled into the Greene's drive, and an aide to the King went to the front door and rang the doorbell.

In her rich English accent, a beautiful honey-blond woman answered the door and asked, "May I help you?"

At that time, the rear door of the second limousine opened, and a five-foot-nine-inch man in a decorated uniform exited the vehicle. On the opposite side, aides were busy preparing a wheelchair. When the uniformed man turned around, Amanda gasped, her jaw dropping in surprise, and her hand flew to her mouth. Then, she called back into the house, "Toby, come quick; the King is here."

That revelation started a scramble of people in an emergency effort to straighten up the living room. Even grandpa chipped in.

As the King approached, Amanda curtsied and said,

"Your Majesty, we're overwhelmed at your presence; please, excuse our humble home and lack of formal attire. We weren't expecting visitors."

"Please, don't trouble yourself, Lady Amanda. We were not that far away and took this opportunity to visit friends."

"Is your friend going to join us?"

"He will be right along; his aide is helping him now."

Amanda waited by the door while the King ran into his old friend, Sir Brian. Then, seeing a man's legs pushing a cart, Amanda opened the door to yet another breathtaking surprise.

"Oh my Lord, Mr. President, forgive me," Amanda held to door open while the President entered through the front door.

The Admiral, true to his training, snapped to attention at the sight of the American leader. King George quietly said, "Stand down, Sir Brian; this is not formal."

"My training still guides me, your Highness."

While the family gathered chairs for those present, Amanda guided the Monarch to Toby's easy chair. King George sat back, his face saying how good it felt. "Lady Amanda, where did you get such a chair?"

The conversation continued; Amanda gave the King a slip of paper with everything he needed to acquire a chair for his use.

Nancy asked, "I am going to prepare tea; how would you gentlemen prefer it, hot or cold?" All preferred hot tea.

The President remarked, "I wish to thank you, Mr. Greene, for your kind admission to your home. The King and I were discussing how much a relief it was to be able to sit back in a setting not governed by protocol and servants. We, too, are human, and there is no relaxation like this except in people's homes." Sir Brian and the King talked for a while, and the First Lady and Amanda hit it off on their first meeting. They traded addresses and promised to write to one another.

Nancy served the tea as the men asked, while Amanda disappeared for a couple of moments, then entered the room carrying a bundle.

She stepped up to the King, "Your Highness, I would like to introduce you to Brian Thomas Albert Greene."

The King's eyes brightened at the sight of the new baby. Then, surprisingly, he asked, "May I hold him?"

"Your Highness, we could have no greater honor," Amanda passed her son to King George VI, with Toby and the President watching over the event.

In the back, Nancy furiously snapped picture after picture with her thirty-five-millimeter camera. "You say his name is Albert?" the King inquired.

"Yes, your Highness. Brian for grandfather, Thomas in honor of Toby's father, and Albert in your honor." The proud mother explained.

"My dear Lady Amanda, you honor me." Only Amanda saw the glistening in the Monarch's eyes. "As do you, Sir Tobias. I saw your colors and sword and sash over your mantle, as it should be."

President Roosevelt added, "Petty Officer Greene, I want to thank you, on behalf of a grateful nation, for your dedication, duty, and sacrifice during your service. You have also made a positive impression on the people of our motherland. Thank you, sir," he finished as he held out his hand in friendship.

Toby stepped forward, took his hand, and said, "Mr. President, this has been a wonderful day for us; you, both of you gentlemen, will always have a special place in our hearts and prayers."

The day wore on, and the visitors indicated they had to depart for the real world. The family surrounded the two leaders, leaving the Secret Service in turmoil. Then they escorted the two to the door and onto the front walk.

After receiving approval from Toby, the King kissed Amanda and her son on their cheeks and whispered well wishes to her. Then he shook Toby's hand for an extended time, giving him his blessings and best wishes. "Sir Tobias, you have my personal address; I would enjoy an occasional post if you wouldn't mind."

"Thank you, your Highness. I would very much enjoy the communications, and we will forward copies of the photographs my mother took if you would like."

"That would be delightful, Sir Tobias; I know many people who ask about you, and with your permission, I would like to tell them about your service in the Royal Navy and the United States Navy. And show your photos the proof that we are still one people under God."

"We will be honored if you would, your Highness."

The two vehicles backed out of the drive, and the driver headed for the airport. However, the driver took an alternate route leading to a private entrance to the airport to avoid unnecessary exposure.

"We shall both be deluged by our news media when we reach Washington, that is if they find out we went on a jaunt without their knowledge," the President smiled.

****

Three months passed before the excitement died down, and the family could return to a normal life. Fortunately, their company-induced celebrity status cooled as well.

Amanda turned Toby down during romantic moments, complaining she wasn't feeling well. During the following days, her discomfort increased, and Toby took her to the family Doctor.

A nurse stayed with Amanda while the Doctor had their receptionist call for an ambulance.

"Doctor, what's happening with Amanda?"

"I'm not sure, but it's clear she is in pain, and her blood pressure is high. So I want to get her to the hospital as soon as possible for further examinations."

Toby called his father and told him to have the family ready to head for the hospital when he arrived. But, unfortunately, all he could say to them was Amanda's in trouble.

Toby raced to the house, and his parents and the Admiral climbed into the car. Toby sped to the hospital as fast as he dared. When they arrived at the Emergency Room, two Doctors stood in a hall talking. Toby rushed to a desk and asked about his wife, Amanda Greene.

The receptionist called to the doctors, who walked rapidly toward Toby, both wearing sober faces. Toby didn't like it, he'd seen that look before, and it was never good.

The doctors guided the family to a nearby room, with everyone feeling the tinges of panic. Every family member clenched their fists to control the rising horror in their mind.

"Mr. Greene, I'm Doctor Edmund O'Conner; this is Doctor Ned Chisum. Your wife came in a few minutes ago; she had no pulse or breath. We worked to bring her back but could not bring her pulse up. I'm sorry, but there was nothing we could do."

Nancy collapsed, and Tom, with Brian's help, laid her on a couch. Two nurses came in and took over her care.

Toby nearly went down, but the Doctors grabbed him and laid him on the floor with a pillow beneath his feet. Additional personnel arrived with a pair of narrow beds with wheels for the two patients and took them to rooms in the emergency section.

Toby was up and alert right away, wanting to know what had happened to Amanda. Doctor O'Conner said, "I am a Doctor of Internal Medicine. We, too, want to know what happened to your wife. She has all the appearance of a healthy lady, which needs a solution."

"Doctor, do what is necessary; I must know what happened," the devastated sailor pleaded.

CHAPTER TWENTY-SEVEN

Before The two physicians left to investigate Amanda's loss, the Admiral asked to talk with them in the hall.

"I am Brian Lacy, Amanda's grandfather. I have some information that may help you determine Amanda's death."

"By all means, Mr. Lacy, the more information, the better our search results."

"Amanda's father was a Royal Naval Officer, and he lost his life in the Battle of Jutland in the First World War. Amanda's mother passed away shortly after. The romantics in England attributed her death to a broken heart."

"You don't accept that, do you, Mr. Lacy?" O'Conner asked.

"No, her cause of death was an aortic aneurysm, quick and final."

The Doctor thought for a couple of minutes, "All the symptoms we have seen; point to such an event. It will give us a start. We'll be out as soon as we can."

Toby Greene and the family sat in an isolated room for privacy. Almost a half hour had passed before Doctors O'Conner, and Chisom returned.

Doctors O'Conner and Ned Chisom quietly stepped through the door and closed it behind them. The family almost jumped to their feet as the Doctors arrived but remained silent, waiting for the report they hoped would end their miserable guesses.

"We have identified the manner and cause of Mrs. Greene's passing. Sometime in the past few months, an aneurysm formed at the bifurcation of her aorta, where her femoral arteries begin. That could have occurred during childbirth when blood pressure can spike. However, this is only a possible cause; no specific evidence exists that birth caused the problem. However, the rupture of the aneurysm was the cause of her death. She did not suffer great pain. Her blood pressure dropped immediately when the thin wall burst, and she went to sleep before falling. It was over in seconds, and she could not have been saved even if she were on an operating table. I'm sorry for your loss. The medical field still has mountains to climb to understand and treat the human body."

The Admiral asked, "How will her certificate read?"

"Mrs. Greenes' death will be listed as natural."

"Thank you, Doctor O'Conner, you have provided the closure the family needs, and thank you for your candor and graciousness."

"I only wish we could be the bearer of better news," then the two men left, solemn faces telling the story of sadness.

Toby and Sir Brian received personal letters from Buckingham Palace. The King expressed his and Elizabeth's deepest sorrow at Toby and the family's loss.

The weeks following Amanda's funeral filled the family with sorrow. Then Toby's adopted grandfather, Brian, handed Toby a letter bearing the exquisite handwriting of Amanda.

My dearest Toby,

If you are reading this, then for whatever reason, I am no longer with you. But, as you remember, we talked about this unfortunate situation, and you must be reminded of our pledge.

Should one of us depart, our promise to ensure our son's safe and complete upbringing became our primary responsibility. You must see to that obligation. We agreed that only a complete set of parents could accomplish the task. And a man is not whole without a mate at his side, who is his mirror character. You must not marry to have a woman present. Your wife must be your mate, which implies an almost duplicate of you. We had that magic, and it is why we were on our way to success in raising Brian. The woman who will share in raising our son must be as dedicated and loving as you; only then can you be happy in her and, ultimately, Brian. I always wanted you to be satisfied, and you will again; I feel it in my heart.

Grandpa has adopted you as his grandson; he loves you as his own. He can help guide you; seek his counsel.

Brian must sense and feel your mate as his mother to accomplish what we want for him. Unless it is necessary, she should always be his mother. If my role must be revealed, Grandpa, you, and she must agree to enlighten him.

Move into the future with my love kept in a tiny corner of your heart. One last important point; time is of the essence. Children begin to remember after the age of three.

We will meet again at His feet.

Your loving wife,

Amanda.

The Admiral also received a letter from Amanda, reminding him of his pledge to her. He never stopped admiring her forethought and determination.

Toby went to grandpa and told him about the letter. "I'm aware of your letter, but not the comments. But I doubt they are much different from mine," as he held up the envelope.

"What do you think of them?"

"My experience with Amanda is simple; if she places responsibilities on you, it will be in your best interest to comply with them as if they were an admiral's orders. Therefore, I intend to do so."

Toby looked at the Admiral as if he were joking or a bit daffy.

The Admiral added, "Let me put it this way, if you fail in your mission, that lady will haunt the hell out of you. I intend to comply and urge you to do the same."

The Admiral's voice and mannerisms convinced the former sailor to reread the letter and plan ahead.

****

Four dark, foreboding days followed Amanda's passing. The former sailor felt as if he was lost at sea, with no hope of life. Tom and Nancy tried to break through his shroud without success. Finally, Grandpa applied proven RN techniques to get through to the Tar.

"Stand at attention, Stoker Greene," the Admiral commanded on the fourth day.

Toby's head jerked up, and he seemed to be propelled by springs, and when he stood ramrod straight, Toby snapped a parade-grade Marine salute. "Sir, Stoker Greene reporting as ordered," he reported.

"Stoker Greene, you will stand firm in your responsibilities, you will see to the care of your son, whom you named after His Majesty King George, and you will continue to live and provide for your family, is that understood?"

"Aye, sir," a soft reply came from the tortured man.

"I asked if you understood, Jack-Tar."

"Yes, Sir," the Stoker bellowed in response.

"Recover," the Admiral growled.

Toby took one step back and did an about-face. He remained ramrod straight for a few seconds, then his head sagged. Another couple of seconds passed, then Toby's head came up, and he took in a great breath and did another about-face.

Tom and Nancy watched in awe as the Admiral broke down the dark barrier engulfing Toby.

Looking at his adopted grandfather, the new man said in a clear and strong voice, "Thank you, Grandpa," and then he stepped into the open arms of his mentor. Nancy, Tom, and

Natalie joined the Admiral in holding Toby's racked frame as his anguish poured from him.

Ten minutes of increasing relief flowed through Toby. Finally, the family took seats, all needing to regain their composure. Rather than allow solemn silence to recapture the atmosphere, Tom asked, did we find a sitter for Brian? Then needs of the present began to take the forefront.

The service, burial, and wake followed in order, giving Toby and the family the needed time and place to begin living again. A telegram from Buckingham Palace drew the family's attention. King George sent his condolences and prayers. However, matters of state and the war prevented his attendance.

****

Toby resumed his agricultural classes, pouring his soul into his studies, which rewarded him with top grades. Brian grew from infant to crawler, giving Grandma plenty to do in monitoring the active boy.

Days became weeks, and they turned into months. Then, finally, six months after the dark days of Amanda's loss, the Admiral and Natalie Longshaw married in the church the family joined. It became the bright spot that promised better times ahead. Brian was growing and began his trials of walking, or in his case, becoming a toddler.

Toby was coming up on his first annual examination from his war wounds. So, he headed for the VA Hospital in Des Moines. On arrival, the former sailor watched the wounded walk and wheeled or pushed in wheelchairs to their destinations. He was happy walking unaided. After checking in with the receptionist, he grabbed a magazine and sat in a comfortable chair.

The magazine he picked up turned out to be the hospital newsletter. The one-time sailor began leafing through the pages, then spotted a page with the caption, "MEET THE NEW HEAD OF NURSING."

Toby turned the page and felt what he thought was an electric shock, dropping the newsletter. Then, after a minute, he picked the paper up and looked closely at the picture of the new Head of

Nursing. The woman resembled a face he'd seen in Noumea, New Caledonia. He was trying to confirm what his heart wanted. Then Toby noticed her left hand holding a necklace attached to a silver coin bearing the face of King George VI. The same necklace he gave a woman he fell in love with in the Coral Sea.

The sailor, almost in a panic, searched for the name of the new department head. There it was, Commander Carol Darcy. Toby felt dizzy, *'Could this be the open door he heard that would lead to a new life?'*

The sailor rapidly walked to the receptionist, "I need to find the Head of Nursing. Can you help?"

"Take the elevator to the third floor, turn left to a receptionist, and they can help you."

"Thank you," Toby walked as quickly as his legs would go. Suddenly he felt nervous. *'What if she didn't remember him? No, that was unlikely, the way she held the necklace. But, what if she had met someone else or was married?'* Flashed through his mind.

The nervous sailor opened the door to an office entitled Head of Nursing. "May I help you?" asked the young lady behind the desk.

"I need to speak with the Head of Nursing, Commander Darcy."

"Do you have an appointment?"

"No, I just got here."

"You must make an appointment, sir; please fill out this form."

"You don't understand; I need to see her now. Would you give her a message for me; it's important?"

"All right, what is it?" her fingers not far from the security alarm.

"Tell her that her knight in shining armor is here," she will know what it means.

The petite woman rose from the chair with a questioning look and knocked on an inner door. Toby heard an exclamation, then the sound of almost running feet. The door flew open, and the figure of a perfect woman stood hidden under a nurse's uniform.

Carol Darcy's hand flew to her mouth as if to stifle a scream. Then she cried, "TOBY," and ran into his open arms. Carol lost control for a moment and sobbed as she clutched him in strong arms. The happy woman held his face in both her hands and kissed him full on his lips. The receptionist stood in the doorway, her mouth open, unsure what to say.

Carol and Toby came to their senses and pulled back. Carol said, “Please, have a seat,” as she waved Toby to a chair in her office. Carol slowly closed the door, smiling at the receptionist, who stood by her desk with a ‘DO NOT DISTURB’ sign in her hand and a broad smile on her cute face. Carol’s eyes were unusually bright, and she had a slight scarlet tinge in her cheeks as she locked the door. Then the receptionist placed the sign over the doorknob.

Carol and Toby spent the next hours covering their lives up to their present meeting. Carol softly took Toby’s hands when he explained the loss of Amanda.

“Toby, I’m so sorry for your loss; I know how much you loved Amanda, and we could have been best friends. What are your plans now?

“I will continue my college classes; I had no idea how deep agriculture could be. This next fall, I and the family plan to prepare the land we have for spring crops.”

Carol Said, “I remember when I was home on the farm in Nebraska. Looking back, I now understand why farming is hard but the best life there is.”

Toby told Carol about the letter Amanda penned and watched her response. The woman nervously fingered the coin necklace Toby gave her on the hospital ship.

Before they knew it, the hospital loudspeaker announced the end of the day’s work. A light tap at the door needed a response. Carol rose and unlocked the door to allow a full view of her office with Toby still in a corner chair. The receptionist announced her departure for the day. Carol told her she would lock the office in a minute when she left.

The two resumed talking until the light from the window began to wane. Toby said he had to get home to take care of Brian, and the family would be waiting.

“Carol, I want to see you again; we still have much to discuss.”

“I agree, and I want to meet your family, especially Brian.”

“Do you like children?” He asked.

“Oh my, yes. I love them. Someday I want to settle down and have my own family,” Toby didn’t miss the slight reddening of her cheeks.

“Do you have someone waiting for you?” He asked.

“Toby, I’m going to be honest with you because this is much too important for either of us to beat around the bush. When we fell in love in Noumea, my father was the only man to have my love. That condition remains to this day. So now, two men have my heart and soul.”

Toby’s head momentarily dropped in relief, and when he looked into Carol’s eyes, he saw tears of happiness ready to fall. Toby’s vision blurred from his joy as well.

Carol wrapped her arms around the former sailor’s neck as Toby’s hands held her tightly in a sealing kiss.

“What are your plans for this evening?” He asked.

“A warm bath and relaxation,” Carol said, her lips curling into a smile.

“May I ask you out for supper?”

“I would love to.”

“I’ll pick you up if you give me your address.”

Carol wrote her address on a paper slip and said, “Will nineteen hundred work?”

Later, the supper allowed them to remove further questions that might come up when Carol met Toby’s family. Toby wasn’t surprised when no issues developed. Carol and Toby spent over an hour at dinner, continuing to cement their futures.

“Carol, would you have dinner with the family and me tomorrow evening? There is more information I have to share with you, and you may be surprised at what I have to say?”

“I would love to meet your family.” The traffic-stopping figure of the woman got up and stepped to Toby, then she placed her mouth to his ear and whispered.

Toby’s eyes widened, his face broke into a broad smile, and he said, “I’ll do my best to be gentle.”

Carol returned his smile, “I know.”

Toby opened the car door for his new future and escorted her to the front door of her apartment. The dazzling lady held Toby’s hands, “I had a wonderful dinner, Toby, and I’m looking forward to meeting the family.”

"That's wonderful; I know you won't be disappointed."

Carol's lips met Toby's, and after a respectful time, they parted with eager hearts looking forward to the following evening.

The next morning, Toby worked extra hard to concentrate on his classes and managed to get through the day. When he returned home, he scooped up Brian for a fun tussle.

"Well, Toby, you must be feeling much better," Nancy said.

"Yes, Mom, very much better, and we're going to have a guest for dinner this evening."

"Ooooh," Nancy extended her surprise. "Do I dare ask about our guest?"

"Mom, you recall the letter Amanda left for Grandpa and me?"

"I'll never forget Amanda's grasp on the necessity of responsibility and her grace in presenting it. We all loved your wife, my dear."

"Very much. However, in keeping with Amanda's wish, I believe God; has opened a door."

"By that, may I assume you have met someone?"

"You may, and if you think about it, you'll know who it is."

Toby's mother was nobody's fool, although she never made it a habit to express her quick and accurate mind.

After a couple of moments, she looked her son in the eye and said, "You went to the VA a couple of days ago; that's when you seemed to liven up. It is a military hospital with nurses all over the place. As I recall, when you suffered amnesia after the sinking of your ship, you fell for a nurse, didn't you?"

"Yes, mother, I did. And as soon as my memory returned, all that went away."

"Yes, it did. But not from your heart, and I'm not judging you or her; I know you both went your way, but tell me, how did you find one another?"

Toby related the facts of his and Carol's encounters and the redevelopment of their romance.

"How do you think she will respond to Brian?"

"I have already told her, and she said she loves children and hoped she would someday have a family. And get this, Carol; comes from a farming family in Nebraska."

"That does sound like a genuine God opened door. Let's see how the evening goes," Nancy agreed.

Toby drove to Carol's apartment, finding her waiting in the late-day sunshine. Nobody would guess she was a full Navy Commander and the head of nursing at the VA. Carol wore a casual white blouse, a trim dark blue skirt, and black flats. Carol's hair had been styled in a rolled pageboy with a white ribbon to hold it from her face. Her dress reflected confidence and that she was active.

At home, the family received Carol with a polite and respectful attitude, knowing her impressive credentials. As the evening wore on, the family warmed to the young woman. The Admiral took to her advancement in the American Navy as her ability to successfully navigate naval politics and pitfalls.

Although Nancy would not admit it, she had positive feelings that this lady would be perfect for Toby and Brian.

Natalie, a Navy brat from birth, whispered to her husband, "Brian, I would bet a thousand dollars this family is going to have a wedding soon."

"My dear, I would not take that bet, it would be a non-winner, and Carol will make a fine wife for Toby. All we must wait for is Brian's response."

Toby rose, left the living room, and then returned with a bright-eyed, unsteady toddler.

With a gleeful giggle, Brian began wandering the living room and, upon seeing Carol, made a beeline toward the lady with his hands stretched before him. Carol, showing perfect white teeth in her wide smile, held her hands open for Brian.

The boy landed in Carol's arms and snuggled onto her neck and shoulder, tightly holding her as if she might get away.

The Navy Commander felt her heart immediately fall in love with the little boy holding securely to her, fighting back the tears clouding her vision.

Then she looked at Toby sitting next to her, and she softly said, "I think I've been accepted."

"I know you have; look at everyone's face."

Carol looked around the room; Tom, Toby, and the Admiral wore full-faced smiles, while Nancy and Natalie were smiling from ear to ear, wiping tears of happiness from their cheeks.

H. Nelson Freeman is a Vietnam Veteran. He enlisted in the US Navy in 1958 and served on five ships. The USS Norton Sound (AVM-1), USS Midway (CVA-41), USS Kitty Hawk (CVA-63), USS Nicholas (DD-449), a Fletcher class destroyer, and the USS Goldsborough (DDG-20). He attained the rank of Chief Machinist Mate. Later he enlisted in the Iowa Army National Guard, serving another 15 years and retiring as a Master Sergeant.

He graduated from Upper Iowa University with a BSPA. After almost 30 years, Mr. Freeman Retired as a Sergeant from the Urbandale Police Department in Urbandale, Iowa. He was a CSI, court-qualified Polygraph expert, and fingerprint and handwriting expert. He now enjoys writing in rural Iowa.

The author's contact is ddgreyhounds@gmail.com.

www.ingramcontent.com/pod-product-compliance
Lightning Source LLC
LaVergne TN
LVHW010540160826
845677LV00013B/2941

* 9 7 9 8 9 8 6 9 3 6 6 0 4 *